Battle at the Rim

Third Novel in the Hollister Series

RICHARD MODLIN

HARTSIDE PUBLISHING
OWENS CROSS ROADS, AL 35763

Battle at the Rim
The Third Novel in the Jack Hollister Series

For further information please contact
www.richardmodlin.com

Printed in the United States of America.

ISBN: 0998542709
ISBN: 9780998542706
Library of Congress Control Number: 2017905735
Hartside Publishing , Owen Cross Roads, AL

Other books by Richard Modlin
Fiction: American Revolution Hollister Series
    Newfound Freedom
    Patriot Apprentice
Nonfiction: Travel Adventure Memoirs
    Chasing Wings: Birding Exploits and Encounters
    Malachite Lion: A Travel Adventure in Kenya

ACKNOWLEDGMENTS

The editorial comments, suggestions, and encourage-
ment of my wife, author and photographer Marian
Moore Lewis, and other members of my writers
group—Rusty Bynum, William Case, William Goodson, and
Sara McDaris—enhanced the quality of *Battle at the Rim*. I
would like to recognize Valdine Atwood of the Machias
Historical Society and former curator of the Burnham
Tavern for providing detailed information on the Battle of
the Rim. Mrs. Atwood also provided a copy of the poem by
Betsy Scott, written in August 1777 from Betsy's experience
and observations of the battle. The Porter Memorial Library
provided historical information and maps of eighteenth-
century Machias, Maine. Carrie Alderfer of ChromAddict
Studio, Huntsville, Alabama, designed the cover.

The Defense of Machias

Betsy Scott

'Twas August on the thirteenth day,
Late in the afternoon,
At the brave town of Machias,
When men were in their bloom,
We heard alarm below the fort,
Which made our spirits fear,
We sent down boats immediately
To see what's coming near.
And when the boats came back
They brought this news we hear,
There were three ships, a brig likewise,
A-coming near.

Two anchored in the harbor's mouth,
The others coming up,
A brig and seven barges
Came to fire against the fort,
They fought a while that afternoon,
But night a-coming on,
They fell below the fort
And anchored in the stream.
And early when the morning came,
They landed on the shore,
Where cannons loud did roar.

They drove our men from out the fort,
And plundered all our goods.
And there they kept possession
Until 'twas almost dark.
And Dawson he commanded them
On board for to embark.
They marched then upon parade
And exercises there
And then embarked on board the brig
The wind it being fair,
To take them up the stream, so bold,
In order for to burn
Our mills, our houses and our barns,
And then for to return.

But when they got in sight of town
Our men on them did fire,
And they received a shot from town,
Which caused them to retire,
And sprung their main mast by the board,
And put them to flight,
They tacked about their brig again
And back they went that night.
Soon as they turned, brave Stillman cries,
"Drive on to the attack,
"For if we fight courageously
"We soon shall beat them back.
"Fight on! Fight on! my hearts of gold!
"For I will fight until I die
"Before to them I yield."

Our men upon the Britons kept
A constant firing then,
And 'fore they got down to the fleet,
They lost a hundred men.
But for our loss it was not so,
As I the truth unfold,
We had one valiant soldier slain.
Who fought with courage bold.
Success onto our officers
That valiantly did fight!
Success onto to our soldiers
Who fought with courage bright!
Success to George Washington,
To Putnam and to Lee,
And as my ditty is ended,
Success to liberty*!*

Betsy Scott authored this poem in August 1777. She lived at the Rim with her father, Sylvanias Scott. Their property, along with Ephraim Andrew's property, was destroyed by the British during the Battle of the Rim, which occurred between August 13 and 14, 1777. The Rim is a narrow tract of land at the confluence of the East Machias River and Machias River. It is situated about two miles east of Bad Little Falls, which is located within the town of Machias, Maine. During the American Revolution, this corridor contained the strategic Fort Foster (captured by the British during the battle) and several farms.

CHAPTER 1
1 BROADWAY, NEW YORK CITY
AUGUST 19-21, 1776

Tension and anxiety had been building for the past several weeks. General George Washington had received an intelligence report that a fleet of 150 Royal Naval vessels from Halifax, Nova Scotia, had anchored off Sandy Hook. The report was about one month old. It said that these well-armed vessels were loaded with troops under the command of General William Howe, but the actual number of redcoats was not noted. A recent, more comprehensive dispatch from a patriot stationed on Staten Island indicated that another British naval fleet had arrived off the island's eastern shore. This fleet brought the new commander of the Royal Navy's North American Station— brother of General Howe, Admiral Richard Howe. The intelligence stated that Admiral Howe's fleet of 130 vessels contained about nine thousand troops.

Washington shuffled the two intelligence reports around his desk. If the admiral's ships carried a force of nine thousand men, he thought, then General Howe's fleet contains about eleven thousand soldiers—there are also more redcoats encamped on that island. "I do believe we are outnumbered," he muttered.

Washington stood and walked into the hall, where a corporal was seated next to a small table.

"Corporal, please find and summon Colonel Reed to my office."

"Aye, sir." The receptionist jumped from his chair and dashed down the hall.

The general returned to his desk.

After a short time, the clomping of several pairs of boots disturbed the silence in the hallway. The sound of those approaching echoed from the staircase and continued down the wooden floor. The noise stopped outside the general's office. Then Washington heard a knock, and the corporal stuck his head through the doorway. "Sir, Colonels Reed and Knox," he announced.

"Gentlemen, enter," Washington said. "Both of you appear to have been in the field this morning."

"Aye, sir," Colonel Joseph Reed, Washington's adjutant, said. "Colonel Knox just returned from a mission to Red Hook. Met with Generals Greene and Putman."

"Aye," Colonel Henry Knox, commander of the Continental Army's artillery forces, interjected. "We also met an envoy of Admiral Howe at the Gowanus Road landing. Came under a flag of truce. Had a letter addressed to a Mr. Washington. Said letter—a civil letter, the envoy insisted—not a military letter. It was a formal request from Admiral Howe to meet with this Mr. Washington."

"Do you have this letter?"

"No, sir," Colonel Reed answered. "I told this upstart redcoat that we have no one by the name of Mr. Washington in our army. That he should return the letter to Admiral Howe and, since we are the Continental Army, have him address the letter properly. 'And what may be the proper address,' the envoy asked? I says to him, 'The proper address is His Excellency General George Washington.'"

Reed and Knox chuckled.

"Protocol," Washington said as a grin appeared on his face. "You did well, gentlemen. I feel the admiral is searching for some sort of reconciliation. I do believe that such a move would not be in our best interest." Washington stepped next to his desk and pushed the two intelligence reports to the front. "The admiral may be somewhat conservative, but his brother is not. These dispatches contain some troubling information. The redcoats are amassing for the invasion we have all been anticipating. Our generals need to be informed and have all the troops fall back to the fortifications in Brooklyn." Washington looked up and faced his two officers. "In a day or so, I plan to visit our people, but I would like you two to go ahead and warn Generals Putman, Sullivan, Greene, and the others. I only wish we had better intelligence on movements of those British troops. Dismissed, gentlemen."

When Knox and Reed departed, Washington called in the corporal. "Please find Midshipman Hollister, Corporal. Have him come to my office."

"And where may you have been?" Washington asked as Midshipman Hollister entered the general's office and came to attention. "Two days ago, I sent the corporal to find you. I have an urgency about which I need to talk to you. I expect my aides and their aides to be available in time of need. Where have you been?"

"A thousand pardons, sir." Jack twitched as he answered. "I was meeting with Major William Blodgett, General Greene's aide. He and I visited the troops stationed at the Old Stone House."

"I hope you learned something from that ragged group of patriots."

"Nothing of importance, sir—not until this morning," Jack said. "One of the scouts from the Flatbush squadron came a-galloping to where the major and I stood. The rider was very excited. He shouted that five of our men, who were patrolling the shore around Gravesend Bay, came running up the Flatbush Road. When they saw the scout, their leader yelled, 'Get the hell to Brooklyn! redcoats—bay full of them. Landing barges coming ashore! We sees about four or five thousand of them damn redcoats ranking on the beach.' Hearing this, the Flatbush scout came galloping to where Major Blodgett and I were standing. As soon as he made us aware of what was happening, the scout yanked his horse to the side and headed off toward the Brooklyn perimeter. That is when I made my excuse to the major, grabbed my mount, and made my way here as fast as I could. The current on the East River made for the ferry's slow progress."

Washington jumped out of his seat. "Invasion has started." He clenched his fists and stepped around the desk.

"Did you get any other information—cannons, armaments, vessels in the bay?"

"Major Blodgett yelled some questions at the scout. But all he said before he galloped away was that the men who alerted him were from Colonel Edward Hand's Pennsylvania unit. Said those men fired a few shots at the redcoats and retreated because there were too many of them. The scout said that Hand's men set fire to whatever supplies they had to leave behind."

General Washington nodded, placed his left hand on the desk, but quickly lifted and fisted it. He shifted to the side. "I need more specific intelligence," he mumbled. "Howe's tactic may be a feint. He has more than thirty thousand troops on Staten Island. Why land only a few thousand? Does not seem to be a major invasion. May be a ploy. Wants me to move Manhattan troops to Brooklyn, leaving the Battery poorly supported." Washington nodded and paced about the office. "I believe Howe plans to invade on the southern tip of Manhattan Island."

Jack noticed that daylight impinging on the office windows was dimming. He relaxed the tension in his legs but still maintained an attentive stance.

"At ease, Midshipman," the general said as he moved about the room. He stopped and faced the window. "Night is approaching. I need to visit our fortification in Brooklyn. Howe's tactic may still be a gambit. Without any good intelligence on the redcoat movements, armor, reinforcements, it is difficult to know what Howe is planning." He turned and faced Jack. "Intelligence. This is what I want to speak to you about."

The general motioned for Jack to move to the up-holstered settee against the wall and seat himself. As Washington was about to sit on a nearby cushioned wing-back chair, he straightened and walked to the doorway. He opened it. "Corporal, please come into the office and pro-vide us with some illumination."

The little soldier scampered into Washington's office, lit some candles and oil lamps, and left.

In the meantime, the general returned to his desk, pulled open a drawer, and removed a bottle of rye whis-key. He poured two shots, turned, moved to where Jack sat, and handed him a glass. General Washington walked to the doorway. "Corporal, I do not want to be disturbed."

He stepped back and closed the door.

"Midshipman Hollister, what we are to discuss now is to be only between you and me." The general returned to the wingback chair. Drinking his shot of rye whiskey, he placed the glass on an end table and seated himself. "You have exemplified yourself since you joined our ranks. During the past eight months, you have shown yourself to be a loyal patriot, a person I can trust." He glanced at Jack.

"Thank you, sir. I have tried to be useful and do what is asked." Jack fidgeted, nervously clasped his hands, and then placed them on his thighs and rubbed them.

"I have a role for you to play, if you feel comfortable to ac-cept it." Washington furrowed his brow, narrowed his eyes, and looked directly into Jack's. "The role is dangerous." The general sighed and laid his arms on the chair armrest. His hands gripped the ends of the armrests. "Usually I place such an assignment to a trusted blackguard, a person to whom life's jeopardies have little meaning. You are young, but I feel you have the qualities that would allow you to accomplish such a mission. It does, however, require, if you accept, that you maintain a constant vigil—in essence, be aware of your backside. But I believe with your aristocratic background, education—"

Washington paused and took a deep breath.

"You are an Englishman who can, with proper precautions, move among redcoats without suspicion. You are a Hollister. Admiral Howe is new to this continent, but he is well aware of the Hollister Exchange and Transport, Limited. The redcoats have been doing business with your family's company since before the beginning of this war." The imposing commander relaxed his hands and continued to gravely stare at Jack. "I need someone to infiltrate the enemy. Live among them. Learn their plans, strategies, strengths, weaknesses—"

Wide-eyed, Jack looked at Washington and blurted, "Sir? You...you want me to be a spy?"

"Aye, lad." Washington nodded slightly. "Recently I sent a man to Long Island to gather what data he could, an American aristocrat. You know him—your friend, Lieutenant Nathan Hale. He volunteered. I really did not feel comfortable putting him into that situation. But he volunteered when no one else would. I had little choice, because, to win this hellish war, we need to know what our enemy is doing. Lieutenant Hale is a young, intelligent, likable fellow, who quickly makes friends. But he also tends to be flamboyant, gregarious. And, I believe, these latter qualities—though I wish to God they do not—I fear they may cause his demise if he becomes known."

"Sir, the British hang spies without question."

"Yes, Jack. I said the role was dangerous—very dangerous."

Jack shrugged. He gritted his teeth, clasped his hands, and then gasped. "Perhaps I should think about this assignment, sir."

"There is not time, Mr. Hollister. Howe's forces outnumber us. And if he attacks Brooklyn or this city, I will have to move our men to safer locations." Washington stood and walked to the window. "I would rather not assign you this mission, but I need information about the Howe's tactics." He turned away from the window. "I recently asked Mr. Christopher Ludwick, a German baker from Philadelphia who recently joined our ranks, to infiltrate the Hessians we captured. Since he speaks German, he has been accepted by them as a deserter from our ranks and interprets for them. By doing so, Sergeant Ludwick has been providing useful intelligence as to how those mercenaries have been assisting General Howe's troops. He also has convinced several of those prisoners to join our ranks."

"Sir, I do not speak German, nor can I cook."

Washington chuckled. "Aye, Mr. Hollister. You are, however, an aristocrat from Great Britain. And that is your key."

"So true," Jack said and took a deep breath. The tension in his muscles eased. "My concern is that I would be not only a traitor to my country but also a deceiver to my family."

"That would be so," Washington said and nodded as he stepped back and edged back against the desk. "In war, deception occurs in many forms, none of which is considered acceptable. But in time of need, a true patriot does what is necessary to further the cause for which he is fighting. I would hope, after all you have been through, you have made America your country. And as for your family, they will never know unless you tell them or you are caught. No matter which, they will eventually accept your decision. As I mention, the decision is yours."

The glow and flicker of the candles disappeared when Jack lowered his head and covered his face with his hands. His fingers scratched his brow as he massaged it. He gave a sigh and raised his head. Looking directly at General Washington, he said, "Without critical intelligence, we are fighting blind. We will lose this war. And all our endeavors will be lost. Only Great Britain will gain. The colonials who fought so hard will be relegated to a life of servitude. I cannot let that happen. I have accepted this country as mine and will fight for its independence. When can I start?"

"First, you need have a higher rank than a midshipman," Washington said. He looked relieved as he stood away from the desk. "Midshipman Jack Hollister, you are, as of this moment, Lieutenant Jack Hollister. We will have a brief ceremony this evening to celebrate your promotion. Colonels Reed and Knox are here, and so are several others of my staff. Colonel Reed can enter the promotion into the log, and it will be mentioned in the report that he will send to the Continental Congress. None of them will know your actual mission." The general moved forward and shook Jack's hand. "Now we must plan the method of your infiltration."

"The idea of being an American spy makes me anxious." Jack followed Washington as the general returned to his desk. The new lieutenant stopped at the front. He scratched his arm and then clasped and unclasped his hands. "Is there any word from Lieutenant Hale? Perhaps I can enter the enemy's territory as he did."

"I have not heard from Lieutenant Hale." Washington picked up a piece of paper and stared at it. "No. You will be ferried to Paulus Point in New Jersey along with a contingent I have assigned to Philadelphia. When you reach the shore, you will leave this group, telling them you are on another mission. I want you to stay in the city for a few days, mingle with the people, listen to what they say of the conflict. Some are Dutch. Others are French Huguenots. I believe most are with us, but I must know their feelings toward Great Britain. New Jersey is our path of escape if New York City falls." The general returned to the side of his desk and seemed to ponder for a moment. "After a few days, you will make your way south to the strait the Dutch named Kill Van Kull. It is the channel that separates New Jersey from Staten Island. A mile or so up this body of water, you will find the little harbor where several fishing smacks are tied. Aboard a gray-hulled vessel whose gunwales are painted red, there will be a captain Joshua Perry. He is one of us and will take you aboard his vessel. Once you are aboard, he will ask that you change into clothing that he will provide, an outfit more appropriate for someone who works aboard a fishing vessel. You will become part of his crew and, once you are at sea, Captain Perry will dispose of the urban attire you were wearing. Perry secreted Lieutenant Hale successfully onto Long Island a month ago. He also delivered Sergeant Ludwick to and successfully removed him from Staten Island.

"Captain Perry has white hair and beard and is usually chewing on a spanish cigar. I believe he is a friend of Captain José Diaz, whom you know quite well. So as not to arouse suspicion, greet Captain Perry as a long-lost friend. You will work with him for a time. Observe the activity along the New Jersey coast and write up what you see. Perry will dispatch your reports to me as opportunity arises. At the proper time, he will put you ashore on Staten Island." Washington crumpled the piece of paper and looked at Jack. "Once on the island, Lieutenant, you are on your own." Washington paused for a moment and then nodded. "However, should I ever need to get word to you, I will send the message to a person of whom you have heard and my staff already knows well: Mr. Manfred McGully, the tavern keeper. Everyone calls him Manny."

"Manny is the owner of McGully's?"

"Aye," Washington continued. "A staunch patriot he is. But the Loyalists are not aware to whom his loyalty is directed. They trusted and respected him. As such, I am sure he will be accepted by the redcoats should their invasion be successful." The general, his brow furrowed, looked directly into Jack's eyes. "But he is also one of my trusted emissaries. Should I and my troops need to evacuate, Manny will maintain McGully's and continue to be our secret courier.

Any message from me will carry my seal and be addressed to a Mr. Carson Rabbit. Do not forget that name. It is code name we use among our couriers. Manny knows this, but be cautious and never divulge the code name." Washington took a deep breath and patted Jack's shoulder. "I am sorry I have to leave you to your own. May our God keep you safe."

Jack blinked his eyes and sighed. "Perhaps not. My capture by the redcoats may not be as dire as we are making it sound to be. About three years ago, the Royal Navy's Atlantic Fleet received a notice from Lord North, the prime minister of Great Britain. It was a request from my father asking that the masters of all British vessels be alerted and on the lookout for my brother and me. My father sent this request when he learned that we were missing after sailing from Halifax aboard an American coastal schooner. The captain of a frigate operating off the coast of Maine raided a pirate camp and unknowingly captured my brother, Ian, along with the survivors of the grounded schooner and some of the pirates and impressed him and the others into the service of his vessel. When Ian's identity was discovered and verified, Admiral Gage, Britain's then admiral in chief of the North Atlantic Station, released him in Boston. With the navy being so meticulous in the conservation of their communications, Admiral Howe may still have a copy of Lord North's letter. I can feign escaping from the patriots and making my way here. The concern is that I have nothing to verify my true identity."

Washington walked around his desk and pulled open a drawer. He sorted through the folders, pulled one out, and laid it on his desk. Opening it, he spread out the missives the folder contained. "Ah, here is what you will need. A copy of the letter Lord North sent." The general lifted it and perused it. "A communication pouch was taken from one of the British vessels anchored in the Charles River when our troops blockaded the city. This letter was in the pouch. That is how I knew who you were from the time we met. This letter is too clean. It will have to be aged and tattered so it will look as if you have been carrying it during your journey."

"When I'm taken by the redcoats, I will be asked how I came to have this letter," Jack said.

"I am sure you can create a likely story."

"Aye." Jack nodded and accepted the letter Washington handed to him. "Seems I came by it when I found the belongings of a fallen rebel. Probably part of the loot the rebel stole from a British courier."

"You will not be immediately believed," Washington said. "They may arrest you—probably will—but the British are an efficient, curious, and thorough lot. They will interrogate you, and of course, you will have the proper answers. You will know details only a true Hollister can know. The letter will also be investigated. And it will be found to be authentic. Do not lose it. Best to keep it on your person." Washington again returned to the front of the desk and faced Jack. "No doubt your anxiety is high, but I do believe this plan will work. After a few weeks of inquiry, I am sure those redcoats will accept you as one of their own."

Jack nodded, swallowed, and sighed. "Aye. I will hide Lord North's letter into my diary." He folded the letter into quarters, removed a notebook from his jacket, gently lifted the edge of its cover's inner facing, and tucked the letter in through the opening. Closing the diary, he laid it on the top of Washington's desk, and pressed down hard on the book, flattening it. "Ah! Now it is safely hidden. When am I to leave?"

Washington dropped his head and smiled. "The men assigned to Philadelphia are scheduled to be ferried across the Hudson in the morning. You should be ready to go with them. But, as of now, let us celebrate your promotion."

CHAPTER 2
1 BROADWAY, NEW YORK CITY
AUGUST 22, 1776

J ack awoke the next morning before daylight. A little draggy from imbibing three tots of Washington's rye whiskey, he drew himself off his cot and ambled to a stand, where a pitcher of water and a bowl sat. He poured water into the bowl and splashed a handful onto his face as he remembered the other officers' jovial bantering at last night's party. It was an amusing party. The other officers, who outranked him, tried to initiate him by telling foreboding, outlandish stories of what befalls a fresh lieutenant. He smiled. I appreciate their jocularity, but little do they know of my real mission, Jack thought. He ran his fingers through his hair, straightened, and looked out the window. Beyond the sky was raising its shades.

A shuffling sound in the hall drew Jack's attention from the window. Someone was moving about. A knock came on his door. He opened it. Billy, General Washington's valet, stood in the doorway holding an armload of clothing.

"His Excellency said you be needin' these fittings."

Jack stepped back and looked. "Come in, Billy. Did not know I was to wear a new uniform."

"No uniform, sir." Billy walked in and unloaded the burden onto the cot. "These is ordinary wear, sir." Washington's valet bent down and lifted a merchantman's waistcoat. "You gonna look like Mr. McGully when you puts on this wais-ket. I sees him when I go to his tavern and gets the general the whiskey he likes. Mr. McGully's always lookin' so proud wearin' his brown wais-ket with shiny brass-colored buttons." Billy draped the waistcoat over the back of a nearby chair.

"Guess the general does not want me to look like a military man when I cross the Hudson."

"Don't know, sir. Just says for you to wear these fittings." Billy returned to the cot and spread out the shirt, breeches, hat, and jacket. "They not need to wrinkle, sir."

"Aye, Billy. Thank you. When I dress, I'll come and find you. You can then inspect me. See if I look like a tavern keeper."

"As you wish, sir." Billy turned and left Jack's room.

Jack surveyed the clothing that Billy brought: buckskin-colored breeches, an off-white linen blouse, striped knee-length socks, and black loafer shoes with brass buckles fixed to the shoes' instep. He pulled on the breeches and slipped on the blouse. Then he sucked in his gut and tucked the shirt in around his waist. Phew, these pants are tight. He sat on the edge of the cot and examined the socks. They were new, silk, and striped. He shoved his feet into them, worked the tops up his calves, and tucked them under the supple pant-leg ends of the breeches that extended a few inches below the knees. After slipping his feet into the shoes, he adjusted each shoe's tongue and snapped the buckle closed. He shook his head and stood.

Only a small mirror in this room, he noted. I can only see my face. Need to rely on Billy's inspection. With his hands, he smoothed his hair. He then turned and looked at what still lay on the cot, a brown jacket and a dark-brown, broad-brimmed beaver hat. He removed the waistcoat from the back of the chair, put it on, and buttoned the seven buttons down his chest. Then he collected the other articles and strolled through the doorway.

Jack found Billy, who was dusting shelves in the library. "Ready for inspection, Master Billy," he said.

Washington's valet dropped the dust cloth and turned. "Aye, sir." Billy moved to where Jack stood in the middle of the room. From a nearby chair, he removed a bib-shaped, rose-colored cloth. As he walked up behind Jack, the valet folded the middle section of the cloth into thirds. He wrapped the cloth around Jack's neck, secured it at the back, tucked its edges in around the neck of the waistcoat, and fluffed its front. "Sir needs a jabot to look proper," he said. "Now, put on jacket and hat, and I will inspect." Billy stepped back, away from Jack, but continued to face him.

Jack handed the hat to Billy. "Please hold this."

"Aye, sir." The valet held the hat by its brim with both hands, but allowed it to dangle down in front of him. "You not button jacket."

"Aye." The new lieutenant slid his arms in the jacket's sleeves, which were long. They extended to Jack's wrists but allowed the blouse sleeves to be exposed. The high-waisted jacket had a long, skirtlike tail that hung to the back of Jack's thighs. He brushed down its sides and retrieved the hat from Billy, placed it on his head, and tapped the center

of its round top. He placed his hands on his hips and took
an akimbo pose. "Well, Master Valet, do I look like a tavern
keeper?" Jack straightened and puffed out his chest.

"No, sir." Billy nodded and grinned. "No, sir. You looks
like a banker. Gonna fit well on the streets of New York."
Washington's valet picked up the dust cloth and snapped it.
A curl of dust sparkled in a beam of sunlight that edged its
way through a window. "Now, His Excellency and the other
officers await you for breakfast. May your promotion serve
you well and keep you safe." Billy turned and continued to
dust the shelves.

Jack watched Billy do his work. He sighed. He closed his
eyes for a moment and pondered the coming consequenc-
es. "Thank you, Billy," he said. The new lieutenant turned
and went into the hall.

The incoherent chatter of men's voices floated through
the back stairwell that led to the lowest level of the old
Kennedy mansion as Jack started down a flight of stairs. A
kitchen and an adjacent large room, originally designated
as the servants' mess, was now being used as the officers'
galley and mess. This change occurred after Washington's
wife, Martha, joined him in New York City, and he moved
his private residence to another vacated Loyalist's mansion
down the block.

The flight of stairs terminated in the kitchen. When Jack
entered, the cook handed him a cup of coffee and pointed
out the breakfast fare: biscuits, a thick gravy, boiled eggs,
and bacon. He filled a plate and headed into the mess hall.
The hall contained several individuals, but Washington was
absent.

"Aye, lookie there," someone with a deep voice called out. "Who's this superb-looking fellow who has entered our presence?"

"Ah, 'tis new lieutenant Jack Hollister," another teased.

Jack nodded, grinned, and found an empty place near several of the younger staff officers.

"Is that the new uniform Continental lieutenants are to wear?" the deep-voiced fellow asked. He sat at the far end of the long dark-wood table.

"Nay," commented Colonel Henry Knox, who sat with Colonel Joseph Reed at an adjacent table. "The lad is dressed to go into the city. No doubt the general has decided to send him on a mission as a courier. With so many disgruntles lurking in the streets and alleys, someone in a Continental uniform presents an opportunity for assault. Is that not so, Joe?" Colonel Knox looked at Colonel Reed while taking a sip of his coffee.

"Aye," Reed answered. "If I were in charge, I would not be sending an inexperienced officer into the midst of unruly Loyalists."

"I say, not to worry, Colonel," Jack said, using his best Oxford accent. Then he switched to a cockney dialect and completed his sentence. "But oie believes oie can chat wi' the best o' them o' Tories."

Several of the younger men chuckled. "'E's a Brit, all right," one bantered and was about to continue when General Washington walked into the room and interrupted him with a statement that made Jack's heart skip a beat.

"To clarify your inquiry, gentlemen," Washington said, "I am sending Lieutenant Hollister on an undercover mission to New Jersey." He stepped to the long table as the cook came alongside of him and handed him a cup of coffee. "It's of little danger to Mr. Hollister, since the residents of the village on Paulus Point are mostly Dutch and support our cause. Some may desire to have their own state on this continent, but most have more anger with Great Britain and side with us."

Jack relaxed. General Washington is not telling these men of my true mission. He is setting the stage to explain my absence from the unit.

"I need to know which of the citizens are the most loyal to us and where to find them," Washington continued. "The possibility is strong that the British will invade Brooklyn and most likely take over the city. With the British garrisons encamped on Staten Island and those who have just arrived with the armada anchored off Sandy Hook, General Howe has a well-trained force of over thirty thousand troops. We are greatly outnumbered. New Jersey is our safest route of evacuation. So I need reliable intelligence on the conditions in that colony across the Hudson." Washington raised the coffee cup to his lips.

He glanced at Jack.

"Your attire will not raise eyebrows when you engage and talk to merchants. And there will be no need for you to use your British accent, though it may be of use in other times and circumstances. They will be more forthcoming if you appear as one of them and not a military man." Washington reached into the pocket of his coat and removed a leather pouch. "This purse contains your credentials. The information is what we spoke of last evening." With an imperceptible nod, Washington handed the satchel to Jack. "A wagon will collect you and the contingent going to Philadelphia within an hour and transport you to the Battery, where a ferry awaits you. Godspeed. May he keep you safe. It is highly probable that we may never see each other again."

Washington extended his right hand. Jack clasped it. As the general turned to leave the mess, he nodded and patted the new lieutenant's shoulder, cast his eyes downward, and strolled out the door.

———————•◦•———————

Jack boarded the unassuming military-style wagon along with three other Continental officers he had never met. The other passengers, Washington's Philadelphia contingent, were a captain and two lieutenants. A corporal drove the wagon. All were dressed in uniforms to give the appearance of the Continental Army. Jack wore civilian clothing. The trip from Washington's headquarters on Broadway to the Battery was short but resulted in jeers as the wagon passed several groups of Loyalist ruffians and merchants along the streets. Most of the business in New York City relied on trade with Great Britain. But since Washington and his troops had arrived on Manhattan Island and the southern end of Long Island, commerce had become strained. Many living and working in and near the city wanted to maintain an alliance with Britain rather than fight for independence.

As soon as all were aboard, the crew of the sloop cast off the lines and allowed the vessel to drift with the current away from the dock. They set the mainsail. With a northeast breeze, the sail quickly filled, and the ferry glided to the south into New York Bay. As soon as the sloop encountered the flooding tidal current, it was pushed toward the mouth of the Hudson River. The crew trimmed and adjusted the sail to catch the wind abeam. As soon as the mainsail re-filled, the sloop swung around toward the Jersey shore, its bow pointed in the direction of New Jersey. Jack looked back at the docks along lower Manhattan, then forward, and seated himself near the bow.

The Philadelphia contingent kept to themselves and sat amidships. No one spoke, but everyone kept watch on the armada of British warships anchored at or near Staten Island, afloat in the narrows and crowding the shoreline near Gravesend Bay.

"I believe those redcoats are invading Long Island as we sail," the captain of the ferry said.

Jack cupped his face in his hands and took a deep breath.

The ferry headed toward Paulus Point and a collection of sheds, barns, houses, and substantial piers on the west side of the Hudson River.

When Jack and the Philadelphia contingent disem-barked the ferry, he immediately noticed that the attitude toward Continental soldiers was more respectful. The several merchants, stevedores, and fishermen gathered on the dock welcomed and assisted Washington's men as soon as they stepped ashore. Horses were readied for the

Philadelphia contingent. When Jack asked one of the fellows for directions to the nearest inn, the man, who was carrying his traveling bag and a couple of smaller satchels, pointed to the street along the wharves. He then swung his arm to the left and said, in a heavy guttural accent, "Rode Duke Inn, there ahead."

Jack thanked the stevedore, conferred with the ferry captain for a moment, and nodded at the officers of the Philadelphia contingent. They glanced at him as they mounted horses. The younger-looking lieutenant waved after he adjusted himself in a saddle. Jack heard the reins snap and watched the riders pull their horses' heads around and trot off. He made his way around several wagons. When he came to Water Street, he crossed it and walked left, in the direction the stevedore had pointed.

A short distance beyond the wharves, Jack sighted a red placard carved in the shape of a duck, hanging from a building down the street. He smiled. "Red duck," he mumbled. As he neared, the partially faded letters shown on the side of the placard came clear and spelled, "Rode Eend Inn en Pub." I'm in the land of the Dutchmen, he thought and chuckled as he entered the doorway.

The entrance opened onto an anteroom with a bar-like desk. To the left was another doorway that led to a flight of stairs. On the right, another door provided access to the pub.

Jack walked in and saw the hotel's logbook and a small bell. He looked around and gave the bell a momentary shake. Within a minute, an attractive woman in her late teens popped through the pub doorway. Her eyes were wide open, as if she were disturbed. She held a pewter tankard in her right hand and a cloth in her left. Her long blond hair swung around from the right side of her head and fell over her left shoulder.

"And what may you want, sir?" she grumbled. She pushed the cloth into the tankard and plopped the mug on the desk next to the logbook.

Jack knew immediately that the bell's harsh chime distracted her attention from something she was doing in the pub. "So sorry for disturbing you," Jack apologized. "The inn was recommended by one of the men on the dock. Might there be a room available for a day or two?"

Her eyes met Jack's. She stepped back, looked down, pulled the logbook closer her, and pondered for a moment, glancing up. "Aye, sir," she said, sighed, and grinned. Her voice had softened and become more melodious. "You wish to stay two nights?"

"Yes. A quiet room, please. Not one over the pub."

"Very good." The young woman looked up. Her eyes momentarily fluttered. A blush warmed her face as she smiled. From beneath the desk, she brought up a quill and inkwell. "Sir will please sign the register. The tavern keeper, Madam van Groot, keeps a special room, a quiet room two floors up, over the kitchen. She charges one quid to rent the room."

"That will be good." Jack rotated the logbook around to him and signed in.

Before he laid the quill down, the young woman was around the desk and had lifted his traveling bag from the floor. With her shoulder, she pushed open the door to a stairway. "Please follow. I will take you to the room." She stepped lightly up three stairs, then turned, and looked back, still smiling.

When Jack gazed up and saw her profile, he noticed that the weight of the travel bag she toted against the side of her slender body accentuated her delicate curves and small breasts. He arched forward and said, "Leave my bag on the step. I can carry it."

She set the bag down, balanced it with her knee, and again flipped her head to the side, causing her hair to swing from one shoulder to the other. She took a deep breath. "'Tis nice of you to offer, sir, but I can manage."

Jack followed a few steps behind and enjoyed the view in front of him. "And what may your name be?" he asked.

She panted for a moment and said, "I am Grishilde van Groot. My mother calls me Hilde."

Jack grinned. "The innkeeper's daughter," he mumbled and then said in a louder voice, "It is my pleasure to meet you, Mistress van Groot."

She coughed. "Hilde, if the sir pleases."

"Aye. Yes, Hilde."

They reached the second floor and continued down a dim, narrow hall past several rental rooms to the door at the very end. Hilde opened the door, walked in, set Jack's travel bag next the bed, straightened, and gasped. She then swung her arm over the bed and said, "The room. I hope, sir, it is to your liking."

"Aye." Jack scanned the room. It was warmly appointed and contained a full bed, rather than a cot, with pillows and a beige quilt. On a small table next to the bed rested a rose-colored oil lamp. A dresser, with an attached mirror, stood against the wall just beyond the foot of the bed. A washbowl and pitcher were set atop the dresser. He walked to the dormer window and looked out. "Hilde, please call me Jack." A view of an expansive field spread beyond the window. Rail and stone fencing divided some of the acreage behind the Rode Eend Inn en Pub. A small herd of black-faced sheep grazed on the outermost meadow. He turned away from the view and faced Hilde. "Yes. The room will do quite well. Thank you."

"Mother will be serving roast duckling for dinner in an hour, Mr. Jack." Hilde stepped out of the room, put her right hand over her mouth, and gazed back into the room before she started down the hallway.

"My name is Jack," he said to her back. A fine young woman, he then thought.

***

Last evening's meal of roast duck on a bed of carrots, potatoes, late corn, and squash, plus the several mugs of local ale that Jack consumed, filled him comfortably. But he felt famished when he awoke in the late-morning hours, as the smell of fried bacon and newly baked bread stimulated his senses. The sun's rays were already beaming through the upper part of the window. He tossed off the quilt, rose, poured water into the bowl, and splashed it on his face. He then got dressed and scurried down the stairs to the pub, where breakfast was being served.

Hilde met him as he walked into the pub. She gestured at a table near the wall and moved toward it. As Jack followed her, he scanned the room. Three men in buck-skin attire occupied a setting near the windows with a view of the street. Travelers, Jack thought. An elderly couple sat alone across from the table where Hilde seated Jack. As he pulled the chair from the table, he noticed four other men, who seemed to have finished their breakfasts and were re-laxing. Two of these stylish men were well dressed—mer-chants or bankers. The other two, who seemed to resemble each other, wore mud-stained, duck-cloth trousers, boots, and broadcloth shirts. Farmers perhaps. Trying to make a deal. He sat with his back to them.

As Hilde began to tell Jack what was for breakfast, the urbane, influential-appearing man shouted, "Mistress Grishilde, would you please bring me and my secretary, Wilton, more of your fine coffee? Oh yes, and I believe the Dekens brothers would also like their cups refreshed."

Jack turned as the gray-haired man's request startled Hilde. He saw that this fellow was gazing at the older Dekens brother and heard him ask, "Would you not, Klaas?"

Klaas Dekens grunted, but his brother said, "*Ja.* I vood like more. An' Klaas too, though he broods." The younger brother paused for a moment and coughed. "He broods not because of you, Mr. Bennett, but at the pennies the British pay for our grain and hops. They vant to make their bier and bread, but not vant to pay for our vork." Klaas grunted again, but the younger brother continued, "Klaas say he vant to burn the grain. Not sell to redcoats. I believe this is good."

"Yes, Mr. Bennett," Hilde said and pursed her lips. "I will bring more coffee as soon as I finish telling this fine gentleman our offerings for breakfast." She turned back to Jack, who was now regarding her, and told him what was on the menu. She took his order and returned to the kitchen. Jack adjusted his chair so he could scrutinize these men.

Bennett nodded, narrowed his eyes, and looked back at the Dekens. "Now, Petre, you know the British. They have the upper hand. Burning what you men have sweated to grow is not wise. The Americans and Washington's army do not have any money. The British do. There are thirty thousand of them on Staten Island, and they are hungry and thirsty. That is your market. Winter is coming. If you want to sell your grain, you will have to sell it to the British. And they will set the price. They leave few avenues for negotiation. You need to convince your brother not to be foolish."

"Ja. I try. He no speak English, but he understand business. He not want to sell for few pennies. I convinced we will burn our fields. Meeting over. We go back to farm. No more coffee. Thank you for breakfast." Petre slapped Klaas on the shoulder. "We go." The two farmers pushed back their chairs, stood, turned, and stomped out of the pub.

Bennett grumbled, raised his eyebrows, and shrugged.

"The other farmers will sell their grain to the British, Mr. Bennett," Wilton said. "Those Dekens brothers are in strong with the patriots. Most likely they will sell their grain to someone in New York—or give it away to Washington's troops."

As Jack glanced at Wilton, he saw Hilde approach with a large pot of coffee, set it on the men's table, turn, and head back to the kitchen.

"Yes, you are right." Bennett clenched his fist and stood. "Come, our ferry for Staten Island leaves in an hour." He and Wilton started to walk out the door. "Mistress Grishilde," Bennett yelled, "our meeting is over. We are leaving. I believe a couple of shillings should cover the breakfasts and extra coffee."

As soon as Bennett and Wilton left the pub, Jack took out his diary and a pencil. Thirty thousand troops, he noted. Redcoats pay almost nothing for local materials and food. He stuffed the notebook and pencil back into his pocket as Hilde moved toward his table.

"My, my," she said as she placed the tray, containing a dish with three eggs, several slices of bacon, and thick chunks of bread oozing with bacon grease, on the table. "You eat well," she said and grinned. Then she spun around and picked up the money Bennett left to pay for his, Wilton's, and the Dekens brothers' breakfasts. She manipulated the coins in her hand and returned her attention to Jack. "I do not know. Mr. Bennett pays well for the services he orders. He is a Tory. Arbitrates for the British in their matters of commerce with the local farmers and merchants."

"Those redcoats must pay him well," Jack said.

"They must, Jack. He does not seem to lack for money. Coffee?" she asked.

"Aye." Jack straightened, picked up the fork, and touched the tines onto the dish of eggs. "I overheard the younger farmer say that the British pay miserably for the goods they want."

Hilde rotated to her left, lifted the large pot of coffee from the table that the group of men had vacated, and presented it to Jack. "Yes. They treat the colonials like peasants. That is why most have no desire to trade with the redcoats. Yet a few do—worried that the British will invade, and if successful, return us to the peasantry and persecution we escaped from in Europe. We came to this new continent for freedom—independence—beliefs Mr. Washington and the men in Philadelphia are fighting for."

"You talk as if you support this fight for independence. You must know that most in Manhattan support the British cause." Jack moved his mug to the center of the table. "Yes, I would like coffee."

Hilde nodded. "Most in New Jersey, both the Dutch and Huguenots, come here to live and worship as they want. We would live like serfs if ruled by the monarchy and nobility of Great Britain." She poured coffee into Jack's mug. "Yes, the American patriots have support in New Jersey."

Jack smiled and nodded. "Then why does this Mr. Bennett treat you so well?"

"He is a philanderer." Hilde stepped away from the table and took hold of the back of a side chair. She sighed. "When he comes from Staten Island to do business, he makes googly eyes at Mama and me. She rents him a nice room. Tells me to give him free coffee. I do not like him. His presence makes me feel slimy."

Jack chuckled. "Where I come from, we call such a fellow a Romeo." He sipped the coffee. "Phew! Good and hot. Perhaps I should get to know him. I need to visit Staten Island."

Hilde gritted her teeth and groaned. "Do you not support the patriot cause?"

"I like to maintain my neutrality," said Jack and chewed his lip. "I am trying to document this conflict between Great Britain and the Americans."

"You are a reporter?"

"You might say I am, though I do not work for anyone. I'm more of an historian, trying to document what is happening between the colonials and the British. My contacts in New York City suggested I go to a fishing village at a place called Kill Van Kull. There, they say, I can quickly be ferried to the Staten Island. Is this Kill Van Kull far from here?"

"Two days on horseback." Hilde relaxed, raised her eyelids, and snapped her head to the side, causing her long hair to swing around from one shoulder to the other. "I know this place. It is south on Bergen Neck—Mama's sister lives along the route—good places for food. Every week Mama sends food and supplies to her, and Auntie Edda sends vegetables home to Mama."

"I have to secure a horse. Where can I find one? Is there a livery near?"

"Petre Dekens makes deliveries for Mama. He has horses." Hilde looked at the ceiling, and then she glanced at the bar, where Madam van Groot was pouring something from a pitcher. "I not seen my aunt since spring. Mama and I went to Uncle Vogel's funeral. I would like to go and see how she is doing. I...I be your guide. Mama will allow this because she know Petre. Trust him. He good man. Aunt good cook; will provide lodging for you and Petre. I will stay with my aunt while Petre takes you to village on Kill Van Kull. Only short distance from where my aunt live. I will return here, to Paulus Village, with him."

"You would make the trip more pleasant," Jack said. A bit self-conscious, he pressed his lips together and glanced up at Hilde. "Is Petre your boyfriend? Will he mind if I am around?"

"Oh no." Hilde chuckled. "He not care. Petre born here. We grow up together. He like my brother."

"Very well, if your mother and Petre agree, I would like for you to be my guide. Perhaps Petre can bring the horses around tomorrow. I need to meet my contact on the twenty-fifth. That is in two days. We will need to leave tomorrow."

"Aye," Hilde said. "I will arrange with Petre and Mama." She giggled and twisted her hands together and then lightly danced back to the pub's bar.

Jack noticed Madam van Groot glimpse in his direction, smile, and nod. It appears I will have a guide, he thought.

CHAPTER 3
KILL VAN KULL
AUGUST 24, 1776

Morning sunlight flowed through the back door when Jack entered the inn's kitchen. Mrs. van Groot, her blouse and apron smudged with patches of flour, stood behind a long table and moved slices of bread from the tabletop to a bowl filled with a yellowy-white liquid. Jack walked to the back door, faced the expansive meadow beyond, took a deep breath, and turned. "How soon before breakfast?" he asked.

"Soon," Madam van Groot said. "Ten, maybe fifteen minutes. Old bread must sop; then I fry it." She laid the last slice into the bowl, lifted it, and then slowly swirled it. "Milk now cover bread and soak through. You like *pain perdu?* Hilde know how to make it good. I teach her."

"I do," said Jack. "Have not eaten such toast since I left England."

"You have bacon. Hearty food, fried bread, and bacon. Too much not good for middle." She rubbed her belly and chuckled and then nodded. "Good for travel. Not get hungry."

Jack smiled. "Aye. As a boy, I was active and loved pain perdu. Our cook back home made it often to rid the pantry of old bread." He walked to the table, fanned his hand over the bowl, and sniffed. "Ah, vanilla. You make the toast like the French, like my mama's cook. She was French." Unconsciously, the tip of his tongue slipped across his lips. "I would cover the pain with marmalade."

"No marmalade. I have honey." Madam van Groot reached to a back shelf, removed a crock, and set it on the table. "Now you go to dining room, so I can finish. Hilde will join you. And after, she help me pack baskets for my sister. Petre will bring horses."

Jack took another whiff of the french toast batter and left the kitchen. Several other travelers had already seated themselves in the dining room. No one sat at the bar. He found a table along the far wall near a window that opened onto the street in front of the inn. Outside, the activity seemed chaotic and hectic. A team of horses pulling a wagon containing several men raced up the street. Within moments another wagon, its team throwing clods of dirt and dust, clattered toward the harbor. Men stood in groups gesticulating. Some shook their fists in the air. Others had both or one hand against their face. They all appeared troubled. He wondered what had agitated the townspeople.

As Madam van Groot placed a stack of french toast in front of Jack, the front door to the inn swung open. Hilde bounded in from outside. "And what, may I ask, were you doing on the street?" Her mother put her hands on her hips and glared as she confronted her daughter.

"Petre has three horses out back," Hilde cried as she shut the door and ran to her mother's side. "Fishermen are rumbling, 'redcoats invading Brooklyn.' They saying Continental soldiers in longboats—rowing fast across river to Manhattan. Boats carrying wounded men. One fisherman sided with longboat that contained a Continental officer. Fisherman said this officer shouted to him, 'Howe's men breaching perimeter around Brooklyn. Frigates coming. Return to your village. Tell everyone to prepare to vacate!' Mama, what should we do?"

Jack wolfed down several chunks of the pain perdu. He gulped a swig of coffee, rose, and pushed himself away from the table. "Hurry! We must leave for Kill Van Kull immediately."

"If all is ready, you must be on your way," Madam van Groot said. She turned and headed to the kitchen. Hilde followed in her wake.

Jack stabbed another lump from the plate, grabbed a slice of bacon, and was about to follow the women when he realized his diary still lay on the table. He stumbled around, grabbed the book, and headed after Hilde and her mother. Behind him he heard chairs scraping and boots clomping onto the floor. Hilde's alarming outburst pressed several other diners, who also had observed the commotion Jack and the women had created, evacuate the dining room.

Petre stood nodding inside the back door when all entered the kitchen. "Must hurry," he snapped and stepped to the large prepping table. "Horses tied at fence. Not safe there. People distressed. They take horses. Must hurry."

Madam van Groot ran into the pantry and returned holding two baskets, their contents covered with a towel. "For my sister. You go. Be safe." As Petre took the baskets of food, Madam van Groot edged next to her daughter and then hugged and kissed her. She looked at Petre and then at Jack. "You protect Hilde. She delicate girl."

"Oh, Mother. You know I can take care of myself."

"Aye. But the men look after you."

Jack and Petre smiled as they sped out the door. The horses were at the rail, where Petre had hitched them.

———•◦•———

Claps of thunder vibrated the air, though the sky was clear. The road out of the village continued on an inland track. But about two miles out, the sporadic, distant booms continued.

"Can we get nearer to the shoreline?" Jack shouted. "Cannons are being fired."

"Ja," Petre yelled. He and Hilde rode in front of Jack. They came abreast of a copse of oaks and maples, margined by a tangle of stunted trees, and then a clearing. The two reined to a stop and waited for Jack to catch up. A path, wide enough to allow passage of a small carriage, led off to the left, through the brush, toward an old farmhouse and a large barn. "No one work farm." Petre twisted in his saddle and shook his head. "Punter, as English say. Ah, but no more—"

"Client, you mean," Jack said, when he halted his horse.

"Aye. Farmer not sell grain to Mr. Bennett. Lose farm."
Petre straightened on his horse. "Ve go to barn. Path go
on to shore from there." He urged his horse onto the path.
"Follow slowly. Many branches hang down."

Hilde turned her horse behind Petre, and Jack followed. They trotted in single file onto the barn, passed it,
and slowed their horses to a walk when the path narrowed
and appeared little used. After a bit over a mile, the tangle
of dense clumps of alders, briars, and jumble of other un-
dergrowth opened onto a grassy meadow. The path continued across this field and up a gradual, dunelike hill.
When the three reached the top, they could see most of
Upper New York Bay; two small, nearby islands; the mouth
of the Hudson River; and in the distance lower Manhattan,
Brooklyn, and Staten Island.

Jack reined in his horse atop the promontory and stared
out across Upper New York Bay. Clouds of dissipating white
smoke and haze drifted near and beyond the narrows.
Plumes of black smoke rose from the eastern perimeter
of Brooklyn. Frigates and barges coasted in the waters between Staten Island and Long Island. The starboard side
of a frigate cruising off Gowanus Bay erupted into jets and
billows of smoke. Within minutes, thundering waves of concussion crashed onto the dune, causing the horses to shy,
stomp, grunt, and whinny.

They all held tight on the reins and brought their
mounts under control.

"Redcoats invading Brooklyn!" Jack shouted. "Appears
the Continentals may be taking a beating." He jostled his

horse around. It snorted. "We have a ways to go. Let's be on our way."

The three spurred their steeds and galloped back down the hill. Where the path narrowed into the tangle of bushes and brush, they slowed to a trot until they passed the barn. Once on the main road, they turned south and galloped for some distance before easing to a slower pace.

They rode for several hours. Petre took the lead. Jack and Hilde followed a few yards behind. The road turned farther away from the coast. Soon the cannon fire faded to the sounds of birds and the hoofbeats of three horses. Above a distant wildwood, a steeple came into view. Petre swung around in his saddle to face his companions. With his right arm, he gestured toward a scatter of farmers working in a field. Nearby a pair of oxen harnessed to a wagon waited. "Harvesting," he yelled.

Jack looked at the idyllic scene and shook his head. They have no idea the redcoats are invading Long Island, he thought.

Several miles beyond the farmers, their village, and the church, the three came to a stream. The sun was at its zenith. They had been riding for about four hours, so they stopped to rest and water the horses. Once dismounted, Hilde removed a pouch of snacks and a canteen of water.

"Bring your canteens," she said. "Mother packed apples, bread, an' finnan haddie. Jack, Englishmen like finnan haddie, don't they? Mama says it comes from Scotland."

"Aye," Jack answered. "A bit strong and salty, but I can tolerate it as a snack." Jack took a swig from his canteen. "Haven't had any since I left Longfellow's in—" Jack stifled what he was about to say—in Machias—shook his head, and faked a cough. I cannot let these two know that I have any connection to Maine. "Sorry," he said, choking and whining. "Must have swallowed a fly." A sheepish grin crossed his face. He swallowed. "Longfellow's, a little public house near where I lived in Plymouth. It was a common bar treat. Made the boys drink more."

"Ja. Thas est so," Petre said. "In my ol' country too, barkeepers make men drink more veet smoked, salty fishes."

"Aye," Jack said. "A practice in Britain and Europe. But in the Netherlands, you people use herring. In England, we use cod and haddock."

"I will eat an apple and some bread," Hilde said as she scrunched up her face. "I eat smoked fish when Mama serves, but do not like it. Too salty and smells like smoky rot."

Jack chuckled. "Unpleasant things taste better to a man when his belly is plashing with beer."

Jack statement made Petre laugh, push out his belly, and rub it. "Tvood be goot to have a beer now." He picked up a piece of finnan haddie and gulped it down.

Hilde shook her head, feigned a gag, and sat down on a nearby log. Jack and Petre settled themselves on a grassy knoll and enjoyed the salty, smoked haddock and chunks of bread. They sweetened their mouths with bites of apple and swallows of water. A smoky, fishy aroma enveloped them. Hilde pinched her nose but continued to chew on an apple. She stood and fed the core to her horse.

Back in the saddle, the three individuals headed south. When the sun was a few degrees above the horizon, the

road approached an overgrown meadow strewn with rip-
ening pumpkins among scattered stalks of maize. Some of
the stalks supported vines of small withering leaves. As the
riders came abreast of it, Hilde rode onto the edge of the
field and halted. She scanned the area as her horse nuzzled
some clumps of grass.

"Farmer Smedt's old farm," she shouted. "When he lived,
he grew corn, beans, and pumpkins all together. And they
still come up every year. 'Field of three sisters,' he called
his farm. Indians, he said, teach him when he first settle
on land to grow these three plants. Like happy sisters, they
flourish best as family."

"Vhen my mama lived," Petre said, "she make pie from
pumpkin." His tongue wetted his lips. "Ah, so good, sweet."

Hilde pointed across the field toward a graying, run-
down cottage surrounded by brush along the front and
a mix of matchstick-sized and mature trees on each side.
"Farmer Smedt lived there among apple trees. Auntie Edda
says house is haunted. Spirits come, she tell me, when pumpkins and apples become ripe." She chuckled. "Auntie Edda
scared. Not go to house in autumn season. But she take
pumpkins that grow near road. She lives not far. A mile."

"Aye," Jack said. "Colonials are very superstitious people." He tugged on the reins and eased his horse back onto
the road.

"Ja," Petre added. "Some see witches." He laughed as he
steered his horse in behind Jack's.

Hilde followed and yelled, "After farmer Smedt die,
Indians come to harvest the pumpkins and apples. They
stay in house overnight. Auntie Edda's old. She hear them

wailing and howling—believe they are ghosts of farmer Smedt and his friends returning to protect the crops. But it is only the Indians enjoying themselves after a day of collecting the fruit."

The three trotted together for five or ten minutes. The road continued past the forest at the margin of farmer Smedt's pumpkin field, and beyond in the distance stood a white, well-kept cottage. Rail fencing and flowers defined its boundaries.

"Auntie Edda's house." Anxious to greet her aunt, Hilde spurred her horse and raced ahead.

Jack and Petre followed leisurely.

The two men watched Hilde stop her horse and dismount, and they saw a small, rotund woman come bounding out of the cottage. They assumed it was Aunt Edda. Her ankle-length outer petticoat was brown, with its front covered by a muslin-colored apron. She wore a beige short coat and a similar-colored neckerchief tucked into her bodice. Aunt Edda did not wear a cap, which exposed her curly white hair. The two embraced.

Aunt Edda knew Petre and hugged him immediately after he slid off his horse. "And who is this, my child?" she asked when Jack dismounted and led his horse to the hitching rail.

"Master Jack Hollister—a reporter," Hilde announced. "He is here to learn how the Americans and the British are cooperating—or not. Jack, this is my auntie, Edda Vogel."

A quizzical, suspicious look crossed Aunt Edda's face, but she walked to Jack and shook his hand. "I have heard the two are in considerable disagreement," she said. "It is not so here. The Lord says we should get along with each other. And that we do." An awkward smile crossed her face as she turned back to Hilde. "Please, let us all go into the cottage."

"Auntie," Petre said as he returned to his horse, "Madam van Groot sends vittles. I bring them."

———————

After Hilde and her aunt had stored what Madam van Groot sent, the sun had set, and the air chilled. Jack brought some firewood in from a woodpile and started a fire in the hearth while the two women set a table of ham, leftover finnan haddie, and some vegetables. Aunt Edda produced a jug of cider. When Petre returned from feeding and stabling the horses, everyone sat down to eat.

"Please bow your heads while I say grace," Aunt Edda said. "Thank you, dear God, for these and other blessings we are about to receive. Please bless my dear sister for sending such tasty viands—" She paused and seemed to ponder for a moment. "Oh, and thank you for providing safe journey for my three visitors. In God's name, amen." Aunt raised her head. "Please—"

Jack interrupted. "I'm not very religious, but perhaps your God will hear my wish. I would like to ask him to protect all my friends in New Jersey from the invaders."

A perturbed look crossed Aunt Edda's face when Jack voiced his request. She gasped. Her hand snapped to her mouth. "Vhat invaders?" she cried.

"Ja! Jack speak truth," Petre said. "Redcoats attack Brooklyn. Ve see, vhen ve ride here."

"Aye," Jack said. "The British forces have invaded Long Island. I believe they're planning to destroy the Continental Army. And they might. General Washington does not have as many soldiers as do the redcoats."

"Vhat are ve to do?" Aunt Edda asked.

"Please, let us not concern ourselves at this time, Auntie," Hilde said as she reached over and put her arm around the older woman. "The British are after New York and its harbors. Everything here has been peaceful. You have nothing the British want. I do not believe much will change if their invasion is successful. They are not interested in the Dutch colonies, because they feel we will remain loyal to King George."

Aunt Edda sighed and lowered her arm. Her brow remained furrowed. She reached to the platter of bread and passed it to Hilde. "Perhaps so. The Lord has been good to us. Please let us now break bread together and speak of more pleasant things."

In unison, Jack and Hilde said, "Amen."

"Tomorrow is Sunday," Aunt Edda said. "I vill tell Reverend van Eyke of the redcoat invasion. Ja, ve all go together to church and pray for General Vashington's army. He vill need God's help."

"I am so sorry—I will not be able to go to church with you." Jack lifted the dish of finnan haddie, took a chunk, and passed the plate onto Petre. "I have to be in the fishing village on Kill Van Kull tomorrow. Want to leave early in the morning." He looked at Petre. "Are you going to show me the way?"

"Ja. I vill." Petre speared a hunk of the smoked haddock and placed it on his plate. "Jack needs to go to fishing village at Kill Van Kull. Not go to church. Vill show Jack de vay and return. Then help Hilde back to Paulus Village. Keep her safe."

Jack nodded. Hilde handed him a bowl with vegetables. "Petre," he said, "these are your people. If you want to escort them to church, you should stay. The road to Kill Van Kull is direct. I should not have any problem finding my way." He forked a slice of ham and passed the bowl to his right.

"No, no. I vill show you the vay."

"Auntie, you and I will go to church," Hilde said. "It will be good to see Reverend van Eyke again."

Aunt Edda put down her fork, rubbed her cheek, and looked at her guests. "The reverend vill be disappointed." Her hand again touched her cheek and then wiped an eye.

Everyone sat and ate quietly for a few moments until Aunt Edda asked Jack, "Who do you meet in village?"

"A captain Joshua Perry." Jack sliced a chunk of ham and pressed his fork into the piece. "He is to ferry me to Staten Island."

"I know this captain Perry," Edda said. "He is old fishmonger. Sometime he come to our church to sell his fish. Irishman he is, but brings good fish and clams." She played with the pieces of food on her plate. "He not come all summer, so no one have much fish to eat." She looked at Petre and grinned. "You bring back fish from Captain Perry when you return?"

"Ja so. Vill bring back fish." Petre had finished off a second round of ham and vegetables and his mug of cider. "Ja, vill do."

Aunt Edda smiled.

"I will try to learn the fate of the invasion," Jack said. "If he fishes anywhere off Long Island or Staten Island, Captain Perry should know what has been happening. Petre and I should learn, and he can let you know, if trouble exists for you or any of the other colonials."

Hilde glanced at Jack and lowered her eyes. "You two are to sleep in Auntie's guest shed. Will you say good-bye before you leave? I may never see you again." She shook her head. "I would hope that not be the case."

Jack tightened his jaw and nodded. "I would also not want that to be the case. I will definitely wish you farewell." Hilde smiled, but her eyes glossed over. "With the invasion ongoing, I will be going into a hornet's nest. Though I'm an Englishman who is wanting to remain neutral in this conflict, I don't know if this is possible. I am uncertain whether I will be able to return. If this conflict ends, I will certainly try to come back."

A sheepish smile formed on Hilde's face. She sighed and nodded as her finger wiped away a tear. "I really would like to see you again."

Sunday, August 25, 1776, the residents of a group of cottages scattered within walking distance of a small Dutch Reformed Church awoke to a chilly dawn. At daybreak Jack and Petre were up and readying their horses for the trip to Kill Van Kull. Wafts of wood smoke mixed with the aroma of frying bacon drifted from Aunt Edda's cottage. She stood at the door and yelled, "Come to breakfast."

While the men were eating, Hilde came into the kitchen with her eyes lowered. A somber look covered her face.

"*Goedemorgen*, Mistress Hilde," Petre said. "You are sad?"

"Yes. I do not enjoy losing friends."

"Ah, Mistress, I vill be returning after I deliver Master Jack."

Jack bit off a piece of bread and sipped some tea. "Aye, you will not lose Petre. All I need is for him to show me the way. He will return as soon as I reach the fishing village, if not before."

Hilde shook her head as she took a seat at the table. "It is not Petre I will miss."

Jack lowered his head, ate the last piece of bacon on his plate, and glanced at Petre, who had finished eating. "It is time to be on our way, Mr. Dekens." Jack pushed himself away from the table and stood. "Hilde, you do not know who I am. But if all goes as it should, I will return. Please do not feel sad about me. I cannot let my, or anyone's, emotions prohibit a duty I must perform." He removed a tricorne from a hook on the wall and placed it on his head.

Hilde jumped from her chair, ran to Jack, and wrapped her arms around him. "I am aware of what Captain Perry does. And I feel you have a secret you cannot reveal. A secret that may be filled with peril." She loosened her hold, stepped away, but kept hold of Jack's arms. "I have seen others follow this same route. They have not returned. We hear some have been hung, or shot, or just have vanished."

Jack felt a tightness in his stomach and a knot in his throat. He sighed deeply.

Aunt Edda compassionately shifted herself next to Hilde and put an arm around her shoulder. "My little darling, it appears you have found a fondness for Master Jack, perhaps a strong affection, but he has a mission he needs to complete. You must let him go."

Hilde released Jack and fell back against her aunt, who wrapped her arms around the girl.

"My little darling, we will put his protection in the arms of our Lord. Today we go to church to pray for his safety and quick return."

Hilde nodded, sniffed, and freed herself from her aunt. She straightened, lifted her head, and looked directly at Jack. "I'm sorry, Jack. I don't know what has come over me. Though our friendship has been very short, I have developed a strong affection for you. But my response has been childish. I am so sorry."

Petre took a deep breath, shrugged, and walked out the back door of the cottage. "I go for the horses."

Jack swallowed and gritted his teeth. "Please do not apologize. Emotions can be overbearing. Sometimes we lose control of them." His eyes softened. "I too have felt a warmth in your presence—" He moved toward Hilde, extended his arms, took hold of hers, and slowly brought her closer. "I would enjoy learning where that warmth might lead. But I have a mission—and I do not know where that duty will take me or what will be its outcome."

Hilde nodded. She started to move closer to Jack, but the sound of horses' hooves startled him. He glanced to the outside, released her, and scrambled to the back door. She came next to him and grabbed his arm. "It's Klaas Dekens," she said. "And he has several other men with him."

Petre approached the horse his brother rode. Jack could not hear what the two were discussing, but by the gestures they made, he assumed it to be important. He looked at the others. Each wore befouled crofters' clothing. They all sported frayed headgear, tricornes, or wide-brimmed Quaker-styled hats, and were armed with muskets, pistols, knives, and swords. Petre nodded and headed back to the cottage, while the others remained on their horses.

Jack stepped onto the porch as Petre exclaimed, "Klaas say they go to the city. He and his friends vant to fight red-coats—help Mr. Vashington he say, like militiamen vould. Klaas vant us to go vit them."

"I would like to," Jack said, "but I need to remain neutral. Should I not, my assignment cannot be completed. However, Petre, if you want, you should ride with them."

Jack and Petre walked to the hitching rail, where their horses were tied. Hilde followed. Aunt Edda stood in the doorway, working her hands in her apron.

"Klaas and his men will ride with us to Kill Van Kull," Petre said, when they reached the hitching post. "They plan to find fishermen to ferry them to Manhattan."

Jack undid the reins of his horse and urged it back. "That sounds like a fine plan, but they will get caught if they sail in daylight."

"They vill go after dark. Fly Dutch flag. Navigate between shoals near Jersey shore into River Hudson and to Paulus Point. Then cross river. Fisherman boat good in shallow water."

"Aye," Jack said. "The redcoats are not interested in Dutch fishermen. So your brother and his men will be safe if they stay close to the river's west shore and cross over after dark. It will be good to have us all go to Kill Van Kull together."

The two men walked their horses to the lane beyond the fence, where the farmers who turned militiamen waited. Hilde followed in Jack and Petre's wake.

As Jack was about to mount, Hilde grabbed onto his shirt. "I will miss you," she whispered. "Please stay safe." She offered Jack her kerchief. "Please remember me."

Momentarily stunned, Jack turned and looked at her. His eyes softened. He accepted the token of affection by gripping its edge with his thumb and index finger and lifted it to his nose. "Remembering you will not be hard. Thank you. I will carry this with me wherever I go and return it when I come back." He tied it to his wrist.

Mournfully, she looked into his eyes, and her head sank.

Jack put his fingers under her chin and slowly raised her head. His face cast a tranquil smile. He gently bent and kissed Hilde on the cheek, then straightened. "I must be on my way."

Her eyes glossed. A tear trickled down the edge of her nose. She lowered her head and tried to catch it with the tip of her finger, but another took its place.

He stepped back, mounted the horse, and gazed down at her. His smile remained as he tugged the rein, urging his horse to the right.

"Godspeed and be safe," Hilde cried as Jack headed the horse toward the waiting militiamen.

Jack glanced toward Petre and Klaas and nodded. They and the other farmer-militiamen nudged their horses toward the main road. With a melancholic look, he tipped his tricorne at Hilde.

"Please, be safe and return," she mumbled.

After touching the kerchief bound to his wrist, he readjusted the tricorne. He dipped its tip, nodded to her, urged his horse forward, and followed the others to the road. Once there, the men headed south.

———•◦•———

After a casual trot, Jack, Petre, and Klaas and his farmer-militiamen arrived just after the noon hour at a little harbor village on Kill Van Kull. There, Klaas and his men went off to find, first, a restaurant or some food and, second, the boatman whom one of them knew, who might transport them to Lower Manhattan. Jack and Petre continued to the wharves and docks to find Captain Joshua Perry's fishing smack.

"A friend described the vessel as a gray sloop with red gunwales," Jack said as he stopped to reconnoiter the harbor. "Should be easy to find."

"Ja. Many know Captain Perry, but not know his boat," Petre called. "Many boats. Most gray—from dirt an' salt. But red topsides make easy to find—if not dirty."

They rode past several derelict sheds. Hidden behind one of the shacks that was skewed at a strong angle to seaward, a vessel sat upright, grounded in mud. Its tired-looking hull was streaked and mottled in hues of green, muddy beige, and gray. Though the paint on the gunwales looked worn, flaked, and peeled, speckles of red paint showed through the dirty topsides. It was not a sloop, but a deep-hulled, gaff-rigged fishing schooner,[1] with a small deckhouse set amidships and another aft of the mainsail.

"Not what I expected," Jack said. "Aye, it has a gray hull and gunwales that were once painted red, but this is not a little fishing smack. This vessel requires a crew of three to six men to work it properly." He shook his head. "But I do not believe it has been away from its dock in the last few years."

As Jack and Petre surveyed the vessel, a shabbily dressed, thickset man emerged from the schooner's aft cabin. A close-cropped white beard covered most of his face. The whiteness of the beard morphed to gray along the sideburns as whiskers mixed with darker strands of lush, disheveled steel-gray hair that covered the man's head. A short cigar stub jutted from the left side of his mouth. He stepped to the rail, removed the gnarly piece, spit, and shoved the nub back between his teeth.

---

1 Gaff-rigged vessels have trapezoidal fore-and-aft sails, where the head edge of the sail is supported or suspended from a spar (the gaff boom). The sail and its boom are raised and lowered on the mast using a line (the throat halyard). Once the sail is raised, it is trimmed by raising or lowering the gaff boom with a line (the peak halyard), which is attached to the outer end of the boom.

Close to what General Washington described, Jack thought. Always chewing a cigar.

"May you be Captain Joshua Perry?" Jack yelled toward the schooner.

"Quién está pidiendo?" the man asked.

Jack nodded. Speaks Spanish. Washington said he was a friend of José Diaz. He bit his lip. His face cast a confident glare and in Spanish he said, "A friend of Captain José Diaz."

"Aye." The man puffed his left cheek and ejected the cigar stub. "Do know the fellow. A mate from my drinking days in Cuba. Harassed those damn British back then, Frenchies too. Any merchantman who carried useful treasures. Aye, I know that pirate." He pulled himself tall against the rail. "Aye, I'm Joshua Perry. Englishman, Dutchman, Spanish, *hombre español*, whoever you want. What is your business?"

Sitting on his horse, Petre's forehead furrowed. He twisted toward Jack and in a quieter voice said, "He speaks in a foreign tongue, but you understand?"

Maintaining his attention on the man on the schooner, Jack answered Petre. "I once had a friend who sailed in the West Indies and taught me Spanish." He shifted in his saddle and yelled, "The name is Jack Hollister. A colleague in New York City told me to make contact with you. I'm on a quest to find a Mr. Carson Rabbit."

Captain Perry nodded toward Petre. "Who's your mate?"

"A guide from Paulus Village. Showed me the way here. He is leaving." Jack turned his attention to Petre. "I have made my contact. I believe, my friend, it is time for you to return to Auntie Edda and Hilde. Tell Hilde that all will be well with me. I am among friends."

"Very good," Captain Perry said. "You can come aboard." He bent down and glanced over the schooner's rail, straightened, and grinned. "A bit muddy below. Enjoy yourself for a time. When the tide returns, I'll cross over with the dinghy. In the meantime, I'm gonna sit back and enjoy a fresh cigar. Your friend Hosie got me addicted to them."

"I go now, Master Jack. May God keep you safe." Petre urged his horse around and started back to the village. "I go find real fisherman. Buy fish for Aunt Edda. Then find Klaas and his friends. And wish them good luck." He spurred his horse and trotted away.

———•◦•———

Not long after Petre rode off, Jack found a quiet, shaded spot some feet from the road within a copse of stunted red maple trees. There he sat almost hidden by clumps of sea oats growing closer to the shore. He ate an apple, the only food he had had since breakfast, and began to doze. He stirred when he felt soreness in his back from lying against a tree, straightened, and glanced at Captain Perry's schooner. It appeared that the vessel's rails had risen. Jack stretched and could see over the weeds that grew along the edge of the copse. Though the sunlight had diminished, there was still sufficient light to see the vessel. He rolled onto his knees, pulled out his diary, and decided to sketch Perry's vessel, but clumps of sea grasses and roses that grew closer to the shore blocked some of his view. He stumbled to his feet. From this vantage, he was able to see the entire vessel and the surface of the water.

Aye, the tide has come in. He shook his head and started to sketch. Captain must be asleep. Dinghy still tied to the hull. For a few minutes, he shaded in the shadowed portions of his sketch, but bathed in warm, muddy, salt-scented air, his eyes again became heavy. He relaxed beside a tree, sat himself down, lay back against its trunk, and fell asleep.

"Ahoy, mate! Hate to wake you from your midsummer's dream, but I came to take you aboard."

Startled, Jack snapped away from the maple's trunk. The pencil and diary that lay on his chest flew forward and landed in the grass. He jumped up, rubbing his eyes. "Where am I?"

"Relax, boy," Captain Perry said. "Did the same on the boat. Damn cigar. Nearly burned a hole in the deck. Smell o' smoke woke me. Then I remembered, supposed to pick you up. Well, here I am."

"Aye, you are." Jack wobbled onto his feet. He straightened. His hands fumbled about his body. "Was writing in my diary. Must have dropped it." He scanned the now-shaded area.

Captain Perry bent down and picked the notebook out of the grass. "Lookin' for this?" He handed Jack his diary.

"Appreciate it," Jack said and accepted the notebook. Unconsciously his middle finger slid under the front cover. He sighed when it touched a subtle, right-angled ridge on the inner facing. Haven't felt that for a while. North's letter; still safe.

"Come. Let's get you aboard." Captain Perry started back toward the shoreline.

Jack shoved the diary into his jacket pocket and followed.

"Get you outta those dandy-lookin' duds," the captain said as he twisted his way around the rosebushes. "Those damn things'll scratch the hell outa you. Smell good, though. Hips make a tasty jam." He allowed Jack to step into the dinghy before he pushed it off the beach and jumped in. "You gotta look like a fisherman. Got some proper duds aboard. And a crock o' hip jam. We'll sup on that tonight." He rowed easily to the schooner.

When Jack boarded, Captain Perry motioned him to walk forward to the amidships deckhouse, open the hatch, and go down the ladder to the second deck. When Jack backed off the lowest rung and turned to face the bow, he found himself in a passageway that ran forward through a dank, compartmented cargo hold. Diffused rays of sunlight that passed through the skylights on the cabin roof dimly illuminated the interior. A strong, nauseous odor of fish and aged wood filled the air. Though the passage appeared recently scrubbed, the shelves, dividers, and decking within the bins were coated in a tarlike slime embedded with scales, skin, bones, and other bits of fish.

Jack swallowed several times while he waited for Captain Perry to come down the ladder. As the captain stepped onto the passage deck, he took hold of Jack's shoulder, urged him to turn around, and pressed him to go behind the ladder and walk aft. A couple of steps beyond was the stern wall of the cargo hold. There Perry reached over and opened an inconspicuous doorway. He then prodded Jack through the opening.

"Welcome to the *Marigold*, Lieutenant Jack Hollister. She's a seaworthy vessel, though she doesn't resemble one."

This grubby wharfie knows me. How can that be?

Jack walked through the doorway into a more brightly lit passage that led to the *Marigold*'s stern. Startled again, this time by what he saw, Jack's eyes widened, and his jaw dropped. The cleanliness of the corridor made this part of the schooner look almost new. The bright work and wood trim shone, and the decking was unsoiled. Outside air flowed through open portholes, freshening the interior and dampening the fishy and moldy odors. The hallway Jack entered led aft to a well-appointed cabin—the wardroom and captain's quarters—located beyond a ladder to a hatch in the after deckhouse. But proceeding the pleasant rear cabin, he noticed two smaller cabins off the passageway, one on each side.

"Arg. Know what you're thinkin', Lieutenant." Captain Perry smiled and closed the doorway to the cargo hold. "In short, my friend, if this vessel's supposed to be an ol' fishing scow, it damned well must look and smell like one. Need to do so if we're to outwit those damn redcoats and accomplish the work our great general wants." He pointed to the compartment on the right. "Your quarters for the duration of your stay aboard"—he chuckled—"the spy ship *Marigold*. You'll find a new uniform in there. And some water and eatables to tide you over to breakfast. We'll talk in the morning. Good night."

CHAPTER 4
KILL VAN KULL
AUGUST 25, 1776

J ack woke, opened his eyes, and then yanked the bed-sheet over his face, blocking the blinding sunlight beaming through the porthole. He rolled toward the bulkhead, trying to push himself deeper into the bunk and to catch a few more moments of sleep. But this was to no avail. He tossed off the sheet, stood, and turned away from the bunk. Fixed to a shelf in front of him was a wash-bowl with a pitcher of water at its side. He poured some water into the bowl, bent forward, and splashed a handful on his face. The breeze wafting through the porthole cooled him as he toweled himself dry. He looked down at the foot-locker. There lay the apparel Captain Perry referred to last evening. Jack gazed at the stack of clothes: local sailor duds.

He plucked the socks from the pile, sat back on the bunk, and slipped them onto his feet. Reaching to the footlocker, he grabbed the white duck-cloth trousers, leaned back, shoved his feet into the pant legs, and stood. The slacks covered his legs to the ankles in soft, loose-fitting canvas. He slid a rope belt through the sash loops, cinched it tight, and knotted it. He then straightened and stepped around the little cabin. Slops. More comfortable than britches. As he bent over to pick up the shirt, a couple of knocks on the bulkhead startled him.

"Arr' you up, boy?" Captain Perry stuck his head into Jack's cabin. "Our cook has breakfast in the crew's quarters, forward in the bow. Finish dressin' and meet me at the after ladder."

"Aye, sir," Jack said, as he slipped the three-quarter-sleeve muslin shirt over his head. It covered his torso to below his waist. He shoved his feet into a pair of leather buckled shoes, grabbed a narrow-brimmed, cocked hat and his notebook, and backed out into the passageway. Captain Perry stood next to the ladder brushing something from his shirt.

"Now those redcoats will take you for a fisherman," the captain said, chewed, and grunted. "We'll need to soil them duds before we encounter any lobsterbacks." He climbed up the ladder, pushed open the hatchway, and stepped onto the weather deck. Jack followed.

The sun had just risen above the horizon when Jack strode onto the deck. He noticed that he had exited from the after side of the little aft deckhouse. Captain Perry directed him toward the bow. The two made their way forward, enveloped in the cool morning air. As they walked along the deck next to the cargo hold, Captain Perry pulled a cigar from a shirt pocket. The strong scent of aged, salted fish and wisps of wood smoke emanated from beneath the layers of tarpaulin covering the hold, flavoring the fresh air. He slid the tobacco roll back and forth under his nose. "Too early to smell the stench," he growled. "Got to put up with that damn stink to cover our toils for independence. Fishermen say it's the aroma o' gold. But we're not real fishermen. In our business, it'll likely to be the smell o' lead to us—or a length of hemp tied about the neck that'll be spicin' our fortunes."

The two men continued forward, past the amidships deckhouse, to a hatch through the deck in front of the capstan. Captain Perry belched a couple of gurgling coughs, laughed, and lifted the cover off a small access way to the *Marigold*'s anchor-cable locker.

"Now that's more appetizing," Jack said as the warm air from below wafted up through the opening.

"Believe cook has breakfast a-comin'," Perry said. He motioned for Jack to go below through the opening. The captain followed slowly, twisting and squeezing his stout body through the hatch as he backed down the ladder. Stepping off the ladder and adjusting his clothing, he said, huffing, "Tight passage. Don't come here much. Cook brings my meals aft. But I wanted to introduce you to my crew. A loyal bunch of scalawags they are."

The schooner's anchor hawsers lay flaked in piles on each side of the narrow, humid compartment with low headspace where the two men stood with their torsos bent forward. Several coils of line hung from an overhead beam, and boat hooks and other nautical paraphernalia were stacked against an after bulkhead. The doorway that led to the crew's quarters, though indistinguishable from its surroundings, passed through this wall.

Captain Perry reached up, wrapped his fingers around an overhead hook, and pulled down. A two-by-four-foot

panel between a pair of studs on the left side of the bulkhead slipped a few inches to the right. The captain slid his
fingers into the space that opened and pushed the panel to
the side, creating an opening that the two men could pass
through.

"A secret door." Jack smiled and straightened as he
stepped over the transom and into the crew's quarters.

"Aye," Captain Perry grunted. "The *Marigold* has many
secrets."

A long, narrow table hung from the ceiling. A rope
on each corner secured it to the deck and kept it from
swinging. When not in use, the table could be raised and
affixed to the ceiling. Attached to the starboard and larboard bulkheads were three bunks, one atop the other.
The upper bunks could be lifted and tied to the bulkhead
to provide more open space and allow the lowest two to
function as sitting space. The crew's meals were prepared
in a narrow galley hidden behind a divider on the starboard side near the rear of the cabin. To the left stood
a wood-burning stove with a rectangular top. A chimney
pipe channeled the smoke into the cargo hold and up to
the weather deck. An obvious doorway on the after bulkhead allowed access to the cargo hold. Oil lamps, hanging from the central beam, illuminated the interior of
this cabin.

A fiftyish, scrawny little man with a stubbly beard and
thinning gray hair wobbled back and forth between the galley and stove.

Captain Perry nodded his head at him. "How's breakfast
comin', Cook?"

Holding a spatula, Cook whirled around to the stove and flipped a pancake. "Bacon and flapjacks 'bout ready. Coffee hot, Mr. Perry. Get yourself a plate. Who's the fellow with ya?"

"This is Jack, a new seaman I took on yesterday. Jack, meet Cook."

"Good to make your acquaintance, Cook."

"Aye." The cook popped back into the galley, darted back with a pitcher in his hand, and poured some of its contents on a griddle. The batter sizzled and steamed. "Get yourselves a plate and sit down. Serve you in a minute."

Jack and the captain ate in silence until the hatchway to the cargo hold opened.

"Phew!" Captain Perry's head snapped up and he twisted toward the door. "Close that damn door, Dillon. Smells like hell in there." Dillon, an Irishman, muscular and weathered, wearing a knit cap, pulled the door closed. A skirt of salt-and-pepper hair extruded below the base of the cap.

Jack shrugged and held his breath until the initial odor was diluted by the aroma of bacon and burned pancake batter.

"Got to pull off those deck tarps covering that hold. Air it out. That stench is getting too strong." The captain turned his attention back to his breakfast. "Sit down, Dillon. Want you to meet our new seaman, Jack Hollister. Jack, Dillon's our boatswain."

Dillon nodded and dropped down next to the captain.

"We're going to get Jack captured by those damn redcoats," the captain said. "Since we're not sailin' until this afternoon's tide, he can help you remove those covers."

"May not be good to sail today," Dillon interrupted. "Redcoats swarmin' all over the bay. Lots of shootin'. Not safe to be tryin' to set fishing lines or tend our nets. Best to weigh anchor tomorrow early, 'fore the tide turns."

A look of concern crossed Jack's face. Why did Captain Perry tell this chap that I'm to be captured by the redcoats? He seems to know more about me than I suspected. His brow furrowed, jaw tensed, and gut muscles tightened. He cocked his head slightly to the right and glowered at the captain.

Perry glared back at Jack. "Relax, boy. I knew of your mission weeks before you came aboard. Washington sent a messenger informing me of his need to infiltrate the enemy. Just didn't know who he was sending. He sent no name. Guess he didn't know if you'd accept."

Jack's tenseness eased. He sighed. "When I agreed to undertake this mission, General Washington said that no one was to know."

"No one in his immediate staff." Captain Perry sat back. "Clandestine assignments work only with the help of a network of loyal people. That includes all my crew. They need to be aware. As I said, they are all loyal to me and our cause." The captain paused for a moment. His eyes softened. "By the way, Washington's messenger is known to you. A young man of about your age named Nathan Hale. We dropped him on the coast of Connecticut. Said he volunteered to gather intelligence for Washington and would cross over to Long Island near the end of this month. He planned to walk to Brooklyn and pass himself off as a teacher."

Jack's eyes widened. "Aye. I do know him. He is a friend. We ran missions from Cambridge to Boston during the blockade."

"Aye. Mr. Hale spoke of your escapades, but the mission you are about to become involved in is more than an adventurous jaunt. We are in a full-scale war. So if the enemy finds you to be a spy, they will hang you."

Jack clenched his fist. Again, he felt a knot form in his stomach. "I understand. General Washington made the danger very clear." He sighed and tried to relax. "Have you heard of Lieutenant Hale's whereabouts?"

"No. Didn't know the jovial lad was a lieutenant. He was not as reserved as you are. Gregarious fellow. I'm afraid that nature might get him into trouble." The captain finished his breakfast. "I believe it is now time to learn how the invasion of Brooklyn is progressing. Dillon, have you any word?"

"Only what I heard at the Loon's Nest, sir," Dillon answered. "Met Gordy, Rik, and the Algonquin, Kitchi, at the tavern last evening. They were drinking with that Irish fisherman named Doyle. Doyle agreed to haul a group of Dutchmen to Manhattan and needed a crew. Our boys decided to help him out." He broke into a coughing laugh. "Militiamen, these Dutchmen called themselves. From Paulus Point, they are—farmers who wanted to shoot it up with Washington. Rik told them that they would probably get themselves shot up. We all drank to those patriots' health." Dillon paused and then said, "Our boys thought they would be back aboard the *Marigold* this afternoon."

"Aye," Jack said with a sad grin. "The intent of those Paulus farmers is admirable. A bold bunch, they are. The fellow who guided me here is the brother of the leader of that group. I hope they will be all right."

"Dissidence generates courage, even in an inept warrior," Captain Perry said. "Hope so too. That Doyle is a crafty fellow, but not a keen seaman. Probably charge those farmers a week's wage for ferrying them. With Gordy, Rik, and Kitchi aboard, all should be well. The Irishman will have to sail along the New Jersey shore to make it safely to Manhattan. After that, those greenhorns are on their own. We'll make our plans when Gordy and Rik and the Algonquin come aboard. For now, you two uncover that cargo hold."

———•◦•———

About an hour past lunchtime, Jack and Dillon removed the tarpaulins and supporting frames from the cargo hold, allowing this vast storage space to air out. They had used the tackle attached to the foremast to hoist the last support frame and stored it atop the others on the larboard side, next to the rolls of tarpaulin.

"Let us go below and have some vittles," Dillon said, wiping the sweat from his brow. He bent forward, untied the lifting line from the frame, and tossed it aside. Straightening, he started to head for the amidships deckhouse, but stopped, turned, and faced Jack, who was scanning the interior of the cargo hold.

Looks like a honeycomb mix of compartments from up here on deck, Jack thought. Guess it is to keep all the different fishes separate. Confusing.

"When he welcomed you aboard yesterday, did ol' man Perry take you to his cabin by way o' yonder deckhouse?" Dillon asked, pointing to the amidships deckhouse.

"That he did."

"Aye. Captain tries to discourage pestiferous kinds from entering into the schooner. Does that to all new arrivals. Tests them." Dillon laughed.

Jack looked at the rear of the amidships deckhouse and could see the ladder, now exposed, he had climbed down, extending from the interior of the deckhouse to the passageway down the center of the hold.

"And today, he brought you to the crew's quarters and galley through the cable locker?"

"Aye."

"Must trust you. Emergency compartment. Fighting equipment. Muskets, shot, powder stored in that locker. Even got a couple of swivel guns." Dillon started walking to the amidships deckhouse.

"Did not see any weapons. Only hawsers."

"Captain keeps them locked up, away from snoopin' eyes. Lots of secret compartments onboard this boat." Dillon entered the amidships deckhouse and stepped onto the ladder. "You should know, 'cept for the captain, this hatchway is how us seamen, visitors, an' redcoats get inside the *Marigold*. Captain goes below through the after deckhouse. Goin' through the cable locker is for escape." He climbed down into the cargo hold. "Come on. I'm hungry."

Jack climbed down the ladder. Even with the covering off the cargo hold, the stench of rotting fish and other revolting odors momentarily nauseated him. He followed

Dillon into the crew's quarters and closed the door behind him. "Phew! That hold stinks bad—like the bottom of a bait box."

Dillon chuckled. "Captain likes it that way. If you look about in there, you'll find boxes of drying an' rotting fish. Scents the hold. Bears out that *Marigold* is a fishing vessel. Those damn redcoat inspectors don't go farther than the bottom of the ladder. Some don't even come down. Almost puke when they pass into the deckhouse above." He laughed. Grasped his belly and feigned a gag. Then laughed again and straightened. "Keeps them lobsterbacks at bay. Keeps them from nosin' around." The starboard bench grated the deck as Dillon hooked his boot against a leg and slid the seat back. He sat and then grabbed the table and scrunched himself and the bench back. "Cook! Got any leftovers? We missed lunch."

———•◦•———

With lunch finished, Jack eased back against the bulkhead and closed his eyes. Dillon fiddled about in a shirt pocket and removed his pipe and tobacco pouch. He took a pinch of the fragrant herb and began packing it into the pipe's bowl as the door to the cargo hold opened. Two middle-aged, muscular men entered. They were followed by a sturdy fellow with jet-black hair, pulled back and tied into a queue, who wore rawhide pants. A sleeveless, open buckskin jacket that hung to his buttocks shielded the latter man's upper body and exposed his weathered, amber-colored arms and chest. He was the oldest of the three. The other guys wore typical seaman's duck-cloth pants and cotton shirts.

"Aha! Our crew has arrived." Dillon put his pipe and tobacco pouch on the table, stood, and faced the arrivals. "Gordy and Rik, meet Jack, the new cargo for delivery to Staten Island. O' yeah, the Indian behind those bums is Kitchi—once scouted for General Washington. Seat yourselves. Cook has some fresh coffee. Brewed it this morning."

Jack got up and extended his hand to the incoming men. Rik and Gordy nodded and grunted, while Kitchi moved into the galley. All ignored the gesture of friendliness.

"Captain Perry told me that you men crewed on a vessel that ferried a group of men to Manhattan," Jack said. "See any of the battle that is being fought in Brooklyn?"

"Aye. Delivered that bunch of novices—farmers—to the island," Rik mumbled.

"Good. They mean well." Jack sat back down and laid his arms on the table. "Met many men like them, who came to this country for independence, found it, and are eager to fight to keep it."

"Aye. They are a resolute bunch," Gordy said.

"What of the British?" Jack leaned forward. "Are Washington and the Continentals safe?"

Kitchi, carrying three cups and a pot of steaming coffee, came to the table.

Rik reached out, grabbed the pot, and poured himself a mugful. "Hugged the Jersey coast into the Hudson. Heard much cannon fire along the way. Crossed the river after dark. Shooting stopped. Gordy and Kitchi rowed those farmers to shore."

Kitchi nodded his head. "Took them into shallows. Patriots not recognize us. Want to shoot—"

Gordy grabbed and banged a mug on the table, splashing some coffee on the table. "Yelled to those damn veterans that we were not the enemy. Just fishermen delivering some recruits from Jersey. Then ol' captain Doyle came on deck and talked to them. Seemed they knew that Irishman. Those Continentals let the recruits come ashore." The seaman pulled a cloth from a hook and wiped the table dry. "All they had to say 'bout the invasion is that Washington visited the fortifications in Brooklyn and had the troops move back to the East River. Someone in the bunch said that Washington is plannin' to evacuate Brooklyn. Set up a defense along the Battery. Not lookin' good for our side."

"What's not looking good?" Captain Perry asked as he walked into the crew's quarters.

"Seaman Gordy was telling us about the invasion," Jack said. "He says that Washington's army may be having some trouble. They are to evacuate Brooklyn and take up arms at the only Continental stronghold that remains, the Battery."

"Aye, General Howe has at least thirty thousand troops." Captain Perry ran a hand through his hair and sat down with the others. "Washington has only about seven thousand. Probably less, now that they been battlin' for the past few days. And the British forces are supported by Admiral Howe's armada of perhaps two hundred fighting vessels. They're all over the lower bay like ants. Some will even be makin' their way to the mouth of the Hudson."

Jack clasped his hands and placed them on the table. He closed his eyes momentarily, lowered his head, and cocked it to the right. "Sounds dangerous out there, Captain."

"Aye." Captain Perry nodded. "We'll let things settle for a day or so. Get some horses and you, Gordy, Rik, an' Kitchi will ride to the bay, examine it, and assess the situation. If all looks good, we'll go fishing on the next morning tide."

———•◦•———

The next morning after breakfast Jack and the three seamen rode to the eastern access to Kill Van Kull. They then traveled north along the shore for about a mile to a high meadow, from where they could scan most of Upper New York Bay from below the mouth of the Hudson River to the narrows between Staten Island and Brooklyn.

Several British frigates patrolled the bay. Frigates and smaller craft filled the narrows. Several large men-of-war lay off the southwest corner of Long Island. Though smoke and flames rose along the Brooklyn shoreline from Red Hook northward, a considerable amount of British activity was centered in Gowanus Bay.

"Deliverin' troops, they are," Rik said.

Jack watched as three spurts of white smoke jetted toward the shore from one of the men-of-war standing off Fort Defiance. Within a matter of moments, he and the others heard the cannons' thunderous rumbles. He pulled a spyglass from a pouch, raised it to his eye, and trained it toward the mouth of the East River. Though his view was obstructed by Governor Island, he could see heavy, gray smoke rising from the inland of Brooklyn. Putman's fort is in flames, he thought. Several more grumbles of cannon fire vibrated over the meadow.

"I do not believe the captain will feel it safe to sail today," Gordy said. His horse's head shifted to the right as he tugged the reins. "Let us return to the *Marigold* and report what we have seen. We will check on redcoat activity again tomorrow morning."

Jack continued to scan the battle before he lowered the telescope and shoved it back into the pouch. Hope General Washington and his troops were able to evacuate, he thought and perused the bay a moment longer before urging his horse around and following the others.

CHAPTER 5
KILL VAN KULL
AUGUST 28, 1776

Noise on the weather deck awakened Jack. He scrambled to the porthole, glanced outside, and saw that the moon still shone bright against a black sky. The crew is already working, he thought. Why did I not awaken? Dressing quickly, he dashed out of his compartment and up the ladder. A warm, southerly breeze flushed around him as he stepped onto the deck and took hold of the after-deckhouse roof. *Marigold*'s subtle movement disrupted his equilibrium. Tide is up, he noted. She is floating. He noticed Captain Perry bracing himself against the helm.

The captain nodded at him. "Stand fast, Mr. Hollister, while the boys ready the *Marigold* for the sea." He gripped the ship's wheel, pushed himself taller, and yelled, "Dillon! Make fast the booms, then send Rik and Gordy to reconnoiter conditions in the bay. We'll sail on the outgoing tide if all has quieted somewhat. Tell Cook to bring some breakfast aft." Captain Perry relaxed and again faced Jack. "Go below to my cabin. I'll be there directly."

———◆———

Cook entered the captain's cabin, carrying a basket of biscuits, a crock of grape jam, and one of butter. He nodded at Jack, who was seated at the table, placed what he had brought on the table, and scampered back into the passageway. "Coffee sitting on deck," he said as he headed for the ladder. But he quickly popped back through the doorway, followed by Captain Perry, who was carrying the pot of coffee.

"Thought we might enjoy this," the captain said as he smiled. "Found this pot full, and it's hot, sitting on deck." He set the pot on the table and smirked at Cook. "Be good if God made us with four or five hands. Some fruit would be nice. Could you bring us some, my man?" he asked.

Cook pursed his lips, nodded, and again headed for the ladder to the deck.

"Jack, reach up to the shelf behind you. There're some mugs. Get a couple, and we'll proceed to enjoy biscuits and jam with our coffee and discuss infiltrating you into the redcoat army."

"I am concerned," Jack replied as he stood, turned, picked up the mugs, and placed them on the table. "With the redcoats swarming all over Brooklyn and, seeming to have the upper hand, I am worried that General Washington may be in serious trouble. I hope he was able to escape and evacuate his troops." He took hold of the coffeepot and poured the steaming, dark fluid into the mugs.

"Not to fear. Washington will not let himself or his troops be caught. Those who know him compare him to a Roman general named Lucius Quinctius Cincinnatus. Like Washington, Cincinnatus was a farmer. He was called from retirement to lead Rome's armies against the Aequians and Sabines. Cincinnatus was victorious and saved the city of Rome." Captain Perry took a bite of a biscuit and washed it down with some coffee. "Washington, also a man of the land, was likewise called to serve his country. He is an excellent military strategist. No doubt, so was Cincinnatus. But there is a difference between these two men. Washington exhibits wisdom, heroism, reason, and a commitment to protect civilization. There is little indication that Cincinnatus had these qualities. Besides, his battles lasted only two weeks, and he only saved a city. Afterward, the man returned to the blissfulness of his farm. Washington's war is ongoing. He is out to save a nation. Who knows where he'll go after we win independence. To many, our excellent general has become a deity. Perhaps he will be called to rule our country."

"You regard General Washington highly," Jack said, "as do I. But I have not heard of this Roman general of whom you speak."

"He lived some time ago. About five hundred years before Christ, I believe."

Dillon popped his head into the captain's cabin. "*Marigold* is ready for sea, sir. Rik and Gordy are off to survey conditions on the bay. Kitchi retired to his bunk."

"Aye, Dillon. Thank you." Captain Perry relaxed back against the bulkhead. "Enough with the accolades to our fine general and leader, Mr. Hollister. Let us get on with the matter at hand." The captain reached into a shirt pocket, removed a cigar, bit off the end, and spat the nub into his empty coffee mug. "Did your redcoat captors ask if you have brought anything to verify your identity as a British subject?"

Jack gasped, clasped his hands, and squeezed them tight. "Aye. I have. A letter Lord North sent to all the vessel masters of Britain's North American fleet, asking them to be on the lookout for two lost Hollister brothers. I have a copy of North's letter hidden in my diary. General Washington gave me the copy he obtained from some rebels who stole from a British vessel anchored in Boston Harbor."

"Hmm—that letter must be almost two years old."

Jack nodded. "My brother was captured and impressed into service aboard a frigate that patrolled off the coast of Maine. When the master of that vessel received the letter, Ian was finally recognized and released to members of our family who lived in Boston." He looked at the captain. "I have yet to be found. The letter will help verify my identity."

"You cannot tell the redcoats that you received North's communication from Washington. How do you propose to tell them how you came by this letter?"

"I will explain thusly to my captors. On my journey south from Maine to Boston, I came upon three dead Continental soldiers. Having not eaten in several days, I examined their pouches for food. One soldier apparently was a courier because he carried a pouch that contained dispatches to Washington and other officers. Lord North's letter was among them. Since it was of value to me, I took it and left the other reports. I found no food, but I did find several shillings. Took them. The coins allowed me to purchase food when I reached a settlement." Jack finished his coffee.

Captain Perry opened the stove's door, reached in, and removed a twig. Then he reached to an insignificant little iron tray attached to the side of the stove and lifted a piece of cord from which rose a paltry wisp of smoke. The captain blew on the smoking end and touched the brightly glowing tip to the twig. When it burst into flame, he lit a candle, then tossed the burning twig into the stove, rehung the match cord, returned to the table, and stared at Jack. He lit a cigar with the candle flame. While exhaling a waft of smoke, he blew out the flame. "Damn!" He grunted. "Yours is a likely story, but it's a bit general. What are you going to tell those redcoats you did before they captured you? They are going to ask you such questions. You've been lost for almost two years."

"Aye, I do have a story."

"Let me hear it," he said and began to chew on the tobacco roll. "Those redcoats are going to look at you with suspicion. I don't want your story to sound incredible." Cigar smoke began to fill the cabin.

Jack shifted about on the bench. He pursed his lips and rubbed his nose. "The early events of the story are true. After the coastal vessel my brother, Ian, and I were aboard wrecked on the coast of Maine in the summer of 1774, we survivors made camp in a nearby cove. There were nine of us, seven men and two women. We remained in the area for some days trying to salvage what we could, but much of the food had spoiled. What was edible ran short. Though snails, clams, and an occasional fish were available, two of us went in search of game. We were gone perhaps three days. When we returned from the hunt, we found the bodies of two survivors. Both had been shot. The others, including my brother, were missing. My hunting friend and I did not feel it was safe to remain in the area, so we left and made our way along the coast to the village of Machias."

The captain puffed out a cloud of smoke, pondered the cigar, and then shoved it back into his mouth and began chewing. "Credible story." He leaned forward, placed his elbows on the table, and rested his head in his hands. "Who do you think shot the two? And where did the others go?" Captain Perry asked as he looked up and stared at Jack. "Those redcoats are going to ask those kinds of questions. They're going to want answers."

"A frigate had been observed cruising off the coast by several persons in our camp." Jack shrugged. "Could have been a British patrol? Pirates? One of the survivors did say that there were pirates and wreckers along the eastern Maine coast. Whoever shot those men took the others prisoner."

"Aye." The captain nodded and continued chewing on the cigar. "Mr. Hollister, tell your redcoat captors that a British patrol took the survivors. Those redcoats have evidence that your brother was indeed impressed into His Majesty's service. Your comments will support what they already know."

"Yes! An excellent point, sir."

"Continue. You are in Machias, a nest of colonial rebels. What now?" Captain Perry exhaled a cloud of cigar smoke.

"Aye. An uncomfortable place that village was for an Englishman to be." Jack squeezed his nose again and wiped his eyes. "Might I open a porthole, sir? The smoke in the cabin is getting rather thick."

"Aye."

Jack pushed away from the table, stood, and released the clamp that held the window closed. He lifted and attached the window to a cord that swung from the ceiling and continued his story of how he would present himself as a British subject. "Though the people were hospitable, I did not feel secure in Machias, even though some residents voiced loyalty to the Crown. I chanced upon a coastal vessel, whose captain professed an allegiance to Britain, and he offered me a seaman's position. The vessel was to take on lumber to supply the army barracks in Boston, but because of the rebellious nature of the Machias community, it departed without taking on cargo. The captain set a course for Falmouth. There he thought the colonists felt kindlier toward Great Britain."

The smoke had dissipated somewhat, but Jack could not stifle a sneeze. "Begging your pardon, sir."

The captain rolled the cigar between his fingers for a short time, allowing it to extinguish. He then popped it back into his mouth and started chewing the nub. "Continue, my boy."

"When the transport anchored in Falmouth, the Brunswick militia met the captain at the dock. He was told there would be no lumber available for redcoats in Boston. The colonel of the militia allowed the captain to resupply the vessel and told him to set sail before nightfall. I and several other of the crew were ordered to obtain sufficient food that would sustain us on to Boston. And that we did.

Back aboard we headed south and then southwest, though the weather threatened as the vessel proceeded. The fury of the storm hit early in the morning. It raged for several hours and blew us well off course."

Jack's story was interrupted as Cook came into the captain's cabin and asked, "Coffee? Still some in the pot. A bit cool, though it is."

Both Jack and Captain Perry lifted their mugs. Cook poured the coffee and departed with an empty pot.

Jack took a swig and shook his head. "Drinkable. Let me continue creating my story."

"Aye. Continue."

"After our course was reestablished, the captain of the cargo vessel decided there was no reason to continue on to Boston. We carried no lumber to satisfy the needs of the redcoats. So the captain set a course for New York City, where he said some form of cargo might be obtained. The trip was ordinary. Being March, a favorable north wind blew mildly. It continued until we were a day or so from Gravesend.

"An hour or two before sunset, the captain could see the coastline. He recognized several landmarks and set a course for the vessel to pass through the mid of the narrows and into New York Bay, expecting that would happen shortly before sunrise. But during the night, we encountered a dense fog. Except for the two jibs, the other sails were lowered. Lookouts were stationed, but we could see nothing beyond arm's length even after the mist whitened in the morning light. As daylight progressed, the captain adjusted to a slightly more westerly course, assuming we were approaching or perhaps already had passed through the narrows. The fog had lessened as we glided through New York Bay. By noon as we move to the west, the shoreline, though still clouded in mist, became visible. The captain had the helmsman steer for the Paulus Point on the New Jersey shore. There, to all our relief, came the command to drop the anchor." Jack took a sip of the now-cold coffee.

Captain Perry chewed on the cigar. "Good story, boy. Convincing, so far. But you arrived here back in March. What have you been doing since them? It is now August."

Before Jack could create an account of his recent activities, he and the captain heard the dull clump of footsteps approaching through *Marigold*'s cargo hold. The after door to the hold opened, allowing a waft of fishy smelling air to invade the captain's cabin. A moment after the door was closed, Rik and Gordy stepped into the cabin to report on their reconnaissance of New York Bay.

"The bay appears quiet," Gordy said. "Brooklyn is burning. A few vessels are cruising off its shore."

"Spoke to a fellow living near the shore," Rik said as he sat down on the bench next to Jack. "He told me that the redcoats have taken Brooklyn. The fellow thinks that Washington evacuated with what troops he had. Everyone assumes Howe will attack the Battery within the next few days."

"Yeah. But nothing happening off Manhattan," Gordy added. "Most of the action is along the south shore of Brooklyn and Long Island."

Just as Gordy was about to sit down, Dillon came into the cabin. "All is ready on deck, sir."

"Thank you, boys," Captain Perry said. "Dillon, find a seat. The rest of you fellows relax. We'll hoist the Union Jack tomorrow and sail on the tide. Maybe we'll go through the narrows and head up the coast for Montauk Point. Be away a couple of days. Then return and drop off our cargo. But maybe not—if one of us comes up with a better plan." He looked at Jack. "He's been inventing a story to tell the redcoats how he come to be here." The captain paused. "But he isn't finished. Got to tell us what he's been doing since he arrived in our waters this past March. Like for you two to stay and listen. Determine if his story is believable." He glanced at Gordy, who was still standing. "Grab a couple of mugs before you seat yourself."

"Aye, Captain. We will lend our ears," Gordy said as he took two mugs off a shelf.

"So you were in Paulus Point in March." Captain Perry chewed on the cigar, stood, and reached to a cabinet behind him. He opened it and pulled out a bottle of rum. "The coffee is cold. We'll have a couple of tots of this stuff to warm our bellies while Jack tells us his story." He pulled the cork and poured the golden liquid into everyone's mug. "Go ahead, Mr. Hollister. Entertain us."

"Not much more to tell if I am creating a false tale." Jack said, slouching for a moment and then straightening. He leaned forward, glanced at Captain Perry, and scanned the crew. "Since I know the sea better than I do the land, my continuance of the journey would be best if I were part of a crew of some vessel. So this is what I will tell the redcoats.

The transport I crewed on remained in the harbor at Paulus Point for a week. The captain spent most of his time at the tavern. He returned one late afternoon, telling several of us that he obtained a commission to transport a shipment of beer, salt pork, and several other items to Wilmington. We were to cross the bay and collect the cargo at a pier on the East River. He ordered us to ready the vessel immediately for the sea.

"I did not receive this news with enthusiasm, since my goal was to get to Boston, where members of my family resided. The voyage to Wilmington would take me south. As the crew and I readied the ship, I considered leaving. But a crew member who had befriended me told me that it would be better to cross over to Manhattan, because many more cargo vessels traveled to Boston from the docks of New York City. And that is what I did. I deserted the transport in Manhattan." Jack paused and sat back.

"Is Cook going to bring food to your cabin, sir?" Dillon shuffled about. "I am a bit hungry. And I am sure the others are also. Perhaps we should go aft to the crew's quarters and continue this discussion."

"The continuance of this story," Jack said, "will depend on how I am to be deposited on Staten Island." He looked at Captain Perry. "When that is decided, it will be easier to create a convincing yarn to support my loyalty to the Crown."

"Aye," Captain Perry said. "Let us go forward. It will be easier for Cook to serve us in the crew's quarters."

———•◦•———

Jack, Captain Perry, and the other seamen finished lunch and sat around the table, bantering ideas that might explain Jack's presence in the area for the past five months. They came up with several stories, some possible, others far-fetched. Kitchi suggested that, during the past five months, Jack had been held prisoner of the Continental forces, but he escaped.

"Possible," Captain Perry said.

"Aye. He is an Englishman, educated, but looks like a dodger." Rik swigged the rest of his rum, chuckled, stood, and stumbled around, feigning a prisoner with a ball and chain tied to his ankle. "Writes poetry. Patriots arrest him for stirrin' up the Tories. Call his writings treasonous."

Captain Perry scratched his head and chewed on the cigar butt. "Could work. But redcoats would suspect he was a patriot plant. They're a nervous bunch."

"He could be a fisherman. Washed ashore," Gordy piped up.

Dillon stood and smashed his right fist into his left hand. "Believe Gordy might have a plan. Here's what we can do. Sail *Marigold* o'er to Raritan Bay an' put in at Perth Amboy. I know the waters. We'll be safe there. Perth Amboy is a town of Scot rebels who do not want anything to do with the redcoats. Across the way is the southern tip of Staten Island known as Billopp's Point. After dark, Rik, Gordy, and I could row Jack o'er, close to shore, and let him swim in and plod across the marsh. We'd do it on the low tide, so he'd get a bit muddy."

Captain Perry nodded. "Aye. Billopp's Point is a nest of redcoats. It's the estate of Colonel Christopher Billopp. He's the great-grandson of the Royal Navy's notable Captain

Billopp, who secured Staten Island for New York City. The colonel has remained a staunch Tory who as a regiment of loyal Tory militiamen encamped on his estate." The captain looked at Jack and smiled. "If the lieutenant can connect with this colonel Billopp and convince him, and the Howes, of his true identity, I do believe we will have a very successful infiltration." Captain Perry chewed down hard on the cigar butt, raised his left eyebrow, and flicked his head to the right. "If not, I'm afraid Jack will be hung as a spy."

Jack shook his head and pursed his lips. "I do not relish that, but Lord North's letter should provide strong, creditable evidence that I am who I say I am. Also, I do not enjoy the thought of swimming into the shallows and having to plod across the mud wet and cold."

"Aye, but sometimes one cannot enter a world dressed to the nines," Captain Perry said. "Especially if one jumps ship to save oneself from disaster."

"Humm," Jack grunted. "I suppose that will make an impression. And, perhaps, move me through the gates and into the hands of the redcoats."

The captain agreed. "If fortune is in your favor, you may be found by one of the young ladies who visit Billopp's wife. I have heard they are fine-looking women and may fancy a handsome fellow as you. This assignment may turn out better than you had anticipated."

"I suppose it is a reasonable plan." Jack sipped the last of his rum, but his face continued to show concern.

Captain Perry shifted on the bench and pushed away the dishes in front of him. "Cook, get us a bottle of rye whiskey. We have a cause to celebrate."

"Fine plan, sir," said Dillon. "And we do not have to sail into the hornet's nest. We can avoid New York Bay. Sail west into Newark Bay and down Arthur Kill along the back side of Staten Island."

A few white clouds drifted to the northwest across the stark blue on the morning of August the twenty-ninth. The warm breeze was insufficient to scatter the clammy air from the deck of the *Marigold*. At about ten o'clock, the flooding tide was reaching its peak. Besides the squawks and squeals of several gulls soaring above, the only other sounds that disturbed the calm were the screech and groan of the hawsers that squeezed around the drum as Jack, Rik, and Kitchi pushed against the capstan's bars, rotating the winch. When the anchors broke the surface, Dillon yelled to Gordy to hoist the forestaysail and jib. The sails fluttered, but the schooner slid slowly and silently into the open waters of Kill Van Kull with the incoming tide. The current carried the vessel westward toward Newark Bay.

Captain Perry came on deck shortly after the *Marigold* reached midstream. He strolled aft to the helm and gazed forward. "It'll be a slow ride, but it is not far. Should make the middle of the bay as the tide turns."

"Aye," Dillon said. "If we raise the mainsa'l and catch what wind we can, make maneuvering easier, sir."

"That it would." Captain Perry walked to the mainmast and started to remove the ties that bound the sail to the boom. "Need a bit of help to haul up the mainsa'l," he yelled.

Jack had finished stowing the capstan bars and hurried to the captain's side. Gordy followed. The two unhitched the mainsail halyard and began hoisting the large sail. When it reached its height, Jack took in the slack on the peak halyard—the line that hauls the outward end of the mainsail gaff—and pulled the end of this spar, which is attached to the head of the mainsail, toward the mast.

"Broad reach the sail to starboard," Captain Perry said.

Kitchi came aft and helped Gordy swing the main's boom to starboard while Jack secured its position about sixty degrees from the vessel's centerline. He then trimmed the sail. It flapped and fluttered as it caught puffs of the transient wind, but these gusts were appropriate to increase the vessel's speed about a half knot.

By the time the *Marigold* reached the lower middle of Newark Bay, the tide had already turned. The southeasterly wind had become continuous, and its force intensified about a knot.

Jack, standing a short distance from the helm, overheard Captain Perry.

"Mr. Dillon, head toward Perth Amboy to the south. Tide's with us, but wind's not. Seems we're gonna have to wiggle our way down Arthur Kill."

"Aye, sir," Dillon responded. "Going to have make a series of tacks. There is ample room, and we keep the mainsa'l's position close-hauled."

"Indeed! Prepare to come about," Captain Perry yelled.

Jack and the crew took positions at the mainmast and grasped the mainsail's halyard.

"Ready mainsa'l for larboard turn. Bring the *Marigold* around to the south, Mr. Dillon."

Jack released the main's sheet. He and the others pulled the spar and sail back to the vessel's centerline as the vessel came about to its new heading.

"Set mainsa'l for close-hauled tack. And strike the jib and forestaysa'l."

Jack pushed the mainsail's boom to an angle a few degrees to the left of ship's centerline and secured it. Gordy assisted Jack while Rik and Kitchi scrambled forward and hauled down the sails in the bow.

"Mr. Hollister, you and Gordy maintain your positions," Captain Perry commanded. "When the *Marigold* nears shore, we'll need to tack to starboard, then after reaching the opposite shore, back to larboard. Gonna wiggle our way down Arthur Kill till we get below Perth Amboy. If all goes well, should be at anchor in Perth Amboy Harbor before sunset."

At seventeen hundred hours, the *Marigold* passed Perth Amboy and continued into Raritan Bay. There the crew turned the schooner and brought her around 180 degrees. The wind continued from the southeast, but its intensity dropped to two knots. With the vessel's heading now to the north, the crew swung the mainsail wide to starboard, raised the foresail, and splayed it to larboard, and then reset the forestaysail and jib. The broad reach of the two large sails captured sufficient air to push the vessel forward against the declining tidal current.

As the *Marigold* moved slowly, Dillon directed the schooner's bow toward Perth Amboy Harbor. Once all the sails were trimmed and halyards secured, Jack strolled forward of the foremast to the starboard rail. He stretched and then ran his hand through his hair. He stood for a moment and then placed his right foot on a gunwale brace, took hold of a foremast shroud, and gazed at the far shore.

"Billopp Point," Captain Perry said as he came up behind Jack. "Ponderin' your future and next adventure, Mr. Hollister?"

"Aye."

"I'm sure all will go well. We'll relax for a day or two and determine what the redcoats are doing. As I mentioned, the residents of Perth Amboy do not take well to redcoats snoopin' about. But there are boys about the town who enjoy snoopin' on Staten Island. So we'll go ashore and sup at the local pub, speak to some of my friends, and learn what is happenin' over there. They'll let me know when it will be safe for you to go over with the least difficulties. We'll make harbor in an hour or two." Captain Perry squeezed Jack's shoulder. "Leave you to your thoughts." He then turned and head aft.

Jack heard him call out to the crew, "We'll be ashore by sunset, as I promised."

———◆———

Three days had passed since the *Marigold* came to anchor in Perth Amboy Harbor. Jack stood amidships next to the starboard gunwale, staring across the water toward

Raritan Bay. He could see Staten Island and pondered his fate once he set foot in this British enclave. But the method to infiltrate him onto the island had not been determined. Not enough information, Captain Perry told him, though he, the captain, or crew members had lunched, dined, or drunk in almost every pub near the harbor for past days. Residents were either tight-lipped or did not know anything. Even the British soldiers who enjoyed liberty in the village, though treated as nonentities by the villagers, spoke little of the invasion or its outcome. Jack straightened and anxiously massaged the back of his neck. A thud against the hull caused him to turn. Captain Perry had returned from shore and pulled himself over the larboard gunwale.

The captain balanced himself on deck and, upon seeing Jack, walked to him. "Ran into a couple of scoundrels, temporizers who use any opportunity to fatten their pockets, but they're ol' friends of mine. Had a brew or two with them. They just returned from doing some work at the Billopp House. Asked them to join me, and you, for dinner." Captain Perry pointed toward the bow and beyond to the shore, where an elaborate estate and manor house stood separate from the village. "They'll meet us at Auralie's Shack, o'er there—not really a shack as you can see. It's a sporting house, so you'll not want to look like a common sea dog, but more dapper, like a barrister's assistant or merchant. Those dandy duds you wore when we met will do. I too will dress for the occasion. These fashionable fellows owe me some favors, so they may provide you a path to infiltrate redcoat ranks. But since they gather light from both ends of a candle, so to speak, nothing should be said of your real mission. They promised that a pair of horses would be awaiting us at Watson's dock in an hour. Be ready."

"Aye, Captain. I will be ready."

———•◦•———

Jack rowed the dinghy the two hundred yards to Watson's dock while Captain Perry sat in the stern thwart chewing on a cigar. After securing the little boat, the two walked to the head of pier. There as the captain's friends promised, a boy of about twelve years of age held the reins of two horses. Captain Perry dropped several pence in the boy's hand and took hold of the leather straps. The boy nodded and ran off. Jack and the captain mounted the steeds and galloped to the opposite side of the harbor. In about twenty minutes, they came to the lane that led to the sporting house.

Madam Auralie, a fancifully dressed, aged woman with well-coiffed hair and from whom emanated a sensuous fragrance, greeted them on the portico. "Captain Perry and Mr. Hollister, I assume." She curtseyed and extended her right hand to the captain.

"Aye, ma'am," Captain Perry said and took hold of her fingers and kissed the back of her hand.

She also offered her hand to Jack. A slight grin crossed his face. He bowed and kissed it.

"Your friends await you at the table." Auralie turned to a snappily dressed waiter. "Escort these gentlemen to the Mr. Staz and Mr. Striker's table."

Jack nodded. He and the captain followed the waiter through an ornately chandeliered reception room, up a wide marble staircase to an elaborate dining room that contained cloth-covered tables arranged with fine china and silverware at each place setting. Staz and Striker's table was next to several windows that looked out onto the meadow and forest behind the manor house.

Jack and Captain Perry, led by the waiter, approached the table. The two well-dressed opportunists folded their napkins, laid them on the table between their place settings, and rose to greet the arrivals.

"Gentlemen, I'd like you to meet my new colleague," Captain Perry said, "Mr. Jack Hollister." He directed his arm toward the man whose pewter-colored hair suggested him to be in his late fifties. "Jack, meet Mr. Staz."

Jack and Staz shook hands.

The captain turned and gazed at the younger fellow. "This is Mr. Striker. A couple of years out of Harvard, did you not say, Mr. Striker?"

"That I am," Striker said as he nodded at Jack.

They all seated themselves. The waiter came and took drink and appetizer orders. Staz had a fondness for claret, so he asked the waiter to bring two bottles of the finest french red wine. All the men requested starters of raw oysters, clams, and a tray of antipasto. A platter of salt-pork-flavored venison collops was ordered as their entrée. These thin slices of roast deer meat were highlighted with a galantine sauce, a sweetened, vinegary gravy with hints of ginger, cinnamon, clove, and rosemary. The entrées came with a platter of roasted potatoes and carrots that surrounded a mound of turnip greens. In Jack's mind, this was a feast worthy of a king's dinner.

When the men had satiated themselves, Captain Perry passed out cuban cigars. Jack declined, but instead accepted the dessert, a tot of rye whiskey.

As the men relaxed, smoked, and drank, Staz asked, "Of what need do you have with us, Perry?"

"A favor, my good man. My friend, Jack, here, would like to return to his homeland, England. He's an Englishman—of aristocratic ties, I might add—who, because of this damn revolution, is having trouble making the safest connections. If he goes to the patriots, they'll probably hold him for ransom. The redcoats will probably hang him as a spy. My crew and I have tossed about a few ideas. But we've all concluded that the best course for him to take would be to connect with an avowed Tory aristocrat, someone like Colonel Christopher Billopp."

"So why does not Jack sail over and introduce himself to Colonel Billopp?" asked Striker.

"There are complications," Captain Perry answered. "Jack was shipwrecked on the coast of Maine two years ago and has been trying to make his way to Boston ever since." He sipped his whiskey. "Jack, tell these two gentlemen your story, so they understand why you cannot confront the colonel on your own."

"If you are a Tory, Boston is not the place to visit," Staz said.

"Yes, I learned that." Jack sipped his whiskey.

"If you are such an important aristocrat, then who the hell are you?"

Jack lowered his head. His face became flushed. The palm of his hands became sweaty. He took a deep breath.

"My father owns Hollister Exchange and Transport Limited of London—"

"Had dealings with the Hollister Exchange," Staz blurted, "and so has most of the Royal Army and Navy."

"Aye," Jack continued. "I was on my way to our office in Boston when the vessel I was aboard went on the rocks"

"Can you prove who you are?"

"Perhaps."

"Let me order us another round," Captain Perry piped up, "while Jack familiarizes you with his unfortunate adventure."

The group sipped their whiskeys and smoked while Jack related the story he, Captain Perry, and the *Marigold* crew concocted to safeguard his survival and to explain how he ended up in New Jersey.

"How did you and Perry connect?" asked Staz.

"I was given lodging and food by some kind Dutch people at the Red Duck Inn and Pub in Paulus Village," Jack said. "While there, some local farmers told me of Captain Perry and said that he might help me get to New York. I found the captain in a harbor on Kill Van Kull aboard his fishing vessel. He agreed to help get me to my destination. I must thank him for his help."

"Aye, Striker and I can get you over to Billopp House. There is to be a meeting of several members of the Continental Congress and General Howe at the Billopp House in ten days. A peace meeting, Colonel Billopp told me. The representatives from the Continental Congress will arrive here, and Striker and I will take them over. Billopp wants Striker and me to visit earlier and arrange for this supposed peace conference. No doubt General Lord Howe and his rotund brother, Admiral Howe, will be there." He looked at Jack. "You know that Lord Howe is the general who led the invasion of Brooklyn. He's a tough ol' bird. I hope you have more proof of who you are than what you told us."

Again, Jack felt anxious twinges zipping through his body. He felt nauseous. His forehead and the palms of his hands moistened. He sucked in a deep breath. "I believe I can convince the general and the admiral."

"Very good." Staz wiped his lips with the napkin. "On the morning of the second of the coming month, a couple of my men will meet you on Watson's Dock. They'll be in a longboat. Do not wear the clothes you have on. Perry, can you provide this man with sailor's garb? Tattered traveler's clothing would be better. He needs to look stressed."

"Aye, my friend," Captain Perry said as he tightened his teeth on the cigar that stuck out of his mouth. "My crew will dress Mr. Hollister in a uniform that will reflect his adventures."

"Second of Sept...September, aye," Jack stuttered, ran the back of his hand across his forehead, and rubbed the back of his neck. "It will be good to be again among my countrymen."

"If all goes well, I'll not be attending a hanging." Staz chuckled.

CHAPTER 6
STATEN ISLAND
MONDAY, SEPTEMBER 2, 1776

Jack, dressed in soiled sailor duds, a tattered jacket, and a small, frazzled cocked hat given to him by Doyle, stood on Watson's Dock. The morning was overcast. There was no noticeable breeze, and a fogbank covered the southern tip of Staten Island. Only Gordy met him on the *Marigold*'s deck at about eight hundred hours. Everyone else had bid him adieu the night before. The seaman silently ferried him in the dinghy to the dock. When the starboard side of the small craft scraped against a piling, the tide was high enough to allow Jack to step off the boat. As soon as he did, Gordy dug the larboard oar deep and pulled. The dinghy spun out and around. The seaman looked up, nodded, and said, "Take care of yourself, my man," and rowed back to the *Marigold*.

Jack attempted a wave, but Gordy was too intent on rowing to notice. Jack moved to a bollard and seated himself. Hope that fog does not come in and delay the crossing, he thought. No sooner had the thought cleared his mind than the fogbank closed in and enveloped the dock. Visibility was reduced to about one hundred feet. Gordy must have known this was about to happen, he imagined.

The density of the fog waxed and waned as Jack sat. After about an hour, he heard the hushed slushing and clunking of working oars. He turned and gazed toward the sound but saw nothing. In a momentary dissolution of the mist, he saw a grayish, misty image approaching, like a phantasm crossing a white sheet. The grayish specter resolved as it neared Watson's Dock. It was a dory carrying six rugged-looking oarsmen and loaded with bundles, casks, and trunks. A tall, muscular helmsman yelled, "Toss oars," as he shoved the tiller hard to starboard, causing the vessel to turn hard to larboard.

The seamen lifted the oars from the oarlock, raised them, and held them vertically, with the oar blades trimmed fore and aft and the handles on the floorboard.

As the open boat glided around and neared the wharf, the helmsman yelled, "Are you Hollister?"

"Aye!" Jack stood and hurried to the edge. While he moved, he put his hand against his back, checking to ensure that his diary was well secured behind his belt.

The dory's side slid easily within inches of the dock without touching it. "We ain't tyin' up. Jump aboard," the helmsman commanded.

Jack did as he was told and landed to starboard of the vessel's centerline, causing the dory to lurch to the right. Catching his balance, he seated himself on a cargo bundle near the bow.

The dory stabilized and drifted slowly. The helmsman pushed the tiller toward the dock, causing the vessel to turn to open water. "Let oars fall," he growled.

In unison, the oarsmen lowered their oars back into the oarlocks and held the blades above the water.

"Give way together!"

The crew dug the blades into the water and pulled together. The dory moved into the fog.

Jack looked aft. He saw the helmsman adjust the tiller fore and aft, and the image of Watson's Dock and nearby shacks dissolved into the moist curtain.

"No talk," the helmsman said. "Listen. There are vessels out here. They be on us before we see them. So listen!"

No one spoke. Only an occasional creak of an oarlock and the quiet slurp of churning water could be heard. Jack stared ahead, hoping to penetrate the whiteness. The dory moved slowly. Then a thump and rattle from beyond urged him to break the silence. "Vessel ahead," he turned and whispered to the helmsman. Jack listened. "To starboard. Approaching."

"Hold water!" the helmsman commanded.

The oarsmen stopped rowing, held their oar blades vertically in the water, and braced themselves against the oar handles. The dory stopped.

Jack heard the water slushing as a large bow cut its surface. Within a few moments, the misty image of a schooner hull materialized in front of him as it passed less than ten yards off the dory's bow. He looked up and saw the vessel's lookouts leaning over its rails. One jumped back, waved his arm, pointed, and shouted, "Longboat larboard!" Several others of the schooner's crewmen turned and glared down at the dorymen.

"Back water!" the helmsman of the dory growled and shook his fist at the schooner as the oarsmen dug deep and pushed the longboat in reverse. "Sound your bell, you damn fool. We've a fog out here," he bellowed at the schooner's stern.

As a sigh of relief vaporized, and the helmsman used the rudder to bring the bow to its original position, he called, "Give way together. Let's get us to shore." He tightened his grip on the tiller and said so all could hear, "Hollister's alertness kept us from getting holed, while the rest of you scoundrels were snoozin' at the oar. Mr. Staz will hear of this."

Uncertain of the consequence of the helmsman's bluster, Jack nervously lay back and cushioned himself against a canvas-covered bale.

About a quarter mile off Staten Island, Jack could see through the haze, across a salt marsh, to several docks that jutted from the shore. The fog is thinning, he thought.

With the improved visibility, the crew began to mumble among themselves. The bow of the dory moved left, redirected away from marshy shoals toward the docks.

Jack looked back at the helmsman. "Where are Mr. Staz and Mr. Striker?" he asked.

"At the Billopp Manor, awaitin' this cargo. They be meetin' us when we secure at the dock."

When the longboat approached the dock, Jack saw Staz and Striker standing at its head chatting with six Hessian soldiers. They casually stood about, several holding their muskets at the hip. The others used the weapons to prop themselves as if the long-barreled guns were walking sticks. The dory slid next to the dock; the soldiers came to attention, set the muskets on their shoulders, and fell into rank. Striker walked down the dock while the oarsmen boated their oars. Jack moved to the side as one of the men came forward, picked up the bowline, and threw it to Striker.

"Mr. Hollister," said Striker, "you will need to go with these guardsmen. They will escort you to the manor house."

Jack stood, and as soon as the dory was secure to the dock, stepped ashore. The six Hessians arranged their rank around him and, on command, marched off to the house, which was about a quarter mile away.

The soldier on his right, who seemed to be in charge, said, "The colonel is not able to see you at this time. He asked that we detain you until he is ready to meet."

Jack nodded. "Aye."

He and the guards marched toward the house, but instead of continuing to the front entrance, they passed it and took a walkway that led behind the manor. They came to the front of a small stone building with a substantial, centrally place door. To each side of the entrance was a barred window too small for a full-sized man to fit through. Once inside Jack noticed the interior had a short wall-to-ceiling stone hallway with four iron doors that opened onto it. Each door had a small barred, oval opening in the center located at about the distance of a man's height from the floor. At the bottom-center of each door, he saw a small, rectangular, latched hatch. I am being detained in a jail, he realized as the sergeant of the guard pushed a key into door lock. The hinges of the door creaked, and its base scraped the floor as the guard pulled it open.

"This is a secure room," the sergeant said. "Many of those who arrive here under the guise of lost souls turn out to be rebel spies. The colonel and our regiment officers will determine if you are real or an infiltrator." He turned to two of the guards. "Search this fellow for weapons."

Jack spread his arms. "You will find no weapons. I do have my notebook. I am a writer."

While the other soldiers aimed their muskets on Jack, the two searchers patted him down, lifted his shirt, found the notebook, removed it, and handed it to the sergeant. He leafed through it. "You write of farmers."

Jack stood silent as the soldier turned more pages.

"Ah, you have written some accounts of the invasion and a description of an old fishing schooner. Is that the one that brought you the Perth Amboy?"

"Aye. The captain kindly took me aboard. He also introduced me to Mr. Staz and Mr. Striker. I am not a spy, and I would appreciate an audience with Colonel Billopp."

"In due time," the sergeant said and returned the notebook to Jack. "I see no subversive writings. While you wait, you can write of your adventure here." He returned the book, put his hand on Jack's shoulder, and pushed him into the cell. "Until later," he said and turned and closed the door.

Jack heard the latch click shut. He looked around the dimly lit, humid, musty-smelling cubicle. Its flooring was a gravelly soil. A cot sat against the wall opposite the door. Next to a sidewall was a table. On its top was a washbowl and pitcher of water. A bucket stood in the opposite corner.

"For now, you will be treated as a prisoner of war," the sergeant said through the oval opening in the door. "A servant will bring you some victuals."

Jack sat on the cot and rubbed his face. At least this jail was aboveground and its walls were not leaking. He gripped his diary and lay back against the cold stones.

———•◦•———

After two days, Jack's anxiety intensified. He walked to the little window that opened to the outside. The day was clear and warm. It is afternoon, he realized, because the African brought lunch about an hour ago. A smile crossed his face, which for a moment abated the nervous pangs gripping his stomach. "The little fellow," he mumbled, "is always apologizing for what he brings. It is basic, porridge usually mixed with nibbles of meat—prison food." He stared out the window. Though he could occasionally hear activity, the grounds that he could see were empty. His apprehensions returned. He placed his forehead against the coolness of one of the iron bars and stood, glaring for another moment at the view beyond the window. Then he turned, sat on the cot, put his head in his hands, and rubbed his temples. "Is anyone going to question me?" He closed his eyes.

A vision materialized of his brother, Ian, standing in the doorway of the Hollister House in Boston. As the retinal glare dimmed, a look of concern covered his face. Jack shook his head, opened his eyes, did not raise his head, but continued to stare into the palms of his hands.

"Perhaps I should have returned to England with the family," he murmured. A tear cooled his cheek as it trickled down. "I could use your help, Brother." He squeezed his eyes closed again. Ian's image vaporized. Another returned, a hangman's noose, glowing and swinging.

Jack popped his eyes open. He snapped to attention, jumped off the cot, and rushed to the little window in the door. "Guard! Guard!" he shouted through the opening.

No response. He shouted again, but to no avail. He returned to the cot. "Have they forgotten me?" He rubbed the back of his neck, then brought his arms to his chest, squeezed them together, and pondered. "I think not." He took a deep breath. His unease remained, but it seemed to diminish like the daylight moving to twilight. The servant will soon bring supper and a candle.

The heavy noise of rhythmic steps, a command of "Halt," and then the release of the door latch caused Jack's stomach muscles to tense. The door opened, and the sergeant of the Hessian guard stepped in. "The colonel will see you. Come with us."

Jack grabbed his diary from the cot and stood.

"Do you plan to write in your notebook?"

"Nay. But I may want the colonel to read what I have written."

"Then bring it."

With Jack in the middle, the guard unit marched to the front of the manor house. On the way, they came upon the little African servant walking to the jailhouse and carrying a pot. A look of surprise crossed his face when he saw Jack and his escort. As the unit passed, the servant turned and followed the soldiers.

At the front door of the simple brick two-story, federal-styled, rectangular manor house, the sergeant of the guard ascended the stoop and knocked. Another African servant opened the door, nodded, and stepped aside. The unit marched into a modestly decorated reception area.

"You will wait here," the Hessian sergeant said. "You men," he pointed to two of the guards, "will remain. The rest of you are dismissed." As the released men departed, the sergeant returned his attention to Jack. "Colonel Billopp's secretary will call you in when the colonel is free." He then walked to door and knocked, did an about-face, and marched out of the house. The servant closed the door to the outside. He motioned to a bench along the wall that faced the door to the inner portion of the house. Jack walked to it and sat down in the middle. The two guards relocated themselves, one at each armrest. They stood at ease, holding their weapons at their sides.

In about fifteen minutes, the door opened, and a lieutenant holding some papers stepped into the anteroom. He nodded to Jack. "Colonel Billopp will see you. Follow me."

The guards came to attention as Jack rose and followed the lieutenant.

Jack accompanied the officer into a hallway. A staircase to the second floor divided the hall. The two climbed the stairs and continued to a central room. They entered. Behind a large desk sat a young man in military clothing. In wingback chairs, located on each side of the desk, two glow-ering officers of high rank sat. The young officer behind the desk stood. "Thank you, Lieutenant, for bringing this pris-oner." He addressed the lieutenant and turned to Jack. "I am Colonel Billopp. Your escort is Lieutenant Peter Quin, my secretary." He moved his arm to the right. "This is General Lord Howe and, on the left, is his brother, Admiral Howe."

The general, a heftily built man with a stern face, pursed his lips. Admiral Howe's face softened. The robust man nodded.

"Please seat yourself on the chair in front of the desk. You are the prisoner who has requested an audience?" Colonel Billopp asked.

"Aye, sir." Jack, holding his diary at his side, walked for-ward, sat on the designated chair and rested the diary in his lap.

"You claim to be a Hollister," the colonel continued. "We all know of the Hollister family and have dealt with the Hollister Exchange and Transport. Some years ago, my father met Lord Hollister. The Hollister company has been supplying the needs of the British military all over the world. And you say you are a member of that family?"

"I am, sir."

"Then why are you in the colonies?" asked General Howe, his brow furrowed.

The account of his presence in the colonies made up aboard Captain Perry's *Marigold* ran through Jack's mind. He started his story slowly. "About two years ago, my broth-er, Ian, and I sailed for Boston. The vessel we were aboard shipwrecked on the eastern shore of the Massachusetts providence known as Maine. Ian was to take over the supervision of the North American office of our family's business. I traveled with him to keep him company. When coastal pirates took over our survivor's camp, my brother and I became separated. I have heard nothing of him or my family since."

"So you say." General Howe nodded, gritted his teeth, and continued to frown. "You have been on this continent for two years. What have you been doing?"

Jack relaxed and attempted to look confident. "Sir, I have been trying to find a way to return to my home in England. In the turmoil the colonies are in, it is dangerous for an errant, undocumented Englishman to find help. I tried to get to Boston, but that city was taken by rebels, and all those loyal to the Crown had evacuated. I then continued on to New York."

Jack paused, took a breath, and proceeded for the next hour to relate his two-year odyssey, using the faux adventures he, Captain Perry, and the crew of the *Marigold* had concocted. He highlighted certain facts he felt would strengthen his account. In conclusion he said, "When I reached Manhattan, the Continentals had taken this city. Though most residents maintained their loyalty, to them I was a vagabond. My clothes were tattered. I had no funds. They viewed me as a hooligan. Then I met this lowly fisherman who provided me with modest employment. That is how I made my way to Perth Amboy. The fisherman introduced me to Mr. Staz and Mr. Striker. The smell of that vessel still remains in my nostrils. Hopefully, it will not be forever. But I am very appreciative of this fisherman's help."

Admiral Howe chuckled. "Aye, those fishing scows do have unpleasant odors. They will eventually dissipate." He signed. "Your stay on this continent has been fraught with many dangers, but my lad, you have survived them well. A tribute to our adventurous English blood. I do believe your account has revealed the jeopardies a young English lad would face during these troubled times. I believe what you have told us and—"

"Wait, Brother," General Howe interrupted. "How do we know this young man is who he says he is? He has given us a good story, believable to some extent. Maybe too believable. But he has given us little to support his true identity. I have some questions, the answers to which only a Hollister would know."

"Yes, yes." Admiral Howe puffed, yawned, scrunched back in the chair, and folded his hands in his lap. "Aye. We must have more proof. Ask your questions, William."

General Howe tightened the muscles in his reddened cheeks, stood, and moved his arms behind him. He locked his hands together at the small of his back and began to pace in front of the desk. Stopping in front of Jack, he glared down at him and asked several basic questions about the Hollister family. He asked the names of Jack's uncles, his cousins, and the name of the Hollister brig that limped, leaking badly into Halifax. Then he asked some more poignant and esoteric questions. Several had no relevance to the Hollister family.

Though Jack had all the right answers, one particular remark the general made angered him. It was when General Howe stated, with apparent conviction, "I remember Lord

Hollister had a black servant, an ill-tempered man, whom he subjugated by having his crew treat him to dreads of the cat-o'-nine tails." Then the general asked, "What was this servant's name?"

"My father never had any black servants," Jack growled. "And, if he did, he would never lash them with any whips or treat them badly in anyway."

"Ah, this occurred before you were born."

"The only gentleman that Father employed to serve our family was a white Englishman, who came from Devonshire. He was hired before I was born, and his name was Auggy. He has been the family butler since Father started the business."

"Yes." The general scratched his head and strolled next to his chair. "You have all the answers, but I am still suspicious. We have no physical evidence to show that you are a Hollister. Learning the details of someone's life would be easy for a clever lad like you seem to be." The general moved nearer to Jack.

"Aye," Jack said. "Please, if you will allow, I came across a document, a letter, that will perhaps attest to my and my brother's disappearance on this continent." Jack raised the diary he held on his lap, opened the front cover, and tore away the cover's internal facing. He removed the letter from Lord North, partially unfolded it, and handed it to the general. General Howe shook the letter open, lowered his head, and peered at it. Jack watched Howe's eyes move as he read the letter.

"This document is old, soiled, but has Lord North's seal, our prime minister," the general said. "How did you come by it?" He turned and passed the letter to Admiral Howe.

Jack related the story of coming upon the bodies of several Continental soldiers, one of whom was a courier. The letter was in the courier's pouch along with other military documents.

"Yes, I have seen this letter," Admiral Howe said. "Lord Edward Hollister, the father of our supposed lost son here, informed our prime minister that his sons, whom he sent to Boston, had been lost at sea. The masters of all our ships received a copy of North's letter, urging us to be on the lookout for the boys or any evidence of their whereabouts."

"Yes," General Howe said, "but having this letter does not prove this man is the lost son."

"Ah, had you read the letter thoroughly, Brother, you would have noticed that there is a description of each lad." The admiral looked up and scrutinized Jack. "This man is older, but matches what the father's narrative states." He paused for a moment and glared at Jack's face. "Except the man before us has a noticeable scar on his left cheek."

"Aye," Jack blurted. "The result of a patriot shot, sir."

The admiral nodded. "Without that scar, this man matches the description. I believe you are the long-lost Jack Hollister." Admiral Howe's face bloomed into a smile, and he clapped his hands.

"Was there any word of my brother?" Jack asked the admiral.

"Aye, indeed. In the summer of 1774 your brother was captured along with a troop of pirates by a marine unit that sailed aboard the frigate, HMS *Buzzard.* All the prisoners were impressed into His Majesty's service. When the master of this vessel, a captain Francklin, learned who your brother was, he released him to admiral Samuel Graves, who returned him to the Hollister family in Boston. That was in the summer of 1775. Later that year the Hollisters of Boston vacated the city and returned to England. As far as I know, your brother is supervising the Hollister Company in London."

"It is good to hear that he is alive and safe. A great weight and worry has been lifted from my shoulders. I have been very concerned. Thank you, Admiral."

"I still have my suspicions," General Howe said, "but if you believe the lad, Brother, he will be your responsibility. What are your thoughts, Colonel Billopp?"

"I will leave the matter in your hands." The colonel nodded at the general and admiral. "I do believe we need to take up the matter of the upcoming meeting with the representatives of the Continental Congress. The meeting is only a few days off."

"Aye," Admiral Howe said. "But first, to clear Mr. Hollister's mind, I will take him on as one of my aides. Since rather few vessels are sailing east, I cannot send him to Britain any sooner than next spring or summer, and then only if all goes well. The majority of naval vessels coming to this shore are bringing troops. Then they remain as part of my fleet. Besides, I need another aide." He looked at Jack. "A uniform of a second lieutenant will be provided for you. You will work in my center of operations. We are headquartering on Governor's Island, an island offshore of Brooklyn. I believe the island will be strategically important."

Jack nodded at the admiral and sat back as General Howe returned to his chair.

"Gentlemen, the meeting with some esteemed visitors from Philadelphia is to take place on the eleventh," Colonel Billopp announced. "All is being prepared. The company of Staz and Striker is handling the arrangements."

"Excellent, Colonel," General Howe said. "I feel we should eat first, and then I will meet with the gentlemen privately. Brother, I would like you and your new aide to join the reception. Colonel, do you know which of the representatives are to attend?"

"Yes. Mr. Edward Rutledge, Mr. John Adams, and a gentleman, General, I know you have heard of, Benjamin Franklin."

"Indeed." The general looked up and wrung his hand. "Let us adjourn. I believe a round of good whiskey is in order."

Colonel Billopp stood and walked to a sideboard. "After, Mr. Hollister, Lieutenant Quin will arrange for your lodging in the manor house. I am sure you will find the house more comfortable than the jail."

CHAPTER 7
BILLOPP HOUSE, STATEN ISLAND, NEW YORK
SEPTEMBER 11, 1776

For the last few days, Jack's time seemed to move quickly. His assignment to a work detail to spruce up the manor house and its grounds kept him busy. But today was the eleventh, the day of the supposed "peace meeting," as General Howe had called it. At breakfast, Lieutenant Quin announced that all personnel be dressed in their best bib and tucker. When Jack finished his meal, he returned to his quarters and put on the naval lieutenant's uniform he had been given.

Jack appraised himself in a mirror and grinned. As a boy, floating around Plymouth Harbor, I imagined myself wearing this attire. The Royal Navy has always fascinated me. He sighed and then pursed his lips. I must remember where I am and the mission I have taken on. For now, I will do what I must. He reached around, grabbed the tricorne, placed it on his head, and walked off toward ballroom located in the center of the house.

This room, rearranged today to accommodate eleven people, contained a long dining table with seating for six on each side and the host at the head. Lieutenant Quin stood at far end, issuing last-minute orders to the three servants and chatting with two other lieutenants and a captain. Jack walked to the group.

"Lieutenant Hollister," Quin said. "I would like you to go outside and position yourself on the stoop. I have assigned two soldiers to the dock. From there, the harbor of Perth Amboy can be seen. The guards are to watch the harbor. When they see the Staz and Striker longboat leave the harbor, they are to ring a bell. Report to me when you hear the bell. It is a clear day, so visibility will not be a problem. The boat will take about two hours to cross the bay, sufficient time to ready the meal for serving."

"Aye, sir." Jack nodded, did an about-face, and headed to the outside of the manor house. On the stoop, he looked at his watch. "Nine thirty," he noted. "If they leave in the next few minutes, lunch will be early." He stood on top of the little porch and scanned the grounds. "It is almost as if I were back in England, home." He shook his head.

About forty minutes had passed when he finally heard the bell ring.

"The Hessian guards will escort the Continental contingent," Lieutenant Quin said when Jack reported. "Now, inform Colonel Billopp and General and Admiral Howe. The colonel wants a formal welcome be given to the representatives and their staff before they enter the house. He expects all the officers to be present. The head servant will inform us."

The welcoming committee hosted by Colonel Christopher Billopp, the colonel's wife, General William Howe, and Admiral Richard Howe met the delegates from Philadelphia on the courtyard just beyond the little porch at the entrance to the manor house. Jack, Lieutenant Quin, and three of Billopp's staff officers arranged themselves in a single rank next to the committee, while several Hessian guards, a troop of redcoats, and members of the colonel's militia were aligned along the carriageway. The three servants, cook, and kitchen workers stood behind the military men dressed in red-and-blue uniforms highlighted with white trimmings, belts, bandoliers, and shining brass and gold accessories. It was a colorful presentation on a bright, sunny September day.

After a few minutes, the carriage from the dock pulled into the courtyard. The Hessian guards who rode on the side and rear of the carriage jumped off. The one nearest to the vehicle's door opened it. Three finely dressed men of short stature exited and strolled toward the three highest-ranking officers. The delegates had not brought staff members. They introduced themselves and shook hands with the officers, who led them into the house.

Lieutenant Quin dismissed the staff officers, soldiers, servants, and other workers. He, Jack, and the colonel's other staff officers followed the visitors and welcoming committee into the house.

The colonel led everyone into the dining room. He took his place at the head of the table. Seated on his right were General Howe, Colonel Billopp's wife, Admiral Howe, and the colonel's staff captain and lieutenant. The representatives of the Continental Congress were seated on left side of the table, with Jack and another staff lieutenant.

When the last person took his place at the table, Lieutenant Quin, who was moving about directing all to their seats, walked to a sideboard and picked up a tray of wineglasses filled with rich, red claret. He placed the first glass to the right of the colonel's wife, walked to the left of the table and set a glass to the right of each visitor, and then returned to the right side of the table to serve the general, admiral, and colonel, and finished the wine distribution with Jack and the staff officers. Quin returned to the sideboard and set down the empty tray and then signaled the servants to bring in the food.

Jack watched this elaborate demonstration of formality and wondered about Lieutenant Quin's place at this ceremonial repast. He smiled to himself, and he lowered his head. The man is not only a secretary but also the house butler, he thought.

Colonel Billopp tapped his water glass to call everyone's attention.

Jack noticed that Lieutenant Quin raised his hand to momentarily still the servants.

The colonel stood and lifted his wineglass. "A toast to welcome our guests from the American Continental Congress."

"Huzzah!" they all called, raised their glasses, and said, "Welcome."

"I would like to introduce the eminent gentlemen." The colonel motioned to the closest man, who was the youngest delegate and the only one with a full head of hair. "Please welcome Mr. Edward Rutledge of South Carolina. Seated next is Mr. John Adams, representative from Massachusetts. And the gentleman farthest to my left, sitting next to our recently found lost soul, Second Lieutenant Jack Hollister, is Mr. Benjamin Franklin from Pennsylvania. Gentlemen, we welcome you to our attempt at reaching a peaceful end to this ridiculous war." Colonel Billopp drank the rest of his wine and seated himself.

General Howe and Admiral Howe stood, reached across the table, and shook hands with each of the delegates. Lieutenant Quin cued the servants and quickly refilled the colonel's glass.

"Mr. Franklin and I have previously met," Admiral Howe said. "He became a master chess opponent to me and my wife. We enjoyed moments of fine cordiality while he was visiting in England." He made a partial bow to Benjamin Franklin. "I am glad to see you again. It would be fine to visit, perhaps play a game of chess, but I am afraid my brother has not allowed time for such trivialities."

Benjamin Franklin rose from his chair and nodded. "I wish we were meeting under different circumstances, Admiral. It is good to see you again." He smiled and re-seated himself.

Trays of ham, mutton, and tongue were brought to the table along with bread, potatoes, and a variety of root vegetables. Lieutenant Quin circulated the table, refilling or topping off the glasses with wine or water. All the guests chatted while they enjoyed the meal. Except for the colonel's mention of the ongoing war at the end of his introductions of the delegates, little was said of the turmoil.

As the meal neared completion and all seemed relaxed and satiated, Jack smiled. It sure would be fine to have one of Captain Perry's cuban cigars—but his thought was interrupted. Benjamin Franklin leaned closer and whispered, "Though I have never met you, I know of you, Mr. Hollister. General Washington's description, to the scar on your left cheek, is quite accurate. I am glad to see you are now established in the enemy's camp."

Jack's head snapped around. He tightened his jaw. His lips parted and eyes widened as he glared at the round-faced man with sleepy but piercing eyes and a strongly receded hairline, who was smiling back at him. A knot formed in his stomach.

Franklin winked and brushed his napkin across his mouth. "Relax," he whispered. "Smile."

Jack shifted in his chair, sighed, and sat back. He took a couple of slow breaths and forced a smile to his face.

"Now we appear to be having a quiet conversation." Franklin took a sip of his claret, raised his head, and faced Colonel Billopp. "Colonel, will you please relay my appreciation to your cook on the fine meal we have just enjoyed."

"Thank you, Mr. Franklin. I will pass your gratitude to the cook." The colonel stood and nodded to General Howe. You gentlemen are here to meet with General Lord Howe. It is time for the meeting to commence."

"I enjoyed your story, Lieutenant, and meeting you," Franklin said as he pushed back from the table. He extended his hand to Jack. As the two shook hands, Franklin turned his back on the others, faced Jack, and slowly straightened, feigning a stiffness in his back. In a low voice that only Jack could hear, he said, "Do not worry when you hear the outcome of this meeting. We are in for troubled times. But you are here to aid our cause. A dangerous mission. May you safely accomplish it." Benjamin Franklin took a deep breath and stretched as he turned to face everyone. "Sorry, gentlemen. My sciatica is informing me that my age is creeping on."

Jack lowered his head and moved to the farther end of the table. The knot that had tightened his stomach unraveled.

"Please follow me," General Howe said. "We will meet in my quarters. Mr. Franklin, will you need assistance climbing the staircase?"

"No, sir. I am fine now. Please proceed."

General Howe's peace meeting lasted about three hours. During this time, Jack and several of the other staff officers, their duties suspended for this time, enjoyed the day on the lawn off the courtyard. At about three thirty, Lieutenant Quin called them to the house. "The meeting is over," he said. "I do not believe it went well."

Jack watched as the three Continental Congress representatives, with brooding expressions, descended the stairway to the reception room. General Howe followed; a frown covered his face. There was no call for a departure toast as was a normal custom when the group collected on the main floor. Instead, Lieutenant Quin called Jack and the staff officers to order and had them align themselves in the entranceway. Everyone glanced up as Admiral Howe, who had spent the meeting in his quarters, came yawning into the room.

"Thank you for your hospitality, General Howe," Edward Rutledge said. "It is too bad we could not reach agreement. And I am sorry you do not wish to recognize the colonists' Declaration of Independence, and as you say, you do not have the authority to repeal the Prohibitory Act and put an end to this conflict."

"Aye." General Howe walked with Mr. Rutledge to the door that led to the courtyard. "I can, however, postpone the conflict if, and only if, the colonies agree to make fixed sums of contribution in lieu of the taxes levied upon by the Parliament. They would also have to agree to end their injurious hostilities."

"You understand, General," Rutledge responded, "there are those who are unwavering in their desire for freedom and independence from the Crown and have the longing to determine their own fate."

"I suppose. It is too bad the colonies are composed of many misanthropes." General Howe stopped in the doorway as the delegates moved onto the stoop. "I feel like losing America is like losing a brother," he said.

Benjamin Franklin faced the general. "We will do our utmost endeavors to save Your Lordship that mortification."

"You know, gentlemen," the general responded, "I view all of you as nothing more than British subjects."

A resolute smile crossed the face of John Adams. "Your Lordship, you may see me however you wish—except as that of a British subject."

General Howe straightened, put his hands behind his back, puffed his chest, and haughtily stated, "Mr. Adams appears to be a decided character. He has shown where his fidelity lies. And I assume you others have hardened your allegiance. I bid you adieu. Please return the hostage we sent to Perth Amboy to assure this momentary truce unharmed."

"As promised, be assured, he has been well taken well care of, General," Mr. Rutledge said.

General Howe nodded, turned, reentered the manor, and shut the door. Disappointed because his offer to curtail the hostilities between the colonies and Great Britain had been refused, he walked to where Admiral Howe stood and took off his tricorne and coat. "Brother, let us go to my quarters. Those ungrateful insurgents refused my offer. Their requests were nothing more than the greatest amount of gewgaw I have ever heard. Our war will continue." He turned and handed his hat and coat to his secretary. "Come with us, Quin. I need for you to record our discussions."

Jack watched as the general, admiral, and lieutenant climbed the stairs. He also heard Howe ranting. "Those damn scoundrels! No better than common villains. The lowest class of human beings they are. They want a war; they are going to get one." As the general neared the top of the stairway, his voice grew louder and angrier. "Brother,

I want your men-of-war stationed off the southern tip of Manhattan Island. Want them to blast that fort. Spare nothing. That city will be mine."

Jack gritted his teeth. He wished there was some way to inform General Washington. Passing the stairs, he walked into the hall that led to the back of the manor and his quarters. As he passed the stairway, he heard a door close upstairs.

I am sure Washington expects to be invaded and has taken proper precautions, Jack thought. He will probably move his troops north. At least he will learn my whereabouts. Mr. Franklin will tell him.

The next morning, September 12, 1776, chaos ruled the kitchen, which was normally the lair of the cook and her staff. But at 6:00 a.m. on this day, it contained General Howe, Lieutenants Hollister and Quin, and Howe's personal guards. Typically, the guards ate their meals with the other enlisted men in the garrison cook tent.

Jack stood to one side, allowing General Howe, dressed in a manner unbecoming of a high-ranking officer, to move about the space with the fury of a whirlwind. Caught up in this draft were Lieutenant Quin and the guards. All were hurrying around the long worktable, grabbing chunks of sweet bread, dabs of butter and marmalades, fruit, and coffee, and gobbling them down. Several times Jack heard someone choke and cough.

"Lieutenant Quin, do you have my uniform laid out?" General Howe barked.

"Aye, sir. In your quarters."

"Did Lieutenant Drummond return from Perth Amboy?"

"He did indeed, sir. Those rebels treated him very well."

"Where is he? I want to be in Castleton by afternoon. Meet with my officers. Proceed with the invasion. Have Manhattan Island in my hands by the end of the week."

"Drummond's a bit under the weather, sir." The lieutenant grinned. "He was soused when he came to shore. Several men carried him to his quarters."

"Get that drunkard on his feet, dressed, and ready for the road in thirty minutes."

"Aye, sir," Lieutenant Quin said. "Do not be too hard on him, sir. He is young and inexperienced in drink." The lieutenant grabbed another chunk of bread, pushed it into his mouth, and washed it down with the remains of his coffee. He stormed up the stairs to the main floor.

Jack heard the manor house front door slam closed.

The general, now gnawing on a banana, turned to his guards. "One of you have the stable hands ready our horses."

The youngest soldier placed the mug he was holding on the table and started up the stairs as Admiral Howe and Colonel Billopp were descending. They collided.

"In a hurry, Corporal?" One of the officers said.

The young corporal grumbled something and continued up the stairs.

General Howe started toward the stairs. "Are you coming, Richard?"

"I will be along later," the admiral said. "The colonel, his wife, and I plan to enjoy a fine breakfast. Several frigates await off the northeast shore. One or two may be at the dock in Castleton. I will be aboard one of them this evening and dispatch a messenger to inform you which. Why the hurry, Brother?"

"I want to confer with my officers to find what needs to be done to complete the invasion." The general started up the stairs. "Perhaps I can surprise that slippery General Washington. The capture of their leader and his hanging would be a proper prize to bring those rebellious colonists to their knees and back under the rule of the Crown." He reached the top of the stairs and disappeared toward his quarters. Lieutenant Quin followed.

Jack was beside himself but had to maintain his composure.

"Lieutenant Hollister," Admiral Howe said, "you and I will travel sanely after I enjoy a fine meal with the colonel and his family and thank them for their hospitality. You may join us if you wish."

"Thank you, sir, but I have had my breakfast," Jack said. "I will arrange with your guards and servants to have your carriage prepared."

The admiral nodded. He and Colonel Billopp climbed the stairs.

Jack poured himself another mug of coffee. He breathed in its aroma, sat at the cook's table, and pondered.

If only a message could be sent to General Washington. Damn. I am not in a position to come to his aid. He sighed several times as the cooking staff cleared the dirtied plates and uneaten foods from the table.

General Washington is an astute man. I am sure he is expecting the redcoats to take New York City. May God be with him.

CHAPTER 8
GOVERNOR'S ISLAND, NEW YORK
AUTUMN AND WINTER, 1776-1777

Cool wisps of air, harbingers of the coming autumn, caressed Jack's face when he exited the carriage at a dock south of Castleton. He flipped on his tricorne and waited for Admiral Howe to step down. Quietly shifting and scraping against the dock ahead was the frigate, HMS *Rose*. When one of the deck watchmen notified the officer of the deck and boatswain of the admiral's arrival, Jack watched the deck crew scramble. Several seamen fell into rank at the side of the gangway. The boatswain stood at the head of the line. The officer of the deck took his place at the top of the gangway. As Jack and the admiral walked up, the boatswain piped his whistle, and then, when Admiral Howe's foot touched the frigate's deck, he shouted, "Admiral on board." The officer of the deck saluted.

The admiral returned the salute and said, "I will be in my quarters. Have Captain Dillard join me."

"Aye, sir. The captain is ashore. I'll notify him as soon as he is aboard." The deck officer replied.

Jack and Admiral Howe strode toward the aft cabins beneath the quarterdeck. As they did, Jack scanned the harbor and the shoreline of southern Brooklyn. Tied forward of the *Rose* was an armed schooner. Several troop transports were tethered to docks up the shore. Five large men-of-war and several frigates lay at anchor off the Brooklyn coast, and a fleet of transports were rafted off Castleton. Many guns will be aimed at the city, Jack thought.

Captain Dillard arrived about an hour after Jack and the Admiral came aboard the *Rose*. The admiral introduced Jack as his aide.

"Hollister?" Dillard mused. "I have heard that name. Yes, the letter from Lord North asking to be on the lookout for the brothers who went missing a couple of years ago. Recently overheard one was found serving aboard HMS *Buzzard* and is now in London supervising our suppliers. So Lieutenant Hollister, you are the other. It is good to meet you, sir. I am glad you are safe. Welcome aboard."

"Thank you," Jack said. "I am glad to be in the service of the admiral."

"Yes, yes," Admiral Howe interrupted. "Captain, the battle for the York Islands is to continue. My brother, General Howe, wants us to concentrate all our efforts on Manhattan in the next days and to complete the invasion."

"Aye, Admiral. The crew will welcome the action. They have been getting weary these days from our idleness."

"Good," Admiral Howe said. "The plan is to destroy the rebels or chase them from the city. Our large ships of battle and available frigates will lay off the island and aim their destruction on the Battery and surrounding city. They will be under the orders of General Howe. Send word to our vessels to be ready to sail immediately." He stood and collected some papers from the desk. "Ready a gig to transport Mr. Hollister and me to the HMS *Renown*. She will be my flagship."

"As you wish, Admiral. The gig will be ready in minutes. I will signal the *Renown* of your coming. She lies just across the water." Captain Dillard nodded, saluted, and left the cabin.

"Though the HMS *Renown* is a relatively new, small, fifty-gun, double-decked vessel, you will enjoy the roominess and comfort aboard her. Captain Francis Banks is the master. A fine man." The admiral opened a satchel and slipped in the papers he was holding. "No time to dally. Let us proceed to the deck."

The setting sun and flocks of seagulls flying seaward made for a deceptively pleasant two-hour journey across New York Bay. No one spoke. Only the splashing-slurping sound of the oar blades stirring the seawater gave voice to the movement of the gig. The ripples and wavelets glowed an orange red when the little transport reached the HMS *Renown*. The boatswain's deck mate piped Jack and Admiral Howe aboard. Captain Francis Banks, a pleasant look on his face, welcomed them aboard. "Good to see you again, Admiral. Welcome aboard, Lieutenant. I assume he is your new aide."

"Aye. This is Second Lieutenant Jack Hollister."

"Your accommodations are ready," the captain said and pointed to two seamen. "These men will escort you to your quarters. Dinner will be served in the officers' mess at twenty hundred hours."

"As always, Captain Banks, your hospitality and ship are impeccable."

The captain, a proud smile on his face, said, "A fresh uniform awaits you, Admiral. One will also be provided for you, Lieutenant." He came to attention and bowed slightly. "At dinner then, sirs."

Jack and Admiral Howe nodded and followed the escorts.

———•◦•———

Following the admiral's orders, on the fourteenth of September, the warships HMS *Roebuck* and HMS *Phoenix*, the frigates HMS *Orpheus*, HMS *Craysfort,* and HMS *Rose* sailed the day before and took up battle positions off Manhattan Island. The two warships anchored in Bushwick Creek on the Brooklyn side of the East River, along with the *Orpheus* and *Craysfort*. The HMS *Rose* patrolled the southern end of the East River and into New York Bay off Manhattan Island.

Though the HMS *Renown* had remained at anchor when the others sailed, a couple of days later, noise on deck woke Jack. The confusion of sound indicated this morning the warship was about to get under way. He scrambled into his uniform, dashed onto the deck, and ran amidships to the starboard rail. From there he saw men in the foremast yardarms unfurling the giant square sails. Forward, several seamen were setting the jibs. Other crewmen forced their weight and energy against capstan arms, attempting to raise the anchors. Admiral Howe, who stood with Captain Banks on the quarterdeck near the helm, motioned for Jack to join them. The vessel vibrated with activity as he sprinted aft and clambered up the ladder to the deck.

"Your demeanor suggests that you find waking a vessel exciting, Mr. Hollister," Admiral Howe said as he observed Jack absorbing the activity going on in front of him. "Seems you have experienced this before. Has the mariner's calling always been a part of your life?"

"Aye, sir. It has since my father taught me the wonders of seafaring."

"Your brother does not share the same aspirations?"

"Perhaps if a desk could sail." Jack smiled. "He was not one for the sea. That is why he asked that I accompany him on the Atlantic crossing."

"Aye, the sea has its wonders, but it is also a dangerous, frightening place.

The massive canvases of the HMS *Renown* flapped, fluffed, and filled. Seamen strained on the sheets to bring the mainsail into trim. "Steerage attained," the helmsman yelled. The warship moved toward center stream.

"Set course, west," Captain Banks commanded.

"Aye, sir. West it is." He rotated the ship's wheel about a quarter turn to starboard. When the bow began a trace toward the New Jersey coastline, the helmsman rotated the wheel slowly back to center.

"We will take our position near the mouth of the Hudson," the admiral said. "The warships *Repulse* and *Pearl* and the schooner *Tryal* will join us." He lifted his arm, opened his hand, and felt the strength of the southeasterly wind. "The winds are light. This vessel will take about two hours to reach its station. Let us go below and have breakfast. With Captain Banks in charge, the *Renown* is in good hands."

As Jack and the admiral descended the ladder to the gun deck, they heard the officer of the deck shout, "Make ready all guns!" The two gave way to avoid collisions with men running to their gunnery stations in response to the order.

After some time, a midshipman entered the officer's mess. "Captain Banks wanted me to announce, the *Renown* and the other warships are now drifting off the tip of Manhattan, sir. He and the others await your orders."

"Thank you, Midshipman." Admiral Howe finished his biscuit and tea and stood. He reached for his tricorne. "Tell Captain Banks to signal the fleet to prepare to shell the redoubts. I will be on the quarterdeck in a moment."

The boy saluted, turned, and departed.

"Come, Jack, let us go on deck."

Looking east from the quarterdeck, Jack saw the troop transports that had been tied to the docks at Castleton crossing the bay and entering into the East River. Then a sail appeared and obstructed his view. The sides of the *Renown* and *Tryal* came close enough to allow a line with an attached waterproof pouch to be thrown from the schooner. The sack was caught by a seaman aboard the warship, who removed a message pouch and handed it to a midshipman. The young officer brought the message to Captain Banks, who handed it to the admiral.

"Aha!" sighed Admiral Howe as he examined the message from the pouch. "From my brother, General Howe. He plans to launch an amphibious assault at fourteen hundred hours. Troop rafts will cross the East River to Crown Point with protective fire from the *Roebuck, Phoenix,* and the two frigates. He asks that, until then, we soften the rim of the island with cannon fire. Captain, you may signal all ships to reposition and commence firing."

"What of the men-of-war in the East River?" Jack asked the admiral. "They cannot see our signal."

"Those vessels are under the command of General Howe," the admiral said as he folded the message and slipped it back into the pouch. "They will follow his orders."

The helmsman brought the *Renown* to about a mile off-shore and pointed its bow into the Hudson River. A staccato chorus of gunnery officers shouting, "Fire!" reverberated from the stem to stern. The *Repulse* and *Pearl* followed suit. The naval guns were answered by cannons behind redoubts and the wall of Fort George. Soon the waters off the southern end were blanketed in billows of white smoke.

Jack held his hands over his ears. Each time a cannon fired, the warship's hull vibrated. Although the shots from patriot guns onshore sent clusters of water jetting skyward just short of the line of British warships, those fired by the British vessels blasted the fortified ground and walls, sending dirt and debris into the air. Some exploded when they hit a canister of black powder, igniting flammable materials nearby. The cannons kept barking. Acrid, sulfurous clouds rose and drifted across the deck of the HMS *Renown*. Jack's eyes burned. He rubbed them and coughed.

At two o'clock in the afternoon, a set of flags was raised aboard the *Renown*, signaling the warships off the southern Manhattan Island to cease fire. One by one the gunnery officer commanded the guns to be cleaned and repaired. Led by the *Renown,* the vessels turned away and headed nearer Staten Island.

Jack looked back at the tip of Manhattan. The southern shoreline smoldered. Heavy, gray smoke curled and billowed from several locations along the east side. The cannon fire from that direction sounded like distant thunder.

General Howe's forces were landing.

———————•◦•———————

Captain Banks and the masters of the other warship aligned their vessels and moved back into position off the south shore of Manhattan Island the next morning. They again began shelling the redoubts at zero eight hundred hours.

Jack strolled the main deck on the side opposite where the cannons were firing. He watched the activity of the gun crews as they went through loading and firing the cannons. With little danger of the shots being sent from shore batteries causing any damage, the younger gun crews fell into a competition attempting to outdo their neighboring stations loading, firing, and reloading.

Nothing wrong with a little rivalry, Jack thought, until he noticed that, in attempting to increase the speed of turnaround, some of the inexperienced seamen were omitting certain important gunnery procedures. Seeing a thin column of smoke rising from a recently fired cannon's touchhole and a man about to shove a couple powder bags into the barrel before swabbing it and the magazine to extinguish any still glowing embers, he suddenly remembered the incident aboard the *Piper* a year ago. Jack dashed to the cannon and slapped the powder man's arm, knocking the bags from his hand. Surprised, the boy dropped the tapping rod, grabbed his arm, and jumped back.

"You could have been blown to bits, had you done what you were about to," Jack admonished the boy. "That powder would have exploded. There is fire in that hole. It has to be extinguished."

The midshipman assigned as gunnery officer to this station was attending a problem two stations aft. He came running. "Sorry, sir," he said. "The rascals at this station are a difficult group. Undisciplined. Impressed from the rookeries of London."

"They need some training," Jack said. "I will speak to the captain."

The midshipman, slightly smaller and younger than the powder man, brandished his sword. He then smacked the boy's head with the side of the blade.

"AWOL," the boy yelled.

The others of the gun crew fisted their hands and jumped forward, ready to attack the midshipman.

"The whack of my sword," the midshipman charged, while raising the sword, "is better than a lash of the cat-o'-nine. Defiance will get you twenty lashes."

The gun crew grumbled but backed off. The powder boy rubbed his head where the side of the sword's blade hit him.

"Man the gun properly," the midshipman commanded. "Load and fire. We have a battle to be won."

"Took some pluck to do what you did," Jack said, smiling at the fearlessness of this midshipman. "What is your name?"

"Robert Drake, sir. My father is a clothier and owner of Drakes in Manchester. His mill produces the military garments. He arranged my entrance into the naval service."

"Good to make your acquaintance, Midshipman Drake. No doubt my father's vessels transport the uniforms made by your father's enterprise. We have not met. I am Second Lieutenant Jack Hollister. We will talk later, since you are now on duty." Jack started to walk off but turned and gave the young man a compliment. "I noted the way you handled this situation." He nodded, adjusted his tricorne, and strolled off amid cannon fire and recoiling cannons.

———•◦•———

Late in the afternoon, the bombardment ended, and the warships again anchored off Staten Island. At dinner Captain Banks informed the other officers of Jack's involvement on the main gunnery deck. "Thank you, Lieutenant Hollister, for averting the accidental ignition of one of the cannons. A prefiring could have greatly damaged this vessel and even killed some men. Seems the gun crews have loosened the firing procedure. I know that some are young, inexperienced, and undisciplined. Midshipman Drake threatened them with lashes. That will calm them for a time, but those urchins will return to their old ways.

Jack raised his arm. "May I comment, sir?"

"You may, Lieutenant."

"While I was a young man in Plymouth, I had many opportunities to visit Royal Naval vessels that came to the harbor. If they remained for a time, and I got to know the officers, I was given the opportunity to observe the training of the ship's crews. Also, I noticed how some captains organized the vessel's work units. There was always one or two experienced men placed into the unit—old hands, masters. These men kept the crews in line."

"Aye," Captain Banks said. "That is a strategy used aboard the larger men-o'-war. The *Renown* is only a 4th-rate warship, small, rarely placed in battle. Mostly used as a troop transport or convoy guard. As such, the navy man vessels like these with knaves and callow fellows. There are few experienced seamen aboard. Perhaps while you are aboard, Lieutenant, for the next few days, you can tutor the midshipmen. Though Mr. Hollister is aide to Admiral Howe, I would like for the duration of this battle to appoint him to oversee the main deck gunnery crews and stations."

"Aye, sir." Jack sat back from the table. "I will be happy to help them. They seem to be an eager group. I am sure the admiral will not mind. He has few activities for me, so working with these young men will pass my time more productively."

"Then let it be so." Captain Banks turned and faced the midshipmen's table. "Gentlemen, for now you will answer to Lieutenant Hollister on matters of training and discipline."

Several indistinct comments rose from the table.

"Do I hear an aye, gentlemen?"

Jack looked to see the expression on Midshipman Drake's face, but before he could perceive a response, a thump against the hull and some racket on the main deck caught everyone's attention.

The door to the officers' mess opened, and the officer of the deck entered. "A message from General Howe, sir." He handed the dispatch to the captain.

Captain Banks perused it, stood, and read, "Our troops have successfully landed on Manhattan Island. They encountered little resistance. As of now they are making their way south to attack the redoubts at the Battery from the north." He raised the message closer to his eyes and said, "The general feels that, by tomorrow, Manhattan Island will be back in the hands of Great Britain. He wants us to continue bombarding until the Union Jack is visible, flying over Fort George."

While others cheered, Jack felt his muscles tighten. He took a deep breath and forced a smile. With the redcoats attacking from the east and south, Washington will escape the city along the west, Jack rationalized. I wish I could have gotten word of the attack to him, but the man is a master strategist.

———————

The next morning the warships were back in line, and as they sailed past Manhattan's south shore, their cannons blasted. They rounded the western corner of the island and cruised up the Hudson for about two miles, each firing fusillades of cannonballs. On the return, the gunners on the opposite side of the vessels lobbed their shots onto the shoreline. As this strategy continued, boredom and fatigue began to affect the gun crews.

Jack leaned against the mainsail mast and watched the activity at the gun stations. Again, he saw a gun crew attempt to rush loading by omitting a crucial procedure. He confronted them. The oldest of the group, a wiry fellow of about sixteen years of age, fisted his hands, raised them toward Jack's face, and growled, "These boys doin' what I tell 'em. This is my station, and these clouts listens to me. No one else. Go 'assle another station."

"You are ready to fire this cannon," Jack said as his muscles stiffened, "but the muzzle is inside the gunport. A slight shift, and you'll blow a hole through the hull." With brow furrowed and jaw tight, he approached the lad. "Roll that muzzle through that port before you pull the cord."

"I got the bloody thing lined up," the defiant gunner said. "Ball'll go through th' hole an' not touch th' paint."

"You're an impudent rascal." Jack's biceps tensed as he flexed his arm. He then ducked to miss the gunner's right hook. From a crouch position, his left fist shot forward and connected just below the boy's ribcage. The impudent fellow flew backward, crashed hard against the cannon's barrel, and slid to the deck, his arms squeezing his stomach.

The boy, choking, doubled into a fetal position and lay moaning.

A friend of the gunner's wielded a belaying pin, but his attempt to swing at Jack was halted by a marine who came to the commotion. "Is all well, Lieutenant?"

"I believe these fellows need to learn a bit of discipline, Corporal. Please escort them to the brig." Jack glared at the two and then turned his eyes on the rest of the gun crew. "Do any of you want to join your comrades?"

The remaining gun crew whimpered and shook their heads.

"Then get this gun back on line." Jack stepped back as the sailors rolled the cannon barrel through the gunport.

Although the Royal Naval vessels continued blasting the shoreline, cannon fire from shore was becoming sporadic. Shortly before lunch, the patriots were no longer shooting back at the British warships. Sooty, gray smoke curled from the shoreline, and occasional flicks of flame could be seen coming from the buildings on and near the Battery. Then someone yelled, "Union Jack, flyin'. Rebels been conquered."

The boatswain's whistle cut through the sailors' cheers, and Captain Banks's executive officer yelled, "Cease fire." Signal flags were raised into the *Renown*'s rigging, signaling the other vessels to cease fire and return to Staten Island.

———————•◆•———————

The September weather remained comfortable; seas were light with occasional fogbanks and sufficient breeze to move the HMS *Renown* at about eight knots. For the next week, Jack and Admiral Howe remained aboard the little warship. For about four hours a day, Jack trained the midshipmen in the gunnery procedures. He also provided them insights into interacting with tough, problematic seamen, and by midweek, he let the midshipmen work with their crews and put some of what they learned into practice. A few minor incidents occurred, but these were easily handled by the budding officers.

However, one confrontation between a seventeen-year-old seaman and the youngest midshipman, a fourteen-year-old, created some moments of anxiety. At the end of a drill, the youngster approached Jack. "Mr. Hollister, I am Midshipman Tommy Pool. It seems handling ruffians is not my calling, sir."

Jack had not seen the confrontation. "Is that where you received that eye that is blackening, Mr. Pool?"

"Aye, sir. One of the crew did not seem to agree with my command."

"Hitting an officer is a week in the brig and at least twenty lashes. Who is the bugger?"

Midshipman Pool nervously worked the hat he held in his hands. "Sir, I would not like to tell the man's name. He's a lazy fellow but is amicable most times."

"I understand, but hitting an officer of the Crown is an offense and must be dealt with." Jack and Tommy strolled to the starboard rail. He motioned for the midshipman to sit on a cannon carriage. "I know who you are, Mr. Pool, and that you are the captain's aide. Under normal circumstances, you are not involved in supervising seamen. But in times of battle, you will very well have to do so. An officer of the Crown is a knowledgeable gentleman who has some authority over the ship's crew. A sailor does not question an officer's order. Midshipman Drake has learned this and stands his ground with a bully. I will mention your unease to him and have him guide in the art of control and the superintendence of men."

"Aye, sir. But Mr. Drake comes from an established mercantile background. I, sir, am an orphan. I do not know my background."

"You are a midshipman, Pool. Many men of unknown backgrounds have attained high office in the Royal Navy. One must have confidence, courage, and perseverance."

"What of the man who hit me, sir?"

Jack pursed his lips and grunted. "Ah, yes. He must be punished. But one of the qualities of command is compassion." He looked Midshipman Pool in the eyes. "You can put a word in on his behalf, but, let me warn you, the one in authority does not befriend his minions." He stepped back and rested against the ship's rail. "Now, go. Join your chums at lunch. I will talk to Mr. Drake."

Midshipman Pool, his brow still furrowed in concern, gritted his teeth, sighed, and then nodded. "Thank you, sir." He stood and walked toward the quarterdeck.

Later that afternoon, Jack spoke to Midshipman Drake. "Midshipman Tommy Pool spoke to me of his unease with an obstinate seaman. He is young and needs shepherding. It would do him much good if you help him along."

"Aye, sir. He talked to me of his conversation with you. I know the bugger who hit him. He has been troublesome since he came aboard. I will arrange for him to be put in the brig for a week. And I will mention that Midshipman Pool asked that his punishment be lenient. The captain will probably agree that he not receive the lashes. Perhaps, with such treatment, this prisoner will become Mr. Pool's guardian, rather than his adversary."

The afternoon sun had sunk to near the horizon by the time the HMS *Renown* was moored to the ferry dock off Fort Stirling near the mouth of the East River in Brooklyn. About an hour later, Jack, with an armful of pouches and loose documents, and Admiral Howe, holding his sextant and telescope, came on deck. A longboat was lowered off the larboard side and allowed to hang just below the gunwale of the vessel. Jack and Admiral Howe walked to the deck above the longboat and joined Captain Banks along with the executive officer and several others.

"Once you are aboard the gig," Captain Banks said, "and seated securely, it will be lowered to the water. The oarsmen will transport you to Governor's Island. It has been our privilege to have you onboard, Admiral. Very good to have met you, Second Lieutenant Hollister." The captain stepped back while several seamen removed a panel from the gunwale. Two burly seamen pulled the swinging longboat against the side of the *Renown* and held it tight. The longboat's helmsman and four oarsmen forward and a pair aft were already aboard. The rugged fellows holding the boat steady collected their lines and stepped aboard. When all were seated, the boatswain aboard the *Renown* yelled, "Lower away."

The open boat gently settled on the water. When the hooks and pulleys at the bow and stern were disengaged, the helmsman and an oarsman in the bow pushed the longboat away from the *Renown*. With the little vessel now adrift, the helmsman commanded, "Stand by oars!" The oarsmen lifted the oars from the middle of the longboat and held them straight up.

"Oars out!"

Together, all lowered their oars into an oarlock, gripped the oar shaft, pushed forward, and held their position, awaiting the next command.

"Give way together!" The rowers dropped the oar blades below the water's surface and pulled back hard. With the tiller shoved to starboard and the longboat under power, it moved away from the *Renown*.

The straight-line crossing to Governor's Island took forty-five minutes. When Jack and Admiral Howe stepped onto the dock, a full lieutenant, two midshipmen, four petty officers, and six seamen greeted them.

Admiral Howe walked to the lieutenant, handed him the documents he brought from the *Renown*, and turned to Jack. "Second Lieutenant Hollister," he said, "I would like you to meet First Lieutenant Gerald Ashton. Mr. Ashton is my adjutant."

Jack and Ashton shook hands. In Jack's grip, the lieutenant's hand felt flimsy. "It is good to meet you, Lieutenant Ashton."

Ashton nodded, turned, and walked to the head of the dock.

Frosty fellow, Jack thought as he scanned his new surroundings. He saw a little boathouse across from the dock. Situated behind it atop a rise was the Governor's

Mansion. It dwarfed the little building. How long will I be here? he wondered.

———•◦•———

September 21, 1776, began as an unexciting, partly cloudy, cool day with a moderate northwest wind that rippled the waters around Governor's Island to a one-foot chop. Jack's lodging consisted of a simple room on the upper floor of a barrack on the south shore of the island. The basic room, with one window, contained a cot, a desk, two chairs, and an armoire with two lower clothing drawers. On a small table along one side sat a washbowl, pitcher, and lantern. He would have the room all to himself.

Jack breakfasted that morning with the two midshipmen, Toby Macklin, a sweet-faced, quiet boy of about fourteen years of age, and Bob Wood, a sixteen-year-old haughty fellow. Jack enjoyed listening to their stories but quickly learned that the two lads had very little in common and had rarely worked together. Midshipman Macklin had whispered to Jack the day the admiral introduced the two of them, "Warn you, Mr. Wood thinks he is the authority on everything nautical and exaggerates most of his stories. He does not take kindly to being challenged."

When the midshipmen had finished their meals and left the mess hall, Jack recalled Macklin's caution, shook his head, and smiled. Today Midshipman Wood said he fought tall, black aborigines in the Hawaiian Islands last year, when he sailed the Indian Ocean off Mombasa. He chuckled and mumbled as he cleared his dishes from the table. "Great adventure," he mumbled, "but those islands are in the Pacific Ocean. That boy's mind is full of fancies." He left the mess hall, crossed the green, and entered the mansion, Admiral Howe's headquarters. The rest of his day and evening were routine.

A couple of hours after he went to sleep, Jack was awakened by someone running through the barracks yelling, "Fire! Fire!" He jumped out of his cot, pulled on a pair of trousers, slipped his arms into a shirt, and dashed out the door.

Others were doing the same. "Not here," someone shouted. "New York City is on fire." Everyone ran toward the boathouse and dock. Across the East River a billowing, waxing and waning, orange-yellow background dissected by a frenzied architectural network of blackened and blazing, exploding, and falling debris released chaotic, curling clouds of black smoke, above which the sky glowed in a ghostly flickering red. The smell of the disaster agitated and irritated those on Governor's Island, but there was nothing they could do but watch.

Like the others, Jack remained, watching from the dock. "I hope all is well with General Howe," he mumbled to himself. "Number One Broadway appears in the middle of that inferno. Only a week since he made that mansion his headquarters."

The next morning as light from the rising sun highlighted great billows of smoke curling skyward from the southern shore of Manhattan Island, Jack trained a telescope to the island and saw mounds of gray ash, twisted piles of charcoaled lumber, partial facades of burned buildings, and tongues of flame continuing to consume what fuel remained. He lowered the scope, glanced around, and noticed Admiral Howe gazing at the destruction across the river. Having been up all night, Jack rubbed his eyes and yawned. Sunday, he thought, a day of rest. "Nothing can be done," he muttered and again looked to see if the admiral were still at the window. He was not. "Probably anxiously awaiting word of his brother and the troops that had been boarded at the Battery." Jack returned to his room and almost immediately fell asleep. He slept most of the day and awoke about an hour before dinner.

While Jack was enjoying his meal, Midshipman Wood came in and announced that Admiral Howe wanted all officers to meet in his office at sixteen hundred hours. "The admiral has a report from Manhattan he would like to share with us."

"We best be on our way," Jack said. "It is near that hour."

He and Midshipman Macklin pushed back from the table and rose. They donned their tricornes and followed Midshipman Wood to the mansion.

A petty officer, standing at the door to the admiral's office, saluted the three officers when they arrived. He opened the door and led them inside. "Seat yourselves," he said and departed, closing the door.

At exactly sixteen hundred hours, Lieutenant Ashton entered the room through a door to the side of the admiral's desk. "Attention on deck. Admiral entering."

"At ease, men, and reseat yourselves," Admiral Howe said as he walked through the doorway. "This will not take

long. I have a report from General Howe that covers the
invasion, fire, and a hanging. Lieutenant Ashton will read
the report."

At the mention of a hanging, Jack's muscles tensed. For
an instant, his eyes widened, but he kept his face sober. He
moved forward in his chair.

The lieutenant accepted the report, scanned for a moment, and then started reading. "General Howe reports
that General Washington and his troops escaped north,
crossed the Harlem River, and took cover in the hills near
Fort Washington."

Jack sighed, slouched in the chair, and relaxed.
Washington had escaped. He was not hung. For the moment, his concentration deviated from the lieutenant's
reading. He missed some of the details about how General
Howe had pursued Continental troops north along the
Hudson River. But then he focused and heard that a small
force of British troops attacked Fort Washington and were
repelled.

"I assume that fort holds a sizable force," the lieutenant said and looked up. "I—I mean, General Howe—plans
to return and take that fort." Lieutenant Ashton returned
to the document he was reading. "The general writes
that he used most of his troops in the pursuit of General
Washington and his renegades." Lieutenant Ashton again
looked up. "General Howe will not stop until he has that
traitor in chains."

Lieutenant Ashton turned a page.

"General Howe and his forces returned across the
Harlem River yesterday morning near the East River," the

lieutenant continued to read. "As the regiment was making its way south, they were stopped by a Loyalist who informed the general that a suspected Continental spy, masquerading as a teacher, was being detained at the Dove Tavern. This alehouse is located near the East River and on the way to the regiment's barracks at the Battery. General Howe and several of his soldiers followed the Loyalist to the tavern. The rest of the regiment continued to the barracks.

"At the Dove Tavern, General Howe found Major Robert Rogers, a retired British ranger who had distinguished himself during the French and Indian War. The major, being loyal to the Crown, had suspected this supposed teacher to be a spy and observed him for several days. The major represented himself as being a Continental spy and befriended the fellow. The major and several of his friends met with this infiltrator and exposed his ruse."

Lieutenant Ashton flipped another page of the report.

"The general interviewed this young man. When he was searched, a diary was found among his possessions that contained descriptions of troop numbers, movements, and drawings of facilities, armament, and fortifications. Confronted with this incriminating evidence, the man confessed to his mission—gave his name as Lieutenant Nathan Hale of the Connecticut Regiment of the Continental Army. General Howe put Lieutenant Hale in the custody of the provost marshal and sentenced him to be hanged in the morning."

Nausea hit Jack as if someone stuck a hand down his throat. He swallowed hard. He lowered his head, held his breath, tried to calm himself. He wanted to cry, scream, and destroy everything and everyone in the room. Slowly this intense pressure dissipated. His face cooled; he raised his head and opened his eyes. He was fully aware of the furniture, the colleagues around him, and their faces and voices, yet it was as if he were still in a dream state. Time had stopped. Movements were slowed. Spoken words droned yet were intelligible.

A nudge in his side made him glance toward the prod. It was Midshipman Macklin.

"Sir, is everything right?"

"Aye," Jack mumbled. "Believe it must be something I ate. My stomach seems riled."

"Some water, perhaps."

"Yes. That would be good. Thank you."

The midshipman stood.

"Where are you going, Midshipman?" Lieutenant Ashton asked. "I haven't finished the report."

"Sir, Lieutenant Hollister is feeling sickly," Midshipman Macklin said. "Something he has eaten had not agreed with him. I will get some water."

"Mr. Hollister, is there something in the report you find troubling?"

"No, sir. I believe I may have an aversion to a tropical fruit I ate earlier. Mango, the cook called it. I will be all right in a moment." Jack looked to Midshipman Macklin. "Please allow the midshipman to fetch me a glass of water."

"Aye. Tart and unripe, mangos can cause a pain in the stomach. Bring Mr. Hollister some water. I will complete the report when you return."

The midshipman returned with a glass of water. Jack drank some and nodded at Ashton, who touched the admiral's shoulder. The man had closed his eyes and had apparently begun to snooze. Admiral Howe popped his head up. "Ready to read on?" he asked.

"Aye, sir," Lieutenant Ashton said, raised the report to eye level, and began to read. "General Howe returned to his office, but before he was able to retire to his bed, the city was aflame. All available men were called out to aid the fire patrols, but their efforts could not avail against the firestorm. Sometime after the midnight hour, the wind changed and blew the flames to the east. One Broadway, General Howe's headquarters and residence, was spared, as were Fort George and all the military facilities at the Battery." The lieutenant lowered the report and folded it. "So ends General Howe's account."

Lieutenant Ashton glanced at the officers, and as he returned the narrative to its pouch, said, "Word came about an hour before I ferried across the river to bring this report that the Continental spy, who was apprehended at the Dove Tavern, went to the gallows with dignity." The lieutenant scanned the group.

Jack felt his stomach again tightening. He took a deep breath. How did my friend die with dignity?

Distraught and dispirited by his restrained emotions, Jack returned to his room and fell on his cot. Stifled tears wetted his face. He smashed it into his pillow, clenched his fists, and emitted a long, muffled, guttural moan. He lay tensed, spellbound by intense desperation, until the depressive

haze seemed to clear from his mind. The pub at the Blue
Goat Inn appeared behind his closed eyelids, diminished,
and reappeared. Professor Morton, a bartender's apron at
his waist, who was holding two mugs, approached. Morton's
illusion faded. The cheerful, ardent face of Nathan Hale
formed and deformed in its place, filling the entire scene.

Jack flipped off the cot. His brow furrowed, teeth gritted, moisture on his face vanished. He was about to yell but
muted the urge and mumbled incoherently what his mind
clearly thought, You helped me into Boston. Got us behind
enemy lines. We feigned espionage. It was a game then. We
were invincible.

Fists clamped, head lowered, he paced about his room.
Then he melted and dropped back onto his bed. Sitting upright on its edge, elbows locked against his sides, he placed
his head in his hands and began to weep. I...I was not
there...when you needed me. Jack lay back on the cot and
blankly stared upward. Depression again enveloped him.
His eyes moistened as he continued to gaze at the ceiling
and closed them. "I am going to miss you, my friend." He
fell asleep.

———•◦•———

The next morning after washing his face and dressing, Jack stared out the window for a few moments. How
does a man die with dignity if he is hung? he wondered
and clenched his fists. "He does not!" He grunted. "Nathan
was a good man. Had a mission. Unfortunately, he went to
it innocently and imprudently. Naïveté can jeopardize any

endeavor and"—he choked—"get you hung." Jack took a deep breath and turned away from the window. He walked to his cot, where his tricorne and jacket lay. The red color of the jacket welled a feeling of resentment in him. "The red-coats hang spies, General Washington warned." He chewed on his lip as he donned the jacket. An anxious twang gnawed his stomach. "Caution. I must remain cautious. I will complete this mission." He flipped on the tricorne and walked toward the door to the hall. "Be the angel at my back, my courageous friend."

———•◦•———

Early in the month of October 1776, a report from General Howe's office arrived. Admiral Howe called a meeting of the naval officers and had Lieutenant Ashton read the report.

The report confirmed that several large regiments of the British and Hessian soldiers occupied Staten Island and that Great Britain had its thumb securely on Long Island, Brooklyn, and Manhattan Island.

A paragraph was devoted to skirmishes with the enemy. Lieutenant Ashton read, "Though minor encounters have occurred between British patrols and Continental rebels in the hilly, swampy regions near White Plains, New York, most of these bands of disorganized insurgents have been exterminated or captured. Some escaped across the Hudson River."

The report mentioned that George Washington had not been heard of or seen.

"So General Howe and his officers," the lieutenant delivered, "assume the rebel leader had slipped through the British grip and fled to New Jersey, though no one is certain to where this mutinous scoundrel and his troops escaped." The report highlighted one hotbed of revolutionaries. "A well-supplied force, estimated to be about three thousand, heavily armed men are now ensconced within Fort Washington. They are under the command of a general Magaw, who, when given the opportunity to surrender, told our envoys that he would 'fight until the last extremity.' General Howe reiterates," Lieutenant Ashton read with emphasis, "that he wants to capture that fort and rid New York of these traitorous rogues. Later this month or early November, he plans to send a large force against this pestiferous anthill and give this general Magaw the opportunity to reach his desired circumstance.

"General Howe surmises that there are many theories of how the great fires started or who may be at fault. But he believes it was probably arson. There were many suspects but little evidence."

The lieutenant concluded the report with General Howe's plan for the winter months.

"The general writes that, with the approach of winter, he feels the ragtag bands of rebels will likely disperse. So the general plans no battles beyond the battle to capture Fort Washington. Troops at some of the outlying posts will not be reinforced until spring."

Up to now, Jack found that Howe's report contained little relevant information to pass on to General Washington, but upon hearing the troop reductions, Jack smiled. Finally, some information, though scant, that Washington might find valuable.

"Thank you, Lieutenant Ashton," Admiral Howe said. "Now that you have heard where our efforts stand to rid this continent of the insurgents, this meeting is adjourned. You may all return to your duties. Mr. Hollister, I want you to take on Lieutenant Ashton's duties for the next few months. I am transferring him to my new flagship, the sixty-four-gun HMS *Eagle*, where he will ready that vessel for my office. You will function as my adjutant."

"Aye, sir. It will be an honor."

On the way back to the barracks, Jack thought about how to provide the first piece of intelligence he obtained to General Washington. I do not know his whereabouts, he pondered as he strolled. Suddenly he shook his fists. "Aha!" He exhaled and looked around to see if the hallway was clear before he entered his office. After closing the door, he began to whisper, formulating his plan. "With Ashton gone, the admiral will send me to General Howe's office in Manhattan with reports. That will provide me an opportunity to have lunch at McGully's Tavern. Perhaps Manny, if he is still with us, will be able to get the information to Washington."

———◆———

The morning Admiral Howe decided to send his brother a report turned out to be warm with only a slight breeze from the southwest, a perfect day for the little naval ferry to sail across the East River. The ferry's crew cast off the lines and raised the sails as soon as Jack seated himself. As the ferry crossed, the helmsman suggested that Jack, upon disembarking, take a left at the head of the dock and cut through the Battery to avoid the ashes, debris, and beggars. "More common folk roamin' city streets now," he said. "The great fire destroyed what meager supplies and lodgin' they once had. Beggin' and thievery ha' increased."

Upon exiting the ferry, Jack took the petty officer's advice and headed into the militarized compound around Fort George. When he reached the statue of King George III, he crossed Broadway and saw the mansion so familiar to him, the headquarters from where General George Washington had once commanded the Continental Army. Now General Howe made this his command center.

No need to go to Howe's office, he thought. I can deal with his aides. They can pass the admiral's dispatches on to his brother.

Jack went up a staircase to the manor's second floor. In the antechamber at the top of the stairs were two desks, one on each side of the entrance to the hallway that led to several rooms. A sergeant occupied each desk, and a pair of armed marines guarded this ingress. The sergeant on the right, an older fellow with a full head of gray hair, recognized Jack.

"Lieutenant Hollister," he said, stood, and saluted. "We never met, but I saw you at the Billopp House. I was one of the general's guards."

"Good day, sir," Jack said and presented the pouch. "Communications from Admiral Howe. I am to give them to General Howe."

"The general is conferring with his adjutants. He asked not to be disturbed."

Jack nodded. "Not to worry, Sergeant. I have no need for any verbal exchange with the general." He laid the pouch on the desk.

"Thank you, sir," the gray-haired sergeant said. "I will pass the reports on to General Howe as soon as he is out of his conference.

Jack bobbed his response, did an about-face, and headed down the stairs and out the door. Lunch. Ferry is to return about fifteen hundred hours, he thought. McGully's Tavern is near the ferry slip, just a couple of blocks north near the commercial wharves that service the East River.

He shrugged, removed a handkerchief from a pocket, and wiped his nose. Rather than return through the Battery, he instead crossed to State Street, then onto Pearl Street, and headed north. The great fire had ravaged the buildings along this street's lower two blocks. Only ash, rubble, and burned, ruined walls now defined the once-vibrant commercial and residential neighborhood. The strong smell of burned wood and other materials that still lingered in the air irritated his senses. Remembering his viewing the horrible conflagration from across the river, he hurried through the destroyed area, staying to the middle of the street and avoiding the light traffic.

That was one hellish fire, he thought. Wind blew. Noxious black smoke billowed onto Governor's Island. We on the island watched helplessly. Lasted most of the night. Then the wind changed. Blew the inferno northwest. Saved some of the mansions on lower Broadway.

He continued Pearl Street to where some buildings stood as burned-out shells. As he neared an intersection, he noticed that the interiors of a few buildings contained collapsed flooring, skewed walls, and fallen beams. Disordered, fire-charred furniture was identifiable amid the ash and rubble in the interior of some of the shops. This is where the fire must have turned, Jack thought. He jogged across the junction, continued his trek for a short distance, and turned east into an alley. He walked cautiously, his hand resting on the hilt of his sword. He encountered no one. Masts and webs of rigging suspended from yardarms came into view as he neared the end of the alleyway. Wharves are ahead, he noted.

The tavern was about a block north of where Jack exited the alley. Though the fires had devastated much of the area he walked through, the way along the East River docks bustled with activity, cartwheels squealed, stevedores howled and complained, and freight wagons stifled traffic. Jack wove his way through this chaos to a doorway under a sign painted in large, faded-red letters:

McGully's Tavern
The Place to Quench Your Thirst

He grabbed the door handle, yanked on it, and pulled the door open. Attracted by the jingling of the bell, everyone inside looked toward the door. Inside, the dimly lit tavern reeked of stale beer, unpleasant sour odors, and tobacco smoke. Except for an occasional loud shout, an inner chatter hummed at the level of a murmur. The interior gloom absorbed the flash of outdoor light when the tavern door closed. Jack's eyes quickly adapted to the dimness. He saw that the patrons had all returned to eating, imbibing, and chatting. His red coat and uniform distinguished authority, but the regular patrons ignored him.

Jack selected a stool from a group of empty ones at the bar. Before he situated himself comfortably, someone grabbed his left shoulder. He snapped his head around and looked up. His eyes lit, and he smiled.

"You have not been here in some time," a throaty voice whispered.

"Manfred...Manfred McGully," Jack uttered. "Manny. Just the man I've come to see."

Manny squeezed Jack's shoulder.

"Manny. I am glad you remained in New York." Jack looked into the man's eyes and lowered his voice. "You've not been found out."

Manny nodded and said, "Let me take your order." He removed paper and pencil from an apron pocket, licked the tip of the pencil, and poised himself to write. "You'll want an ale. Several slices of beef, bread, and perhaps a carrot or two."

Jack nodded and then whispered, "I have a message for Mr. Rabbit."

"Mr. Rabbit is busy delivering somewhere. Secret routes he takes." Manny slipped Jack a piece of paper. "Write. I will collect your dispatch when I deliver your food. Its delivery, I must warn, may take some time to reach the destination."

"Is he safe?"

"Aye. As safe as one can be in these times."

CHAPTER 9
GOVERNMENT ISLAND, NEW YORK
SPRING 1777

Word came from General Howe's office at the end of November 1776 that the eight-thousand-man force of British and Hessian soldiers he sent successfully captured Fort Washington and renamed it Fort Knyphausen, after the Hessian general who led the attack. Jack noted that more than two thousand Continental prisoners and a large cache of supplies were taken. The redcoats now had complete control of Brooklyn, Manhattan, and the territory to the north along the Hudson River. General George Washington and his remaining troops were now on the run.

The winter months were severe, but a report came at the end of January 1777 that excited Jack. General Washington and a small force had crossed the Delaware River and captured the fort at Trenton, New Jersey, in a surprise attack on Christmas Day. The nine hundred Hessian soldiers manning the fort were taken as prisoners.

The stores of food and powder that were confiscated were used later that week to aid the Continental Army when it attacked the village of Princeton, New Jersey. Washington's troops ousted General Charles Cornwallis's army from Princeton with the aid of local Continental forces and militia that came from the surrounding colonial states. General Howe's report said that, after a few minor skirmishes, British troops had been isolated in the village of New Brunswick. The traitor George Washington pushed north and established his headquarters at Morristown. "I do believe that for now we will dispense with the Jerseys and concentrate British efforts on Philadelphia," Howe wrote at the end of the report.

Elated, Jack bit his cheek to stifle a smile. General is upset, he noted. This war is not going according to his plan. His remark at the end of the report is meant to pique our concern.

"Cornwallis is a good general," Admiral Howe said. "Between him and my brother, I am sure this is only a setback." He folded the report and started back to his office. "Lieutenant Hollister, you and the midshipmen can return to your duties."

———————•◦•———————

The month of March brought gusts that blustered across southern Long Island and squeezed through the cracks in the window frames of the barracks. They blew over the top of the partitions that defined Lieutenant Hollister's quarters, causing the flames of candles that he had just placed on the outer edge of his desk to flicker. Wisps of the waxy vapors that curled upward quickly dispersed. Orange reflections fluttered, flashed, and flitted about the room's walls like drunken butterflies. Jack shuddered in the momentary chill that whirled by him as he stood and peered through the window behind his desk into the darkness across the East River toward Brooklyn. Large flakes from a thin spring snowfall swirled beyond the pane. Pellets of sleet smashed against the glass like popping corn.

Six months ago, Washington's men—patriots—were retreating and dying over there, trying to evade the British onslaught. Jack squeezed his arms across his chest, pursed his lips, lowered his head slightly, and continued to stare. Some I knew—worked with. Now I am the enemy. Why did I let myself be talked into this mission? He shivered, turned, and sat down.

Setting his elbows on the desk, for a moment Jack cradled his head in his hands. I did...I did overhear Admiral Howe say it. At last evening's officers' meeting, he said he planned to send a fleet to avenge the loss of the *Margaretta* and the other outrages the rebels of Maine had inflicted on Great Britain. Jack shook his head and ran his hand through his hair. Washington has little interest in Howe's desired assault on a town far from where military action is concentrating. He's in Morristown—too busy to be interested in Howe's rant. He continued to tussle his hair, and then he slammed his hands on the desk. Damn, he said to himself, it may only be the admiral's want for revenge, but if it comes to pass, his want could destroy a town of wonderful people—people who have helped me.

Jack pulled open a drawer and took out a piece of writing paper. He slid the inkwell and quill holder closer to his right side. "Must inform them," he mumbled and then cautiously raised his head and scanned the room. "I'm alone." Jack looked at his watch, which lay on his left. "Three thirty in the morning. Everyone's asleep."

He lifted a quill and dipped the nib into the ink. His intelligence might be of no value to Washington, but the people in Machias needed to know. Then he touched the nib to the paper and paused, scratched his eyebrow, and pondered. General Washington said I should be cautious. Little he could do if I'm found out. A letter warning the people of Machias, if it falls into wrong hands—he nodded and continued to scratch his eyebrow—would surely jeopardize my position and my life. His fingers tightened on the quill's shaft. Those people have to be warned. But to whom should I write this message? Closing his eyes tight and clenching his jaw as if to ward off a black cloud, he let his mind wander. Charles. He wanted to shout the name but instead grunted and softly smiled.

Charles Bowden, Jack's friend and mentor, Jeremiah O'Brien, Benjamin Foster, the Reverend Lyons, and the other Machias militia leaders had devised a simple code to send secret messages. They designed an icon, to be added to the message, to indicate how the secret portion of the message was being transmitted. And to indicate that a letter contained a secret message, the address also needed to be coded. The group accepted placing the suffix "Esq" after the name of the individual to whom the letter was being sent.

Jack laid the quill down and reached under the desk-top. He ran his fingers gently along the inner side of the facing to the left corner. There he felt the small vial hidden there. He extracted it, raised it to eye level, and swirled it. The liquid was a translucent yellowish-orange color. He pulled away the stopper and smelled the contents. His head snapped back. "Phew!"

Jack snorted and wiped his nostrils. "Burns. Horseradish, lemon." He resealed the vial, set it next to the inkwell, and picked up the quill. Then reaching across the desk, he moved one of the candles nearer, leaned his face closer to the paper, and dipped the quill into the black ink. In the top-left corner of the sheet, Jack drew a small fruitlike image surrounded by blade-shaped leaves. He sketched a similar image in the upper-right corner. "Aah. The impresa for invisible ink," he whispered to the paper. "Hope my friends remember."

Dipping the nib into black ink, he began to write the visible part of the message, leaving additional space between the lines.

March 22, 1777
Dear Charles Bowden, Esq.

It has been some time since we have last been together. A year or more I do believe. I hope my letter wishing you luck on your new venture in life finds you in good health. I heard that you, the fine Loyalist you claim to be, have moved to that Hotbed of Colonial Rebels, Machias. For what reason, I do not know. You were always the venturous soul, and I am certain you feel your knowledge of carpentry will be of more use in that distant and turbulent frontier.

Some fine objects have come from that coast. And my brother, who supervises the family business, Hollister Exchange and Transport Limited of London, has told me that the Crown receives much of its material for masts and spars from the timber growing there. But I believe shipbuilding is more active and prosperous closer to Boston. Perhaps you should reconsider your location. Nevertheless, I wish you luck and prosperity, but please be cautious and take care of yourself. These are dangerous times, and you are in the midst of those traitors to the Crown. I hope we again can meet at a more favorable time. I remain your loyal friend and colleague.
Jack Hollister

Jack picked up the blotter, tapped the nib against it, laid the quill next to the inkwell, and blotted his letter. Then he removed another quill with a clean nib from the tray. He manipulated it between the fingers of his right hand, took hold of the vial of invisible ink with his left hand, unstopped it, and dipped the nib into the pungent liquid. He started to write the secret message in between the lines of visible black ink.

Dear Mr. Bowden,

At this time, I cannot tell you where I am or what I am doing, but please disregard the portion of this letter written in visible ink, though I do hope my letter finds you and my other Machias friends in good health. I wrote the visible letter for the benefit of those who may chance to see it. The information below is of considerable importance.

As Jack wrote with the invisible-ink concoction, the script appeared in a soft, yellowish color and was visible. But as it dried, the message faded away. The starkness of black ink masked the slight discoloration the concoction left on the paper. Someone with a trained eye could visualize the discrepancy, however. So to confuse the eyes more, Jack periodically wetted the tip of his finger with invisible ink and dabbed it randomly in the margins of the paper and other blank spaces, creating discolored blotches. The blotches and invisible script would reappear as a dark brown-black image when the paper was placed on a hot stove top or heated over a candle flame.

A day ago I overheard Admiral Richard Howe, Commander-in-Chief of the North American Station of the Royal Navy, order his officers to prepare an attack on the city of Machias. Seems he received word that the colonial rebels in the Machias area are planning a naval invasion of Halifax now that much of the British fleet is stationed off Long Island, Staten Island, and Manhattan, leaving Halifax not well defended. He also mentioned that the capture of the Margaretta and the killing of its captain must be avenged. The admiral gave no date as to when the attack should take place, but I suspect, if it comes to pass, an invasion could take place later this year. You and I have seen what the British are capable of when we visited Falmouth. I surely would not want that to happen to my friends in Machias. I implore you to inform the residents of Machias to make preparations for a possible attack. I remain your loyal friend. Please take care.
Jack

Jack looked at the letter, sighed, and laid the quill back in the tray. He picked up the piece of paper by its corner and fanned it over the desk. He examined the letter carefully to see if any of the invisible part could be noticed. Smiling, he placed it back on the desk and folded it into thirds and then looked across the room. I have no official seal and surely cannot use the seal of the Royal Navy, he concluded. Since it is only a letter to a friend, it does not need a seal.

From a drawer in the desk, Jack removed an envelope. He addressed it.

> *To Charles Bowden, Esq.*
> *Somewhere in*
> *Machias, Maine, Province of Massachusetts*

"Now to post this letter," he mumbled, walked to his bed, and removed his jumper and breeches. He then sat on the edge of the cot and stared at the envelope that lay on the desk. Standing, he returned to the desk, blew out the candles, and returned to bed. "I'll be delivering a pouch of messages and orders to the admiral's brother's office in Manhattan tomorrow. McGully's Tavern is a short distance away. Perhaps Manny will be working as before. He can get my message to Connecticut and on its way.

CHAPTER 10
GOVERNOR'S ISLAND, NEW YORK
MARCH 1777

The lions of March still prowled through the nooks and crannies of Governor's Island and the byways of lower Manhattan. Windowpanes and naked tree branches shuddered when these mystical winter beasts howled and moaned. The growls of these whirlwinds woke Jack. He shivered as he untangled himself from the blanket that had kept him warm during the night. "Damn," he mumbled when he realized that he had forgotten to feed the little wood stove that heated his room. With the still-warm parts of the blanket wrapped over his shoulders and around his chest, he stumbled to the little woodpile next to the stove.

"Maybe there are still some embers hot enough to ignite a flame." His body trembled, and his teeth were on the verge of chattering. He opened the stove's door and blew into the firebox. A waft of smoke and ash jetted and curled toward his face. He hopped to the side until the dust cloud cleared and then looked into the firebox. "Aye." Inside were some glowing embers and transitory licks of flame. He reached to the woodpile, grabbed some kindling, and tossed it into the firebox. With his hand, he fanned the embers. When the new pieces of wood finally caught fire, he added two larger chunks. He shut the door to the stove, though some thin slips of smoke escaped, leaving his room scented with a strong campfire odor.

With the blanket still draped over his shoulders, he hobbled to the washstand and splashed his face and then dried it, dressed, and brushed his hair. The fire in the little stove was crackling when he put on his officer's woolen red jacket. The envelope containing the Machias letter, stark on the black desk, glared at him. He picked it up and stuffed it in an inside pocket, sighed, and patted the area of the jacket covering the pocket. Before pulling on his boots, he straightened the tangled bedclothes and covered the cot with the blanket that he had tossed on the back of the chair. Then, with his hands, he brushed bits of lint from the jacket, buttoned it, and walked into the hall.

An aroma of baked bread and fried bacon moistened his mouth as he walked down to the galley.

"Hear you're going to cross over to Manhattan this morning," Toby Macklin greeted. Toby, a clean-cut, pale youth sporting a crop of tousled, rust-colored hair was the youngest midshipman on Admiral Howe's staff.

"Right," Bob Wood, an older midshipman at the table, resounded. He seemed to display minimal concern for military decorum by having the top part of his shirt and his jacket unbuttoned. "Second lieutenants are errand boys, Toby," Wood said as he looked at Jack.

"Midshipman Wood," Jack countered. "That may be so. It is part of the job. Not glorious, but a rung on the ladder to advancement. Since you seem to have little care for your image, it may be some time"—Jack scowled and flicked his head to the side—"or perhaps never, for you, Midshipman, to receive a promotion. That shirt should be buttoned completely. Your military appearance should be proper."

Midshipman Macklin covered his mouth with his hand and chuckled.

"Sorry, Lieutenant, but you are not my commanding officer," Wood answered. "Around here I do as I want."

"Aye. Your haughtiness will haunt you someday, Mr. Wood." Jack raised his head and walked to the table where the cook had laid out breakfast food.

Midshipman Wood shoved his plate away from him, smacked down his eating utensils, rose, and stomped out the door.

As Midshipman Macklin was leaving the galley, he walked to where Jack had seated himself. "Beggin' your pardon, Mr. Hollister, but I want to apologize for Midshipman Wood's arrogance. He was out of line, but I do believe he is not happy being in the Royal Navy. He is from Long Island and told me that his father, who held the rank of captain, insisted he enlist. But I believe he was forced into the service. He is not happy here."

"Your apology is not necessary, Midshipman," Jack said. "I understand the young man's dissatisfaction. During my time in the service, I've known two such unhappy men. One was released, and the other deserted." Jack looked at Toby for a moment and then lifted his cup and took a swallow of the tea.

Midshipman Macklin nodded, turned, and departed. Jack finished his breakfast, contemplated Midshipman Wood's discontent for a moment, and finished drinking the tea.

The cook came to the table. "If sir has completed his breakfast, I will clear the table."

"Aye. And thank you," Jack said.

———•◦•———

Though the northeast wind subsided somewhat, it continued to churn chaotic waves in Buttermilk Channel. The officers' barracks blocked the gusts when Jack exited through a south-facing door. As he rounded the building and made his way to the road ringing the island, cold blasts hit him full in the face. Lowering his head, he grasped the jacket's collar with one hand and gripped the brim of his tricorne with the other. He continued along the road for about one hundred yards to a path that progressed slightly uphill, away from the shore, and across an expansive green. It led to the centrally located Admiral House, a federal-style mansion and headquarters of Admiral Richard Howe.

Jack's muscles tightened as he headed up the path toward the Admiral House. A couple of strong drafts buffeted his right side. He turned and lowered his head into the wind, squeezed his grasp on the tricorne, and continued. Once he had negotiated a short flight of steps and reached the mansion's portico, the wind's grip released him. He shivered, freed the hold on his clothing, took a deep breath, and walked to the door. After nodding to a marine guard, he entered the manor house. The tenseness in his body calmed when he felt the warmth inside.

As he walked across the reception room, he glanced up the stairway to the second floor. Admiral Howe's quarters, he thought. He continued to the side of the stairway to a room that contained the officers and enlisted men who administered the daily duties of Howe's command. He stopped at the desk of a young seaman.

"I am here to collect the dispatches the admiral has for his brother, General Howe," Jack said.

"Yes, yes, Lieutenant Hollister," the seaman said. "Have them here." He reached to a shelf below the desktop and brought up a leather pouch. He handed it to Jack. "The admiral requests you deliver them posthaste."

Jack nodded. "Must be of great importance." He accepted the pouch and grinned. "Or perhaps the admiral and his brother are planning a ball for some ladies from the city."

The seaman smiled. "Lieutenant, that's not possible. You know the admiral has a serious case of gout. He'd have little use for ladies from the city."

"Aye." A grin brightened Jack's face as he turned and walked out of the administration office.

———•◦•———

Once outside, Jack stood for a moment in the entryway of Admiral House and looked to the right. From the portico, the buildings of Lower Manhattan and the Battery were clearly visible. Though where he stood was in the lee of the wind, he could see that the waters of the East River were churning angrily. He grabbed and squeezed tight the jacket's cloth near his neck, scrunched his shoulders, lowered his head, took hold of the beak of the tricorne, and walked down the steps. On the walkway, he turned toward the docks on the East River. As he moved beyond the protection of Admiral House, the northeast winds encased him, impeded his movement, and buffeted him to the left. With a sturdier grasp on his jacket and tricorne, he increased the length and strength of his stride and crossed the green to the river's edge. With very few barriers, the wind continued to batter him. Upon reaching the shore, Jack sheltered himself behind the left side of a boathouse.

The door on the riverside of the boathouse opened, and a petty officer leaned out. "Come inside and warm yourself, sir," he said, "'fore we ferry you across. Sure of a stinger, tha' wind is."

Jack nodded, rolled around to the door, and jumped into the shed before the wind had a chance to trash him more. In addition to the sailor at the door, six burly men were scattered around a wood-burning stove inside.

"We're to ferry a courier o'er to Manhattan," the petty officer said. "You must be him, Lieutenant?"

"Aye, Petty Officer. That is who I am." Jack looked out the window at the sloop straining against its moorings. The lines holding it to the dock were stretched tight.

"A tempestuous day to be on the river, sir. We'll be usin' the longboat, 'stead of the sloop. Goin' to be fast goin' o'er, bit sloppy an' wet, but fast. Wind goin' to make rowin' easy on the goin', but the mates'll have to use a bit of muscle and dig deep comin' back. The sloop would shoot across the river like a shot, but it'll not return against the wind."

"Guess I'm in for a tad of excitement, Petty Officer," Jack said as he walked nearer to the woodstove.

"Aye, sir. Have some tarpaulin to cover you. Keep you dry."

"Thank you, Petty Officer. Should not be too much splash in a following sea."

"Aye." The petty officer turned to his crew. "Get your oars. Let's go and fight the tempest."

As soon as the sailor on the little pier tossed off the bowline, the longboat drifted backward with the current. When the vessel had coasted about twenty feet from shore, the six rugged oarsmen leaned forward and dug the blades deep and, with all their might, hauled back on the oars. With the release of their groans, the longboat moved forward, counter to the current. They continued to strain against the oars as the petty officer pushed the tiller to starboard. The bow rotated through the current and pointed to the southern tip of Manhattan. The oarsmen maintained a constant rowing rhythm, but with less effort because now the boat moved with the current and with the wind behind and slightly to starboard. They made good progress.

Jack scanned New York Bay. Three Royal Navy frigates rode at anchor nearby. They brought his brother to mind. Ian sure did not enjoy his tour aboard one such vessel. He pushed away the tarpaulin that protected his left side from the spray, readjusted his position on the seat, and looked past the stern of the longboat. Docked along the Brooklyn shoreline was the sixty-four-gun warship HMS *Eagle*.

Admiral Howe's new flagship, Jack noted. He scanned the *Eagle* and thought of his brother. I wonder if Ian would have enjoyed being aboard such a larger vessel more. I doubt it, even though the accommodations might have been better. A grin lit his face but disappeared when his eyes locked on the freight brigs docked forward of the *Eagle*. Ian surely didn't like being aboard the Hollister brig when we made our Atlantic crossing. Especially when the hulk began to leak. He removed his hat and scratched his head. I wonder what he's doing. It's been long since we have communicated. He shrugged and turned his head toward lower Manhattan.

The longboat crossed the confluence where the East River entered Upper New York Bay and the wind and current-driven chop diminished. Coming abreast of and in the protection of the southern end of Manhattan Island, the petty officer moved the tiller to the left. On an almost-flat surface of water, the longboat's bow pointed toward the Battery and small docks at the southeast corner of Manhattan. Within a few minutes, the crew rowed the longboat between two docks, boated their oars, and allowed the slight current to push the vessel next to the left side of a pier. Two sailors on the pier caught the mooring lines tossed by the longboat's crew and secured the lines to the dock.

"Passenger ashore," the petty officer announced.

Jack disembarked from the longboat and walked the short distance to State Street. On his right stretched blocks of burned-out buildings, rubble, and ash from the great fire that had occurred back in September. On his right stood the military hospital, lower barracks, redoubts, and fortifications associated with the Battery. The fires had missed the barracks and the mansions along the lowest block of Broadway. He clutched the satchel destined for General Howe's office and patted his jacket. My letter is safe. He continued along the left side of Water Street to Fort George. To avoid the panhandlers and other displaced persons, he entered the Battery and cut across the green below the fort to ramparts along the shoreline. Rounding to the west side of the fort, Jack headed along the promenade to King George square and the beginning of Broadway. On his left was a huge mansion, Number One Broadway.

Jack glanced at the statue to King George III, shrugged, and crossed to General Howe's headquarters. No need to go to Howe's office, he thought. I can deal with his aides. They can pass the admiral's dispatches on to his brother.

When Jack entered the mansion and reached the second floor, the sergeant at the reception desk said. "Lieutenant Hollister. Back again?"

"Aye," Jack said and handed him the pouch for the general. Because of the wind, I have a few hours to enjoy the city. The naval ferry will not return until later this afternoon when the outside gale subsides. Until then I plan to visit McGully's Tavern and enjoy a plate of his delicious roast pork."

The sergeant's eyes narrowed in alarm, "You know, Lieutenant, that tavern is a haunt for rebels and reprobates. Make sure you maintain your guard."

"Thank you for your concern, Sergeant. I agree the place does cater to ruffians and displaced sailors." Jack grinned. "But I am familiar with the place and find it acceptable."

"I can send a marine with you. Those boys don't have much to do and would like an unusual break."

"That will not be necessary, Sergeant, but thank you."

"As you wish, Lieutenant."

Jack saluted, turned, and returned to the stairway. On the way down, he adjusted his jacket and then patted the area of the jacket covering the inside pocket. He heard the crunch of the envelope and continued to and out the door of General Howe's headquarters. He headed back to the east side of Manhattan and entered the dim, gloomy alley that led to the wharves. He noticed there were more indigents roaming about, more than had been in this alley last fall when he passed through about a month after the great fire. *There looks to be a pauper in every nook and cranny. The damned red coat will surely attract their attention.*

"Hey, mate!" An unkempt fellow older than Jack seemed to have popped out of a darkened corner. "A military man like you can spare a few pennies to one the fires left destitute." He leaned toward Jack and held out his hand.

Before Jack could answer, three more slovenly scoundrels about his age materialized. The group surrounded him. Within a blink, he swung his arms across his body. His right hand grabbed the hilt of his sword and his left the dagger's handle. Before the older fellow could jump back, the tip of Jack's sword had creased his throat. The blade of the dagger flashed in the eyes of the other three blackguards as he poised it at shoulder height toward them. "That is no way to behave when asking for alms from a gentleman of His Majesty's Navy," Jack declared.

The mature fellow dropped to his knees. "I meant no harm, sir," he cried.

Jack's eye caught the rascal, who stood to his left, moving his arm behind his back. The scamp brought the arm forward, brandishing a knife, and lunged toward Jack.

With a quick twist and sidestep, Jack's rotated to the right and away. He swung his sword up and around. The blade sliced the scalawag's wrist. His knife skittered over the cobblestones. Blood squirted. The scoundrel yelled, gripped his wrist, slowing the red plasma oozing over his fingers. He fell backward onto the bricks. His villainous partners ran to his aid. The older man jumped to his feet and ran off down the alley.

The commotion attracted two royal marines, who drew their swords and dashed to Jack's assistance. "Are you all right, Lieutenant?" the marine corporal asked. The two would-be attackers cowered beside their injured comrade.

"Aye," Jack said as he sheathed his sword. He pointed to the bleeding man. "I believe that one will need to be stitched up in a hurry."

"Not to worry, sir," the marine said. "We have a place for scoundrels like these. A year or two at sea will teach them a love for their fellow man. There's a frigate at anchor in need of some hard-bitten men."

"Aye," the other marine said. "If they survive, they will be a disciplined lot the next time they set foot on land." He pulled his pistol and moved toward the complaining rogues. "You be on your way, Lieutenant. We'll take care of these fellows."

"Thank you, gentlemen." Jack sheathed his dagger, straightened, and patted his jacket. He felt the envelope containing his letter to Charles Bowden crunch. Sighing, he looked in the direction the beggar had run. "Don't bother chasing down the older fellow. He was a real beggar." Jack reached into his pocket, jingled some coins, and continued through the alley. As he approached the wharf, he turned left toward McGully's but almost ran headlong into another vagrant. Stumbling back, Jack realized this was the older man who had approached him earlier.

The beggar also recognized him, turned, and was about to run, but Jack yelled. "Hey! Hold up. Don't run. I am not after you. Got something for you." Jack put his hand in his coat pocket and clutched the coins.

The beggar stopped and looked back.

"I do have a few pennies and a shilling," Jack said as he approached. "You did come on a bit strong. And those ruffians didn't help your cause." He extended his fisted hand toward the beggar, who stood with his mouth open.

The beggar pulled himself together and said, "Never meant you any harm, sir. I'm at my wit's end. Desperate. Lost my business to the fire. Have a wife and two young ones. Been days since they ate."

"Here. Take these. It isn't much."

"I thank you, kind sir." The beggar sheepishly smiled, opened his hand, and allowed Jack to let the coins fall into it.

"No one is after you. Go take care of your family. But the next time you approach an almoner, be cautious and a bit less aggressive."

"Aye. Those are thoughtful words, sir. I shall try to abide by them." The beggar scooted off toward the alley.

Jack smiled and took a deep breath. As he continued on his way, a feeling of warmth relaxed the tension in his body.

As he neared the tavern, the street filled with a confusion of sailors, stevedores, and horses. Empty carriages and wagons headed for the wharves as loaded ones moved off, their wheels crunching down onto the bricks that paved the street and wharves. Instead of an aroma of burned wood, this zone of commerce smelled of horses, urine, dried fish, tar, cordage, algae, and decomposition. Clouds of flies hovered over dung piles. Men in fine clothing vigilantly moved about within this bedlam.

When Jack reached McGully's Tavern, he pulled the door open and made his way, between the scattered lunch crowd seated at the tables in the dimly lit room, to the bar and found several empty stools away from a group of sailors. He sat down on one.

Manny leaned over the bar and faced Jack. "I see you've survived the winter without being found out."

"Aye." Jack put his hand onto his jacket over the interior pocket and pressed. He felt the envelope. "I need to talk with you—quietly."

"When I saw you come through the door, I knew it was not for enjoyment. Let me take your order and pass it on to the cook. When I return and serve you, we can talk. No one here suspects. I believe they don't even give a damn." He motioned to a bartender. "The lieutenant needs a pint."

A tall, sinewy African near Jack's age nodded.

"I'll place your order." Manny went into the kitchen.

"Tuppence, sir," the bartender said as he set a full mug in front of Jack. He picked up the coins Jack dropped on the bar and returned to where a group of sailors sat, chitchatting.

Manny soon returned carrying a tray and put it on a counter behind the bar. He removed the various dishes that contained Jack's lunch and set them in front of him.

Jack noticed the edge of a piece of paper sticking out beyond one of the plates Manny placed in front of him. The paper was folded several times.

"Your entrée, sir, and," Manny said, "as you ordered, roast pork, boiled cabbage, and bread." His eyes narrowed as Jack fingered the paper partially hidden under the dish. "A message to a Mr. Carson Rabbit," he whispered. "I believe you may know him." He glanced around. "Now then, pray tell, what further need do you have of me?"

Carson Rabbit? Jack's eyes widened for a moment. He felt his heart skip a beat. Haven't heard that name in some time. He sighed, then reached into the inner pocket of his coat, and slowly pulled the edge of the hidden envelope toward the middle of his chest. "I need to get a message to Machias as soon as possible."

"Aye," Manny said in a hushed voice. He saw the corner of the envelope. "Slip it under the large dish when you finish. I will collect it when I clear your area." He placed the last dish in front of Jack. "You need a fill on your ale?"

Jack nodded.

Manny straightened and swung the tray under his arm and leaned toward Jack. "Perhaps you may have questions after you read the message addressed to Mr. Rabbit." As he returned to the kitchen, he motioned to the bartender to bring Jack another ale.

Jack drank what beer remained in his mug, took up the fork and knife, and cut the chunk of pork into small pieces. Laying down the knife, he picked up the bread, broke off a chunk, and placed it on the edge of the dish. He bent forward, slipped his fingers under the dish, and skidded the message Manny had brought him onto his lap. Using the piece of bread, he shoved a bit of pork onto the fork and passed it to his mouth as he looked around to see if anyone was watching or looking in his direction.

"Your ale, Lieutenant," the bartender said.

Jack looked him in the eye, shuffled, and reached into his pocket. He collected some coins and dropped two pence onto the bar. The bartender took up the coins and returned to the group of sailors.

After seeing that the coast was clear, Jack, using his left hand, lifted the note from his lap. He glanced down, raised it slightly to the level of the bar, and partially unfolded it. The address line contained, To Mr. Carson Rabbit, NYC. The note was sealed with a stamped blob of red wax. He immediately recognized the imprint, though somewhat distorted, as a twisted shield that contained two bars and three mullets and a crown from which a spread-winged bird seemed to be rising. Washington's coat of arms!

He gingerly lifted a loose edge, tore it free of the wax, and unfolded it completely. Though cursively written in light-colored ink, the message was clear:

My dear Mr. Rabbit,

Based on the results that have recently developed, I no longer feel the need for your services. All has gone somewhat as planned. Our labors from now and into the future will be concentrated on the land. But there is still a great need for those with nautical capability.

May I suggest you rid yourself of those Tory chains post-haste, but carefully, and by whatever means, travel east. Boston and beyond are good for the balance of summer and hold strong opportunities for your talents. Besides, you already have contacts in that direction.

I wish you Godspeed. Be safe. Perhaps we will again meet someday. Until then, I remain your friend.

G. W.

Jack lifted his head and closed his eyes. As he leaned his head back, the roughness from the collar on his red coat scratched the back of his neck. His muscles tightened. He crunched the message in his fist.

"Message of concern?" Manny asked as he returned to Jack's table. "Have you completed your meal?"

Jack lowered his head. "Aye, my friend. You may remove the dishes, but leave my mug of beer."

"You have a message for me to deliver?"

"Aye, I do." Jack lifted his serviette with his left hand and slowly began to wipe his mouth as he slipped his right hand into his coat. He cautiously removed the envelope from the inside pocket, keeping it hidden behind the napkin. When Manny picked up the platter, Jack folded the napkin, covering the letter, and placed it onto the platter. "Could some stealthy means of passage to Paulus Point or the Connecticut coast be arranged in the next few days?" Jack whispered as Manny bent to retrieve several other dishes.

Manny straightened, placed the dirty dishes on a nearby table, scanned the room, pulled a cloth from his belt, again leaned over, and began wiping the bar. "Aye," he hinted. "A private departure is what is needed?"

"Affirmative, Mr. McGully," Jack said. "His Excellency is engaged in Morristown with the challenges of upcoming land missions. The intelligence network he has established has become effective. So he suggests I leave the British ranks and move on to more useful endeavors."

"Aye. A trip can be arranged," Manny said. "Finish your ale while I take these dishes to the scullery." He turned, tossed the washcloth onto the counter with the stack of dishes, and quickly slipped Jack's letter from the folded napkin into the gather of his apron as he wiped his hands. "I'll return in a moment."

Jack sipped his ale and gazed around the tavern. Most of the patrons had left. Two men sat at a distant table. It appeared they were in a quiet discussion. Jack looked down the bar. The sailors had departed, and the bartender was drying mugs. He stared down at his mug and ruminated. I need to liberate myself of these lobsterbacks and make my way to Boston or Beverly. Manny's return disrupted his thoughts.

Manny picked up the wiping cloth he had thrown onto the counter and hunched against the bar next to Jack. "Paulus Point is an anthill of redcoats," he said. "To get away from these teabags, Connecticut would be a better sanctuary. Go to New London, a fishing village with many patriots."

"Aye," Jack said. "But a dangerous route for one trying to escape."

"Aye, that is so, for a patriot. But you, being a naval officer of the Crown, could travel as McGully's emissary. I go to Oyster Bay—a redcoat stronghold—every Wednesday to purchase seafood. There are patriots among the fishermen. They would have few qualms about ferrying an agent of independence to safety. Your letter to Mr. Bowden will travel a similar route."

Jack looked directly into Manny's eyes. "Your plan sounds good."

"Aye. Once in Oyster Bay, you change from a military uniform to the clothing of a seaman. Then you will be secreted aboard a fishing vessel."

"I do not want to get you into any trouble, Manny."

"You will not. Occasionally, one or more British military persons travel with me to Oyster Bay. If we are stopped, there is always an explanation why those persons are aboard. Not to worry. All will go well. Should I plan for you to travel with me?"

"Aye," Jack said. "I cannot give you a specific time. I must create a reason for having to stay in the city for more than one day. Today is not a problem because the winds are against returning." Jack sat back on the stool. "I will come a day or two early and be ready to travel."

"Right you are, sir. I will be ready."

Jack slipped off the barstool, nodded at Manny, and left the tavern.

CHAPTER 11
LONG ISLAND, NEW YORK
APRIL 1777

A misty breeze wafted about the wharves and scented the air with the sweetness of spring flowers and cherry blossoms, diminishing the moldy, burned-wood, and salty odors that usually flavored the South Street waterfront of Manhattan. With few clouds in the sky, the sun shone brightly, warming the air on this first Monday in April 1777. Commercial and harbor activity seemed light. The Governor's Island naval ferry, carrying Lieutenant Hollister, approached the Water Street pier. Jack was assigned to deliver Admiral Howe's pouch containing messages for General Howe's headquarters.

As the crew secured the longboat to a piling, Jack stood, picked up the courier pouch destined for General Howe, took hold of a rung on the dock's boarding ladder, and balanced himself on the moving ferry. He turned to the crew and said, "Thank you, gentlemen. I will see you in a few days. The admiral gave me leave until Thursday." He climbed the short distance and stepped off onto the dock.

Little has been done with the buildings the great fire destroyed, he thought as he scanned the adjacent street. Trash and ash abounded everywhere. "Best I make my way to the general's office by going through the Battery," he mumbled and set his course. "I will drop off the pouch and return to McGully's." He walked off the pier onto the street, turned left, and strolled toward the army's lower barracks. As he walked his mind strategized.

If all goes well, Wednesday, Manny will transport me to Oyster Bay. By the time those on Governor's Island realize I am missing, I should be in Connecticut.

Reaching General Howe's headquarters, Jack handed over the courier pouch to the sergeant at arms. As he was about the turn and leave, the sergeant handed him another purse of reports in exchange. "General's communications for the Admiral," he said.

Jack nodded, accepted the new courier pouch, turned, and headed down the stairway to the front door. He shook his head as he crossed Broadway and considered what to do. Hope there is nothing important in this damned bag. Manny can arrange to have it delivered after I get away.

Completing his official errand, Jack gritted his teeth, squinted his eyes, glared forward, and set off at a brisk walk back toward the East River wharves and McGully's Tavern. It usually took an hour to cover this distance. But with the disruption in his plan created by the unexpected packet that needed to be delivered, he hastened his stride. He reached the alleyway that led to the wharves in thirty minutes. Along the way, his right hand fondled and gripped the hilt of his sword. Just in case. But this time no one accosted him as the thieves had on previous occasions. He approached McGully's overhead signboard, reached the door, and pulled it open. Once inside and his eyes adjusted to the darkness, he chuckled. Tea time. And this is not a tearoom. He proceeded to the bar and found the bartender absorbed in wiping the drip tray beneath the beer spigots. "Mr. McGully about?" he asked.

"Out," the bartender answered without looking up from his chore. "Be back shortly. A mug o' beer while you wait, Lieutenant?"

"Aye." Jack slipped a stool away from the bar and sat down. He sighed and clasped his hands atop the bar. How did he know who I am? Then he looked up, glanced across the bar, and saw his reflection in the mirror. He smiled. As the bartender set a mug full of beer in from him, he took a swig.

An hour later and his second mug now empty, the sound of the kitchen's back door opening and closing nudged Jack back into reality. Manny strolled into the pub. "Good to see you, my friend. It has been a while."

"Aye," Jack said. "I am ready to travel."

Manny nodded. "Wednesday we go." He reached under the bar, pulled out a short-barreled flintlock pistol, a bag of powder and shot, and a compass that was tied to the drawstrings of a leather bag. He placed the things on the bar and slid them across to Jack. "Put this gear together for you. Stuff for your journey. Must be ready. There'll be those who will try to stop you. But until we depart, stay off the streets. I have a room for you upstairs." Manny turned and walked to the kitchen door. "Take the gear and come with me. I will show you to the room."

Jack slid off the stool and followed Manny. "What about this uniform? And Howe's office gave me some messages to be delivered to the admiral."

"Keep the uniform. It will be useful as we travel to Oyster Bay. Once there, you will be given a change of clothes. Leave the courier's purse with me. When I return from Oyster Bay, I'll have one of my people give it to a sailor to deliver. No one will know where the pouch came from."

"Thank you. That damned sack gave me some concern."

"Don't concern yourself." Manny thought for a moment. "On second thought, it might be best to take that courier purse with us. If a need arises, an official pouch may prove important. Now, let me show you to your room."

Jack followed Manny up a rickety set of back stairs to a room that contained a cot, a chest with a washbowl and pitcher upon its top, and a bucket against a sidewall.

"The bartender will bring you food and water," Manny said as they entered the room. "You can trust him. Now, get some rest. You'll need it. Your journey to the Maine territory will be arduous and dangerous. The ferry across the East River leaves before sunup." Manny dipped his head and backed into the hall. He closed the door to the room.

"Safe for now," Jack muttered, sat down on the cot, and sighed in relief. This room reminds me of Billopp's jail. Another prison—before another adventure. He slipped off the red coat, undid his belt, and lay back on the cot.

———•◦•———

Dim morning daylight that illuminated Jack's room woke him. He stretched and shoved himself to a sitting position, yawned, and rubbed his eyes. Atop the chest, within reach, lay the pistol and compass Manny had given him. He retrieved the gun and examined it, ran the tip of his finger on the scrolling carved into the handle, and put his nose near the oiled barrel.

What a nice piece. I wonder why Manny gave this pistol to me. Looks so elegant. The gun felt comfortable in his grip. He sighted down the barrel and aimed at different objects. When he sighted on the red coat hanging on the wall, he also saw his scabbard and sword, which he had hung over the coat. He raised his eyes from the gun and stared at the army uniform and its accessories and smiled. "Manny knows best," he mumbled and grinned. "Without that uniform and sword, I will be unarmed." He relaxed, punched the pillow, and lay back on the cot.

After a few minutes, he swung his legs off the bed, twisted, and dropped them over the cot's edge. "An item of even more value," he whispered as he removed the compass tied to the leather sack. He prized apart the drawstrings and opened the bag. Inside he found a map, removed it, and inspected it— the route along the coastline of Connecticut. Hand drawn, rough, but beneficial. He traced his finger along the route. What are those periodic Xs? He opened the map further and found Manny's scribbling. Ah, yes. Way stops. Safe places to camp. "That man thinks of everything. I will not get lost."

Shortly after Jack finished washing his face, the bartender brought him breakfast. Jack cleared a space on the chest for a tray that contained some ham, bread, a small crock of jam, and a pot of tea.

"Mr. McGully asks tha', if you do go out, you not wander far from the tavern." The African fellow put down the tray. "'E says, soldiers in the streets nervous. Have been nettlin' single men driftin' about the city. Declarin' 'em spies. Arrestin' 'em—even arrestin' their own kind." The bartender straightened and began to back into the hall. "Mr. McGully asks you stay about. Not look suspicious. Besides, it's wretched outside, rainy, cold."

"But I am a lieutenant in this blasted army."

"No mattah, sah. Masqueradin', they calls it. They hanged a lieutenant last year." The bartender scratched his head. "Course, he were a rebel."

And friend, Jack thought as he looked up and handed the fellow a couple of pennies. "Thank you. Tell Mr. McGully I will take his advice."

———•◦•———

Jack and Manny McGully met behind the tavern early Wednesday morning. The innkeeper stood in the darkness at the rear of a wagon. When Jack, carrying his travel bag, came outside, he let the door close. Hearing the door clack, Manny raised an oil lantern and beckoned him. "Over here. Throw your pack in the back. Come, partake of yesterday's biscuits and a slice of cheese. Vittles to fortify you for the journey. Also have coffee."

A pair of draft horses, hitched to the front of the wagon, fretfully shuffled and whinnied as Jack approached. "Breakfast, Mr. McGully? How considerate."

"Thank you," Manny said as he passed Jack on his way around the wagon to the horses that were munching on hay and oats. "At this time in the morning, the cooks are cherishing their last snores of the night. In an hour, they'll be lighting the fires in the kitchens. We need to be on our way before then." Manny removed the feeding bags from the horses, untied them, and guided them to the water trough. He then climbed aboard the wagon.

Above, a bluing sky migrated westward and in its path extinguished the pinpricks that had blazed through the overhead darkness.

"Finish, Lieutenant," Manny commanded. "We've a ferry to catch."

Jack gulped down the coffee and left the mug on a shelf attached to the barn. He ran to the front of the wagon and climbed onto the seat next to Manny. "Let us be on our way."

Mr. McGully pulled the reins to the left, and the horses sauntered away from the trough and onto the road. He urged them to a trot. Manny and Jack traveled north along the East River to just below Blackwell's Island,[2] which they reached at sunrise. At the river's edge, one of Manny's friends owned a large barge that he used to ferry wagons, carts, and boxes of cargo across to Long Island. They boarded the barge when the river's tidal level was nearing the morning's high tide. This allowed the horses and wagon

---

2 Today named Roosevelt Island.

to remain relatively dry and mud free when driven off the road and down a gradually sloping embankment to the ferry's ramp.

"Why did we come way up the river to cross?" Jack asked once they were aboard and the wagon and horses secured. "The river has greater width here."

"Aye," Manny answered. "Too much traffic and too many redcoats at the Brooklyn ferry. They ask too many questions. Only the river, its tides and currents, will challenge us here."

Once a few other pieces of cargo were hauled aboard, the shore side ramp of the bargelike ferry was lifted from the mud and raised to an angle a few degrees above the deck and secured. Several muscular, robust men poled the rectangular hulk away from the shore and out into the river. When the men's poles could no longer contact the bottom, they switched to large oars. Though the tidal currents were relatively negligible, this means of propulsion required considerable strength to move the heavy platform across the downward flow of the river. Contrary currents and a northern breeze fought the rowers. In the early part of the crossing, the ferry's course angled to the south. At midriver its forward end came around to an easterly heading. When the ferry came into the wind shadow of the island, a slight upriver flow swung its bow northeasterly. With the aid of this current, the oarsmen were able to ease up to keep the barge headed toward shore. About fifty feet from the river edge, the oarsmen switched back to the poles and were able to maneuver the barge's leading end to the beach. It came aground about ten feet from the shore. Two men ran forward and lowered the ramp. This provided a dry access up a sandy incline.

Manny climbed onto his wagon, jumped onto the driver's seat, and grabbed the reins. Jack came up the opposite side of the wagon.

"Thank you, my friend," Manny shouted to the master of the ferry and snapped the reins.

"Pleasant trip, Mr. McGully," his friend yelled back and waved. "Restraints securing the wagon are disconnected. See you on the return."

Manny snapped the reins. The wagon lurched forward. The deck of the barge snapped, groaned, and rumbled as the wagon wheels rolled down the ramp. Manny guided the horses up the embankment to the road. "We should make Oyster Bay harbor by nightfall.

The trip was basically uneventful along the maintained easterly road on the north side of Long Island. The two ran into three different redcoat patrols assigned to scrutinize travelers. Though signaled to stop and be recognized, most of the officers and sergeants who were in charge knew McGully and his grocery wagon. To ease his trips and avoid undue inspections, Manny promised that on his return he would bring the patrols several bottles of whiskey. And he kept his promise, but most times what he brought was a cheap, rotgut whiskey.

"Those boys," Manny told Jack and chuckled, "don't know good whiskey. Their only care is that it makes them drunk."

As Manny had estimated, the two men reached Oyster Bay at sunset. Jack scanned the bay. "Appears to be many small craft anchored about," he said. "Some new and others looked well used."

"All fishermen," Manny said and pointed to a sloop off the distant shore. "Captain Danby's scow. He'll get you to Connecticut. He and his three boys are herring fishermen, but the mackerel are about now. Spawnin' time for them. Greasy little fishes, but tasty and sell well. The Danby crew will be goin' out to catch them."

"Aye," Jack said. "They are good grilled over an open fire."

"You may not think so after you have had your fill. It may take Danby several days to get you to a safe port in Connecticut. That's all those boys eat while at sea." Manny halted the wagon near a short dock with a tall pole that had a bell hung partway up. He grabbed the bell's cord and gave it three good yanks. The loud clangs echoed across the harbor. "That's their signal. They be rowin' over shortly."

As Jack watched, someone on the Danby sloop climbed into a small open boat, took up the oars, and smartly rowed toward the dock.

Manny climbed off the wagon. "This is where we are going to part, my friend." He looked around the area and up and down the shoreline. "The only redcoat I see is you. That the little boat's comin' to pick you up. Once aboard, remove the coat. Danby has some seaman duds for you. Come down off the wagon so I can say my good-byes."

Jack reached behind the bench, grabbed his travel bag, stood, and jumped to the ground.

Manny walked to him and hugged him. "Be safe, my friend. Perhaps one day we will meet again."

Jack felt a sad warmness move through his body. A tear moistened his eye. "Yes. Perhaps so. We both covet dangerous assignments. You also must take care. If my defection is successful, I will be free to aid my patriot friends in Maine."

The two hugged again, separated, and shook hands. Manny climbed aboard the wagon, waved, and snapped the reins. The wagon slowly moved toward the road.

Within twenty minutes of Manny McGully's departure, the Danby open boat, a moderate-sized fishing dory, pulled to the dock. The oarsman, a pleasant-looking fellow of about sixteen, tossed Jack the painter. "If you would, wrap it around the piling, sir," he said. "We must get on. My father and brothers are waiting. Before you board, you will need to remove the military coat. Don't want to attract attention. I am Peter, and you must be Jack."

Jack nodded, glanced around for possible redcoats, and saw none. He caught the rope and threw a single loop low around the piling. He handed his bag to Peter and climbed into the dory. When he sat down on the stern thwart,[3] Peter pulled on the bowline and sat on the thwart amidships. The painter slipped from the piling, and the dory drifted away from the dock.

---

3 A thwart is a seat in a rowboat.

Peter took up the oars, dug the blades deep, and in one sweep, rotated the dory and pointed it toward the Danby sloop. He rowed with ease. "Dad and my brothers—I'm the youngest—want to get you across the Sound as fast as can be. They want to head for the Connecticut River. Shads are beginning to run. A boat load of those fish will fatten our purse, my dad says."

"Mr. McGully said you fish for herring and mackerel."

"Aye. We do, but shad is a big herring and can be caught for only about two weeks in the early spring. Mackerel are about all summer."

"I have never eaten shad."

"Bony they are, but very good roasted over hot coals. It is the roe that everyone seems to favor. Mother fries the shad egg sacks in butter. Excellent flavor and no bones."

"Fried caviar. You are making me hungry."

Peter laughed. He turned to judge the distance to the sloop. "Few more strokes, and we will be next to the *Annie D*. Dad named the boat after my mom. She passed away last year—consumption."

"A terrible disease. I am sorry." Jack glanced up and saw the other Danby men standing next to the starboard rail. Amidships, a rope ladder hung over the vessel's side. The *Annie D* was a square-topsail, gaff-rigged sloop of about forty feet in length. Its mast rose from the hold, which took up most of the forward half of the vessel. A low deckhouse was situated between the hold and the helmsman's cockpit located in the stern. The entire vessel appeared to have been freshly painted.

Peter maneuvered the dory against the *Annie D*'s hull next to the ladder.

Captain Danby welcomed Jack as soon as he climbed over the rail. "You've met Peter," he said, as he and Jack shook hands. "Those two ruffians are his brothers. The one with the hair under his nose is Roger. He's the oldest. And Sam, who does not want his hair to be cut. So it spurts out all over and makes him look like a South Pacific fuzzy-wuzzy." He laughed. "No matter how they look, they're good boys. Hard workers."

The two brothers frowned and glared at their father, but both snickered and welcomed Jack.

Peter came aboard holding the bowline of the dory. He guided the boat aft and tied it to the transom.

"Get the sails up, boys. Let us make for the Sound 'fore the sun sets." Captain Danby stepped away from the rail, walked aft, and stepped into the shallow cockpit. He took hold of the ship's wheel and said, "Peter, take Jack below and show him where to bunk." He turned his attention to Jack. "Mr. Hollister, get out of those redcoat duds. There will be a change of clothes in the cabin."

Peter pushed back the cover over the deckhouse hatch, gripped its frame, and dropped into the cabin. Jack followed, climbing down the three rungs of the ladder into the cramped quarters. He looked forward. A central table, suspended from the ceiling, was raised out of the way. Affixed to each bulkhead for about half the cabin's length was a continuous bench. Its underside provided storage space. Just above the height of a seated man were additional shelves. These contained numerous nautical items, tools, seashells, and books. Beyond the main cabin were six-tiered bunks, two on the side bulkheads and a pair on the forward wall. A narrow slot, but a man can sleep comfortably, Jack mused. A wispy odor of musty urine caused him to turn and look aft. The vessel's privy sat behind the cabin's ladder to the deck. He rubbed his nose and stepped forward.

"Your new attire," Peter said and pointed to some clothing scattered on the lower forward bunk. He walked to it, reached down, and lifted the cot, exposing a storage space. "Store those redcoat duds in here." He chuckled. "You can dream on them."

The two men stabilized themselves as the *Annie D* rolled slightly to starboard.

Peter squeezed around Jack and made for the ladder. "We're under way. Need to get topside and stand my watch. You change and come up. When there are heavy clouds to the west, the setting sun makes colorful scenes.

"Aye. But colorful clouds mean possible rain by morning." Jack nodded and waved as Peter darted up the ladder.

———•◦•———

The blanket of gray clouds colored the sea's surface as the *Annie D* hiked to larboard, rolling and twisting in the turbulent four-to-six-foot pewter-colored waves. Her course heading was set to the northeast, toward the Connecticut shore. The thirty-knot southwest wind blew the foaming, curling crowns from their fleeting pedestals and sprayed them across the sloop's deck. With her mainsail reefed and storm jib stretched, the *Annie D* groaned with each gust and clapped as the vessel pitched up and down. Straining shrouds and rigging hummed like a poorly tuned cello.

Jack, balancing himself against various braces, frames, and beams, stuck his head out the deckhouse hatch. A few feet in front of him he saw Roger Danby standing in the cockpit, whirling the ship's wheel back and forth, attempting to maintain course as the *Annie D* rose, swung, and dove. Seawater glistened and drained off his oilskins. At that moment, as if the sloop dove underwater, the bow smashed into a wave, allowing much of its contents to wash down the deck and over the deckhouse roof. Cold seawater poured onto Jack's head, down the ladder, and into the cabin. The wave crashed into Roger, hard enough to push him aside. Luckily, several ropes tied about the man's body kept him from being washed overboard.

Roger pulled himself up against the wheel and cursed loudly.

"Close that damned hatch," Captain Danby yelled. "We don't need the water in here."

"Sorry," Jack said. "That wave took me by surprise."

"You're about the same size as me," Sam Danby said. "My oilskins will fit you if you want to go on deck." He worked his way to the back of the left bunk and removed the foul-weather coat and pants that hung on the bedstead and tossed them to Jack. "A pair of boots is under your cot."

When Sam returned to the table, Jack squeezed forward, grabbed the boots, and stuck his feet into them. He then stood and stumbled back to the ladder. Dressed in heavy, bulky foul-weather gear, he seated himself on the ladder's lowest rung.

"The Norwalk Islands." Captain Danby looked up from his charts. "If you're going on deck, make sure to keep a hand on the safety line. Those seas can wash you overboard."

"Good advice. I will." Jack stood, climbed onto the ladder, reached up, and pushed the deckhouse hatch open. The sounds of the wind and crashing sea intensified. He heard Captain Danby yell to him, "Keep a lookout for the islands off Norwalk. They're arranged in an easterly line, with a bunch of little ones scattered in between. If Roger has us on course, they should be off to starboard. Manressa Island should be off to larboard."

Jack pulled himself onto the deck and noticed the wind and waves had lessened a bit. Roger had set the *Annie D* to run with the waves. This maneuver lessened the stress and disorder on the sloop. The pitch of the bow had softened, allowing Jack to falter less as he made his way forward to the mainmast. Though it was about four o'clock in the afternoon, the heavy clouds reduced daylight considerably. Nevertheless, from where he stood, he had a clear view off the larboard side, though the shoreline was lost in fog and rain. He glanced back to the helm.

"We're off the islands," Roger shouted. "Norwalk Harbor about six miles to larboard."

The mainsail obstructed Jack's view to starboard, so he crouched and looked under the boom. Two darkened areas, like shadows cast upon a white sheet, one behind the sloop and one off the beam, indicated large, fog-shrouded islands.

Suddenly, Roger spun the ship's wheel to the right, causing the *Annie D*'s starboard to lay deeper and her bow to turn rapidly into an unplanned jibe. The mainsail slapped and flapped. The storm jib fluttered. "Jack!" he yelled. "Push the boom left. Secure the mainsa'l sheet when the canvas fills." He then stomped his foot hard on the cockpit deck. "Dad, Sam, Peter, on deck now!"

Jack whirled himself to the front of the mainmast. After releasing the mainsail sheet, he jumped onto the deckhouse roof. He laid his body weight against the boom and pushed on it. The boom swung to starboard. Gripping the sheet and balancing himself against the vessel's roll, he threw a loop around the nearest bit and held the rope tight. He let the line slip through his hand as the sail filled and the boom stabilized. The Danby men stumbled onto the deck while he secured the mainsail sheet.

"What in the hell is going on?" Captain Danby growled as he relieved Roger at the helm.

"Frigate off the larboard bow!" Roger screamed. "I'm headin' for the fogbank between the islands."

With the *Annie D* now headed across the ocean's turbulence, activity aboard returned to chaos. The sloop rolled and dove as northeasterly traveling breakers smashed into and over the starboard side. The men held their stance and balance with the aid of safety lines. Captain Danby fought the ship's wheel to keep a straight course. Jack watched the movement of the frigate as the brothers trimmed the sails.

With the wind now streaming over the vessel's beam, the sloop increased in speed and frenzy.

"What's that damn frigate doing?" shouted Captain Danby.

"She has seen us," Jack answered. "Her bow is turning in our direction."

"We're about a mile from the fogbank," the captain roared. "And it'll soon be dark. Keep those sails trimmed and tight. Release a bit more canvas on the mainsail. We need to stay out of range of that bitch."

Everyone heard the blast of a cannon and the scream of the ball as it flew past the stern.

"They're shootin'! Get that mainsa'l full up."

Jack joined Peter and Sam at the boom and helped untie the reefing cords. Once all were removed, Roger started pulling on the mainsail's throat halyard to raise the sail to full height, an operation that could normally be done with ease if the vessel was taken off wind. But with the frigate in hot pursuit, this could not be done. Captain Danby held the vessel's course.

Jack, Peter, and Sam joined Roger on the halyard. With every man hauling, the sail was inched up the mast against the resistance of the wind. When the sail's head reached the topsail yardarm, Roger jumped back and secured the hauling line. Peter and Sam pulled the peak halyard tight, readjusting the position of the gaff. They then trimmed the storm jib.

A second blast from a frigate cannon sent a ball splashing short of the *Annie D*'s transom.

"That damned fog is drifting seaward," Captain Danby shouted. "Peter, get up the mast and unfurl the topsail. Need the speed."

Peter dropped the sheet he was holding and scampered up the mast. "Wind's strong, Dad. Chance that sail is gonna rip away."

"Get up that goddamn pole and let that sail fly!" Captain Danby adjusted the ship's wheel and took the *Annie D* slightly off wind.

The edge of the mainsail shuddered as Peter climbed the rungs that held the large sail's luff against the mast. With the roll of the *Annie D*, the mast flailed wildly back and forth. The young man kept his arms around the mast and his knees squeezed tight against it.

"Damn boy is climbing without a safety line," Jack shrieked.

"He's done that before," Roger roared. "Only had to fish him out one time."

Within a few tense moments, Peter reached the topsail yardarm and untied the binding that kept the rectangular topsail furl on the yard. He then scampered down the mast while Roger hauled in the topsail halyard, raising the yardarm toward the peak of the mast. Jack and Sam adjusted it to catch the wind. Once the topsail billowed and tightened, they secured the lines.

With the topsail full, mainsail and jib trimmed, the *Annie D* rolled and pitched but increased its distance from the frigate. Captain Danby fought the ship's wheel to keep the bow headed straight for the fogbank, though waves smashing against the bow and starboard side tried to force the sloop left. Jack and the brothers held on tight to safety lines and whatever else they could to keep from being knocked down or washed overboard.

"Fog just ahead," cried Captain Danby.

Water splashed onto Jack's face when he looked up.

The frigate fired two more rounds as the *Annie D* passed headlong into the curtain of dense mist. The cannonballs followed but fell short of their target.

After a short time of crashing blindly through curling, foaming, dull-gray waves, Captain Danby rotated the ship's wheel to the left and yelled, "Trim the sail! Gonna run with the wind."

The turmoil softened as the winds, now coming from behind the *Annie D*, pushed the sloop to the northeast. "Sam," the captain called, "take the helm and maintain this course. Peter, you, and Jack, stand the watch. Roger, get some sleep. I'm going below."

The fog continued well into the night, but eventually began to diminish. The wind still persisted to blow from the southwest, but its speed dropped to about six knots. The ocean's surface calmed to a chop. Sometime after midnight, the sky blackened, and the northward fleeing puffs of cumulus clouds were vividly edged in moonlight. The air cooled, and the humidity dropped.

Captain Danby returned to the deck. He scanned the glistening sea. The sparkling path cast by the moon illumed and darkened with the passing of the clouds. "Sam, set course more east. Let's get away from the shoreline. Should be off the Connecticut River by morning. With the damned lobsterbacks blockading waters off Norwalk, we're going shad fishing, boys. Everyone keep a watch out for those red-coats." The captain turned to the bow as Roger came on deck. "Peter, you doing well?"

"Aye, sir."

"Good. Stay on watch. I'll relieve you before sunup." Captain Danby gripped the deckhouse rail. "Roger, take the helm. Sam and Jack, go below and get some sleep."

Sharp squawks that filled the gaps between the soft groans and moans of the *Annie D*'s hull woke Jack. A dull reddish glow filled his eyes as he opened them. Still in his daytime clothes, he rolled out of his bunk, slipped on his shoes, and stumbled onto the deck.

Outside a ragged, blood-orange cloud bank blazed along the horizon, dull at first and then radiating a chang-ing kaleidoscope of hot colors across the bluish firmament. Its most easterly midpoint continued to brighten until the dazzling, fiery ball rose from the caldron. Circling and following, raucous gulls filled the glowing air around the *Annie D*. Jack watched them and noticed that the rising sun was off the starboard beam. He turned and looked at the helm.

"They smell the fish stench arising from *Annie D*'s wet decks," Captain Danby said. "We're nearing the mouth of the Connecticut. Be there by sunset. If there are no frigates patrolling, we'll head into the river and put in at Saybrook. If the winds cooperate, in the morning we'll continue up-river to Chester, about twelve miles. From there you can catch Warner's Ferry. It crosses the river. Connects Chester Village with the King's Road to Norwich. I have a trusted friend in Norwich Town by the name o' Toby Conley, who sails a freighter up and down the River Thames between Norwich and New London. He is always looking for a crewman. He will allow you to work your way to New London. There, Toby will help you find a coaster that will take you to sea. Good place to start your journey back to Maine."

CHAPTER 12
TO NEW LONDON, CONNECTICUT
APRIL 1777

A spring chill ran through the air as Jack walked up onto the deck of the *Annie D*. In his hand, he carried a travel bag. He stood in front of the helm and gazed at the wooded shoreline across the Connecticut River. Birds chirped from the woods and sea gulls squawked as the sun stretched its beam over the treetops.

After almost two years, I am returning to where my adventure began. He smiled.

"We're going to be heading south this morning, down the Connecticut River," Captain Danby said, his hands gripping the handles of the *Annie D*'s ship's wheel. The sloop's tethers held the vessel to the pilings of a narrow pier. They strained against the downriver current. "The boys—they'll be on deck shortly—and I will miss you, even though our association was short." The captain released the wheel, stepped out of the shallow helmsman's cockpit, walked to Jack. "Let's go ashore for a moment." He patted Jack's shoulder. The two walked to the starboard rail, climbed over the gunwale, and jumped onto the dock. "You'll need to tend the lines. After you cast us off, go to the little tavern o'er there." Captain Danby pointed to a ramshackle cottage next to a marsh. "The proprietor knows you're comin'. He'll have breakfast victuals awaitin' you. I told him to take care of you. After you finish breakfast, go down the road. The ferry there will take you across the river at about ten o'clock. Here, take these shillings. You'll need them."

"Very kind of you, sir." Jack looked surprised at the support the fisherman provided but was hesitant to accept the money. Instead he gripped his bag and tossed it onto his shoulder.

"It's quite all right," Captain Danby said with a smile. "General Washington's network provisions our loyal patriots. You are one of us, fighting for the same cause, Lieutenant Hollister."

Jack bit his left cheek and curled his lip; he lowered his head, raised his right arm, and ran a knuckle under his eye. "Thank you again, sir. Would you also thank General Washington, if you ever get to see him?"

"That I'll most certainly do." Captain Danby's big arm enveloped Jack as the man hugged him. "I most certainly will. It's been good to meet you, Lieutenant. May you have a safe journey." The captain climbed back aboard the *Annie D.*

Peter Danby pulled himself out of the deckhouse hatch and onto the *Annie D*'s deck. Roger and Sam followed. Almost in unison, the three brothers called, "Safe travels."

"Let's get down the river," Captain Danby yelled. "Cast us off, Jack. Them shads are awaitin'."

Jack dropped his bag at the head of the pier, ran to the pilings, and untied the *Annie D*'s binding. The river's current carried the sloop into the river as the brothers raised the mainsail. Captain Danby brought the bow around and faced it downstream. All waved and shouted, "Good luck."

He raised his arm to acknowledge the *Annie D*'s departure, but those onboard were either facing in the direction the sloop headed or involved in some work. Jack strolled to the head of the dock, watched for a few minutes as the *Annie D* glided downriver, and then picked up his travel bag and walked to the tavern across the road. A little, rotund man wearing a stained apron met him at the door and directed him to a table. Owner, he assumed. The tavern contained no customers.

"Please sit," the roundish man said and sniffled. "I have eggs, kippers, bread, and tea. Business improves when the ferry crosses over. No place to eat across the river."

"That will be fine." Jack sat at the table, leaned back, and closed his eyes. When he opened his eyes, the tavern owner was still at his table. "Is there anything else?"

"Just thinking." The owner fiddled with the apron. "You're a fine-looking young man. Your captain said you were traveling to Norwich. Perhaps you will have time to enjoy the village. I have a lovely niece who lives there—a handsome woman, hardworking. She weaves and make fine clothing. She is of marriageable age, but says she enjoys her life as it is. I would rather she not be a spinster, so I told her I would send her a fine young man, though she says not to." He grinned and nodded. "I am sure she would find you an interesting man."

Jack looked up at the owner. His jaw dropped. He shook his head. "Sorry, but I will not have time nor am I in need of a companion. I am on a mission and cannot deviate from my course. Perhaps another time."

A frown crossed the owner's face. He lowered his head. "Aye, sir. That is too bad."

Jack grinned and continued to shake his head. "Please bring my breakfast." He watched the owner walk into the kitchen.

Strange fellow. Lonely. Meddlesome. Surrogate father, no doubt.

After a short time, the owner returned with the eggs, smoked herring, and other food items. "Captain Danby paid for the meal, so eat and enjoy. He stops in occasionally. His sons are also fine men but are not interested in going to Norwich. The captain must think much of you. You must be important to him."

Jack raised his eyebrows. "I cannot imagine why. I am only a voyager." He glanced down at the food and began to eat. The tavern owner turned and returned to the kitchen. Jack chewed the last piece of bread and sucked down the tea, rose from the table, and headed out the door.

Phew, good to out of there, away from that fellow. Feel sorry for the niece. Probably the woman is happy and content living at a distance from her uncle.

He tossed his bag over his shoulder and headed for the ferry landing. I wonder how many rogues and highwaymen have accepted that uncle's offer. With his free hand, he ran his fingers through his hair. He pondered as he walked. That tavern owner could be a redcoat informant. That is the way Nathan Hale got caught. He befriended a man who turned him in. I do need to be careful.

———•◦•———

Jack sat on a bale near the front of the ferry and watched the ramshackle tavern shrink as four burly men poled the raft to the middle of the Connecticut River. The men struggled against the river's mild current to keep the ferry facing toward the far shore. As they neared the opposite side, a countercurrent eased the struggle and pushed the boat upriver. The pole men knew the whims of the river. After about twenty minutes, the front of the ferry ground in the soft mud just below the end of the access road to the King's Highway. After the men secured the long poles, they lowered the ferry's ramp, allowing passengers and cargo to be unloaded.

Jack picked up his travel bag, bid good-bye to the ferry master, walked down the ramp onto the road, sighed, checked his timepiece, and strolled the short distance to the highway. To the right was the coach stop, a clearing in the surrounding forest with several benches where travelers could wait. The ferry master told him that the Hartford-to-Norwich coach would be along around the noon hour. The time being ten thirty, Jack dusted the pollen from a bench and sat. He scanned the area.

After about a half hour, three people arrived aboard an open wagon. A dapper man reached behind himself and pushed three large luggage bags against the side of the wagon. He then climbed off and unloaded the bags.

Seated next to this man, an elegantly dressed, plump woman holding a purse stood. She leaned forward and embraced the wagon driver. He was an older, worn-looking fellow dressed in farmer's clothing. The driver appeared to be surprised by the woman's warm gesture. He looked up at her face, smiled nervously, and stuttered, "Thank you."

"Hum," Jack murmured and ran his hand through his hair. The old fellow seemed to relish the fondness. Perhaps he knows her.

The dapper man set the travel bag on the ground, extended his hand, and helped the stylish woman off the wagon. She carried a small bag with her. As soon as her feet were planted solidly on the ground, the wagon driver, with the glowing smile still on his face, trembled momentarily, looked forward, and snapped the reins. The horses jolted away. The driver, sitting straight and proud, never looked back.

The two seated themselves on a nearby bench.

Shortly after the wagon departed, the man nodded at Jack and in a bass voice said, "The coach should be along within the hour. Though it's usually late, today the weather is good, so it may arrive as expected."

Jack nodded back.

The man returned his attention to the woman.

Impressed by the dapper man's deep voice and the clarity with which he enunciated his words, Jack eavesdropped. When he overheard the woman tell her companion that she was hungry, Jack's stomach grumbled. Breakfast had been some time ago. He continued to listen.

"Colchester." The dapper man responded. "The coach will stop at the inn in Colchester to exchange the team of horses. There we will have time to partake of food and drink." He then raised his head and regarded Jack. "Are you traveling far?"

"New London."

"Aye." The man smiled. "Perhaps you will join us for some vittles. The Colchester Inn, where we end our journey, has a pleasant tavern."

"Thank you. I will enjoy that. Breakfast was some hours ago," Jack said, took hold of his bag, placed it onto his lap, opened it, and removed his diary. "Please excuse me. I need to record my morning observations. I am a traveler and would like to remember my impression of the ferry crossing lest I forget."

The man acknowledged. "There will be time to talk onboard the coach." He returned his attention to the woman.

Jack wrote for a few moments, laid the pencil on a page, closed the notebook, and shuffled his hand about in the travel bag. He felt the handle of the little pistol, squeezed it, and then touched the hammer. He slid his fingers along the barrel and sighed.

Loaded, but not cocked. He removed his hand from the bag, took a breath, sat back, and glanced at the couple. They know each other well. I wonder what they do. He shrugged and reopened the notebook.

Dampened by the surrounding forest, the sound of horses galloping on the highway alerted Jack. He shut his diary, returned it to the travel bag, and cinched the bag closed.

Within moments, the coach came around the curve. The driver slowed the four-horse team to a walk and brought the coach to a stop aside the clearing.

"Colchester an' Norwich," the driver yelled. "Board."

The coach driver's assistant scrambled off the seat, dropped to the ground, collected the luggage bags, and secured them on the coach's rear cargo rack. He then came around, grabbed the door handle, and opened the coach door.

Jack allowed the man and woman to board first, and then he entered.

An elderly woman sat on the far corner of the seat against the coach's back side. Next to her sat a younger one—probably in her thirties, Jack estimated. The couple took the seats across from them. The younger woman removed some baskets from the seat next to her and set them on the floor. Jack seated himself in the cleared space and laid his bag on his lap. The assistant driver closed the door and climbed back onto the driver's seat.

The coach shuddered as the horses whinnied and snorted and yanked the vehicle into motion. Within moments, the driver had the team in a gallop. All those inside braced themselves against the bumps and jars and, though the seats were padded, settled in for the rough ride. The elderly woman uttered a stifled cry. This urged the younger one to remove a pillow from a basket and place it behind her back.

"Mother does not travel well," she turned to Jack and said. "So far, she has done well on the trip from Hartford. But from here, the road becomes bumpy."

"Perhaps she should change seats with you," Jack said and shifted closer against the side of the coach. "She is sitting directly over the wheel, where the jarring is the greatest."

"Yes. But we are moving, and it would be difficult to change," the young woman said.

Jack grabbed the window frame and handle next to the coach door and swung himself across to the open seat next to the well-dressed woman. "Now you two can slide over."

"Thank you. My name is Martha Newman," the young woman said as she slid against the coach's side. She helped her mother move to the middle of the seat and then leaned across her lap. She collected the pillow and stuffed it behind the elderly woman.

"I am Jack Hollister, traveling to New London," Jack said as soon as the two women were settled and somewhat comfortable.

Martha was about to acknowledge him but was interrupted by the dapper fellow.

"Hollister? I've heard that name." He looked at his companion and shook his head. "Have you heard that name?"

"No, Jonathan. I have no recollection."

"Boston, I believe," Jonathan said with a grin. "There was an English exchange there before the patriots took that city. Yes. Yes. A lucrative business. Dealt close with the British army and navy." He glared at Jack and squinted his eyes. "You are English. Are you related?"

"Aye, from Great Britain I am." Jack swallowed and bit his lip. "As a sailor aboard a merchant brig, I have heard of the Hollister Exchange. It is well known." He looked at the dapper man and sighed. "Ah, to be so lucky as to be a true Hollister, I would not have to suffer the rigors of being a common Jack. Alas, I have no connection with that company."

Jonathan wagged his head, gritted his teeth, and scowled. "From where do you hail in Britain?"

"Yorkshire."

"I find it odd that you are not connected with the Hollisters of Plymouth." The well-groomed man cocked his head inquisitively and then shook it. "To have such a prominent name and not be related."

"Indeed. I am an orphan and do not know my true name." Jack grinned and squinted his eyes. "I took the name of my ward, a kindly woman, whom everyone called Holly Ester. Aye, the name rings in comparison by its pronunciation." He sat back and spelled, "*H-o-l-l-y-e-s-t-e-r*. My dear sir, too many question makes one suspicious."

Jonathan straightened and sat back. He appeared confused, turned, and glared out the window.

"Sorry to disappoint you." Jack tried to appease the dapper man, but he rubbed his goatee and turned to ponder the passing countryside.

"I am sorry to hear you are an orphan," Martha Newman said.

"Thank you," Jack replied. "My life has been good so far, but I do have one regret. I came to the colonies to find a new life but instead found myself in the middle of the revolutionary turmoil that is going on here. This is a wonderful place. It is too bad the British and the Colonials cannot find agreement."

"Where are you bound for, Mr. Hollyester?"

"New London, Martha—err, I mean, Mistress Newman."
He shifted about, attempting to ease his bottom. "I have
been told that in New London there are coastal freighters
where I may find a billet and make my way to Massachusetts."

"Are you planning to take the coach to New London?"

"No, Mistress Newman. A friend gave me the name of a
master of a smack that lighters cargo between Norwich and
New London. I will join his crew and be transported down
the River Thames to New London."

"Then you'll be staying in Norwich," Martha Newman
said. "My aunt has a guest house. It is near the waterfront.
I'm sure she would enjoy having you as a guest. Since I will
be staying for some days to settle my mother, I would be happy to show you around and help you find the boat captain."

"That is very kind of you. I would be honored if you and
your mother would join me and the others when the coach
stops at the Colchester Inn."

"Yes. An opportunity to stretch our legs and have some
water would be delightful."

———————

About two hours after the coach departed the Warner's
Ferry stop, it came to a halt on Main Street in front of the
Colchester Inn, a blue-gray, two-storied federal building
with a veranda across the front.

Jack looked out the window and noticed that several
small groups of onlookers had congregated nearby to

scrutinize the passengers. Two young men from the inn approached the coach. The assistant driver handed them the luggage bags brought by the couple and then opened the coach door, allowing the passengers to exit.

Jack stepped out of the coach and aided Martha's mother off. He then held his hand out to help Martha. The three strolled onto the veranda. The women entered the inn, but Jack watched as the smart-looking twosome, who had not yet identified themselves, stepped out of the coach. He also noticed that the eyes of the bystanders widened. These viewers began to chatter excitedly and gestured toward the couple as they walked into the inn.

"The two that traveled with us, are they important?" Jack asked Martha when he entered the inn. "Do you know them?"

"The man's features appear similar to one I saw on a posting in Hartford some time ago. I believe"—Martha twisted her head to the right and watched the pair enter the inn—"it was to advertise the presentation of a Shakespearean tragedy. The woman, I have never seen."

"Perhaps they are noted entertainers."

"Come," the gentleman said, "let us sit and refresh ourselves." He smiled at Jack, Martha, and her mother. "My companion, Viola Teasdale, an up-and-coming soprano." He looked over at her and smiled and then put his arm around her. "Yes, my dear, a famous soprano you will one day be, but first you must master the musical language of Italia." He turned his attention back to the group. "Mistress Teasdale and I would enjoy chatting with you. Mr. Hollister, being a sailor, you must have many adventurous tales to tell. And these two lovely ladies—"

"Excuse me, sir," Jack interrupted. "Who are you?"

"Ah, yes. Sorry. My arrogance. I seem to think I am more famous than I am," the man replied. "Being an Englishman, Mr. Hollister, I assumed you knew who I was." The dapper man straightened and extended his hand. "I am Sir Jonathan Drugger, actor from the court of King Edward III. I am here touring the colonies. And, like you, I am finding it difficult to move about this country. Frustrating how this disagreement between Great Britain and the colonies disrupts the enjoyment of this fine country. Please excuse my inquisitiveness in the coach. You would be better off if you were one of the Hollisters."

Jack nodded and accepted Jonathan's hand. "How do you do, Mr. Drugger. It is good to meet you." Jack said as he turned, thinking to walk into the dining room. "I regret we will not have time get to know each other."

"Yes, that is too bad," Jonathan said. "Come, let us refresh ourselves before you continue on your trip aboard that bone breaker of a coach. My treat. Viola and I are staying here at the inn. We have a performance this evening."

Jonathan placed his hand on Jack's shoulder. Following the women, the two strolled into a large, open room where tables were arranged to serve customers and lodgers. When the waiter seated them, Jonathan ordered a round of flavored sparkling-water drinks.

"I am sorry," he said. "But would anyone prefer a libation?"

All shook their head.

"Then let the order stand."

About fifteen minutes after the drinks were served, the assistant coach driver barged into the room and announced, "Norwich coach ready. Passengers need to board."

Good-byes were bade to the performers.

"I hope your evening goes well," Jack said as he stepped down the stairs from the veranda.

"In a week, we will be in New London," Jonathan said. "We are scheduled aboard a transport to New York City. And then from there, on to England and home."

"Safe voyage." Viola scampered down the steps and hugged Jack.

"Viola is warmhearted," Jonathan said, smiling. "Especially to handsome young men. It is her nature."

"Thank you, Viola." Jack stepped away and put his foot on the step-rung of the coach. He helped Martha and her mother to board and then turned toward Viola. "Perhaps you, I, and Mr. Drugger can meet in New London. Will you be performing in that city?"

"Yes, yes, we are." Viola presented her hand. Jack bent down and kissed it. He then pulled himself aboard the coach. "Sir Jonathan will hang posters about the city advertising our presentation."

Jack leaned out the coach window. "I will watch for them."

The coach driver snapped the reins, and the team of horses yanked the vehicle into motion.

As soon as the coach cleared the city center, the driver urged the horses to a gallop. Jack settled back and looked at Martha. "An interesting couple," he said. "I have never met actors before. I would have enjoyed getting to know them. Though I must admit, the way Mr. Drugger spoke with such pomposity and self-assurance, I suspected him to be a dodger. I am cautious. Since I have been in the colonies, I have found that there are many who enjoy taking advantage of others."

"Yes," Martha said. "One must be careful when traveling. Connecticut does have redcoat spies, deserters, and renegades. Most are found along coastal routes. Our watchmen and militia are always on their guard."

The road ran smoother toward Norwich, but when a coach wheel hit a pothole, Martha's mother, who had fallen asleep after leaving Colchester, snorted and bumbled herself awake. "Oh my!" she said and straightened. "Ah, the young man is still with us, Martha."

"Yes, Mother. The trip has been so jarring and dusty, I have not had a chance to introduce you." Martha glanced across the compartment. "Mother, this is Mr. Jack Hollyester. He is a sailor and writer from England. Jack, this is my mother, Mrs. Victoria Wrotham of Hartford, Connecticut."

Jack nodded. "A pleasure to make your acquaintance, Mrs. Wrotham."

"Likewise," Martha's mother said and looked up at her daughter. "Are we almost there?"

"Not much farther, Mother. Mr. Hollyester needs lodging for a day or two. I was planning to ask Auntie Helen if she has room in her guesthouse."

"That would be fine, my dear." The elderly woman turned and looked out the window. The road was passing through a valley of meadowlands decorated with leafy islands of boscage. On the left flowed a slow river. Everyone inside the coach leaned as the road deviated to the right. The route ran up out of the valley, flattened, and continued past groups of houses that became more densely concentrated. The gravelly highway blended to cobblestone as the vehicle entered the city. At about five thirty in the evening, the coach came to a stop at the station located between two brick buildings.

"Norwich!" the driver yelled.

Jack opened the coach door and jumped out. He helped Mrs. Wrotham and Martha down while the assistant driver removed the women's luggage from the coach. Once the bags were placed on the street, the assistant driver caught the attention of a young man standing next to an idle livery wagon near the coach station. The fellow brought the wagon over and loaded the luggage. After Martha and her mother collected themselves, the livery man helped them into the wagon and seated them. Jack climbed aboard and sat next to the driver. Martha gave the driver her aunt's address, and they all got under way for a short trip.

When the livery reached the guesthouse, Martha's aunt was sitting in a rocker on the porch. She warmly greeted her sister and niece as the women walked up the stairs. Jack paid the driver and joined the women. Martha introduced him to her aunt, Mrs. Helen Cormier.

"Auntie Helen," Martha said, "Jack needs lodging for a night or two. Would you have a guestroom available?"

"Martha said you were a sailor and writer," Aunt Helen said as she frowned and cocked her head to the side. "Sailors do not stay long, writers do, but usually cannot pay. Which hat will you be wearing while you are here?"

Jack raised his eyebrows and grinned. "A sailor, ma'am, but I will pay for my lodging. I came to Norwich to find a captain Toby Conley. He is to transport me to New London, where I hope to find a vessel that will take me up the coast to Boston or farther."

Aunt Helen lowered her head and thought for a moment. "Aye, I do have an empty room. One of my tenants, a teacher, is away for a few weeks. I can put you in his room. He will not mind."

"Thank you. That is very kind of you."

"It is on the second floor at the top of the stairs. The bed is firm and the room furnished to meet the needs of a gentleman." Aunt Helen looked around for Jack's luggage and then realized he was carrying a pack. She nodded at it. "All your essentials are in your bag?"

Jack raised his travel bag slightly. "Yes, I travel light."

Aunt Helen led him inside the house and pointed out the stairway to the second floor. "Dinner will be served in the dining room at seven o'clock."

"Thank you, ma'am." Jack nodded and headed toward the stairs.

———••———

The next morning at breakfast, Martha informed Jack that the grocer down the street occasionally dealt with Captain Toby Conley. The grocer told her that the captain had an office in a shack on Wharf Road. His vessel, when he was in town, was tied to a dock on the south shore of the Shetucket River. "It is near where the Shetucket joins with the Thames," she said. "The vessel, a bateau of some length, is named after his deceased wife, Tessie." Martha finished her breakfast and then continued, "The grocer also told me that Captain Toby likes to be home on weekends. He loads the *Tessie* on Mondays and departs the dock near evening. He usually returns on Thursday or Friday. Today is Wednesday. You may be staying in Norwich longer than you planned."

"Aye." Jack cupped the coffee mug in his hand, lifted it, and took a sip. "Perhaps that will be a blessing. I will have time to rest. My travels have been trying in the past weeks. I can go to the dock on Thursday. Perchance Captain Toby will have returned."

"Yes. The distance to New London is not great."

———•◦•———

Jack, bundled in a blanket, sat on the porch most of Thursday morning. Overhead, heavy, gray clouds concealed the sun. As Martha came out with a mug of hot tea, Jack asked, "Do you think it is going to rain, or snow?"

"Well, whatever it does, does not matter," Martha said as she handed him the mug. "Our neighbor has lent me his carriage. It is covered. We can leave for the harbor after lunch. You can drive. I will show you the way."

A smile erased the despondent expression Jack wore. "Thank you." He checked his watch. "That will be good."

As the street to the harbor turned, then straightened and began its gradual descent into the river valley, Jack glimpsed of the city along the waterfront. He tightened the reins to slow the horses as they progressed down the slope to the bridge over the Shetucket River.

"When we cross," Martha said, "make a right turn onto Wharf Road. We'll watch for an old gray shack with Conley's sign by the river. It hangs from the porch. Should he not be there, we can ask along the wharves if anyone knows of his arrival."

"Aye," Jack said.

The horses, disturbed by the bridge decking, hesitated as they started across. Jack snapped the reins, urging them on. Seeing the sparkle and flow of the Shetucket River through the spaces in the flooring and feeling the span sway and vibrate, the worried horses wavered but continued. Their heads erratically rose and fell and twisted side to side. Simultaneously, they lifted their heads when their hooves touched solid ground. Jack thought he heard the horses sigh in relief. He pulled the reins, directing them to the right. The carriage rumbled as its wheels bumbled over the Wharf Road cobblestones.

"There!" Martha waved and pointed ahead toward a ramshackle, gray half house. "Conley's signboard."

Jack turned the horses toward the side of the road and stopped next to the cottage.

Martha climbed down from the carriage and checked the door. It was closed. She returned and boarded the vehicle.

"On to the wharves," Jack said and popped the leather straps.

About one hundred yards ahead, the carriage came to a stretch of riverbank where eight narrow docks protruded into the river. A boardwalk connected the group together. Muscular men walked back and forth along this walkway, lugging boxes and pushing carts. Several bateaus, two sloops, and a small schooner were tethered to the docks.

"A working waterfront." Jack scanned the area, chuckled, and said. "Though it does not have the organized chaos of New York or Boston, it reflects in a small way its own sense of disorder." He stopped the carriage in a nearby clearing and prepared to disembark. "It would be best if you stay aboard the wagon. A waterfront is no place for a fine woman." He handed Martha the reins and climbed off the coach.

Jack walked along the wharf to where a group of men were unloading one of the bateaus. He watched for a moment and approached the one who was holding a tablet and leaning against a piling. "Are you the foreman of this gang?"

"Aye, that I am," the foreman said. "Who's askin'?"

"Jack Hollister. I am looking for Captain Toby Conley."

"Aye. I know Toby. And what do you want of him?" The foreman reached up and pushed back his cap. He glared at Jack and furrowed his brow.

"A friend told me to contact Captain Conley." Jack saw the foreman tense his jaw, raise an arm, and fist his hand.

"An armed British sloop arrived yesterday under a flag of truce. Captain of this British vessel came ashore. He was askin' everyone if they knew a lieutenant Jack Hollister. Captain said the lieutenant went missing—kidnapped or maybe deserted. That sloop came from New York City. You wouldn't, perchance, be the Lieutenant Hollister they be lookin' for?"

Jack's body temperature rose. His muscles tensed. "I need transportation to New London," Jack said. He narrowed his eyes. "Captain Danby of Oyster Bay, Long Island, suggested I contact Captain Conley."

"You know, Mr. Hollister, we don't take well to red-coats infesting our waters. For all I know you may be a redcoat spy." The foreman dropped the tablet and moved toward Jack. He nodded to several of the stevedores. They immediately dropped what they were carrying and approached.

Jack backed up, put his hand in his pants pocket, and fondled the handle of his pistol. "I am not a British spy, and I am not a deserter. I am a traveler and journalist. One of my colleagues, a close friend, was hung by those lobster-backs. I am trying to escape them. Return to Maine and rejoin the patriots with whom I fought."

"Aye." The foreman stopped but continued to glare at Jack. "Would I know this friend of yours?"

"Lieutenant Nathan Hale of the Seventh Connecticut Regiment."

"I know of this lieutenant. He was from Coventry. A hero, he was." The foreman relaxed but did not let down his guard. "And the Danbys, never met them, but heard they're loyal patriots. But what do you have to prove what you're saying is true?"

"Nothing that I can share for fear of putting civilian patriots in New York and New Jersey in jeopardy. All I can tell you is that I fought in the Battle at Machias in 1775 and helped in the capture of the HMS *Margaretta*."

The foreman nodded, turned, stooped over, and picked up his tablet. "Get back to work, you louts. We've a boat to unload," he yelled and again turned his attention back to Jack. "I've heard of that battle. Captain Conley will be in this evening. You can find him in the morning. He breakfasts at the Whale Tavern." He pointed to the two-storied building next to Conley's shack. "I will tell him you are looking for him."

"Thank you." Jack walked back to the carriage. The stevedores, who earlier were about to accost him, now paid him no attention.

"Did all go well?" Martha asked.

"It did indeed," Jack answered, picked up the reins, and turned the horses back to the bridge. He held them to a slow walk as they returned to it. "Captain Conley will arrive this evening, and I am to meet him for breakfast in the morning."

"May I join you?"

Jack looked over at Martha. "Yes, if you like."

———————•◦•———————

The weather remained overcast the next morning. Martha again borrowed the neighbor's carriage and horses. On this trip, Jack took his travel bag. When Martha questioned his reason, he said, "If Captain Conley agrees to take me to New London, I would like to remain nearby to avoid any suspicion. The foreman of the stevedores I talked with yesterday told me that a redcoat patrol came by looking for a deserter. The person they described made that foreman suspicious of me. Seems my explanations satisfied him. There may be others who question. If the captain hires me as a crewman, that may stifle the inquisitors." He threw his bag into the carriage. "I will secure lodging nearer the harbor."

"I am sorry to hear that." She sighed. Disheartened, she spoke more softly. "I'm disappointed that you are leaving. I knew you were not staying, so I wanted to show you our town."

Jack climbed aboard the carriage. He let Martha drive the team.

When the two reached the Whale Tavern, Martha turned to Jack and said, "I will not join you. If your time permits, perhaps you will stop by for Sunday dinner. Auntie Helen cooks a wonderful meal of chicken, potatoes, and other trimmings. You can consider it your farewell dinner. She serves at two o'clock."

"Thank you," Jack said. "I would be honored. I can make the walk to your aunt's house; though it is mostly uphill, it is no more than a mile." He reached behind the seat, picked up his travel bag, and exited the carriage. He stood for a moment and looked up at Martha. She extended her right hand. He took hold of it and kissed its back. "I will try to visit on Sunday."

Martha smiled and snapped the reins. The carriage moved down Wharf Road. Jack watched it until it turned onto the bridge.

———•◆•———

Pungent cooking odors and dense tobacco smoke burned his eyes. Jack rubbed his tearing eyes as he sat at an empty table in the dim innards of the Whale Tavern. He listened to the chatter that surrounded him. Most was abstruse and incoherent. While his eyes cleared, and adjusted to the tavern's interior, he overheard someone tell of a Nantucket whaler who was captured off Rhode Island by the Royal Navy. Its crew was impressed and cargo confiscated. The gruff voice then said, "Those damned lobsterbacks got New Londoners riled and on edge."

The scrape of a nearby chair made Jack look up. He saw a brawny fellow in his fifties, with a face hidden by a heavy beard, rise from the table and slam the chair forward. His partners, jolted by the bearded man's action, stared up at him. "Cain't let them redcoat wharf rats irritate you, Toby," one of them said. "Them lobsterbacks ain't gonna attack your bat'o."

Toby? Jack looked up. Captain Toby Conley?

"Makes me madder'n hell to have our boys dragooned by the British," Captain Toby Conley said. "Most o' them Nantucket crews are not Americans, but Indians. Not even their battle. But they gonna be forced to fight against us." The captain stepped away from his group. "'Scuse me, gents. I'm to meet some cargo my foreman said needed to be transported to New London right quick. Hear anyone askin' for me, tell 'im I'm at the bar."

"Gonna sail right into the bees' nest, are ye, ol' Toby?" Captain Conley's heckler gibed, choked, and chuckled.

"I be at the bar," Captain Conley said and limped off.

As soon as the captain seated himself at the bar, Jack rose and walked over to his side. "I overheard one of the boys at the table call you Toby," he said. "I am to meet a captain Toby Conley. By chance you would not be him?"

"Aye, sir. Captain Toby Conley I am." He slipped off the stool and extended his hand. "You must be the cargo I'm to transport."

The bartender came over. "Can I bring you fellows something?"

"Aye," the captain answered. "I'll have my usual mug of coffee." He glanced at Jack, who nodded. "Bring us two mugs. Perhaps a sweet, Mr.—I didn't catch your name."

"Jack Hollister. Please call me Jack."

"Aye, Jack." Captain Conley again looked up at the bartender. "Bring us some sweet bread."

"I need to get to New London," Jack said, "and from there onto a vessel headed for New England as soon as I can."

"I should say so, Jack. My foreman tells me the redcoats are looking for a fellow like you. Say the fellow is a deserter. Left his post on Governor's Island. Say he's a rebel spy."

"It appears your foreman was told more about me than he let on. Without putting my friends in jeopardy, all I can say is I must join my patriot friends in Maine."

"Understand." Captain Conley nodded. "Redcoats are not popular in New London, so when they do come into the city, they come as a troop. A party of them arrived last week. Put some posters up. Our militia monitored their movements. They departed as quickly as they came. My foreman says the posters name you as a deserter." He stared at Jack. "I saw the posters. They have an image of a handsome sandy-haired fellow, but without a scar on his face. The image resembles you, but you have a scar on your left cheek. Rather noticeable, it is. I assume it is a battle scar?"

"A musket shot grazed me when I got too close to the fight for the HMS *Margaretta*."

"Aye. Heard of that battle. The rebels in Maine captured that vessel and killed the captain. That was two years ago." Captain Conley took a bite off a chunk of bread, chewed it, and sipped his coffee. "Perhaps to be safe, you should change your name to"—he grinned—"to Carson Rabbit."

Jack's eyelids widened and jaw dropped slightly. "You've heard of Mr. Carson Rabbit? Seems General Washington's intelligence network has a greater embrace than I thought."

Captain Conley grinned and nodded. "Aye, it does indeed. Patriots loyal to the call for independence are everywhere, Mr. Rabbit."

Jack smiled. The two men sat in silence and enjoyed the sweet bread.

Captain Conley slugged down the remains of his coffee, leaned closer to Jack, and said, "Since you are known in Norwich, and there are British zealots here, who, for a few shillings, would inform on you, I believe it best that you get to New London as soon as possible."

"I am ready to leave when you are ready."

"Tomorrow, before sunrise." Conley slipped off the stool. "Come. We'll go to the office, where you can stay the night. Since those damned Tories have ears, you should contact no one. Some will sell their mother for a guinea. Quarters at the shack are a bit uncomfortable, but I have a blanket or two and a pillow. You can sleep on a bench or on the floor. My foreman will bring you some victuals. You'll survive."

"Aye, I will." Jack finished off his food, picked up his travel bag, and followed Captain Conley to the tavern's exit. On the way to the captain's shack, he thought of Martha and her invitation to Sunday dinner. His stomach grumbled.

———————

The moon hung in the east, the sky around it brightening from black to blue. Jack, Captain Conley, and one of his men, a ruggedly built, tanned fellow with a queue of long, jet-black hair flopping against his back, strolled down Wharf Road to a little dock. It jutted into the water where the Thames and Shetucket Rivers united. Conley's man pushed a cart loaded with crates and a pair of ten-foot boat oars. The air was cool, and a slight wind blew from the northwest.

"Good day for running downriver," Captain Conley said. "When we make the channel, the sail can be raised, an' we can sit back an' enjoy the scenery." He put his hand on Jack's shoulder. "The fellow ahead is Joey. If need be, he can row *Tessie* from here to New London without takin' a break. He can also choke a bear, should one need to be choked." The captain chuckled and massaged his beard. "Hey, Joey! Want chu to meet our passenger, Mr. Carson Rabbit."

Momentarily struck by the unexpected name change, Jack stumbled but caught himself before the man with massive shoulders stopped and turned toward him. Jack smiled and extended his hand. "Good to meet you, Joey."

"Joey's a Pequot," the captain said as the Indian's big hand crunched Jack's. "Lot of them around here. Good, loyal hard workers. Great whalers. Them's the ones I got riled about in the tavern, when I learned those damn redcoats captured that whaler and impressed the crew. Toilin' the Arctic waters for a year or two and, just as they're approachin' home port, that damned lobsterback gunboat run 'em down. Some of Joey's friends were part of that crew. Joey can tell you 'bout them. What say you, Joey?"

The big fellow only grunted and fisted his hands.

The captain's rant continued. "That whaler had no defense. Carried no cannons. Boys had no chance. Makes me goddamn mad, so I'll do what I can to rid this side of the Atlantic of them arrant bastards."

When the group reached the *Tessie*, Jack scanned the vessel. He had never seen a bateau but heard that the French used them in Canadian waters. The craft had a high, strongly raked, peaked bow and stern. But *Tessie*, a larger bateau, differed slightly by having a small, centrally located, panel with a flange for attaching a rudder. This modification flattened *Tessie*'s stern peak. Jack estimated the bateau's length to be about thirty-five feet. She had a six-foot beam, with widely flared sides and a flat bottom. Vessel is perfect for transporting cargo up and down rivers, Jack thought.

Joey loaded the crates amidships and laid the oars atop of them. Leaving the longboat tied to a pier at the head of the dock, he returned and climbed aboard. Jack took a seat in the bow, and Captain Conley slid the rudder into its fitting on the stern and attached the tiller pole.

"Cast off the lines, Joey," the captain said, "and pull us into the river."

Joey freed the boat of its bindings, pushed it away from the dock, and set the oars into the locks aft of the load of cargo. Standing with his back to Jack, the rugged Pequot grabbed the oars, leaned forward, dug the blades deep, and pulled. The bateau slid quietly toward the middle of the Thames River as Captain Conley brought the bow around to a downriver heading.

"Step the sail," the captain commanded.

The Pequot stopped rowing and boated the oars. He then crawled over the crates of cargo, untied the mastsail complex from the larboard gunwale, placed the bottom of the mast into its base on the deck located a few feet from where Jack sat, and knelt. He secured the mast in the base by pushing in the lock pin. Joey then stood and undid the lashes that held the shrouds, the sail and its rigging, boom, and gaff against the mast. All of them fell free. After attaching the shrouds to the gunwales, he pulled them taut, adjusted the mast vertically, and secured the fixed rigging. Then he hoisted the sail, trimmed the gaff, and pushed the boom to larboard. When the sail caught the wind, he trimmed it, and the bateau glided downstream with the wind.

Jack was amazed. It took the Indian less than five minutes to switch from rowing to sailing.

"Should be a fine ride, if this breeze holds," Captain Conley said. "When we near New London, we'll pick up the outgoing tide, an' that'll help."

Conley kept the bateau in midstream as Joey tweaked the sail. About a mile downstream, the sun cleared the treetops, illuminating a few easterly hillsides and the yellowing canvas. A tattered cloud blanket slipped unnoticed overhead and covered the spring sky. Though the air temperature warmed, Jack felt comfortable in the jacket he wore.

At Walden Island the Thames turned more southerly. Joey pulled the boom a bit closer to the vessel's midline and relieved Captain Conley at the helm. The captain maneuvered himself forward and sat down on a crate and faced Jack. "Last week there were two privateers fixing for runs off Boston," he said. "Good port, New London, for such vessels to take on supplies. Royal Navy seems to keep its distance. There's talk that an armed, medium-sized downeaster is to make harbor for provisions. She's being mastered by a Mainer and crewed by Marbleheaders. May be in port while you're there. Good vessel to get on your way."

Hearing this, Jack snapped out of his daze. "Aye. Just the vessel I would be searching for. How will I know her?"

"You'll need to listen. There will be word on the docks. But be wary of what you hear. It can also be a guise lobsterbacks use to entice and kidnap callow fellows."

"Thank you, Captain." Jack straightened his coat and took a deep breath. A sense of self-reliance surrounded him. "I have dealt with Marbleheaders. They are a stalwart lot. But I have no desire to go to Halifax."

"Understand," Captain Conley said, "nor do I. Though Nova Scotia is beautiful in summer, I'm told. But that schooner will no doubt be stopping at some down east ports on the way. Passage aboard that vessel would be a rapid way to get you to where you want to go. And there may even be some excitement along the way."

"Agreed. I will keep an ear out."

The captain returned to the stern and relieved Joey of the tiller. In a short time, the Thames rounded past the mouth of Horton Cove and returned to its southeasterly trek to Long Island Sound. Joey again trimmed the sail, sat back, and relaxed. After a short time, the bateau's placid, tranquil glide downriver sent Jack into a doze. To stay alert, the captain lit his pipe, and Joey remained soundless but watchful.

They had traveled a little over a third of the way to New London. The cloud cover began to break, and the steady northwest breeze dwindled to occasional puffs. The sail fluttered and swayed, rendering Jack fully alert. The vessel lost headway, and Captain Conley had difficulty maintaining steerage.

"Joey, man the oars," the captain commanded. "At this speed, we'll not make New London till next week."

Within a few moments, the big man's strokes fell into a soft, splashing rhythm, causing the bateau's bow to surge and gurgle as it cut a path downstream. This harmony continued until the current of the outgoing tide embraced the bateau and aided the vessel onward. Joey's cadence slowed.

About four hours later, as the tide slacked, Joey dug the oars deep. Captain Conley turned the bateau and aimed its bow at a small dock on the northeast shore of Bream Cove. He ordered Jack to drop the sail. The captain found an empty slot among several other bateaux and coastal sloops. Several men stood on the dock, and one caught the bateau's bowline that Jack threw. He pulled Captain Conley's vessel forward and secured it against the dock.

"Back so soon, Toby?" one of the men yelled.

"Aye. Had to make a special trip. Not stayin'. Goin' return as soon as I deliver my cargo. Sunset about four hours away. Plan to be north of this town by then."

Jack jumped onto the dock and tied the stern line to a piling.

Captain Conley came ashore carrying Jack's travel bag, while Joey unloaded the crates onto the dock. The captain walked to Jack and handed him the bag. "You're here." He pointed to the complex of buildings clustered to the left around the cove. "There's some inns on Tilley Street. You'll find the privateers, when they're in"—the captain swung around and pointed right—"docked up the north shore. Not far. You will see their masts. Good luck."

Jack nodded. "Thank you for taking your time to transport me here." He extended his hand, but the captain turned and returned to the crates. A puzzled look crossed Jack's face. He furrowed his brow and cocked his head to the side.

"The privateer you are looking for is a sizable vessel," Captain Conley yelled back. "I did not see her when we arrived. If the rumors are sound, she should be here in the next day or so. Now be off with you."

Jack lifted his bag, walked off the dock, crossed the wharf, and maneuvered his way between carts containing fish, oyster, potatoes, lumber, or other supplies. At an alley leading to Water Street stood a tavern. Jack asked a fellow for directions to Tilley Street. He pointed the way. "Just up the block," he said.

Captain Conley is in a hurry to return. Hope all is well with him, Jack thought.

CHAPTER 13
NEW LONDON, CONNECTICUT
MAY 1777

It had rained during the night, and in the morning, when Jack left the bakery where he had had breakfast, the streets were nearly dry. A thin, misty fog still softened the air, though beams of sunlight were breaking through the clouds. He breathed in the sea-flavored air and strolled toward the larger wharves lining the Thames River. As he approached he saw, occupying several docks, the masts of some coastal schooners standing out against the yards and rigging of two transport brigs. Moored offshore, several large vessels were being serviced by a flotilla of lighters or awaiting dockage along the wharf.

Anchored on the distant side of the river floated a large, down east schooner. It caught Jack's eyes and excited him. Likely a vessel from General Washington's navy. He smiled, flicked his eyebrows, and increased his pace to the wharves for a closer view. Could it be the privateer Captain Conley spoke of?

"Came in last night," a grizzled old seaman on a fishing smack tied to the dock on which Jack stood examining the distant vessel called up to him. "Flying no flags. Several of her crew came ashore 'fore daylight." He pointed to a longboat beached about a quarter mile away. "That's their boat. Rugged-looking bunch. One o' them, an older fellow wearin' a long, dark coat an' a bicorne, had a limp. Figure he were their captain."

Jack looked down at the fisherman, who was now concentrating on coiling a length of rope. "Thank you. Did you see where they went?"

"Nay. But figured they are down at the Crab Tavern. Fellows like them, that's where they rendezvous. Ne'er been there. But if ye do, better take a weapon." He returned his attention to the alga-covered rope.

"Where is the Crab Tavern?" Jack asked.

"Down Water Street. Gray shack sittin' on pilings," the fisherman said, never looking up from his task.

"Hmm." Jack swallowed and put his hand in the pocket of his coat. His fingers felt the handle of the pistol Manny McGully had given him. "Thank you again, Mister," he said as he touched the pouch of shot and powder he had secured to his belt.

"Aye," the old fisherman grunted.

"Passed that tavern yesterday," Jack mumbled as he walked onto Water Street. "It is near that alley that leads to Tilley Street."

A shack, indeed. Two-thirds of the Crab Tavern, which fronted on Water Street, sat on solid ground. The other third was supported by about thirty weathered, slimy, barnacle-wrack-encrusted pilings that extended from the mud of a tidal creek to the flooring of the stained cedar-shingled building. As he approached, Jack could see that many of the shingles on the side had fallen off, and the paint on the framing around the two windows appeared gnarled and flaking. One of the corners that held the signboard, advertising the Crab Tavern's Water Street entrance, had fallen free of its rusted hanger. Jack had to tilt his head to read the sign, now hanging vertically over the boarded entranceway. The building's windows onto the street were also covered over.

Jack stopped, glanced at the tavern's facade, and shrugged. A tarnished meeting place for infamous patriots. He walked past the building and looked back. The sunlight, after burning off the remaining fog, now brightened the leeward side of the tavern.

On a bench next to a serviceable doorway sat two rough-looking men. Both wore blemished duck-cloth trousers, navy-colored cotton pullovers with the long sleeves nearly pushed to their elbows, and narrow-brimmed tricornes. Each had a dagger stuck in a wide, worn leather belt strapped around his waist. Both men smoked a clay pipe and seemed to be enjoying the sun's warmth. No doubt crewmen from the mysterious schooner.

Jack hesitated but then walked to the boardwalk that led to the porch on which the sailors sat. They looked up as he approached. One, a bearded fellow with a patch over his left eye, removed the pipe from his mouth, stood, and faced Jack. "Is there something you be lookin' for?" he asked.

"Aye. Passage to Maine," Jack said.

"What make you think we be goin' that way?"

"A friend, Captain Toby Conley, told me that a Continental privateer was to make New London harbor sometime this week." Jack moved closer to the two men. "Thought you might be off that large schooner anchored across the way. My name is Carson Rabbit, and I thought I would ask."

The other fellow, who wore a red neckerchief, removed his pipe and rubbed the bowl against his thick but trim mustache. He glared at Jack, blinked his eyes, and turned his back to the sun. "Step closer. You look familiar, but never met a Carson Rabbit, though I hear the name do surface in some circles." He scrutinized Jack further. "Cannot say where we are bound, and our capt'n does not take passengers. He be looking for a couple of able seamen though." The mustached man stood and stepped back, continued to inspect Jack. He fiddled with the pipe and then chuckled. "It is them duds you are wearin'. You ain't no seaman."

Biting the inside of his lip, Jack took a deep breath. "I am familiar with the ways of the sea. I have fought its anger and enjoyed its passivity. The clothes I wear are traveling clothes."

"That scar on your cheek, where did you get it?"

"Musket shot." Jack fingered the scar. "A battle some years ago."

"Have ye heard o' the *Piper*?" The mustached fellow shoved the pipe back into his mouth, put his hands on his hips, and furrowed his brow."

"Perhaps so." Jack felt a nervous twitch in his stomach, and caution activated his mind. He asks probing questions. If these men are not who I think they are, my answer may put me in jeopardy.

"What do you know of this vessel?"

"A Marbleheader that hailed from Beverly, Massachu-setts," Jack said.

"Aye."

The two men took positions on each side of Jack. His height reached to their shoulders.

"You may be a patriot," the beard said, "or a redcoat spy. No matter. We'll let the captain decide." He nudged Jack to the door. Opened it and pushed him in. The mustache followed and closed the door. "May have a prospect for you, Captain, sir," the beard announced. "A jack-a-dandy just stopped by. Calls hisself Carson Rabbit. Say he wants to be a jack-o'-the-sea an' get to Maine."

Jack's eyes acclimated to the interior dimness. In front of him was a table, and an elderly man sat it. His back was to Jack. Scattered around the room were about twelve to fifteen burly seamen, some standing and others sitting or lounging. All, except the old man, looked at Jack.

"If he's a sailor, we might be able to help him," the cap-tain said quietly but did not lift his eyes from the table. "Step around to the front, Mr. Rabbit. Like to get a look at ye." Spread on the table lay a navigational chart. It was illu-minated by a single candle that the captain clenched in his left hand. In his right hand, he gripped a magnifying glass, held it a few inches from his right eye, and studied the map.

Heard that voice, but cannot place it, Jack thought as tension tightened his leg muscles. He removed his hat and stiffly walked around to the front of the table.

The captain did not look up from the aged, partially faded, chart. He set the candle and magnifying glass to the side and laid a parallel rule on a plot. "We'll make for

Nantucket, Robert, resupply, stay out to sea, and head north around the cape. Should make Marblehead in a week if we can avoid the redcoat patrols. Of course, we will try to pick a prize or two."

"Aye."

Jack looked up just as the bearded fellow responded.

"If Mr. Rabbit turns out to be a spy, Robert," the captain continued, "you an' the boys take him out back, shoot him, and push his corpus into the river. It won't be found till we're gone.

Jack did not notice that the captain's mouth fell open when he glanced up at him.

"Bless my goddamned soul," the captain blurted.

Hearing the profane yelp, Jack snapped his attention back to the elderly man seated behind the table. He stared at the man's face. His knees weakened. His heart thumped several extra beats as his jaw dropped. Within a moment, a smile covered Jack's face. He dropped his hat as his arms reached out to the captain. "Mr. Smoke—Mr. Horace Smoke! Or should I say, Captain Smoke."

The old man exploded out of his chair with such intensity that the table flipped forward against Jack. With his massive hand, Mr. Smoke slapped his desk to the side and it went banging across the floor. "Damned my soul, Jack Hollister." He threw his arms around the young man and embraced him with fervor.

Jack remained stunned. He tried to speak but could not.

Mr. Smoke released his hug, stepped back, grabbed Jack's shoulders, pushed him back, and held him at arm's length, looking into his face. A smile lit up the captain.

"This man's one of us! Welcome Jack Hollister to our fold, my boys, a veteran of the Battle of Machias." He released his hold on Jack, who stumbled back.

"Aye! Midshipman Hollister," someone with a French accent shouted from a darkened corner of the Crab Tavern.

Jack looked around. For the first time in many months, he felt safe and comfortable. He was among friends, Marbleheaders, old shipmates. Then he saw two men approaching and recognized them.

The burly one extended his right hand and said, "Bonjour, mon ami," and then wrapped his left arm around Jack and kissed him on the cheek. The thinner fellow came up and joined in the embrace.

"Gunner Gaspar," Jack blubbered. "Boatswain. You really do not know how relieved I feel to be among friendly faces." Tears flooded Jack's eyes. "It is so good to see you, Captain Smoke, and my friends from the *Piper*." He looked about the room. "I do not see Mr. Bowdon. Is he not among you?"

"Nay," Captain Smoke said. "Aboard the schooner *Balch*. They are lookin' for British prizes off Nova Scotia. We'll be meetin' up with him soon." The captain turned to the table where he was seated earlier and lifted his mug. "Gentlemen Chandlers, let us raise our glasses and toast your new second mate, Mr. Jack Hollister."

Taken aback by Mr. Smoke's enlistment of his services, Jack recoiled. He tensed, but when the room filled with the men thumping their mugs on whatever solid object was near and shouting, "Huzzah," he eased, though his jaw remained unhinged. Slurping, knocks, and bangs continued until someone cried, "Mr. Smoke's told us about ye, Mr. Jack. How ye helped capture of tha' sloop-o'-war, *Margaretta*."

"That was two years ago," Jack muttered. "And much has happened since—to our country, General Washington, and to me."

"Aye indeed," Captain Smoke said. "But the battles continue. And will, till every damned redcoat and Loyalist is off our land. Let us now return to our vessel." He put his hand on Jack's shoulder. "I came here to find a qualified mate. And, I have found one. Mr. Hollister is a sailor more capable and loyal than I had ever expected to find. Our business here is finished."

"True indeed. Captain Morris o' the *Piper* made Mr. Hollister second in command when Mr. Bowden left," First Mate Stokes added. "A very capable seaman 'e is."

Gaspar shouted, "He teach *Piper* gun crew to shoot. He good master gunner."

Captain Smoke's announcement continued to perplex Jack. Horace Smoke is an old and dear friend, but do I want to remain in this fray? Seems I am continually being bound by others or by circumstance. "Captain Smoke, am I being impressed? You have not asked that I join your crew. Nor whether I am available."

"Aye. That I haven't." Mr. Smoke removed his hand from Jack's shoulder and returned to his chair.

Feeling tense, Jack twisted his hat in his hands. He glanced at the captain, took a deep breath, and sighed. I do need to get to Machias, he thought. His mind calmed. I could not be among a better group of men. They are loyal patriots.

The captain looked at Jack. "Please excuse my bungle. We are not redcoats—you are not being impressed. My enthusiasm got the better of me. Let me explain. My vessel, the *Chandler's Liberty*, lost its first mate in a gale off Boston several weeks ago; a capable Marbleheader he was. Though there are other able, loyal Marbleheaders aboard, most have limitations. First Mate Stokes, whom you know, is the most capable of the bunch. I promoted him upon the loss. Colonel Glover, of the Twenty-First Massachusetts Regiment, oversees these sailors and plans to assign Stokes as master of another privateer once we return to Beverly. I was told that I could find a replacement here. Many New London seamen are loyal patriots and very skilled. But I need a special man, one who knows well the vagaries of the sea and can confront its whimsies. If I found such an accomplished man, he'd become my first mate after Stokes leaves. Finding you is the best that could have happened." A doubtful glance crossed his face. "I should have consulted you before I assigned you to my crew. I have no mind of your past activities or future, but I do hope your loyalties have not changed, and you will join us."

"Much time has passed since I have been among more loyal and trusted friends," Jack said. "I have a very strong need to return to Machias as soon as possible. If this can be done, I would be honored to become a member of your crew."

Captain Smoke rose, clasped and shook Jack's hand, and then he stood, smiled, and asked, "Why the haste to return to Maine?"

"The redcoats plan to avenge their losses. Machias must be warned." Jack moved away from the table. "I will explain once we are under way."

"Finish your drinks, gentlemen," Captain Smoke commanded. "Prepare to pull for the *Chandler's Liberty*. We weigh anchor on tonight's high tide."

———•◦•———

Captain Smoke grappled with the tiller as if it were trying to resist his efforts, glowered, and roared commands as the *Chandler's Liberty* crew rowed for their vessel, growling, "Dig those damned oars deeper! Throttle that dawdling! Maintain rhythm." As soon as the longboat scraped against the schooner's hull and before anyone had time to toss the painter, he grabbed the rope ladder and started to climb toward the rail, yelling, "Jack, follow me. We need to talk." He grabbed Jack's shoulder as soon as he cleared the gunwale and pressed him toward the after hatch of the deckhouse. "What is this intelligence you have of Machias?"

"Ad...Admiral Howe," Jack stuttered, "planning to invade the city."

The captain kicked open the hatch and waved his arm down the ladder. "Below. My quarters. We can talk in private."

Jack climbed down, followed by Captain Smoke. Behind them, under the helm, were the captain's quarters.

"Sit! Tell me what those redcoats are planning." Captain Smoke reached to a shelf behind his bed and removed a jug of rum. He poured a tot into a pair of mugs that sat on his desk and offered one to Jack. "Now speak."

Jack took a sip of the rum. He nodded. "Early this spring the Howes and several of their field commanders, upset over General Washington's victories in New Jersey, held a meeting." Seeing the captain tighten into a defensive mood upon hearing his statement, Jack explained, "General Washington, because of my English aristocratic background, asked me to covertly infiltrate the British forces after he secured Boston and transferred his headquarters to New York City. He needed reliable intelligence on redcoat movements and strength. I accepted the mission. That is how I became involved with Admiral Howe and learned of his frustration with losing the *Margaretta* and the death of her captain at the hands of the Machias militia. He also fears that the Machias militia will invade Halifax. To achieve revenge, he wants to eliminate the rebels, as he calls the Continental soldiers, and destroy their city."

Mr. Smoke slugged down his tot of rum and relaxed. "You sure took on a dangerous mission."

"Aye. Shortly after I became a spy, a close friend, attempting a similar mission, was captured in New York City and hanged at the order of General Howe." Jack brushed his hand through his hair.

"Aye. Lieutenant Nathan Hale, the lost hero of Connecticut."

Jack nodded. "Yes. An engaging fellow, he was. His death greatly angered me. So, when I learned of the admiral's plans, I wrote a letter to Charles Bowden informing him and had it secretly sent. I have no idea whether he will ever receive it. But my contact in Manhattan gave me a letter from General Washington informing me of the establishment of a highly organized intelligence team that he had created, and he released me from my mission. I immediately arranged to desert the Howes and make my way to Machias. I do not want the people of Machias to face a redcoat invasion."

Captain Smoke poured himself another tot. "Beverly first," he said. "Resupply. Then set our course for Machias." He gulped the rum, slammed the mug down on the desk, stumbled to the ladder, and climbed the first few rungs. With his shoulders through the deck hatch and silhouetted against a reddening sky, he yelled, "Mr. Stokes, make ready for the sea. We sail on the outgoing tide." He dropped back to the lower deck and returned to face Jack. "Let's dine and talk of old times." He extended his arm and waved forward, toward the mess.

About thirty minutes after Jack and Captain Smoke had sat down to dinner, they were joined by First Mate Stokes and several of the crew. When all had finished, the captain stood and strolled to a rear counter in the wardroom where a sextant, two parallel rules, and a compass lay atop a navigational chart. Several oil lamps hung over the table. From a cubbyhole above him, he removed a folder and returned to the table. He took a document from the folder and laid it in front of Jack.

"Before you are the credentials that permit me to use the *Chandler's Liberty* as a private vessel of war and engage the enemy as I see fit," Captain Smoke said and placed his finger on the certificate. "My letter of marque, sir."

Jack had heard of these permits that allowed masters of nonmilitary vessels registered in the country that issued the letter to pursue, capture, confiscate, and sell the cargo and vessel of any enemy nation. The letter was a license to piracy. He looked at the document and saw the official signatures of George Washington, John Glover, and John Hancock, president of the Second Continental Congress. An impressive group. "So, the *Chandler's Liberty* is a privateer?" Jack asked.

"Aye. That she is," answered Captain Smoke in a boastful voice. "A well-armed, topsa'l schooner with a deck length of a hundred and ten feet. She was built on an island in Englishman's Bay to the specifications prescribed by General Washington and Colonel Glover and launched last summer. She carries ten five-pounders, two twenty-pounders,[4] and six swivel guns[5] and is crewed by twenty loyal Mainers and Marbleheaders." Using his fingers, the captain snatched up the letter and put it back into the folder. He turned and limped toward the rear counter. "Come. I will point out our course to Beverly. It is a parlous one. We'll

---

4 Cannons aboard an eighteenth-century vessel were identified by the weight of the shot they fired; e.g., a 20-pounder cannon fired a twenty-pound cannonball.

5 Small bore, rotatable cannons that can be moved and mounted anywhere on a vessel.

have to sail away from the coast. British patrol near shore. But we'll be in the sea lanes. The crew would enjoy coming upon a merchantman from Great Britain or Nova Scotia. We have yet to take our first prize." He straightened and turned around toward the table where Mr. Stokes and several other men still sat. "Mr. Stokes, is the *Chandler's Liberty* ready to sail?"

Stokes pushed back from the table and stood. "Almost, sir. Topsa'ls set. All that's left is to set the jibs, staysa'l, and hoist the fore and main. Tide will turn in an hour, an' the current will be in favor. As you commanded, sir, anchors be hauled after dark."

Captain Smoke nodded.

Stokes turned and headed for the ladder leading to the weather deck. The other sailors followed.

Alone in the wardroom, the captain and Jack stood and moved to the table where the navigational charts were laid out. When they reached it, Captain Smoke explained his anxiety in wanting to depart clandestinely. "There's always British frigates on patrol in Long Island Sound. Don't want to meet up with one tonight. So, we sneak out in the dark."

"Aye," Jack said with smile and a nod. "Good timing. New moon. Tonight will be particularly dark. We should be able to slip away unseen."

The captain bent over and perused the chart. "Show you our course." He put his finger on a speck offshore of Massachusetts. "Nantucket," he said. "Be east of the island by sunup. Later we'll go northeast past the Cape of Cods and west to Beverly. Should be there in a week or two." He straightened and took hold of Jack's shoulder.

"Come let us go on deck. Our schooner should be ready to get under way."

After extinguishing the candles and lanterns below, the two men felt their way up the ladder to the deck. When they passed through the hatchway, they entered a night broken only by overhead, starry pinpricks that cast the sails in a ghostly luminescence. Though crewmen scurried soundlessly about the unlit deck, only subdued clunks and clanks disturbed the peace. Like a phantasm, the *Chandler's Liberty* glided seaward before the anchors splashed through the sea's surface and were secured against the hull.

After a sound sleep in his assigned cabin below, Jack came on deck as the sun rose above the horizon. With all sails full and taut, the *Chandler's Liberty*, her deck hiked to starboard, cut through the one-foot chop at about eight knots. A good speed, he thought as he stood near Mr. Stokes, who commanded the helm. The sky was clear, and the sea color had changed from its usual dark green to a viscous royal blue. "The Gulf Stream flow should quicken our speed northward," Jack said.

"Aye," answered Stokes as he gently tweaked the ship's wheel to maintain an easterly heading. "If some o' the boys throw out some fish lines we could have 'delfin'[6] for dinner. They abo'nd in these waters."

---

6 Fish in the genus *Coryphaena*, commonly known as the dolphinfish or mahimahi.

"Unusual, drab-colored fish," Jack said. "Only seen specimens in the Royal Museum."

"Beautiful they are, when they come outta wa'er." Stokes made a quick turn on the wheel to stabilize the schooner as it propelled over a five-foot swell and then dove into the trough. He then continued, "Blue with yellow bellies, almost golden, they are, but fade fast outta wa'er." He bobbed his head. "Damn good eatin'."

"Should I call a couple of men to stream out some fishing lines?"

"Nay. They be here shortly. They readyin' for breakfast now."

Jack turned and looked aft. He saw a gray blob shrinking away on the western horizon. "Was that Nantucket behind us?"

"Aye. Passed it just before sunrise."

"Someone going to relieve you, Mr. Stokes, so you can go to breakfast?" Jack asked when he heard the cook ring the ship's bell. "There is a fine smell of bacon coming from the galley."

"Aye, Gaspar. He takes the helm after breakfast."

"Good. Then I will go below and join Captain Smoke for breakfast. Thank you for telling me about that fish. I will look forward to seeing one alive and fresh, and of course, have it for dinner." Jack nodded and walked to the hatchway that led below deck.

———◆◆◆———

So far during this trip, Captain Smoke did not assign Jack any specific responsibilities. Because he was the second mate, his duties were nothing more than those of a glorified boatswain. But, so far, First Mate Stokes had taken care of everything necessary to get *Chandler's Liberty* under way and, since they departed New London yesterday, everything was progressing smoothly. Stokes had assigned only five crewmen to the tasks necessary to sail the schooner. With the southwesterly wind maintaining a constant velocity and the sea being relatively calm, Jack had very little to do.

After breakfast, he relaxed on his bunk, brought his log up to date, and then chatted and played cribbage with several off-duty crewmen until the cook called lunch. Jack satisfied his hunger with an apple, biscuit, and a mug of coffee and started for the deck to relieve Gaspar at the helm, but met the Frenchman coming down the ladder.

"Mr. Stokes say go below," Gaspar said when he and Jack met at the door of the mess. "Have lunch. Then relax. I take the helm for the afternoon, Stokes say." Gaspar continued into the room.

Jack climbed the ladder to the deck, steadied himself, and made his way aft to the helm. There he found Mr. Stokes leaning with his back against the ship's wheel and watching six excited and alert crewmen, who were scattered about the stern, trolling. Jack smiled. "Are they catching anything?"

Startled, Stokes snapped around and glanced at Jack. "Aye," he said, nodding. A grin appeared on his face. "They catch maybe five or six delfin, a bonito, and a small shark. They usin' the bonito and shark for bait."

A whoop and holler erupted from a couple of men on the larboard side attempting to haul in a line. Their arms were cocked and tense, and the line wrapped around their fisted hands. They strained and stumbled backward, trying to pull the force fighting for freedom to the schooner's hull. Several crewmen who were fishing nearby dropped their lines and jumped into the tug-of-war. The five men grunted and groaned, yelled, and cursed as they pulled and stumbled against their forward skid. Suddenly the line went slack. And they all fell back into each other and heaped onto the deck. One of the men jumped up, grabbed the line, and looped it several times around a nearby bit. Another one scrambled onto his knees and began pulling in the slack, allowing the largest and most muscular man to throw a loose hank of the rope across his back before it began to stream seaward. The others gripped the line and braced themselves against the gunwale. Then for a moment, the tension lessened as a marlin speared through the surface, rocketed skyward, and fell back with a tremendous splash and a great jerk on the fish line.

A gasp exploded from the fishermen. "Too much to handle," someone yelled. The lead man yanked his dagger free and slashed the line. Again, the group scattered backward, but this time, they maintained balance.

Jack's and Stokes's eyes glared seaward at the foaming, rippling spot where the large fish disappeared. For a moment, they saw the fish line zing below the sea's surface.

"That must have been several hundred pounds of fish," Jack cried, holding his hands on his head. "Never have I seen anything like that."

"We'll be hearin' o' tha' monster fish for many a year," Stokes said, shaking his head as he watched the now-silent fishermen all bending over the rail, staring at the diminishing ring of disturbance, hoping their quarry would resurface.

Jack sighed. His tension eased, and a grin brightened his face. "Aye. By tomorrow the men will embellish its virtues, and in a week, that fish will become a legend." He walked to the rail, smiling as the crewmen began to disperse. "Too bad Cap'n Smoke was not on deck to see this excitement."

"Aye, too bad. But the captain'll hear of it, all right," one of the fishermen said. "We catchin' eighteen of those delfin for supper should make him happy. Some o' them should go about ten pounds. They're big too."

Jack nodded, grabbed he ship's rail, and looked toward the horizon. Several of the crewmen went below to tend to cuts and rope burns. Three returned to the stern and played out their fishing lines. But the serenity of fishing and the excitement of catching fish abruptly ended when the lookout, stationed in small crow's nest situated at the junction of the lower topsail yardarm and foremast, yelled, "Sail on horizon, starboard."

Within seconds the crewmen retrieved their fishing lines, stashed them out of the way, and congregated at the starboard rail.

"Notify Captain Smoke of the sighting," Jack commanded a nearby seaman as he walked across the deck.

"Aye, sir." The sailor ran to the deckhouse, jumped through the hatchway, and slid down the ladder.

Sixty feet below the foremast lookout, everyone on deck scanned the horizon, but no one could see any sails. Jack jumped onto the rack of deadeyes,[7] gripped a foremast shroud, and climbed two-thirds the way up the ratlines. He removed the spyglass from his belt, scanned the starboard vista, and sighted topsails protruding above the horizon roughly south-southeast of the *Chandler's Liberty* heading. He estimated the distant vessel to be about ten to fifteen miles away and heading west.

From his perch, Jack saw Captain Smoke come on deck and walk rapidly to the helm. First Mate Stokes followed. They talked, and Stokes came forward and yelled to the lookout.

"Where tha' vessel?"

"South-southeast, sir."

Stokes scampered back to the helm.

Jack held tight to the nearest shroud and locked his left leg over a ratline as he felt the schooner roll to starboard. He heard the creak and rumble of the sails being reset and trimmed, readjusted position, pointed his telescope over the *Chandler's Liberty* bow, and scanned the horizon in the direction of the distant sails.

Within an hour, those on deck could see the sails. From his position in the rigging, Jack was able to identify the

---

7 A deadeye is an item used in the standing and running rigging of traditional sailing ships. It is a rounded wood block that is encircled by a rope or an iron band and pierced with one or more holes perpendicular to the plane of the disc. Deadeyes can be used singly or in groups to receive the lanyards necessary to tighten shrouds or other stays.

vessel. He swung around and yelled to the helm. "Brig! Flying British transport ensign." He saw Captain Smoke wave to him to return to the deck.

"Lookout," the captain shouted. "Is she being escorted?"

Jack reached the deck, looked up, and saw the lookout twisting about, scanning the horizon.

The lookout shouted, "There are others—ahead and following—several leagues apart."

Jack scampered to the helm.

With Stokes now at the helm, Captain Smoke, with Jack in tow, made his way amidships. "Call the men to general quarters," he commanded. "Use the pipe. We have no bell." The captain handed Jack a boatswain's pipe.

Jack grinned. He had heard Royal Navy boatswains use the pipe to welcome officers and other noted individuals aboard ships. He attempted blowing it several times himself and realized he was not musically inclined. He had never heard it used to call a crew to general quarters. Scratching his head, he again tried to blow the whistle, which resulted in a couple of off-key peeps.

"It's a whistle," Captain Smoke said after seeing Jack fumble with the pipe. The captain pressed his lips together and whistled a low note that quickly swung to a higher note. "A couple of loud shrill blasts that sound like that will do. Now blow into the damn thing."

"Aye, sir. Thank you." Jack took a couple of breaths, pursed his lips, and puffed into the boatswain's pipe. He emitted a low-volume squeal. Then he blew stronger. The tone he produced started low and wound to a super-charged shrill.

"Tha's it!" the captain said and chuckled. "You'll make a musician one day. Now give me a couple more blasts."

The piercing screech roused the crew. They hurried to the assigned stations, removed protective canvas covers from cannons, wiped down guns, collected loading gear, and opened the gunports. "All ready on the line, sir," Gaspar shouted.

"About three leagues from the prize," Jack called to Captain Smoke.

"They know we're here," the captain barked, "but they continue to run. Doin' nothin' to avoid bein' captured." Smoke moved next to Jack, who stood by the starboard rail. "Raise the American flag. Have starboard one fire a shot toward her. That'll get their attention."

"Frigates on larboard beam!" The lookout yelled down. "Four, maybe five leagues off."

The starboard-one cannon fired as Jack and the captain scampered across the deck to the larboard rail. Within moments, its acrid exhaust wafted over them. Jack rubbed his eyes and glared out to sea. The sight of not one, but two, frigates under full sail bearing down on them startled the two men.

"My God! We're outgunned. Let's get the hell out o' here," Captain Smoke cried. "Stokes! Break off chase an' head northeast."

Jack dashed amidships and released the sheets that allowed the foresail to be trimmed as the schooner swung to its new heading. Other crewmen did the same for the mainsail, topsail, and jib sails. Within less than two minutes, the canvases billowed and *Chandler's Liberty* pivoted around almost immediately and started smashing through the chop on the new course heading.

Jack looked aft. The two warships also changed course. Smoky white jets shot from the bow gun of each vessel. He saw two spouts erupt when the cannon balls hit the ocean surface off the stern.

"They're outta range," Captain Smoke said, "but they're fast. If we can maintain our distance till the sun sets, we can get away. Sun be settin' in an hour. Then they'll cut off the chase. Tell Gaspar to keep the gun crews at their stations." He scanned the deck and rigging. "Keep those sails trimmed!"

"Aye, sir," Jack said as he ran to the starboard-one gun station. Once he informed Gaspar of the captain's orders, he joined the rigging crew to assist in keeping the sails trimmed.

Running with the wind, the *Chandler's Liberty* sliced swiftly through a following sea, away from the setting sun. The frigates, separated from each other by several hundred yards, followed. They fired intermittent salvoes, but First Mate Stokes diverged from a straight course with periodic, slight zigs and zags. Even though one shot hit the ocean's surface near enough to throw a spray of water on deck, the rigging crew remained calm and focused and kept the sails taut and in trim.

Jack and Captain Smoke stood by the taffrail,[8] assessing the danger to the armed schooner. About three leagues behind them, the two Royal Navy frigates continued to pursue. With the sun diving below a sanguine horizon, both

---

8 The taffrail is a deck rail located at the stern of a vessel.

vessels appeared exaggerated and glowed as menacing reddish-black silhouettes, each occasionally belching a blaze of orange smoke.

"Like fire-breathing sea dragons, they are," Jack said. "They appear to be closing the distance between us."

"Aye," Captain Smoke said. "Need to stay ahead twenty more minutes. They cannot shoot accurately off the bow. If one of those frigates comes sideward of us, we're in danger."

Jack nervously stepped away from the rail and moved to the left side of the schooner. He kept his eyes on the frigates. Highlighted by the setting sun, they appeared as shadows dwindling with the diminishing twilight.

Captain Smoke moved next to First Mate Stokes. "Their visibility is becoming difficult. Slowly bring us more easterly, about ten degrees. Those frigates will follow. Before the moon rises, it'll be too dark for them to see us. If we make quick a shift to the north during the darkness, I believe the frigates may stay the course to the east—if they continue the chase—while we will be heading north. If the winds hold, in an hour the distance between us will widen. Hopefully, by the time the moon rises, we'll be out of their sight."

Jack returned to the helm. "I will inform the crew that we need to run silent and dark, Captain Smoke."

"Aye, do that, and tell Gaspar to keep the gunnery crews on alert."

Jack started down the starboard side of the *Chandler's Liberty* to pass the word when the frigates again fired their cannons. One of the cannonballs flew over the stern, missing Captain Smoke and First Mate Stokes by inches and crashed through the after portion of the starboard gunwale.

It did not explode, but tore away about twenty feet of the *Chandler's Liberty*'s side above the deck before splashing into the ocean. The nearby gunnery crew extinguished a small fire that erupted from a destroyed oil lamp.

While Stokes countered the schooner's inertial response to the impact, Captain Smoke grabbed a nearby stanchion and regained his composure. "That was a goddamned lucky shot," he growled. "A little less altitude and it would have taken out the entire stern. It's getting very dark. Give us ten more minutes, Stokes, then swing us to the north. Can't see 'em, but I believe those lobsterbacks are about a league or so behind us."

"Is all well here?" Jack cried as he scrambled back to the helm. He arrived before the smoke from the little fire had cleared.

"Aye," Captain Smoke said. "Mr. Hollister, instruct Gaspar to be ready to fire the aft cannon to cover the noise the rigging crew will make when they reset and trim the sails when I give the command to change course." Captain Smoke paused for a moment as Jack prepared to go forward. "Ah yes, snag a couple of fellows to rig safety lines along the starboard gunwale. Don't want anyone falling through that broken gunwale and overboard. Tomorrow the torn rigging can be secured. And the carpenter and his mate can make temporary repairs to the *Chandler's Liberty*'s wounds. Was anyone injured?"

"Nay," Jack replied. "Only some minor cuts from flying debris to some of the gun crew stationed near where that cannonball destroyed the gunwale. They are sound. Gaspar patched them up."

"Good! Step lively now. Alert the crew to the course change." The captain stepped back and removed the speaking trumpet that hung on the binnacle.

"Aye," Jack said. "Allow me some minutes to ready the crew, sir."

"Aye." Captain Smoke nodded as Jack headed toward the middle of the schooner. He assigned two sailors who were sitting on the deckhouse roof to string safeguard around the damaged area of the vessel. Finding Gaspar supervising the forward gun crews, Jack relayed the captain's message to fire the 20-pounder in the stern to cover the schooner's course change. "Make haste, Gaspar, my friend. Captain Smoke wants the *Chandler's Liberty* to be headed north in a matter of minutes."

Gaspar and gun crew dropped what they were doing and scrambled to the stern of the vessel.

"Extinguish all lanterns and stand by to—" Jack's command to the rigging crew was interrupted by Captain Smoke's command to change course. The roar of the 20-pounder also added to the mix-up. He stumbled to the side and grabbed a nearby stanchion to keep himself from falling as the schooner laid hard to the left. Sails flapped and fluttered, the hull and masts creaked, and several unsecured barrels rolled across the deck. Two of the barrels slid through the damaged area and fell into the sea. Regaining composure, Jack yelled, "Set the booms and trim the sails."

Darkness furthered the confusion on deck. But within a matter of minutes, the *Chandler's Liberty* was gliding smoothly, her bowsprit point toward the isolation around the North Star.

With less volume to his voice, Captain Smoke commanded, "Lookouts, eyes aft! Silence on deck!"

The sloshing of the schooner cutting through the
ocean's surface and an occasional groan from a mast or
the hull were dampened by the wind. Men spoke in whis-
pers and Captain Smoke did not issue any further orders.
Sometime between the hours of ten and eleven, a half-moon
rose in the east. The moonbeams, periodically masked by
masses of the northeasterly drifting cumulus, highlighted
the ocean surface like a moving spotlight.

With the rigging crew focused on their duty, Jack scrambled up the larboard mainmast ratline. About three-quarters of the way up, he secured himself by locking his right leg
around a shroud. He swung his body out and, with his eyes
and the aid of a telescope, scanned the sparkling, moonlit
patches on the ocean's surface around the *Chandler's Liberty*.
From his vantage in the rigging, he could see for about two
or three leagues behind the vessel. He hung in the lines
and watched for any unusual configurations. He did this
for about an hour and did not see anything that would suggest the schooner was being pursued. He slid the telescope
back into its case that hung from his belt and climbed down
to the deck.

"Are we being followed?" Captain Smoke asked as he
came up behind Jack.

"No."

"Those frigates either continued on the original course
or gave up the chase. For now, I believe the night will remain quiet." Captain Smoke walked with Jack to the mainmast. "Have Gaspar release the gunnery crews. Make sure

there are lookouts posted on the bow, stern, and rigging. It's late. And all have missed the evening meal. Earlier I sent word to the cook to fry up those delfin the men caught this afternoon. I can smell that he has complied with the request." He took a deep breath and patted his belly. "Ahh, that odor could stimulate hunger in a gorged bear. Hurry. Pass my orders and come below." Captain Smoke turned and headed toward the deckhouse hatchway.

———•◆•———

Hammering, thumping, crashing, timber-cracking noises on the deck above his cot woke Jack. He blinked his eyes and looked toward the main passageway. It was dimly illuminated by daylight passing through several small skylights built into the roof of the deckhouse. He propped himself onto his elbows. Carpenters repairing damage to the gunwale, he thought. Damn. Slept late. He scrambled off the cot, stood, and tried to brush away the wrinkles on the shirt he had forgotten to remove last night. Grabbed the pair of pants from a peg next to the cot and slipped them on. At least I removed my pants before I bedded myself. He tussled his hair, hoping to organize it into some natural arrangement, and headed to breakfast.

When he finished eating, Jack anxiously hurried up the deckhouse ladder. As soon as his head rose through the hatchway and he glanced east, he saw that only about half the sun had risen above the horizon. A fluffy bank of pink-and-orange-colored clouds seemed to be cushioning the ascending fireball. A smile filled his face. It is still early. I'm not late.

He was about to step onto the deck, but had to duck away to avoid colliding with a long board the carpenter and his mate were lifting over the deckhouse.

"Sorry, sir," the carpenter said. "Hope our pounding didn't wake you."

Jack frowned and lowered his head as the carpenter and his mate laid the plank near the damaged starboard gunwale. "Everything is well, gentlemen. Carry on." His frown morphed into a smile as he walked the short distance to the helm. "Helmsman, what is our heading?"

"North, sir."

Jack scanned the horizon behind the schooner. The Royal Navy frigates were not following. Instead a squirt of water a couple hundred yards behind caught his attention. Whale. He turned and looked toward the bow and into the rigging. Two lookouts were stationed against the rails in the bow, one watching the starboard side and the other watching the sea to larboard. A lookout was poised in the little crow's nest on the foremast. Captain has set the sea watch, he noted.

Except for the carpenters' sawing and pounding, the morning passed uneventfully.

Captain Smoke came on deck at about 1130 hours and walked next to Jack, who was watching a small flock of Atlantic puffins cavorting off the larboard side. "Unusual-looking bird," the captain said.

"Aye, sir. It is their colorful beaks that attracted me." Jack turned his attention to the captain. "We see them off the coast of England occasionally."

"Must be a breeding colony nearby. They're usually scattered out to sea." Captain Smoke looked to where the carpenters were working. "Would like you to sight on the sun and estimate our position. You'll find the sextant in a starboard cubicle in the deckhouse next to the ladder. We should be somewhere off the Cape of Cods."

"Aye, sir." Jack rushed off to get the navigational instrument. He returned on deck with the sextant in his hand and found a stable position near the *Chandler's Liberty* taffrail. Peering through the instrument's eyepiece, he sighted on the sun, adjusted the little mirror, and noted the angle between the sun at its zenith and the horizon. To determine the most accurate latitudinal position of the schooner, he took several readings. Jack returned to Captain Smoke, who stood next to the helmsman. "Our position is forty-one degrees, eighty minutes north, sir."

"Aye, Jack. Thank you. We're off the Cape of Cods. Provincetown is forty-two degrees north." Captain Smoke nodded. "Prepare the crew to make a course change." He turned his attention to the helmsman. "When Mr. Hollister signals that the rigging crew is ready, change course to two hundred and seventy-five degrees west."

With the wind blowing from the northwest, Jack knew the change in course would cause the large sail booms to swing around to larboard. He warned the carpenters before scurrying amidships to inform the rigging crew. Once he gave his command, he signaled the helmsman, who turned the ship's wheel slowly to the left.

The *Chandler's Liberty* rolled easily to larboard as the schooner's bow came around to a westerly heading. For a few moments, the sails fluttered, the masts and hull creaked, and the rigging slapped and rattled. With the sails trimmed and secured, and the booms angled to the left, the schooner glided toward the Cape of Cods shoreline, which lay beyond the horizon.

"Foremast lookout," Captain Smoke shouted. "When ye see land, yell out." He turned to Jack. "At the first sight of land, we'll run parallel to the shore till we pass Provincetown. Then we'll make for Beverly." The captain pondered for a moment, removed his cap, and scratched his head. "Don't know how far we're from shore. If we don't sight land by sunset, need to lower the main and foresa'l. Slow the speed. Continue with the jibs. Post extra watches. Don't want to run up the beach."

The large sails were lowered before Jack went to the very late evening meal. First Mate Stokes took over the supervision of the deck. The northwest wind continued for most of the night, moving the *Chandler's Liberty* along at about two to three knots. Two additional lookouts were stationed around the bow and another rode on the bowsprit. About two o'clock in the morning, Mr. Stokes ordered the leadsman into the chains[9] to take depth readings every fifteen minutes. At four o'clock in the morning, the wind shifted

---

9 Small platforms on the side of a vessel to provide a wide purchase for the shrouds and a platform for a man sounding the depth.

to the northeast, and its velocity dropped to three knots. The change chilled the air, issuing an onslaught of fog. To slow the vessel, the jibs were shortened and their position trimmed to the new wind direction. The schooner's speed slowed to about one knot. The helmsman could barely maintain steerage.

Subtle changes in the sound of the moving vessel caused by the wind shift brought Captain Smoke on deck. Jack followed shortly. Anxious about the possibility that the *Chandler's Liberty* might run aground, both men had slept fitfully. Every alteration in the vessel's attitude agitated them.

"Depth, Mr. Stokes?" Captain Smoke asked.

"Last mark, about ten minutes ago, lead did not kiss the bottom, sir."

"Jack, go forward. Have the leadsman to take a mark every five minutes."

"Aye, sir." Jack scurried toward the chains, which were located near the bow and passed the captain's command. The leadsman responded by tossing a three-pound plumb bob with all his strength as far as he could ahead of the *Chandler's Liberty's* bow. It splashed into the water. The lead line followed, spinning free off a reel, following the lead as it rapidly sank. Suddenly the line went slack. The leadsman quickly pulled in the access until the line came vertical and taut. He pulled the line up about a yard and dropped it. He felt the lead plumb hit the bottom. Quickly he retrieved the line; sliding it through his hand until he felt a depth marker, examined it, and called out, "By the mark, six fat'oms."

"About thirty-six feet of water below the keel," Jack said, as he dashed back to the helm to inform Captain Smoke.

The captain immediately became animated and shouted, "Drop the anchors!"

A group of crewmen scrambled to the forward end of *Chandler's Liberty* and released her bow anchors. The heavy hooks raced for the ocean bottom, pulling chain and heavy rope from a below-deck locker. As anchor lines rumbled through the hawser holes, the schooner's hull vibrated and bumbled; all went silent when the hooks hit the seabed. The vessel continued forward for a short distance and came to a jerky stop, when the anchors grabbed the bottom.

"We're less than a mile offshore," Captain Smoke exclaimed, "an' tide's low. Any closer an' we'd be kissing bars and shoals. That damn fog's no help either. I want some men with good ears on watch. Need to hear any boat noise goin' on out there." He paused and scanned the soupy darkness. "Mr. Stokes, inform the crew they can only whisper on deck. Mr. Hollister, have a man ring the ship's bell every five minutes till this fog lifts." The captain pulled his cap tighter on his head, moved next the larboard rail, took out his pipe, and lit it. Several puffs of tobacco smoke drifted around the edges of his mouth. The pleasant odors of the smoke mixed with those of fried salt pork.

Cook was preparing breakfast. Jack's stomach grumbled as he and the sailor he assigned the duty to ring the bell passed near the captain. They overheard him mutter, "British warships don't usually come this near to shore. But one can't be too cautious." Jack nodded as he gripped the rail above the deckhouse hatchway while the sailor continued to the mainmast, where the ship's bell hung. Jack swung through the hatch and dropped to the deck below.

The ship's bell had been rung fourteen times, and the sky began to lighten, but being on deck was like viewing the world from beneath a cool, wet, white sheet. One's hand could barely be seen at arm's length. The crew was forced to move about with the aid of safety lines. The sea surface was calm. The only sounds around the vessel came from an occasional squawk of a seagull or the gurgle of the bubbles when the hull bobbed over a swell.

Jack returned to the weather deck at midmorning. A light, offshore breeze brushed his cheeks when he exited the hatchway. He turned and looked forward. The fog had dissipated somewhat. He now could see the entire deck, but the images of masts, rigging, and other gear above were still fuzzed in mist. At the mainmast, he looked up and saw foggy wisps and globs streaming and drifting toward several shards of azure brightness.

The bell ringer continued to ring the ship's bell to warn the presence of *Chandler's Liberty*. The rigging crew was active, preparing to get under way. First Mate Stokes shouted, "Haul the anchors!"

Within thirty minutes, Jack could see the shoreline. Looks like I could almost jump ashore onto those sandy dunes, he mused.

With the sails set and trimmed to catch the breeze, which increased to about five knots, coming across the beam, Stokes gently steered the *Chandler's Liberty* for open water. The schooner, with her larboard side hiked, sailed smoothly along but slightly away from the coast, to the north.

The vessel cleared the northern end of Cape Cod shortly after the noon hour. The day had cleared, and all clouds deserted the sky. Jack took a sighting on the sun and estimated the latitude to be 42 degrees north. He relayed the vessel's position to Captain Smoke, who gave the command to bring the schooner's course to 290 degrees. This brought the *Chandler's Liberty*'s bow around to the northwest.

"If this wind holds, we should sight the coast off Beverly by daylight tomorrow," Captain Smoke said. He scanned the deck and considered the rigging. "Have the lookouts keep a sharp eye out. Report any sails. Lobsterbacks run patrols from Boston to Falmouth tryin' to catch us off guard."

As twilight of the approaching day lightened the sea and sky, the foremast lookout shouted, "Land ho! Off larboard bow."

Upon hearing that land had been sighted, First Mate Stokes scrambled from his seat next to the mess table and dashed up to the weather deck. Jack followed. Both men sighted on the coastline through their spyglasses.

"Aye," Mr. Stokes said. "We're off Marblehead Neck." He pointed toward almost barren rock offshore of what appeared to be the main landmass. "Marblehead Rock little o'er a mile. Helmsman, point the bow more to the north."

While the *Chandler's Liberty*'s large sails groaned, creaked, and the vessel laid more to starboard, Mr. Stokes clutched Jack's shoulder and urged him forward toward the bow. When they reached it, he took a sighting on a large island. "That be Cat Island[10] off to starboard. Beverly Harbor lies inland from there."

"Sails ahead, 'bout six miles," the foremast lookout yelled.

Both men swung their telescopes toward the bow.

"Brig," Jack said. "Heading seaward." He bent himself against the rail and held his breath to get a steadier observation. Several minutes passed as he peered through the scope. "The *Olive*. Have not seen her in two years."

"Aye, indeed," Mr. Stokes said. "The prize we took returning from Falmouth. A joyful encounter. She's been equipped as a privateer."

"Mr. Stokes, take o'er the helm," Captain Smoke said as he came up behind the two men. "Take us in. The tide and wind are good. Mr. Hollister, have the deck crews make ready for the harbor. We should be at anchor or at a dock by the noon hour."

---

10 Today Cat Island is known as Children's Island.

CHAPTER 14
MID-MAY 1777
BEVERLY, MASSACHUSETTS

Several days after the *Chandler's Liberty* arrived in Beverly, Colonel John Glover came aboard and promoted First Mate Stokes to captain. The colonel assigned Stokes the command of an armed brig and ordered him to patrol off the coast of Virginia. Stokes sailed two days later. The colonel also reassigned about a dozen of the *Chandler's Liberty* non-Marblehead crewmen to other privateers. Over the next week, these vessels headed to sea. Most of the *Chandler's Liberty* Marblehead crewmen, who remained unassigned, stayed ashore. With land and families in Beverly, Salem, and Marblehead, they were content and happy to stay onshore until called back to duty aboard the *Chandler's Liberty*.

Stokes's first-mate position onboard the *Chandler's Liberty* had to be filled so the vessel would have a full complement of officers. At Captain Smoke's recommendation, Colonel Glover elevated Jack to the rank of first mate.

Three weeks had passed and, with repairs completed after the second week, the *Chandler's Liberty* continued to remain idle and in port. The delay to return to sea made

Jack and Captain Smoke restless and eager to be under way. Food and sundry provisions had been loaded, but gunpowder and shot were not. Colonel Glover said he had a sufficient supply and promised to provide Captain Smoke with the ammunition. But that was a week ago, and during that time, he had furnished several other privateers. Colonel Glover had not been seen aboard the *Chandler's Liberty* for some time.

Jack exited Captain Zachariah Stone's house, where he and Captain Smoke secured lodging for the time it took to repair the *Chandler's Liberty*. At the beginning of the American Revolution, Captain Stone had turned part of his home on Front Street into an inn. When Jack strolled down the hillside to the harbor on Water Street, an overwhelming odor of drying fish stimulated his nose. Everywhere he looked, he saw fish drying on racks and platforms behind residences and in empty lots. Not only was Beverly a refuge for patriotic privateers but it also served as the harbor for a profitable codfish fishing fleet. To preserve the codfish to sell and export after unloading, the catch was cleaned, split in half or filleted, salted, and hung or laid out to dry on this south-facing hillside.

Fish Flake Hill. An appropriate name for this place. Jack smiled and rubbed his nose. He headed toward a small cottage at the base of the hill, where Gaspar and several of his expatriate friends from Quebec had rented. Frenchmen know how to prepare a fine breakfast, he noted. A fine way to ease the doldrums of this place.

The odors of baking, sweet spices, and wood smoke tickled Jack's nose when he entered the little cottage. His stomach complained of hunger. He headed for the kitchen.

"Monsieur Hollister," Gaspar said. "Seat yourself, s'il vous plaît. Pierre will fry you some crepes."

"Merci," Jack said. "My mouth waters for those delicacies"

"Très bon. Sirop et sucre sur la table."

"And pieces of smoked meat." Jack reached to the middle of the table and pulled a pan of bacon toward him.

"Oui. Le bacon. It is cold. But good." Gaspar grabbed a pot off the stove, brought it to the table, and poured Jack and himself a cup of coffee. He pulled out the chair next to Jack and sat down.

"Do you know where Colonel Glover is?" Jack asked as the two waited for a dish of crepes. "He brought us food and shipboard supplies, but no ammunition. Captain Smoke wants to sail, but without gunpowder and cannonballs, we could not go far."

"Oui. Men at Dixey's Tavern say colonel go to find powder. I hear Loyalist have casks hidden somewhere to north. The colonel used his reserve to supply boats that sailed last week."

"Aye," Jack said. "I too would like to depart this place as soon as we can. I need to get to Machias before the English. Perhaps we can help find that store of gunpowder the Loyalists have hidden. We could befriend a Loyalist or two. Fill their blood with a little spirit. Loosen their tongues. A secret is not safe with a drunkard. Their hoard cannot be too far away."

As Pierre served each man a plate of crepes, Gaspar grinned and nodded. "You not let grass grow under feet, Monsieur Hollister. Votre es impatient."

"Aye. That I am. Shall we plan?"

"Oui, oui." Gaspar looked over at Pierre, who was listening to the conversation. He said something to him in French and then returned his attention to Jack. "I ask if Pierre and his friends would like to join us. He not speak English well."

"Ah, oui oui," Pierre said, nodding rapidly and rubbing his hands together.

Jack smiled. He pushed back from the table. "I will tell Captain Smoke of our plan. Then, since I am English and not known in this town, this evening I will spend time at Dixey's and bind with some Loyalists. We will need horses and a wagon. Can you have your men secure them? Pistols and muskets are aboard the *Chandler's Liberty*. I am sure Captain Smoke will allow us to use them." Jack stood and nodded at Pierre. "Thank you for breakfast." He then turned to Gaspar. "I'll go now and tell Captain Smoke of our plans."

Jack found Captain Smoke smoking his pipe and reading a newspaper in the sitting room of Stone's Inn. He scanned the area. There were no others in the room. He nodded when the captain lowered the newspaper and acknowledged his presence.

"Hoping someone would come and join me," Captain Smoke said. He reached over the side of the chair and retrieved a bottle. "Hate to drink alone. Join me for a tot of rum?"

"Aye." Jack seated himself in the cushioned chair located opposite the one in which the captain sat. He accepted a glass of rum. "Gaspar and I have a plan to secure some of the gunpowder and other ammunition we need." Jack explained the plan.

"Your plan sounds dangerous," Captain Smoke said, shaking his head. He squinted his eyes and curled the left side of his lips. "Those Loyalists are not going to give up the gunpowder without a fight. Besides, Colonel Glover is searching for some hidden stores of gunpowder. We should wait until he returns."

"If we do, we may be here for some time. Like you, I am anxious to get under way."

Captain Smoke scratched his head and laid his pipe on a side table. He took a swig of his rum. "The town has eyes everywhere. How do you, Gaspar, and his five scrappy fellows plan to move about together without raising suspicion?"

"This is the time of the year when farmers around here do the first haying of their fields. The wagon can be loaded with hay once we are beyond the town's boundaries. Our weapons will be concealed under the hay. A wagon of hay should not attract attention." Jack leaned back and took a sip of rum.

Captain Smoke rubbed his chin, picked up the unlit pipe, and placed it between his lips. He pondered for a moment. "Aye. Your time with the redcoats has given you experience for covert actions. Your plan may succeed, if you can learn where the Tories hide their ammunition." The captain tried to light his pipe. "So, you plan to spend a few evenings at Dixey's getting to know the punters." He removed the pipe from his mouth. "It's true. No one in town knows much about you. You've kept rather quiet. I heard they think you're a passenger that arrived on the *Chandler's Liberty*—a writer by the name of Carson Rabbit. Some folks I've met are suspicious of you, but I've heard no jeopardizing remarks. It is good that you are using General Washington's nom de guerre while we are in Beverly." He took another swallow of rum and refilled his glass. "If you learn where those Tories hide their gunpowder and go after it, it must be with great care. I don't want any of our men injured. Gaspar's Frenchmen are also part of our crew. The crew cannot be injured."

"Aye, sir. We will make the raid after dark. We will need weapons that are secured on our schooner."

"Very well. You can have them." Captain Smoke passed the bottle of rum toward Jack's glass. "Join me in another?"

"Thank you, but no. If the raid is successful, and when we are back out to sea, I will have a tot of rum to celebrate. Now I plan to stroll to Dixey's Tavern and drink with a few Loyalists. There are not many in this town, but I have met a few since we arrived. I learned it is always useful to know what the other side is doing."

Captain Smoke grinned. "Your spying experience has taught you well. Take care." The captain returned the bottle of rum to the floor next to his chair.

The sun had already set when Jack exited Stone's Inn, took a right turn, and walked about a block to Dixey's Tavern. Once inside, he found two merchants he had befriended a couple of days earlier. They were sitting alone in a far corner. Jack's earlier meetings with these merchants led him to believe that the men were more inclined to agree with British ideology than that of Colonial Americans. He bit on his lip, adjusted the strap connected to the satchel that hung from his shoulder, and sauntered to their table. "May I join you fellows?"

John, the stouter of the merchantmen, looked up and smiled. "Aye, Mr. Rabbit. Please join us," he said. "Perhaps you can entertain us with more of your adventures."

"Yes. I am glad you find my stories interesting." Jack pulled a chair away from the table. But before he sat down, he bent toward the table. "It appears you gentlemen are drinking ale? I shall get myself a pint." He straightened and turned toward the bar. "Shall I bring a refresher for the two of you?"

Both men smiled. "That would be delightful," John said.

Jack returned to the table and sat down. Several minutes later the bartender followed, carrying a tray with three pints of dark ale. For the next hour, Jack entertained the two men with a fictitious story about the Battle of Brooklyn. He intimated that General Howe allowed him aboard his vessel to record and observe the redcoat battles that drove the George Washington's troops out of Brooklyn. He watched how the two men reacted to his tales, to determine whether they were indeed loyal to the Crown.

At one point Robert, the leaner of the two merchants, lowered his head and whispered, "Oh, John, it would have been wonderful to stand alongside our gallant men and fight for the king." He paused and pondered for a moment. "Ah, but no. Here we are relegated to standing behind a counter selling buttons and pins to calash-crowned, corpulent colonials."

John pursed his lips and nodded.

Jack had heard what he wanted. Two Loyalists trapped in a town of patriots.

John and Robert straightened. Both looked dejected. They turned their attention to Jack. "Mr. Carson, how are you able to move about Beverly without raising suspicion?" John asked.

"For one thing, my friends," Jack said as he looked the two in the eye, "the fact that I just arrived as a passenger aboard a known continental privateer as a journalist from Great Britain did not arouse any suspicions. Secondly, I try at all costs to avoid entering a political discussion, show no favoritism, and voice no opinions. As a writer, I listen, observe, and relate my stories to whomever asks." Jack took a swig of his ale. "Gentlemen, I do not stay long in one place. From here I will go to the east overland. Eventually, I will secure passage to Halifax. From there I plan to sail for England before winter arrives."

"You are staying in the same inn as the captain of the vessel that brought you here," John said.

"Aye, that I am," Jack said. "Expedience. Captain Horace Smoke, whom I found to be an honorable man, knew of Captain Stone's inn. His knowledge saved me the trouble of having to search for a billet in a town not known to me."

"What of the rest of the crew?"

"They are Marbleheaders and have family in the area. Captain Smoke is from eastern Massachusetts."

"How soon will you be leaving?"

"Within the next few days. But I have a problem. I do have a weapon, a pistol, but I have not been able to secure ammunition. You gentlemen, being merchants, would perhaps know where I may purchase shot and powder?"

Robert looked at John. He bit his lip. "We have none in the store. The patriots have confiscated what quantities we had."

Jack nodded and lowered his head. He wrapped his hands around the glass of ale, looked down, moved the drink toward himself, and momentarily closed his eyes. Then, raising his head, he whispered, "There are other Loyalists about, are there not? Where do they obtain their supply?"

Robert was about to answer, but John interrupted. "Stop by the store tomorrow afternoon, and I will have what you need. For now, we should end this discussion of ammunition." John looked up. His brow furrowed. "Mr. Carson, please tell another story while we finish our drinks. The hour is late. Tomorrow looks to be a trying day."

The three finished their ales while Jack related his experience of catching delfin fish from the deck of the *Chandler's Liberty*. As they stood to depart, Jack said, "I will be in the store before you close. Thank you for what you will do. You will be reimbursed for your trouble." John nodded.

Instead of returning to Stone's Inn, Jack headed to Gaspar's cottage. He knocked, and the door was answered by one of the Frenchmen. The hour being about ten o'clock, the group was in a heated game of cribbage.

"Ah, Jack," Gaspar said as the first mate entered the little sitting room. "Did you learn anything?"

"Learned about the merchants. I believe one of the merchants, probably the one named John, will be visiting the Loyalists' hidden supply of ammunition tonight or in the morning. I convinced him that I needed gunpowder and shot before I leave for Halifax. He told me he would sell me some tomorrow afternoon."

"Come. Sit." Gaspar poured Jack a glass of wine.

"Aye. Thank you, Gaspar," Jack continued. "The two merchants live above their store located on the Boston Road near Water Street. Can you send scouts to watch the store starting tonight? Should one or both merchants leave, the scout should secretly follow but not confront them. The scouts should be able to return with information about the location of the Loyalists' ammunition cache and how well it is guarded. We will attack tomorrow night." Jack sipped the wine and sat back. His eyelids closed. He did not hear Gaspar say, "Très bon, mon ami."

———•◦•———

Shortly after lunch, Captain Smoke, looking for Jack, arrived at Gaspar's cottage just before the four scouts who watched the merchants' store returned. They barged into the cottage with their report. The leader, a burly man, started to relate what the patrol had observed. "We see merchantmen leave store after midnight. They ride up the Boston Road for maybe ten miles to a dilapidated barn. Storekeepers go behind barn and continue along a not-so-used path. It cross open meadow. We wait. Tories ride into the woods on far side of field. We follow." The burly scout scratched his beard. "Damn trail. Much weed and brush. Only wide enough for two horses. We stay in forest. Go slow. Then see campfires and lights of lanterns—"

The youngest scout jumped off his chair and interrupted. "Aye, aye. We dismounted. Snuck ahead on foot—"

"Steady, lad," the burly scout said, grabbed the boy by his shirt, and pulled him back into a chair. "I tell report." He looked up at Captain Smoke and Jack. "Aye. We dismount and go 'head like Indians to edge of clearing. See storekeepers. They stand next to a stone shed—shed looked like well house. We stay in forest because lanterns light up clearing. Storekeepers, they talked to guards. The guards carry muskets—"

"How many guards?" Jack asked.

"Five, we saw."

"Did the storekeepers go into the building?" Captain Smoke asked.

"Aye. With two guards, they go, carry torches. When merchant come out, he carry box. Guard warn, 'What inside box will blow your hand off if it get near fire.'"

"Gunpowder!" Smoke slapped a tabletop. "You found the Tory hoard. How far from here is that arsenal?"

"Maybe fifteen miles," the burly scout said.

"Très bon, mes amies." Gaspar grabbed a bottle of wine, pulled the cork, and poured each man a glass. "You do good. Now drink, eat, and rest. Tonight, we dress like renegades an' go for munitions. Captain Smoke, you have bad leg. You not come with us. You make *Chandler's Liberty* ready for sail tomorrow. We get gunpowder. It be aboard in morning."

———•◦•———

About an hour before midnight, the men were ready. They had dressed in dark ragged coats and blackened their faces with charcoal. Several wore wide-brimmed hats and others knit caps, except the two brothers from a Wampanoag village on Marblehead Peninsula. These two were dressed in buckskin and had decorated leather headbands. Some Frenchmen and the Marbleheaders wore bandannas around their necks. These could be used to cover their faces during the raid. For the same purpose, Jack, Gaspar, and two others tossed a lightweight Indian blanket around their shoulders. They were well armed with swords, daggers, pistols, muskets, and bows and arrows.

About twenty men congregated behind the cottage, where a wagon, with a team of horses and two other saddled mounts, waited. Gaspar and one of the scouts climbed onto driver's seat, while another fellow hopped into the wagon bed.

"Attack must look like done by outlaws. Be silent," Gaspar ordered before the raiders mounted. "No speak French. No kill guards—unless is needed. Use knife or club. Shoot gun only if need to. Cover faces." Gaspar snapped the reins. The horses began to move the wagon. "We not leave together. Not want to draw attention. Go by different routes. All meet on Boston Road." Gaspar maneuvered the wagon onto Water Street.

Jack mounted a horse and turned to the group of men standing about, waiting to depart. "Gentlemen, your attention. Divide into three groups. Each will have a scout. My group will leave now. The next in five minutes and the last five minutes after. Should any fall behind or get delayed, meet at the old barn about ten miles up the Boston Road. Godspeed." Jack spurred his horse, and he and four others headed off toward Front Street.

———•◦•———

By two o'clock in the morning, Gaspar's band of renegades had all assembled in front of the dilapidated barn off the Boston Road. The dim radiance from the moonlight that filtered through the overcast sky illuminated the barnyard. But when the scouts guided the troops behind the barn onto the narrow path that led into the forest, the riders eased up on the reins and allowed the horses to follow the piloting steeds.

Since the wagon was too wide to negotiate the path and would make too much noise, Gaspar assigned the man who had ridden in the bed and one of the riders to remain at the barn and guard the wagon. He mounted the horse and rode to join the column that moved into the forest.

The riders rode slowly, quietly, and surely through the blackness. They continued until glimmers of light from campfires and lanterns in the clearing surrounding the arsenal silhouetted the lead guide. He snapped up his arm. Almost in unison, the column stopped. A second rider came next to the guide. After a moment, the guide signaled everyone to dismount. The only sounds heard as the men got off their horses were noises a woodsman would associate with nocturnal critters scampering about the forest floor. Crickets chirped, and flying insects buzzed.

As silently as possible, the raiders scattered and hid along the edge of the clearing, but as they took up positions, occasional strange twitters cut through the din. These delicate warbles sounded like those made by waking birds. It was the Wampanoags using subtle cheeps and chirrups—Gaspar's signals to organize the troops.

Jack, kneeling behind some lush cinnamon ferns, scanned the clearing. He then clutched his musket and crawled to his right to where a compatriot hunkered behind a boulder. He tapped the fellow on the shoulder. When the Wampanoag turned, Jack pressed two fingers on the Indian's left bicep, then raised his arm into the light radiating from a nearby campfire, and pointed one of the fingers toward the stone building and the other to the right.

The Indian stretched higher and directed his attention toward the arsenal. There he saw one guard slouching against the building and another a couple yards away but approaching. The Wampanoag let out a little squeal, followed by a low whistle. In response, a peep responded from a short distance away. He grabbed his bow, stood, removed an arrow from a quiver, set it against the bow's string, and pulled it back. He aimed, squeaked again, and released the arrow.

A swish, thunk, and a cry of "Ohow." Simultaneously the two guards twisted and dropped to the ground.

"Fine shot," Jack said as he stood, pointed the barrel of his musket toward the clearing. "You and your brother have removed the guards from this side. Let us go forward."

A musket barked as Jack and the Indian moved into the open area around the arsenal. More of the raiders entered the open flickering tract, their weapons pointed at the arsenal. A flash blazed from the arsenal's gun holes. The musket ball splintered a small tree trunk. Then a muffled "argh" came from inside the stone building.

Though he could not see him, Jack heard Gaspar yell from somewhere near the entrance to the arsenal, "Les guardes sont morts. Effacer pour entrer."

"The guards are dead," Jack translated. "We can enter the building and get the gunpowder and ammunition, and other weapons we need."

The Wampanoags and several men heard him and headed for the building's entrance. Jack grabbed a lantern off an outside wall and followed them. Inside the only thing they found were scattered stacks of black powder casks, some full, but most empty. Jack estimated that there were several hundred casks. He figured that each full drum contained a thirty-five-pound mixture of charcoal, sulfur, and potassium nitrate. There were no muskets, shot, or cannonballs found in the arsenal.

"Attention," Jack shouted. A dozen men gathered around him. "Each man grab four powder casks and tie them to your horse. Take more if you can. Walk your horse, but we must hurry. The sky is already brightening."

Gaspar gave the same order in French.

Within thirty minutes, eighteen raiders removed about sixty-two full or nearly full casks of gunpowder. The building still contained more than eighty full casks.

"What to do with what remains, mon ami?" Gaspar asked Jack. "Le Loyalist soit très, très fou, when find gunpowder missing et leurs gardiens ont été assassinés?"

"Torch the arsenal," several men nearby hollered. "Throw the dead guards inside. They'll go up with the blast."

"Oui," Gaspar said.

Though tense, Jack smiled and sidled next to Gaspar. "The blast will be heard in town. It will bring many of the curious onto the Boston Road."

"Ah," Gaspar shook his head. "Not good. We not blow up." He waved everyone out. "Go; put gunpowder in wagon. Do quick. Take to Bass River pier and load aboard *Chandler's Liberty*. Then Captain Smoke sail. We be gone by time Loyalists trouver et réaliser."

"That would be best," Jack said and hauled out two more casks.

The brightening sky sent trickles of light through the forest canopy and illuminated the path. Chilled morning air condensed the dense vapors that rose from carpets of sphagnum, fogging the way ahead. Gaspar's men moved slowly in a single file along the trail, some leading their horses and others riding, their vision blurred by the mist and near darkness. As the raiders reached the wagon hidden behind the dilapidated barn, they loaded the casks of gunpowder onto the wagon and rode off individually or in small groups. Some men headed to the pier on the Bass River. Others returned to their homes. Jack and Gaspar unloaded what casks they brought and followed the wagon down the Boston Road to the pier. The Wampanoag Indians followed for a short distance and then turned off toward their village near Plymouth.

The sun had risen above the horizon when Jack, Gaspar, and the loaded wagon veered onto River Road. Jack noticed an empty wagon followed by a small group of riders hastening away. When they reached the pier where the *Chandler's Liberty* was docked, they were greeted by a cloud of dust.

"Colonel Glover and some of his militia just left," Captain Smoke said from the schooner's bow. "Brought us cannonballs, grapeshot, muskets, and musket balls. But no gunpowder. Hope you were successful."

"Aye, Captain," Jack answered. "At least the colonel kept part of his promise. We found gunpowder, but no Loyalist ammunition or weapons. Need men to help unload and store these casks."

Captain Smoke did not have to issue a command, because eight muscular crewmen had gathered on the dock as the cloud of dust dissipated. Onboard a deck crew was readying the schooner to get under way. As the men hauled the powder drums aboard, several crewmen lowered a longboat that would be used to tow the schooner into the outgoing current.

Jack followed the last cask aboard. He hurried to the bow and felt the *Chandler's Liberty* drift to freedom as a seaman slipped the final cable from the dock. Believe the vessel shivered, he thought and smiled. He turned and watched four oarsmen in the longboat trying to maneuver the schooner into the flow of the ebbing tide.

Jack left the bow to clear the way for several crewmen who were trying to set a pair of jib sails. As he strolled aft, he had to be mindful of the crews hauling the foresail and mainsail. To catch the northwest wind, the large sail booms were swung larboard, so he continued aft along the starboard side. Amidships he stopped to assist in the retrieval of the longboat. Once this vessel was aboard and secured, Jack continued to the helm. He stood at the starboard rail, gazed into the rigging, and for a few moments appeared mesmerized by the widespread sails, wind, and motion of the schooner.

Captain Smoke, who stood in command of the ship's wheel, looked at Jack and said, "A beautiful and energetic sight, when our angel spreads her wings and is reborn, 'tis it not?"

Jack did not respond but kept staring into the confusion of ropes, poles, booms, pulleys, and canvas.

"When we first got under way aboard the *Pegasus* some years ago, you also fell into a trance. I remember Captain Hargrave—may he rest in peace—came to you and put his arm on your shoulder. Then I overheard him say, 'Let us watch our angel unfold her wings.' I believe the reawakening of a sailing vessel still fascinates you."

His lips pursed, eyes glassy, Jack turned to the captain and smiled. "Aye. I still enjoy the experience."

Captain Smoke turned the wheel to the left, and *Chandler's Liberty*'s bow rotated east into the Danvers River. The schooner's sails caught the southwest wind and continued down the waterway. "In an hour or so, we'll be in the Atlantic. And if all goes well, in four or five days, we'll be enjoying a mug of ale at Burnham Tavern."

CHAPTER 15
MACHIAS, MAINE
SUMMER 1977

For two days after leaving Beverly, the *Chandler's Liberty* sailed comfortably toward the northeast, pushed by gentle winds, beneath a partly cloudy sky. But on the morning of the third day, the crew awoke aboard a schooner drifting to contrary breezes under a gray overcast. To the south and west, the edge of this cloud blanket was clearly visible a few degrees above the skyline. An ominous, dark-gray wall, diffused below and curling above, blurred the horizon in the northeast.

When Jack turned his telescope toward the north, he saw an angry, churning sea preceding the tempest. "In for a blow," he yelled. "Nor'easter coming quick. Helmsmen! Come about. Bear southeast. Riggers! Reef and trim the sails. We will take the wind from behind." He scampered to the deckhouse hatch and shouted to the men below. "Batten hatches and hang on."

Just as the *Chandler's Liberty* turned her back on the approaching squall line, the stern lifted, and foam and cold seawater rushed down the deck toward the bow. The bowsprit dove and speared the sea surface. Then the bow abruptly rose, throwing water and spray upward, causing the forward gush to stop, reverse, and scuttle aft along the sides and overboard. Many of the crew trimming the sails fought to stay upright. Several fell and were washed down the deck, grabbing for any holdfast that would keep them from being swept overboard. The schooner rolled deeply to starboard and then pitched upward and laid to larboard. Another fuming wave bashed the stern, again throwing everything into turmoil.

The violent squall lasted about ten minutes. Then, as if Neptune had dumped his cistern, a torrent of blinding, nearly horizontal, rain began. The cold wind whistled and moaned through the rigging. The schooner's hull groaned, creaked, and howled. The *Chandler's Liberty* tossed and pitched as it raced to the southeast, pushed by forty-knot winds.

Jack assisted the helmsman, a fellow named Jocky, at the ship's wheel. Jocky was a strapping Scotsman identified by the straggly wool-knit cap (which Scots called a *thrumm*) that he always wore. Except for Jocky's head, which stayed relatively dry and warm, both he and Jack were soaked to their skin, because there was no time to retrieve and don oilskins. Jack and Jocky had time only to tie themselves to the rails near the cockpit. When they did, Jocky ripped off the thrumm and handed it to Jack. "You're a wee fellow whose head may become a mite cold. Here, don this cap. Keep your noggin' warm."

Jack accepted the thrumm without question and quickly pulled it onto his head. He nodded to the Scotsman, as saltwater drained off the cap, down his face, and burned his eyes. He then grabbed the handles of the ship's wheel, aligned his legs with Jocky's, and leaned against the big man's frame. Together the two men fought to keep the schooner on a straight course.

Several of the deck crew, caught in the open, huddled in safe places. A few managed to get below deck. No one was washed overboard or injured. The storm continued through the day and began to weaken near sunset.

When Captain Smoke sent a crewman to relieve Jocky at the helm, Jocky and Jack stumbled to the deckhouse hatchway. Completely drenched, cold, and shivering, they slid down the ladder. At the bottom, Jack removed Jocky's thrumm, squeezed the water from it, and handed the cap back to him. "Thank you, my friend."

The helmsman removed his dripping shirt and hung it over one of the ladder's rungs. He took the knit cap and spread it out on a shelf. "Aye, matey. My head big. Much hair to keep it warm. I not need thrumm. I put to good use." He nodded and smiled at Jack. "We go to mess. Eat. Have hot coffee."

As the two men entered the passageway, a couple of crewmen carrying blankets met them. "Captain says you get outta those wet duds," one of the crewmen said and raised a blanket up next to Jack. "Strip. I'll wrap this blanket around you. Then you men can warm yourselves with some hot coffee. Cook has a pot a-goin'."

The other crewman did likewise for the helmsman.

Their naked bodies covered by the blankets, Jack and Jocky looked like two barefoot, wet-headed monks when they walked into the mess. Several men in the room chuckled.

The cook poured steaming coffee into two mugs and set them on the table.

Though Jack's body warmed, his teeth continued to chatter. His hands shook when he wrapped them around the mug. He sat down at the table and took a sip of coffee.

"You boys did well," Captain Smoke said. "Cook, feed these men." He returned his attention to Jack and Jocky. "After you fill yourselves, crawl into your bunks. Cook, gimme a couple of glasses." The captain reached into the bag he had brought, pulled out a bottle of brandy, and filled each glass about three-quarters full. "This'll warm your innards. Drink it and hit the sack. Don't want to see you till mornin'. The storm's abatin'. *Chandler's Liberty* can continue without you."

Jack finished the apple he was eating, threw the core over the side, and looked up at the clear blue sky. A chilly northeast wind pushed the schooner on an easterly course. He walked amidships where several crewmen sat on the deckhouse roof, repairing a storm-torn jib. The large bundle of canvas covered their laps. Each man wore a three-fingered glove with a thick leather patch that covered his palm. Jack watched as the crewmen used the leather patch to push, with considerable force, a long needle through the canvas. When the spike passed halfway through the patch and sailcloth at the edge of the tear, the repairer reached under the gather of sailcloth, grasped the needle, and pulled it and its attached length of twine through the sail. He then pushed the needle through the sail from the underside, grasping the spike near its point and pulling it up, and then tightened the stitch. The man then started to push in another stitch.

"A bad tear?" Jack asked.

"Aye," one of the men said. "Gonna take us several hours to repair the gash."

Jack checked his timepiece. Almost the noon hour. He returned to the deckhouse hatch, climbed down to the inner deck, opened a nearby cabinet, and removed a sextant. He returned to the weather deck, took several sightings on the sun, and calculated *Chandler's Liberty*'s position. Latitude forty-three degrees, one minute north. Jack returned to the lower deck, stowed the sextant, and knocked on Captain Smoke's cabin door.

"Enter!"

The captain was standing at his desk, peering over a nautical chart.

"Where are we, Mr. Hollister?"

Jack told him the schooner's position.

"Aye." Captain Smoke examined the chart closer, touched his finger to the map, and slid it at an angle for a short distance. "Stay the course. Have the lookouts watch for land. We are not far from the southern head of Nova Scotia."

"Last night's blow took us quite far to the east," Jack said as he moved nearer the desk.

"Aye. When land is sighted, change course to north. If the wind continues from the northeast, the new heading will take us toward Grand Manan Island. Should sight it tomorrow. Then we'll jibe and head northwest toward the coast of Maine. Keep an eye out to larboard. Near sunset, if the weather stays clear, should see Seal Island. The island is about half the way to Grand Manan."

"Aye, Captain," Jack said. He exited the captain's quarters, returned to the deck, and informed the lookouts to stay alert.

Within an hour, the foremast sentinel shouted, "Land ho!"

Jack grabbed his telescope and rushed to the bow. Before he brought his glass to his eye, he noticed a cloud bank on the horizon. He did not see any landmass, but the gathering of clouds provided the evidence he needed. He returned to the cockpit and shouted the command to change the schooner's course to north and trim the sails to starboard.

The eight-knot northeast wind, now blowing abeam, filled the canvas, causing the *Chandler's Liberty* to hike to larboard. Her speed increased to twelve knots. Cold spray and seawater spurted over the bow as the vessel crashed through three-to-five-foot waves. Several crewmen strung a safety line along the lee side of the vessel. The forward deck remained awash in seawater, which kept most of the deck crew aft of amidships.

As the afternoon progressed, wind velocity decreased, and the height of the waves diminished, righting the schooner's deck and slowing its headlong rush.

"Jocky, go below," Jack said. "I will take the helm. Relax. Warm up. Have supper."

"Heading north, sir," the Scotsman said as he moved away from the ship's wheel.

Jack gripped the wheel handles. "Aye, helmsman. Inform Captain Smoke that you were relieved. Appreciate it if you would toss up my jacket. The air has taken a chill."

Jocky nodded as he stepped from the cockpit and headed to the deckhouse hatch. Moments after the helmsman disappeared down the ladder, a heavy wool sweater shot through the opening. "Cain't find jacket. Sweater'll do."

Jack stretched forward and pulled on the sweater. "Thank you, my man."

When the sun neared the western horizon, sheets of high clouds began to glow a whitish pink. Their color deepened to orange as the blazing globe lowered. Streaks of reds appeared and painted sparkling wine-colored ribbons on the sea's surface. As the sun lay on the horizon, a small black blob sat almost in its center.

"Island to larboard," the foremast lookout shouted.

"Aye. Lookout." Jack shouted, acknowledging the sighting. "Seal Island. On course. Captain Smoke knows these waters," he muttered to himself as he watched the sun drop below the horizon.

———◦◦———

Jack was on deck shortly after sunrise the next morning. He and Captain Smoke stood near the bow. The men pondered on the nearing massive landmass in the distance, perhaps three miles away. Jack trained his telescope on the island. Though the sea surface where they sailed was broken by a one-to-two-foot chop, he saw the periodic swells break into foamy explosions on the boulders and rocks at the base of the massive, craggy, reddish-colored cliff. Though the summit of this flat-topped headland was devoid of trees, he could see that about a mile away from the brim of this promontory grew the beginning of a thick forest. Grasses, stunted bushes, and other meadow vegetation carpeted the surface of the headland and skirted down the cliff for a short distance like a green blanket. From the lowest margins of the vegetation, the two-hundred-foot precipice was composed of vertically aligned barren, razor-edged, and rugged slabs of rock. It appeared that whatever encountered this crag would immediately be ground to splinters.

"No safe harbor there," Jack said anxiously.

"Aye," said Captain Smoke. "South Head of Grand Manan Island. Usually covered in fog and bathed with cruel winds."

Jack lowered the spyglass and looked at the captain. "I would not like to venture too close."

"Aye. Time to point our vessel to the northwest." Captain Smoke swung his arm toward the misty landmass that, for as far as the eyes could see in both directions, lay to the left against the horizon. "The coast of Maine. We'll parallel it. Should make Machias Bay this afternoon."

———◆·◉·◆———

"Cross Island, to starboard," Jocky yelled down the deck-house hatchway.

The northeast wind had freshened, stirred up three-foot whitecapped waves that bashed the starboard side, but pushed the *Chandler's Liberty* to just off the mouth of Machias Bay by lunchtime. Upon hearing the helmsman's report, Jack pushed back from the mess table and stood to go on deck.

"No room for tacking," Captain Smoke said. "Channel's too narrow. Must be towed into the bay. Jocky's a good wheelman. He likes to announce our position a bit in advance. Finish your lunch. There is time to prepare to enter the bay." The captain checked his timepiece. "Our schooner should be nearing the east side of Cross Island. Too many shoals to go into the bay from this side. Water to the west of the island is deeper."

Jack relaxed and readjusted himself on the bench. He finished a bowl of beef stew, sopping up the gravy and pushing bits of potatoes and carrots onto his fork with a chunk of bread. He then stood, but before he could leave, Captain Smoke laid his fork next to his plate and again checked his clock.

"We're off the bay," the captain said. "Good position. Bring the schooner to a stop, lower the longboat, and prepare a crew to tow us up river."

"Aye, sir." Jack went aft toward the ladder leading to the deck. He grabbed the speaking trumpet from a shelf, climbed up, and then located himself forward of the helm and looked toward Cross Island. The schooner was about a half mile beyond the western tip of Cross Island. He shouted through the trumpet, "Strike mainsa'l and foresa'l."

The deck crew loosened the hawsers, and the large sails scraped and rattled down their mast. The sailors gathered the canvases, furled, and secured them onto

the booms. With only the jibs catching the wind, the
Chandler's Liberty slowed.

"Strike jibs and a lower longboat."

As the men worked, a small brig scooted seaward past
the *Chandler's Liberty* as if it were standing still. Its deck was
stacked with long fir trunks and finished lumber. The captain of this brig waved and called out a welcome.

With all sails struck, the schooner pitched and tossed
over the choppy sea as it drifted away toward open water.
The crew lowered the longboat off the leeward side. A boat
crew of six oarsmen and a helmsman climbed down rope
ladders and boarded the open boat. When the longboat
came forward of the schooner's bow, a line was tossed to
it, and the boat crew secured it to a stern bit. The oarsmen
dug deep, rotated the bow upstream, and proceeded to tow
the *Chandler's Liberty*. Going was slow, because the men had
to row against the wind and the beginnings of an ebbing
tide.

"Go to lunch and relax." Jack dismissed Jocky from the
helm and took over, keeping the schooner aligned with the
longboat.

The schooner came abreast of Bare Island and passed it
on the right, staying midstream in deeper water. "Sounding
man, to the chains," Jack called.

A man broke from a group, grabbed the lead line, and
headed toward the bow.

"Entering shoal waters. Need to know depth." Jack
shouted to the fellow.

"Aye, sir."

As the longboat oarsmen pulled the *Chandler's Liberty* through the mouth of the Machias River, the late afternoon sunlight illuminated the tall fir and birch trees along the eastern shore to their evening brilliance. A straight line between light and dark slowly descended from the top of the trees to their bottom. It was as if a shade were being slowly drawn downward in the west.

Captain Smoke watched as evening approached. "We'll move upriver. Anchor north of the Machiasport logging docks."

"Aye, sir." Jack worked the wheel as the oarsmen pulled the vessel. With the midtide flowing seaward faster, the job became more difficult. It seemed to Jack that the schooner was standing still. Ahead lay Salt Island and Round Island. Captured the *Margaretta* off Round Island, he thought and scratched his head. Wonder what would have happened if that British war sloop had not run aground?

Though a slight breeze generated patches of ripple waves on the river's surface, the movement of the vessel against the current generated a slushy groan, disturbing flocks of sanderlings that exploded from exposed sandbars. The little shorebirds darted around and between flights of herring gulls.

The current forced the schooner to the left. The leadsman took a sounding and sang out, "Two fat'oms!"

Jack rotated the ship's wheel to starboard. As the bow turned, the towline became taut, but the schooner moved slightly to midriver. He straightened the vessel, and its starboard passed Salt Island about a half mile off.

Ahead from the left shore jutted several piers and docks. A brig was being loaded with lumber at the most substantial dock. As the *Chandler's Liberty* passed the little harbor, the river narrowed, and the tidal current increased. Jack turned the wheel to larboard and allowed the schooner to slowly slide closer to shore.

"Depth, fathom and half!"

"Drop anchors," Jack shouted.

The schooner jolted to a stop when the bow ground into a sandbar. The current slowly pushed it backward.

"Take up slack on anchors." Jack secured the ship's wheel amidships. "Secure the deck for port." He then called to Captain Smoke. "Machiasport, sir. *Chandler's Liberty* at anchor."

"Aye, First Mate. Call the longboat to the side and secure it next to the hull. We'll use it to go to shore. There should be wagons and horses available for hire in the village. We'll go to Machias and sup at Burnham Tavern this evening. If you wish, you can find lodging there.

"Good morning, Jack," Captain Smoke said. "I am glad you came down for breakfast. I did not want to leave without a good-bye. I am sure you are staying in Machias, but I must be back at sea. Want to finish my coffee—then I'll return to the *Chandler's Liberty*. The crew is anxious to earn a living. Our trip from New London to here has not been laden with lucrative spoils. Though our mission is to harass and capture enemy vessels, we have not done so. As you know, when a vessel is taken, it provides revenue, and if the vessel is taken as a prize, it provides additional riches. The crew depends on these treasures. It has been some time since the *Chandler's Liberty* has taken a prize."

"Aye," Jack said as he pulled a chair from the table. "I understand. Yes, stay I must. I need to find out if the letter I sent, that the British plan to attack, was ever received in Machias. If not, I must alert this village for the possibility of a British attack."

"A mission you must accomplish." Captain Smoke pushed back and stood. He picked up his bag and threw it onto his shoulder. "Good-bye, my friend and good luck. Should you meet with Mr. Bowden, the Balches, or the pirate, Dunkin, please give them my regards." The captain turned and limped toward the exit.

"Thank you, Mr. Smoke," Jack yelled before the captain passed through the door, "for bringing me back to Machias. And please thank your crew. I will miss them. Perhaps we will meet again somewhere. Sail safely."

Jack toyed with his breakfast. Without Mr. Smoke, I do not have any contacts in Machias, he worried. He laid his fork next to the plate and lowered his head in his hand. It has been two years since I have been here. I am sure things have changed.

"Beggin' your pardon, sir," a voice said. Jack felt a hand softly laid on his shoulder. "Are you not feeling well?"

His head popped from his hand, and he looked toward the person who had touched him. "I am well. A bit sad. My friend has departed, and I may never see him again."

The woman's eyes widened, and she slapped her hand to her mouth. "Mr. Jack Hollister," she said in a muffled voice.

"Madam Burnham?" A smile appeared on Jack's face. "Aye. I am he."

"It has been so long." Mary Burnham bent toward him and wrapped her arms around him. "My husband, John, had mentioned that he had provided you and Horace Smoke lodging last evening. Is Mr. Smoke with you?"

"No. He has returned to his schooner. He is not staying, though I am."

"It is good to have you back. I am so happy to see you. There will be no charge for your breakfast. Are you staying with us long?" Mary released Jack and straightened. Her reddish face glowed, and her hands worked her apron.

"Aye. And thank you." Jack adjusted himself in his chair. "I do not know how long I will stay, but I do have important information to discuss with the town leaders. Who now supervises the village?"

"Colonel Foster. He still oversees the militia and is the president of the Committee on Safety. You remember him. You fought with him when the HMS *Margaretta* was captured. I have not seen him in here lately, though. Reverend James Lyons still preaches. But perhaps the person you do not know is Mr. John Allan. He came from Nova Scotia. Impressed George Washington with his knowledge of the Indian culture, so with His Excellency's recommendation, the Continental Congress sent Mr. Allan to manage the affairs of the Passamaquoddies and the Maliseets in our area. He usually takes care of town matters when the others are absent."

"Then it is this Mr. Allan I must meet."

"Perhaps you would like more coffee?"

"Thank you, but I must meet Mr. Allan. Where may I find him?"

"Longfellow's Tavern."

"Thank you, Madam Burnham."

About a week had gone by before Jack and John Allan connected at Longfellow's Tavern. When Jack had resided in Machias during 1774 and 1775, he, Mr. Smoke, and Charles Bowden rented rooms at Longfellow's. So when he entered the day John Allan was there, Mr. Longfellow introduced the two men.

"What can I do for you, Mr. Hollister?" John Allan asked, took a sip of tea, and looked up at Jack.

"I posted a letter some months ago, addressed to Mr. Charles Bowden. The message is of great importance to the village of Machias."

"Yes, yes. Indeed, the letter did arrive near the end of May." Allan sipped his tea and set the cup down. "Mr. Bowden has been at sea aboard the privateer *Maire Balch*. Believe that schooner is somewhere in the Gulf of St. Lawrence. No one knows when it will return. I did not read the letter but gave it to Colonel Foster, who takes charge of matters in Machias. He knew of you. I will contact him. Colonel Foster spends his time at the barracks the militia built at the Rim. Where are you staying?"

"Burnham Tavern."

"Very good. I will let him know." John Allan returned to meditating and his tea.

"Thank you, Mr. Allan." Jack departed Longfellow's and headed back to Burnham Tavern.

———•◦•———

John Burnham closed the tavern after the lunch hour on the thirtieth of June at the request of Colonel Benjamin Foster. The colonel called a meeting of the Committee on Safety. He also asked several other town notables to attend to hear Jack read and discuss the letter he had sent. By two o'clock in the afternoon, members of the committee—Reverend James Lyons, Major George Stillman, Captain Stephen Smith, Lieutenant Colonel Phinneas Nevers, two O'Brien brothers, and the Indian agent, John Allan—seated themselves in the tavern. Several militiamen and several Indians from the Penobscot, Passamaquoddy, and Maliseet tribes, who were brought by Mr. Allan, also joined the meeting. By the elegant clothing they wore, Jack took the Indian attendees to be either elders or chiefs. Colonel Foster had asked Jack to describe his concerns and how he came by the information of the possible British attack.

"Many of you know Mr. Jack Hollister, who lived with us for a while and exalted himself during the battle for the HMS *Margaretta*. He sent a letter a few months ago warning of a potential attack on Machias by the Royal Navy." Colonel Foster looked at Jack, who was seated at a front table. "Mr. Hollister has returned to us, and I would like him to explain this warning. This is a serious matter—a worry our people have been harboring since the capture of HMS *Margaretta* in 1775 and the HMS *Diligent* and *Tatmagush* later that summer. I am sure those captures did not make the redcoats happy. But today, I am happy to have Mr. Hollister back. Mr. Hollister, the committee awaits your report."

Jack came forward and, for the next hour, related what he had done after leaving Machias in the fall of 1775. He concluded with, "Being born in the British aristocracy, I was, with some skepticism, accepted into the redcoat inner circle. Admiral Howe promoted me to the rank of lieutenant and took me on his staff. As such, I became privy to the plots the Howe brothers were planning and the activity of the British military. This intelligence I could pass on to General Washington. At one of the strategy meetings, Admiral Howe voiced his desire to seek revenge on Machias. He noted the death of Midshipman Moore, one of his favored officers, and the loss of the HMS *Margaretta* at the hands of the Machias rebels. He also stated that Machias needed to be destroyed to quell the ongoing rebel activity. 'Those rebels have plans to enlist Canadian-American sympathizers and attack our fortifications at Halifax.'" Jack paused for a moment. "Some of you remember that a year ago the town of Falmouth was laid to waste by the Royal Navy. That bombardment was an act of revenge ordered by Admiral Howe. So you know what General Howe and Admiral Howe can achieve. I did not want such a tragedy to be inflicted on the people of Machias. Therefore, I wrote the letter of warning." He noted concerned expression on the faces of the men. "This spring, General Washington informed me that my service as a spy was no longer needed. He suggested I desert the service and come back to Machias." Jack returned to his seat.

Colonel Foster came forward. "Mr. Hollister paints a grim picture. Gentlemen, we must prepare for an invasion. We will begin immediate reinforcements of Fort Foster at the Rim. I have about forty militiamen barracked at the fort. They can heighten the redoubts and place logs beside the river. With the first sign of enemy vessels in the bay, the pole barrier can be strung across the Machias River to prevent any vessels from coming near the city."

"When the British arrive, they will come in force," Reverend Lyons interjected. "We have too few fighting men. Our militia is not strong."

"Aye." Colonel Foster walked forward and grasped the back of a chair. "I will send a proposal informing the Honorable Congress of Massachusetts Bay of our plight and ask that they send reinforcements."

"Sir." John Allan stood. "My vessel, the *Marisheete*, is lying idle. It has several cannons and swivels aboard. These can be removed and placed in more strategic locations." Mr. Allan turned and was about the sit back down but caught the eye of a robust Passamaquoddy at the back of the room. He quickly straightened. "One more thing, Colonel. I will enlist the service of our Indian allies. They have many warriors eager for the excitement of the battle."

Jack looked around at the Indians, who were standing along the wall. Though their faces were stoic, several of them nodded.

"Their assistance would greatly benefit our cause and definitely be appreciated," Colonel Foster said.

"Lookouts should be placed at strategic locations along the coast," Major Stillman responded. "I will enlist some men to station themselves on Beal Island, Roque Island, and Cross Island. They can quickly inform us if any Royal Navy fleet comes near—"

Captain Smith interrupted. "Additional temporary fortification can be constructed. I do believe Libby's Hill will give us an excellent vantage. The hill offers a southern view of the river. I can have redoubts constructed. Also, sir, redoubts can be raised below Libby's Hill at White's Point."

"Indeed," Colonel Nevers said. "I will fortify some locations near the falls. We have several important mills along the river that will need protection."

Colonel Foster grinned and nodded. "Gentlemen, it appears we are all in accord. Let us go and prepare a welcome for our invaders. Thank you, Mr. Hollister, for bringing us this warning. It is too bad Mr. Bowden and the Balches will not be present to enjoy another victory. With reinforcements and additional fortifications, I do believe we may have the advantage."

—◆—

For Jack, the next six weeks went by quickly. He busied himself by interacting with the various militia groups and helping them with strengthening fortifications along the Machias River. He joined the team ordered to construct the pole barrier that would be strung across the river to prohibit naval traffic. Helping float large fir logs to the location where Colonel Foster decided to place this barrier exhilarated him. Roughly the site was a narrowing in the river about a quarter mile upstream from Fort Foster and the Rim. Except for the mosquitoes that pestered him in the evenings and on calm days—being July, the blackfly season had passed, thank God—Jack enjoyed spending time as a lookout camping on Starboard Island. He was grateful that several families on island brought him vegetables, fish, clams, and lobsters, and on occasion, they invited him to join them for a home-cooked meal.

The headland on the south shore of Starboard Island provided him a commanding view of the Atlantic Ocean. Jack could see vessels approaching Machias Bay from the east and west. During his sojourn on the island, he spotted only a single frigate. The vessel was about six miles off and heading northeasterly into the Bay of Fundy.

Travelers arriving in Machias from south and central Maine would sometimes bring information of British fleet movements along the coast. One individual from the Castine region mentioned that he had seen a large convoy, escorted by frigates, enter lower Penobscot Bay. Reverend Lyons, who questioned this individual, told Jack that he learned the British were quite active in Penobscot Bay. They purchased lumber from several mills along this bay that were operated by individuals loyal to the Crown. They used fir logs for masts and lumber for the construction of barracks and other military buildings. The man from Castine said he would keep his eyes and ears open for any unusual naval traffic and report back the next time he came to Machias.

Though Jack remained busy, he had an opportunity to enjoy some leisure time. The month of July passed without incident. Spending an evening with John Allan at Longfellow's, he mentioned that he hoped the townspeople would not become complacent. Mr. Allan assured him that this was not the case.

———————

On the afternoon of Wednesday, August the sixth, the visitor from Castine entered Burnham Tavern. He stopped by the table where Jack, John Allan, Reverend Lyons, and Colonel Nevers sat, enjoying an afternoon ale.

"May I join you gentlemen?" he asked. "The last time I came to Machias you seemed to be quite interested in the movements of British naval traffic. About a week ago, several fishermen sighted four warships under full sail between Vinalhaven Island and Matinicus Island. They were headed east."

"Aye, please join us," Reverend Lyons said as he shifted to the left, opening a space for the man to pull in a chair. He then introduced the man to the others. "This is the visitor that brought me the information on the activity of the British Navy in the Penobscot Bay several weeks past."

"Aye," Jack said. "I remember. Sir, would you care to have a pint?"

"Thank you, I would," the man said and extended his hand to each man at the table and then seated himself. "Gentlemen, I'm a merchant dealing in jewelry, and I travel widely to acquire articles. The name is Phineas Gordon."

"Good to make your acquaintance, Mr. Gordon," Jack said. "Please tell us more of this sighting you mentioned."

"It is not unusual to see a Royal Navy fleet passing by," Mr. Gordon said. "But for some reason, the fishermen who saw it said it looked like those boats were on a mission. Under full sail, they were, and closer to Matinicus Island. The fishermen told me that the vessels paid them no attention, while other naval vessels usually pull close and either harass the fishing vessels or purchase a catch from them. Gentlemen, these fishermen told that the fleet was composed of three frigates and a brig." Mr. Gordon accepted a mug from the waiter and took a sip.

Jack's brow furrowed. He pursed his lips and then pushed away from the table. "Gentlemen, I need to get to the post at Starboard Island. Thank you, Mr. Gordon, for providing us with this information." Jack stood, grabbed his hat, and checked to determine if he had brought his telescope. "Please tell Colonel Foster of this, and let him know where I have gone."

Jack dashed out the door, mounted a horse, and headed south at full gallop along the road on the west side of the Machias River toward Machiasport. He continued south, past the little village harbor near the mouth of the Machias River, for about eight miles. The road ended at a small forested island, accessible by crossing a bar where some fishermen lived. He borrowed one of their small bateaux and rowed across the sound to Starboard Island. From the southern tip of this island, he could see across the mouth of Machias Bay to Cross Island, located on the bay's eastern side and south into the Atlantic Ocean. He stayed on Starboard Island for a week.

On the morning of the thirteenth of August, after the fog had cleared, Jack saw two frigates approaching. They were about five miles off. He focused his telescope on the lead vessel. The *Rainbow*, he thought. Know that vessel. Howes' vessels. Battle of New York.

As soon as he lowered the scope and looked up, two more vessels came clear on the horizon, their bows pointed landward.

Jack hastened toward the bateau and rowed to shore. He beached the boat on a small strip of sand, ran to the fisherman's shack, thanked him for caring for his horse, mounted, galloped along the bar, and proceeded onto the road north. It took an hour to get to Burnham Tavern. He barged in.

Since it was past the lunch hour, only a few patrons were in the tavern. Luckily for Jack, Colonel Foster and Captain Smith, having taken a late lunch, were still at their table.

"You've seen something, Jack?" asked Colonel Foster.

"Aye. A fleet of warships are coming into Machias Bay."

"We should go to the fort immediately." Colonel Foster touched the napkin to his mouth and stood. "We'll collect a few men on our way to the wharf across from O'Brien's Shipyard. I have a longboat there. Captain Smith, go ready your men."

On the way to Front Street, Colonel Foster collected five militiamen. They all boarded the longboat and rowed downstream toward the fort. They had gone about a mile when the sails of a vessel came into view.

"Holy hell!" Colonel Foster stood in the bow and cried out. He shook both his fists in the air. "That brig coming upriver is towing eight barges. And they are loaded with marines." He turned and yelled to the oarsmen, "Pull for shore. We'll hurry on foot. It's only about a half mile."

As soon as Jack, the colonel, and the militiamen reached higher ground, they broke into a run. They entered the fort from the north side. Major Stillman had the men aligned behind the redoubts and breastworks, with their muskets trained on the approaching brig and barges. When the redcoat marines started to approach the shore, the patriots opened fire, turning back the initial onslaught.

The marines who had come ashore scampered back to the barges, which were rowed to cover behind the brig.

After about an hour, Captain Smith and his men arrived and reinforced the few men at the fort. Defensive shooting continued until after dark.

Jack, Captain Smith, and several men left the fort and rowed the longboat back to Machias. They met with John Allan aboard his armed schooner, *Marisheete*.

"The attack has come," Captain Smith said.

"Aye, we heard the commotion," John Allan said. "How is it at the fort?"

"All is well, so far," answered Captain Smith. "We've repelled their first attempt. Kept them to their boats. Damned redcoats. Hundreds of them came on barges towed by the brig *Hope*. Seems they thought we were more numerous. We are in a bind if they learn we have fewer than fifty men. Are there any reinforcements?"

"No," said John Allan. "The Honorable Congress did not support Colonel Foster's proposal. Reinforcements are not coming from Boston. We'll have to do with what we have.

Jack scratched his head, spotted a small cannon lying idle forward of the *Marisheete's* foremast, and inspected it. "One or two of these would do well at the fort."

"They would indeed," answered John Allan. "There is little ammunition for it. Take it and what cannonballs remain." He moved to a small rack that contained four swivel guns. "Take these also and those pouches of scrap metal. The swivels shoot that junk. They will also shoot stones. There are two kegs of powder stored under the shelf. Take them also."

"We need some strong anchors and cable," Captain Smith said. "The pole barrier must be reinforced and anchored in place."

"O'Brien's Shipyard can provide those needs," Allan answered.

Jack picked up the pouches of scrap. "Gentlemen, take that cannon, the swivels, and ammunition to the boat. We will pull across the river and get what we need from the O'Briens."

On the morning of the fourteenth of August, the militia men had the swivels and little cannon set in place.

"The cannon has a very short range," Jack said as he adjusted the weapon's position and angle and tested the windage. "These little guns have little accuracy." He motioned to two fellows nearby. "Grab the muzzle and lift, please." The men raised the barrel enough for Jack to place a block of wood under the front of the carriage. This gave the cannon's barrel a slightly higher angle.

"Load it." Jack sighted along the top of the barrel. He nudged the cannon slightly to the right, sighted again, and then blew on the end of the glow rope and placed it to the touchhole.

The little cannon belched and then blasted a cloud of white smoke.

Those behind the redoubts saw the ball splash about thirty feet from the HMS *Hope*.

Jack adjusted the aim. "Load!" He again fired.

This time the little cannonball hit the brig's hull with enough force to splinter a few boards. The patriots gave a cheer and started shooting their muskets at the brig and barges. After several more cannon shots and several blasts from the swivels, the HMS *Hope* suffered some damage in the area of her bow.

Jack and Colonel Foster heard the captain of the HMS *Hope* yell the command to haul the anchor. The men saw the barges collected to the side and rear of the brig as it slipped downstream on the ebbing tide.

"Those redcoats will not be satisfied until they destroy us," Colonel Foster said. "When they return, they will come with greater resolve. We've killed some of their marines and damaged that damned brig. I believe we should abandon the fort and man the defensive positions closer to Machias. Should the enemy breach the pole barrier, they'll have free access to the village. Major Stillman and Captain Smith, take twenty men to the redoubts on Libby's Hill. That promontory will offer you a good vantage for marksmen. I believe a cannon has been placed there. A few of your men can dig in at White's Point, below the hill, a good site. It is closer to the river.

"Mr. Hollister, find Mr. Allan. He may have additional guns on his schooner. Also, check with Allan—ask if he successfully convinced the Indians to join our forces."

"Aye, sir." Jack grabbed a musket and prepared to leave with Major Stillman's troop.

"Lieutenant Colonel Nevers," Colonel Foster growled. "Where the hell is he?"

"He stayed in the village last night," Jack said. "Said he wanted to fortify the area near the falls. Planned to enlist the help of the men in town and a few lumberjacks to help. He thinks that defending the mills above and below the falls is extremely important. They are the livelihood of Machias. The O'Briens said they and their men will also defend this area."

Jack found John Allan at Longfellow's, having his usual cup of tea. He explained Colonel Foster's defensive strategy. "Are the Passamaquoddies and Maliseets going to join us?"

"Aye. They are." Mr. Allan sipped his tea. "The chiefs have sent word to their villages for warriors. I believe we can count about forty or fifty warriors. There are only eight Penobscots in Machias. They came to Machias representing the tribes from the Castine area. They want to protect their trade, so they said they would join us. You know all these men love a good fight."

Jack grinned. "That brings our number to about one hundred and fifty. Far short of the force the redcoats sent."

"Aye, but we will do with what we have. I don't believe the British understand the military strategy used by American natives. If all goes well, it will bewilder those redcoat marines."

Another pot of tea arrived at the table. Jack poured himself a cup. The waiter also brought some afternoon scones.

John Allan refilled his cup. "Lieutenant Colonel Nevers assigned some men to collect the rest of the swivels I had aboard the *Marisheete*. Used them to fortify the area around the falls. Also, the men from the mills and some of their wives found old muskets and brought swords, knives, and pitchforks. Said they'd use them if there were a charge. I do believe the defenses are good there. The colonel is a good leader."

Several of Colonel Foster's militiamen entered Longfellow's Tavern. "The colonel asked if we could take the remaining cannon from your schooner to Libby's Hill?

"Aye, gentlemen. Help yourselves."

"I will go with these men," Jack said as he stood to leave. "I would like to lead a small patrol to the Rim to monitor the British movements."

Jack and three militiamen returned to the fort, but by sunset they saw no British activity. As the sun dropped below the horizon, temperatures cooled, clouds rolled in, and fog enclosed the area. Just before midnight, the patrol heard noises on the river and along the shore: voices, squeaks, and rattles, thumping of oars on a deck, muddy squishes, and other clamors.

"Those marines are using the cover of the fog to attack the fort," Jack whispered. "Let us retreat to the forest and take cover."

The patrol heard sporadic gunfire, but no one knew at whom the redcoats were shooting. Several buildings in and near the fort were set ablaze. Then about four o'clock in the morning, a blast occurred at the fort. Jack and the men saw the fireball, laced with black smoke, rise from the fort.

"They've found the gunpowder stash in the arsenal," one of the men said. "There were two casks we could not take.

Then a large fire near the explosion erupted and lit the fort in orange.

"There go the barracks," someone said.

Shortly after the barracks fire, several farm buildings blazed on the Rim outside the fort. Then the concussion from an intense burst shook the area. Black smoke curled upward within a fireball to the west of the Rim. The explosion occurred in the river. Within seconds, splinters of wood fell into the trees.

"The log pole barrier has been ruptured," Jack said, raising his musket and then scratching his head.

The patrol remained in place until sunrise. Then they saw that Fort Foster had been destroyed. Additionally, a barn, some farm buildings, and a mill along the East Machias River were on fire. Scurrying about the Rim were the redcoat marines. They seemed confused because they found no patriots. The HMS *Hope* and all its barges lay at anchor near the southwest shore of the Rim.

"Let us return to Machias and inform Colonel Foster." Jack waved his musket and the four men headed up a slight hill and deeper into the forest.

———•◦•———

In the afternoon of August 14, 1777, the attackers, aided by a flooding tidal current and upstream breeze, appeared off Machias. The force included the HMS *Hope*, with its load of Royal Marines occupying the barges that were being towed by the brig. Also, the captured sloop, which the redcoats had reinforced, followed. The brig anchored to the west of Libby's Hill and White's Point. The sloop went farther upstream. The barges scattered themselves near the larger vessels. All British guns were trained on the shoreline buildings of Machias.

Jack and the patriots, atop Libby's Hill, had their cannons and muskets trained on the invaders. Colonel Foster, Captain Smith, and thirty Indians, who manned White's Point, had their guns readied to repel the attack. A scouting troop of Indians headed to the west bank and hillsides of the river.

As patriots and Indian allies watched from shore emplacements, they saw a scurry of activity around the vessels. The marines in barges, expecting to be fired upon, attempted to take cover behind the brig and sloop. The patriots waited for the redcoats to fire their broadside guns, but after about an hour, not one had fired a shot. The HMS *Hope* and sloop hauled anchor, turned, and started downstream against the current. The barges followed. The Indian scouting group started running about the hills and shoreline forest, howling and whooping.

Across from White's Point, one of the barges turned toward the buildings on the west shore. Several marines, standing on the deck of this vessel, held torches. The Indians began shooting. One of the torch holders fell. The barge quickly retreated to the middle of the river.

Though the men on Libby's Hill cheered, Major Stillman felt uncertain of this turn-and-run strategy exhibited by the redcoats. He instructed several men to load a cannon on a wagon and haul it to the west side of the river. He, Jack, and thirty men scampered down the hill after the wagon. In about a half an hour, they reached Libby's Point, a small exposed nipple of land projecting into the Machias River across from the Rim. There they engaged the retreating attackers, which were about one hundred yards off shore, in an all-out gunfight.

The redcoats were again thrown into disarray, but they returned fire. The HMS *Hope* assisted by firing grapeshot from her quarter-deck cannon. Then the brig ran aground off the shore of the Rim.

The patriots heard officers aboard the brig order the marines to come aboard and take cover. With many marines killed or injured, the soldiers called to the vessel that, because of the dead and injured, it was too difficult to get aboard the brig or sloop.

The firefight continued into the night. The patriots tired and, low on ammunition, retreated to Machias. Major Stillman, Jack, and their men returned to Libby's Point in the morning along with additional troops led by Colonel Foster. Stillman's men scattered themselves along the shoreline. Jack and several fighters fired the cannon, though the size of the cannon made this ineffectual.

Colonel Foster and his men, with a larger cannon in tow, continued south along the shore of the Machias River to Manchester Point. Colonel Foster's strategy was to keep the three frigates anchored off Round Island from sending boats upstream to aid the HMS *Hope*. Manchester Point offered a clear view of the mouth of the river and Round Island.

The tide raised the HMS *Hope* sufficiently to refloat her. Officers aboard the brig commanded oarsmen in the barges to tow it to safety. The oarsmen rebelled, yelling that they were being fired upon and wanted to take cover behind the brig or reinforced sloop.

Since the patriots had mostly exhausted their supply of cannonballs and scrap metal the night before, Jack instructed the men to load the cannon with rocks. This worked. When the *Hope* slid closer to the west shore, the stones peppered its hull and bow and inflicted some damage by splintering boards and rails and injuring marines in the barges.

As the day progressed, the HMS *Hope* again ran aground, this time closer to where Stillman's militia were posted.

Jack's rock slinging and militia musket shots made attempts by the marines to tow the brig to freedom difficult. Several of the oarsmen refused to row; instead they lowered themselves below the barges' gunwales for protection.

"Row! You scurvy rats, row!" Jack heard a brig officer yell. "If ye refuse, I'll blow your head off."

Desperate, Jack thought and shouted to his crew to fire another salvo of stones.

The sloop, able to withstand small-arms fire, came between the brig and shore. Doing so gave several barges the protection needed from musket balls and flying rocks.

Again, freed from the river's bottom, the HMS *Hope* slipped downstream, this time aided by an ebbing tide.

The patriots chased the vessel along the shore, firing their muskets. But a torrential downpour, moving upriver, prohibited further pursuit and brought the Battle of the Rim to an end.

Jack, Major Stillman, and a troop of men joined Colonel Foster at Manchester Point. They arrived after dark. All remained encamped.

The next morning, August the sixteenth, the sun rose bright. Jack looked toward Round Island and saw much activity on the island's shore and around the frigates. Before lunch, sails were unfurled aboard the war vessels, and within an hour, two frigates, HMS *Hope*, and the sloop headed out into the Atlantic Ocean. One of the frigates remained. It later hauled anchor and headed east.

————•◦•————

Several days after Great Britain's attempt to invade and destroy Machias failed, Jack, Colonel Foster, and several other officers and men of the town met at Burnham Tavern for celebratory drinks. One of the officers stated that the militia had surprised the crew of the HMS *Blonde*, which on that day was anchored on the eastern side of Machias Bay. Crewmen from the *Blonde* had put ashore on Cross Island to collect freshwater. The patriots seized the sailors, carrying water buckets, and took them prisoner. The Machias militia attacked the frigate, capturing it and its commander. The HMS *Blonde* was one of the four vessels that had come to destroy Machias.

Colonel Foster waved tavern owner John Burnham to the table. "Another round for all, Mr. Burnham. These men deserve recognition. The enemy came. We repelled them. Though some property was lost at the Rim, the Siege of Machias was averted, and the battle ended with us triumphant. We sustained only one fatality, while the British lost more than a hundred men." The colonel glanced at Jack and returned his attention to the group. "Gentlemen, we need to give special recognition to Mr. Jack Hollister. Though we all suspected that someday the British would return, we may have become complacent waiting. Mr. Hollister's warning brought the British threat to the forefront, giving us time to prepare. I do believe that without his concern for the welfare of Machias and its people, we would not have befuddled the redcoats as we did. Let us raise our glasses in a toast to Mr. Hollister."

Everyone stood and yelled, "Huzzah!"

———•◦•———

By the end of August, the elation of the battle at the Rim had diminished. Though Jack took part in removing the pole barrier placed across the Machias River and other projects that were undertaken to repair the fort, he become weary and restless. He spent time with several fishermen and loggers. The O'Briens even offered to hire him at the shipyard or at one of their mills. But in his accustomed quest for adventure, these activities did not interest him. Rather than brood at the end of a day over a mug of ale or something stronger, he went to Libby's Hill and pondered his future while watching the sunset illuminate the eastern turn of the Machias River beyond White's Bay.

I did not remain in the colonies to become a laborer, he thought. I need to return to the sea. This fight for independence is not over. General Washington is somewhere in Pennsylvania. How can I rejoin him?

One evening as he meditated on the changing colors of the clouds, a familiar schooner rounded the turn in the river. Its light-colored hull and sails glowed a warm golden-orange in the setting sun. It turned northward toward the village of Machias. Jack pulled his spyglass from his belt and focused on the oncoming vessel. Her name appeared bold in black letters, *Maire Balch*. He scanned the vessel fore and aft. There at the helm stood a tall muscular man. Crewmen scurried about the deck, preparing the vessel for harbor. Near the bow, another lean, dandy-looking fellow stood with his black-leather-boot-covered right foot resting on the starboard rail. He wore a purple cape with white trim. A tricorne sat askew his head of thick, shoulder-length hair. A tall, bushy ostrich feather that projected up from the right side of the hat vibrated in the breeze. His right hand rested on the hilt of a long sword, its tip stuck in the gunwale, bracing him in a gallant stance.

Jack suddenly shook with laughter and jumped from the stump on which he had been sitting. The heat of excitement reddened his face. "Mr. Bowden and pirate Dunkin!" he cried out. "The vessel to my future has arrived."